DARKNESS FOLLOWS

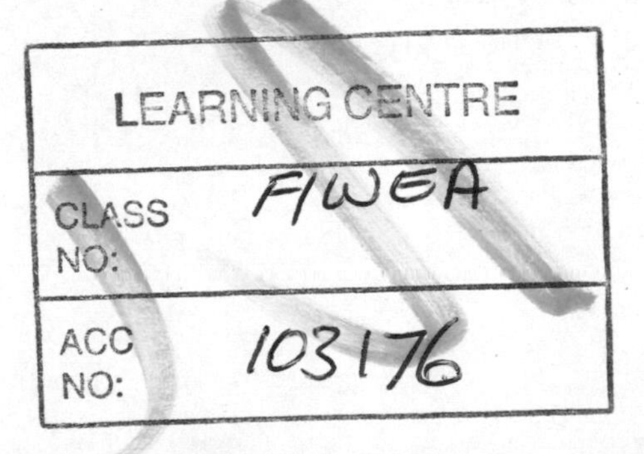

L.A. WEATHERLY

LOVE IS WEAKNESS

To be trusted is a greater compliment than being loved.
– George MacDonald

Prologue

May, 1941

Amity Vancour's trial had been going for eight days.

Mac Jones's footsteps echoed as he approached Courtroom Four, his eyes on the guard. He kept his shoulders relaxed, a slight saunter to his step.

A pair of golden scales hung from the ceiling. They were in the Libra building of the Zodiac: the twelve-domed capitol complex that housed President Gunnison's regime. Far away outside, downtown Topeka buzzed with traffic.

Restricted – by official arrangement only, read the sign.

Mac showed his pass. "Okay if I sneak in?" he said with an easy grin – what his girlfriend Sephy called his *resist me if you can* look. Being short always helped. Who was wary of a guy only five foot three?

The guard hesitated and then shrugged. "Yeah, suppose. It'll be wrapping up soon for the day anyway."

Hiding his tension, Mac pushed open the heavy panelled door and slipped inside.

Though barely May, the courtroom felt steamy, the gallery a solid mass of double-breasted suits and flimsy feminine hats. *No surprise it was packed*, Mac thought grimly. Everyone wanted to see "Wildcat" go down.

Amity Vancour was up on the stand. Her sleek dark hair fell past her jawbone. Weariness etched her unsmiling face. Two Guns with pistols flanked her. Nearby, a moving-picture camera whirred on three spindly legs.

"No," she said, her voice level. "That is not what happened."

"Don't *lie*, Miss Vancour," said the prosecutor. "I'll ask again..."

No seats. Mac stood with a knot of people near the back. He spotted Chief Astrologer Kay Pierce at the prosecution's table and his muscles relaxed, though Pierce was one of his least favourite people.

Good – she was here. He'd grab her once she had finished and somehow wheedle the information he needed out of her.

It was the only reason he'd come. He could do nothing to aid Vancour, not now. Watching her, Mac felt the familiar, helpless anger. If the timing had been only slightly different…if he'd met Vancour *after* she got hold of the documents proving the corrupt Peacefights, instead of before…

He grimaced. *Let it go.*

Vancour still wore the pilot's gear she'd been arrested in six weeks ago. A dark bruise stained one olive cheek. She looked nothing like the laughing young woman Mac had met the night she'd been out dancing with Collis Reed. "Collie", she'd called him.

There was no sign of Collis in the room.

The prosecutor rocked on his heels. "But isn't it *true*, Miss Vancour, that you're a cold-blooded murderer?"

She sat straight, unmoving. "No, it is not."

"Yet on March 13th, you won a Peacefight against the former Central States – and then *shot your opponent down* as he parachuted to safety!"

"*No.* Our planes were both sabotaged. My wing exploded when I—"

The judge banged her gavel. "Speak *only* when asked a question."

"Admit it, Wildcat!" the prosecutor sneered. "You killed him because he was going to report you for taking bribes, *isn't that right*?"

One of her fists clenched. "No," she said. "Cain's men tried to kill me so that I couldn't tell what I knew. The other pilot was killed so that there'd be no witnesses. I—"

"Ah, I *see.* Yet prior to this, you called the World for

Peace 'outdated' and claimed that pilots should make money however they liked!"

"That's not true! I never—"

"Silence, Miss Vancour!" barked the judge.

A photographer passed Mac a camera. "Hold this, buddy?" he whispered.

Mac took the large, boxy instrument. The guy rummaged in a bag and pulled out a flashbulb; he reclaimed the camera. "Thanks."

"Pretty lively. Has it been like this all along?" muttered Mac, watching the front of the courtroom.

The photographer nodded as he inserted the new bulb. "No one's listening to a word she says. Half the time they don't even let her speak." He quickly caught himself. "Well, of course not – she's guilty as sin."

Don't worry, pal; I'm the last guy who'd report you for being a threat to Harmony, Mac thought. He propped himself against a column, his eyes still on Vancour. "Sure is," he said. "Good thing they caught her."

Yeah. Terrific. Thanks, Collis.

A large Harmony flag – Gunnison's flag – hung on the wall, its red-and-black swirls a corruption of the old yin-yang. Mac knew Vancour must hate seeing that every day. Hell, it was hard enough for him.

The Western Seaboard, Vancour's home country, had fallen to the Central States's illegal army just days before she was captured. The newly-reformed "Can-Amer" now extended from the west coast to the Miszippi River.

Only Appalachia, stretching beyond that to the eastern shores, remained free from John Gunnison's rule on this continent.

For now.

"Then after the murder, you broke into the World for Peace building with your accomplice, *didn't you*?" demanded the prosecutor.

Something flickered in Vancour's eyes. "I broke into the World for Peace building, yes. I didn't have an accomplice." And Mac, watching, thought this was the first lie he'd heard her tell.

"Oh no? Ingo Manfred! We know you tried to plant a bomb, Miss Vancour. We found your failed device! The fingerprints match!"

"*No!*" she burst out. "I took documents proving that Peacefights had been thrown – that it all led back to Gunni—"

The judge's gavel went wild. "Miss Vancour! I will *not* tell you again!"

The Guns stepped close, pistols ready. Vancour's attorney lounged back in her chair, legs crossed, one foot tapping the air. Mac thought she needed only a nail file to complete the picture.

Vancour took a deep, shuddering breath. "This is a farce," she said, so quietly he almost didn't hear.

That was the word, all right, he reflected bitterly, still slouched against the column. And what was happening in the other courtrooms was just as bad.

The world had erupted when news of the thrown Peacefights came out. There'd been no fights since. The World for Peace – the governing body trusted for generations – was in tatters.

As well as declaring himself president of the new Can-Amer, John Gunnison was chairman of the investigating committee. Somehow, thought Mac, Johnny Gun, who'd orchestrated the whole web of corruption to put himself in power, had emerged a gladiator for justice.

Seventeen honest World for Peace officials had so far been hanged.

Inside his trouser pockets, Mac's hands were fists. *We'll bring him down,* he promised himself.

Suddenly he caught sight of Walter. The *Topeka Times* editor sat like a large, rumpled lion at the end of one of the benches.

Their gazes met. Walter's flicker of relief matched Mac's own: now they wouldn't have to try to meet later.

Walter waved Mac over and moved down his bench. "I think we can make space for a young man as important to Sandford Cain's office as yourself, Mr Jones," he rumbled in an undertone.

The woman beside him had been about to protest. At the mention of Cain – Gunnison's right-hand man – she glanced apprehensively at Mac and said nothing.

Mac was Cain's assistant. *A young up-and-coming star of the Gunnison regime,* he'd been called.

He slipped onto the bench. "Thanks," he said. At the

front, the prosecutor was conferring with the judge. Vancour slumped in the witness box, eyes closed as she rubbed her bruised cheek.

Under the buzz of whispers, Walter murmured, "Any news on what we talked about?"

"Yeah," Mac said, his voice just as low. "It could be big, Walt. Exactly what we need to get rid of the bastards."

Walter shot him a look but didn't comment. The prosecutor had begun again; you could hear a penny drop.

Everything Vancour had done was being twisted beyond recognition: trying to expose the corruption, her first arrest in Angeles, escaping the Peacefighting base to help confront Gunnison's troops.

Collis's name wasn't mentioned – though Mac knew he'd been in it up to his neck.

"Peacefighting!" boomed the prosecutor. "Let me read you the official definition, Miss Vancour." He whipped out a piece of paper. "*So that the world shall never again experience the horrors of war, all disputes between nations will be resolved by Peacefighting: two honourable combat pilots going up against each other under a strict code of rules.*" He slapped the paper down. "Did that mean *nothing* to you?"

Vancour sat very still. From her expression, she was trying to contain some deep emotion.

"It meant a lot," she said softly.

Mac sighed and scraped back his unruly brown hair. For the hundredth time, he wished he'd known the crucial role Vancour was fated to play. He could have tipped her off about who "Collie" really worked for.

Everything might have been different.

Finally they let Vancour off the stand. She sat at the defence table massaging her temples, not looking up.

As conversation mumbled through the gallery, Walter leaned close. "All right, tell me."

Mac brought his attention sharply back to the matter at hand. In a whisper, he told Walter the news.

"It'll be a big extravaganza," he finished. "Both him and Cain up on a stage together – exactly what we need. I just have to verify the date with Pierce."

"Finally." Walter let out a breath. "Will we have time to prepare?"

Mac nodded, keeping his gaze on the front of the courtroom. "Sephy thinks there's a date early next year that Pierce might choose. It's perfect, Walt. It gives us a chance to—"

"Madeline Bark to the stand," announced the bailiff.

Mac fell silent. Vancour's head snapped up. She twisted in her seat to look behind her.

The courtroom doors opened. An auburn-haired woman wearing a tailored skirt and a jacket with broad shoulder pads entered. Her high heels clicked against the floor. She didn't look at Vancour as she was sworn in.

The prosecutor smiled. "Now, Miss Bark, you're a

special advisor to President Gunnison, is that correct?"

Vancour sat bolt upright at this. She gaped at the woman who Mac knew had been a trusted family friend.

Bark fiddled with a golden Libra brooch. Her lipstick was very red. "Yes, I work for Mr Gunnison. I used to work for the World for Peace."

Keeping her gaze firmly from the defence table, Bark testified that "Wildcat" was a loose cannon. "Always, from the time she was a child," she said, her voice stilted. "A… rebel, I guess you'd say."

"You knew her late father, Truce Vancour?"

"We were Peacefighters together."

Bark explained what the world by now already knew: twelve years ago, Amity's father had thrown the civil war Peacefight that divided the Central States from the Western Seaboard. It had put Gunnison in power.

Mac glanced at Vancour. She sat staring fixedly at Bark, her expression one of deep sorrow – impotent anger.

"And how did you feel when you realized what Truce Vancour had done?" asked the prosecutor, his tone sympathetic.

Bark cleared her throat. "Oh – shocked, of course. As was President Gunnison. This was only a few months ago; some new evidence came to light."

Mac gave an inaudible snort. Nope, Gunnison had had *no idea* that the fight that put him in power was thrown. But now his "discovery" let him justify the Western Seaboard takeover: the wrongfully divided countries, reunited.

"Part of me suspected at the time that Truce might have thrown it, which horrified me," Bark went on. "Naturally, we all wanted Mr Gunnison to win, but manipulating Peacefights was unthinkable." For the first time, her eyes flicked nervously to Vancour and she stumbled: "I talked him into…I mean, I talked *to* Truce about it, and…"

Mac's eyebrows lifted.

Vancour's chair scraped the floor as she lunged upwards, her hands on the table. Her voice was hoarse. "*What* did you just say?"

The courtroom went silent. "Sit, Miss Vancour," said the judge icily.

"You talked him into it," whispered Vancour. "*How?* What did you—?"

"*Now!*"

Mac tensed as the Guns started for her, pistols drawn. *Sit down!* he wanted to shout. Vancour didn't move. For a long moment she and Bark remained locked in time, Bark's wide-eyed gaze meeting Vancour's own.

Belatedly, Vancour sank into her seat, looking dazed.

She didn't say another word throughout the rest of Bark's testimony.

It was over for the day. As the rustling crowd got to its feet, Walter clapped Mac's shoulder.

"Good luck finding out the date," he muttered. "Don't let her suspect anything. What will you do?"

Mac glanced at Kay Pierce. In the hour he'd been here she'd shown astrological charts to the prosecutor several times. She'd also joked across the aisle with Vancour's defence attorney.

"See if she wants to go out for a drink after her long, tiring day," he said. "We're buddies. She likes me."

Walter smiled slightly. "Everyone does; that's why you're so good. Let me know what you find out."

Mac nodded and started for the front of the courtroom. Kay Pierce stood talking to the prosecutor. Nearby, Guns flanked Vancour, waiting for the room to clear before taking her away.

As Mac approached, he took in her drawn, weary features – and with a pang, recalled the single time he'd met her, that night in The Ivy Room. She and Collis had been out on the dance floor, holding each other close. She'd gazed at "Collie" as if he'd made her every dream come true.

Collis had looked at her the same way…but then, Collis was a consummate actor.

So was Mac. He had to be.

He leaned against the prosecution's table, waiting for Kay to turn around. Vancour looked over and saw him.

Her nostrils flared in recognition. Bitterness creased her face. "Figures," she breathed. "*You* work for Gunnison, too."

No one would have guessed Mac's feelings. His half-smile and shrug said only, *Yeah, that's how it goes sometimes.*

The Guns jerked Vancour around and cuffed her. "If you see Collie, tell him..." she started, and then broke off. She ducked her bruised face towards her shoulder. She was trembling. When she spoke again, her voice was hard.

"No," she said. "Don't tell him anything."

As the grey-suited Guns took Vancour away, Kay turned. "Mac!" she said, beaming. "What are you doing here?"

"Felt like seeing the great Miss Pierce in action," Mac said with a grin. "Want to grab a drink?" He was acutely conscious of Vancour just exiting the courtroom, hustled between the Guns.

Mac didn't know the exact details of Vancour's arrest – only that Collis had been involved. Inwardly, he winced at a sudden mental image: "Wildcat" up on the gallows with a noose being cinched around her neck.

He hoped she'd be so lucky.

"WILDCAT" FOUND GUILTY

Angeles Advent, May 4th, 1941 AC

The sensational "Wildcat" trial of former Peacefighter Amity Vancour has now drawn to a close. Vancour, arrested in Topeka on March 25th, was today found guilty of first-degree murder and of deliberately losing Peacefights for financial gain. Sentencing is expected imminently.

"Vancour made a mockery of Peacefighting just like her late father," said President Gunnison. "Her punishment will never make amends for what she did, but with the help of the stars we'll create a truly Harmonic society."

Our gloriously reunited nation of Can-Amer is lucky to have President Gunnison steering us through these troubled times...

Chapter One

March, 1941

Wind and rain churned the tree branches. I stood hidden in the twilight shadows, gazing down the drive at the farmhouse.

In the light from its open doorway I could see Collie, his broad shoulders hunched against the wet. As he talked with the farmer, he motioned to a used auto with a *For Sale* sign in the yard. The farmer nodded and beckoned him in.

I pressed tightly against a tree. *Be careful, Collie. Don't let him know you're a pilot.*

The storm had been a stroke of luck. After we'd escaped the battlefield hours before, we'd flown the Firedove as far as its fuel tank would take us. Nothing was as distinctive as a Firedove's roar, but under the rumble of thunder and wind it seemed unlikely we'd been heard.

In the gathering darkness, we'd landed in a nearby field and hidden the Dove in a dilapidated barn. The barn's condition hinted that we might still be in the Western Seaboard. I peered into the lashing darkness, wishing I knew for sure.

Yet even if we were still in our home country, it might not be ours for much longer.

Cold rain darted down my neck, but my shiver was from revulsion as I recalled bombers, tanks, soldiers: all supposed to exist only in history books. That morning Gunnison had attacked the Western Seaboard. All of our Peacefighter pilots, myself and Collie included, had flown into battle. We'd lost.

This day – March 18th, 1941 AC – would live in infamy for ever.

I straightened with a jerk as the farmhouse door opened. Collie and the farmer shook hands, then Collie jogged through the rain to the auto, not even glancing towards my hiding place. The whole country was on the lookout for "Wildcat". My photo had been front-page news for days.

A few minutes later, we were cruising down the road, rain streaking against the windscreen. I shrugged off my wet jacket. "What happened?" I said. "Where *are* we?"

The faint glow from the dashboard showed Collie's features – his broken nose, his strong chin and full lips. His sandy hair was damp; he swiped a hand through it.

"Western Seaboard still," he said, shifting gears. "He was listening to the news on the telio. Nothing about you, for a change. Gunnison's attack has distracted everyone."

I studied him anxiously. "And?"

Collie blew out a breath. "It's bad, Amity. His troops are still advancing. Now towns are surrendering without him even having to do a thing." He grimaced. "Hell, I think half the country *wants* him to take over, no matter how crazy he is."

Gunnison was crazy, all right. In his speeches he talked about using "the power of astrology" to "maximise Harmony and weed out Discordant elements". I sat motionless, recalling his henchmen, the Guns, arresting a woman. Blood had run down her battered face as she was shoved, sobbing, into a Shadowcar and taken away – just for having the wrong birth chart.

My brother could be taken too, if he was discovered.

The rain beat against the roof. "Thanks, Dad," I said.

Collie glanced quickly at me. "Don't say that."

I sighed and dropped my head back against the seat. I'd learned only hours before that my father had thrown the fight that put Gunnison in power. I knew in my heart it was true.

Collie was watching me. "Hey," he said. "Come here." He reached his arm out. After a beat, I slid across the seat towards him. He pulled me close against his side and kissed my hair.

"Don't do this to yourself," he murmured. "No matter what, Tru was your dad. You've got to let it go."

I wanted to relax into Collie's warmth but couldn't. "How can I? It changes everything."

His arm tensed. The windshield wipers swished back and forth a few times. "Why?" he said. "Just because you found out he did something bad?"

"'Something bad,'" I echoed ironically. "This goes a little beyond that, Collie."

"All right, but…he was still the same person."

My throat was tight. "No," I whispered. "He wasn't. I wouldn't even have *been* a Peacefighter if it wasn't for him. If he was capable of doing this…then I never really knew him."

Collie started to speak and stopped, his expression conflicted. We drove through the rain in silence. The worst thing, I thought, was that I'd never know Dad's reasons. He'd been dead since I was thirteen.

The night before his fatal plane crash, I'd found him drunk in the kitchen. He'd said I was braver than he was – that he thought I'd be a Peacefighter too one day.

I'd perched stiffly on a kitchen chair, longing to really understand him…and ashamed that Peacefighting wasn't what I most wanted to do. I wanted to be a transport pilot. I knew I'd never, ever tell him.

Dad had mentioned his mother, a former Peacefighter who'd died when I was three. "Oh, she had no idea," he snorted.

"About what?" I'd asked in a small voice.

And he'd stared at me as if he'd forgotten I was there.

"Nothing," he said. "Times change, don't they? She knew what it was like for her, but not for me. And if you become a Peacefighter, all you'll know is what it's like for you. No one can judge your actions unless they've been there. Got that? Nobody."

"Dad...you can tell me anything."

His smile hadn't reached his eyes. "Maybe someday. When you're a Peacefighter too. It's the only thing worth being, Amity...I always knew that."

The headlights streaked through the rain. I felt made of glass: he'd been talking that night about throwing the civil war Peacefight. What words could he have possibly used to explain?

Collie still seemed tense. Abruptly he took his arm from my shoulders. He pulled us off onto an overgrown dirt road and killed the engine. High overhead, stars were caught in the pine trees' dark, prickly branches.

He exhaled and stroked the steering wheel up and down. "All right, look...I'm just driving aimlessly here. We need to decide what we're doing."

I nodded and pulled a weary knee to my chest. "How are we doing for money?"

Collie's hands slowed and then stopped. Finally he gave a small, sour smile. "We're fine. More than fine."

"What? How?"

Twisting towards the back seat, he snagged his flight

jacket. He drew a brown envelope from the inside pocket and opened it, angling it towards me.

Cash. Lots of it.

I quickly took the envelope from him and flipped through the bills. "How much *is* this?"

"Almost ten thousand credits."

My gaze flew to his. "The Tier One fight," I whispered, and he nodded.

I'd been told to throw it. I'd pretended to agree. It had been a set-up to try to kill me. After I went on the run, Collie was told to throw the fight instead. He'd fought fairly, but still lost in the end.

The result had given Gunnison the right to extradite all so-called Discordants from the Western Seaboard. My brother Hal had been named one. He was still in hiding in a neighbour's house, if he hadn't been discovered yet.

The envelope felt cold in my hands. I stared at Collie. "But…you tried to win that fight."

"Sure, but *they* didn't know that." Collie took the envelope back and rifled through the bills, his expression bitter. "Hendrix called me into his office and paid me just after I landed."

"And you *took* it?"

His head snapped up. "Of course I took it. What was I going to say? 'No, I refuse, you're all corrupt'?"

When I didn't answer, Collie dropped the envelope and gripped my fingers. "Amity…come on," he said in an undertone. He stroked my hair. "I hate it too, but we're going to need money. How do you think I bought the auto?"

The wind whispered through the pines. I sighed and rubbed his palm with my thumb, circling his Leo tattoo – a souvenir from his life in the Harmony-obsessed Central States.

"Okay. Yes," I said. "You're right."

Wordlessly, Collie cupped his hand behind my neck and kissed me. For several heartbeats I took refuge in the feel of our lips together. When we drew apart he rested his brow against mine.

Neither of us spoke. Finally Collie cleared his throat. "So…I was thinking we should head for the coast, maybe up around Puget."

"Puget? What's there?"

His eyebrows rose; he gave a short laugh. "Well, there's getting the hell out of the country before Gunnison takes it over, for one thing."

I frowned. I leaned back against the seat's cracked vinyl and rubbed my forehead. "Collie, no…the main thing is to get hold of those documents again."

He stared at me. "Amity…"

"They still exist – they have to!" I'd told him already how I'd trusted a police officer with the documents after my arrest. "Can't your contacts do anything?"

The contacts who'd helped Collie escape the Central States were shadowy figures to me. A guy named Mac Jones was the only one I'd met; he and Collie had talked in The Ivy Room the evening my team leader, Russ Avery, was murdered.

That night I'd broken into Russ's house and found out everything I believed in was a lie. A date book, newspaper clippings, notes in Russ's handwriting about his thrown fights – it was all there. Later, I'd discovered documents in Madeline's office safe that implicated the World for Peace at the highest levels. Everything led back to Gunnison. It was enough to bring him down, if we could just get hold of it again.

I pushed away what else I'd discovered: Madeline's betrayal of me and her affair with my father. She'd been like an aunt to me, growing up.

Collie's jaw was stone. He hadn't spoken. Outside, a night bird gave a long, plaintive call.

"You...don't want to try," I said slowly.

"No. I don't. And if you're sane, you won't either."

"You can't *mean* that! Gunnison's busy taking over our country right now – everyone who's already in hiding will be in even more danger! What about Hal?"

Collie winced at my little brother's name. All I could think of was the look on Hal's face as Ma and I had closed the trapdoor over him. The tiny room under a closest was in the home of someone I wasn't even sure we could trust.

"I know," Collie said roughly. "But, baby, there's nothing we can do about it."

"But—"

"*Listen to me!* It is *over*, all right?" He kissed my hand and clutched it. "Either that cop tried to help you, or he turned the evidence in. Either way, it's been destroyed – probably shoved in a furnace the second he handed it over to someone."

The news of what I'd found had broken days ago, mangled beyond belief. I started to reply. Collie gently put his fingers over my mouth. His eyes were dark green in the shadows, locked on mine.

"The whole world thinks you killed another pilot to cover up taking bribes," he said. "No one will believe a word you tell them. It's like I've said all along – Gunnison's going to win, and there's nothing anyone can do to stop him."

A weight pressed on my chest. I stared out at the dark, dripping trees.

"I hate it as much as you do," Collie said in a low voice. "But the *only thing* we can do now is escape. Grab a steamer to somewhere – the European Alliance, maybe, or up to Alaska. Amity...being happy together, living a long life together...that's all we can do to fight this. And it's not a small thing."

My heart clenched. Collie turned me to face him; he caressed my cheekbone with his thumb. I could feel his skin's warmth, the slight roughness of a hangnail.

"You can't always be a hero," he whispered. "Sometimes just surviving is the best that you can do."

Chapter Two

May, 1941

The train stopped with a hissing lurch.

Though I'd thought I didn't care where we were going, I found myself craning with the others, trying to see over the tangled press of bodies in the boxcar. Bars of sunlight broke up the gloom, showing people's greasy heads and rumpled clothes.

I glimpsed a station platform that seemed abandoned. It was May but snow still dusted the ground. The plain wooden building looked as stark as a gallows.

Beside me, a girl named Melody shivered and rubbed her arms. She'd tried to talk to me these past few days, offering up information about herself even when I barely responded. She'd been a student, she told me. She had no idea why she'd been found Discordant.

"I guess my stars were just wrong," she'd said, sounding sad; resigned. As if she really believed, like Gunnison said, that astrology held the answers for a Harmonic society.

She hadn't asked about me. Everyone already knew, or thought they did. Apparently my trial had been required viewing. When Gunnison's men had first herded us all into the boxcar, I'd seen dread on people's faces as they recognized me.

"But...but if we're going where *you're* going, then..." one woman had stammered, and then fell quiet, her face leaching of colour.

Now the only sounds in the boxcar were worried whispers and the distant mutter of Guns talking outside. I stared at the slats that sliced across the barren landscape. That wall was the only possible escape route. People had tried already, of course – tried until their hands bled – but the flat metal bars were immovable.

There'd been a time when I'd have tried too – when nothing could have kept me from straining and pulling with the others. Though only one person, I'd have thought I could make a difference.

Now I knew better.

I still wore the leather flight jacket I'd been captured in. Gently I touched the folded square of paper nestling in one pocket. My muscles tightened. I ran my finger over its soft creases.

Ma. Hal. I brought their faces to mind, savouring

every detail. I prayed that Hal was still safely hidden – that he and Ma were both all right. I knew I'd probably never see them again. The thought numbed me.

Stay safe, I begged my family silently.

Once I'd have believed that Collie would help them. At the thought of the man I still loved – though I wished I didn't – a wrench of pain left me hollow. Surely none of this had actually happened?

Yet it had.

A gust of wind blew snow into the crowded boxcar; it skittered at our feet. People were still murmuring, wondering why we'd stopped. The smell of sweat and urine hung in the air.

Melody started to say something. Then her eyes widened and she clutched my arm.

"Listen!" she whispered.

The whine of approaching engines. I tensed as I strained to hear. Were they autos? No, they were higher in pitch...

We all jumped as a pair of Guns appeared outside in long wool coats and fur hats. The Harmony symbol was a dark wound above their hearts.

One of them unlocked the slatted wall's padlock. They heaved together and the wall rattled open. You'd have thought, after so many days, that we'd have rushed them – tried to clamber right over them and escape away over the fields. Nobody moved.

A Gun made a face as the smell hit him. "Filthy Discordant animals."

An older man, still dignified despite everything, glared at them. "We were only given a single bucket," he said in a clear voice. "So who exactly are the animals?"

Anger leaped over the Gun's face. He raised his pistol and I flinched with the others, wishing feverishly that the man had kept quiet.

The other Gun grabbed his comrade's arm.

"Not these," he said. "Let them find out there's something worse than a lousy bucket."

The Guns motioned us out of the boxcar. There were no steps to help with the sheer height. My limbs felt stiff after days in the cramped space; I staggered as I dropped to the ground.

The air was cold on my clammy skin, but it briefly felt good. And now I could see other Guns, standing nearby cradling rifles. Several sat on snowmobiles, revving their engines. The vehicles' sleek lines and grilled fronts looked like they belonged to a different century than the clattering, steam-belching train.

We'd seemed such a crowd in the car, but as everyone emerged I could see there were less than thirty of us – men and women of all ages and colours, with grimy skin and rumpled clothes. Gazes fell away from each other. A sense of shame hung over everything.

During the journey people had listened to each other's stories with fascinated dread. This one was "pure" Discordant with a faulty birth chart; that one had declaimed Gunnison and been made Discordant on the spot. Gunnison wasn't choosy. Pretty much anyone he didn't like was a threat to Harmony.

The grey-haired man who'd spoken up was the last off the train car. He hesitated, eyeing the high drop. One of the women in our group started forward. Before she could reach him the Gun who'd drawn his pistol on us stretched a hand up.

For a split second I had a sense of the world being sane again – and then the Gun grabbed his arm and yanked.

The man pitched forward with a startled cry and fell hard onto the ground. The Gun kicked his prone form viciously. "That'll teach you to mind your manners, Grandpa," he hissed.

Stony-faced, the older man struggled to his feet. His nose was bloody. The Gun scanned us, lip curling. He waved his pistol northwards, where a snow-covered road sliced across the fields.

"Walk," he said.

The fields wound through a steep valley. The snow hadn't melted at all here; we slogged through it for what seemed hours. In places there were deep drifts and wetness bit at my calves.

On the train people had tried to guess where we were. Once we'd left towns behind, all anyone had known for sure was that we were heading further and further north

– surely not far enough for Alaska.

Where was this place? The upper Yukon? The Inuvik Territory?

The cold knifed into you, clutched at your bones. My leather jacket wasn't fleece-lined; it felt as if I was wearing nothing at all. As we trudged in a long, straggling line, the snowmobiles roared along beside us, sometimes darting ahead and then racing back. One of the Guns did a figure eight, whooping and calling to his comrades.

Melody struggled by my side. I didn't know why she stayed so close to me – maybe because we were the same age, nineteen. She wore a dress with a light wool coat over it. Stockings. Boots that had probably been perfectly adequate for city sidewalks kept cleared of snow.

One of the girls was crying. A matronly woman had her arm around her. To my shame, as my gaze lingered on them I felt mostly jealousy over the older woman's long fur coat.

"Do you think it's true...about the place where everyone said they're taking us?" asked Melody dully. She had a round, pretty face and blonde hair. She was limping by now; her stylish boots were soaked through.

"Yes," I said.

We all knew what fate probably awaited us, though on the train the words had only been spoken in fearful whispers. I should have been scared too, but somehow couldn't summon up the energy. None of it seemed to matter any more.

Melody shivered and hugged herself. "Maybe it'll be all right," she murmured. "Maybe they're not as bad as everyone says."

Ahead, the older woman patted the younger one's arm. From the jut of her chin, I could guess what she was saying: *Don't let those bastards win. You have to keep going, no matter what.*

I'd thought that too. I had a sudden flash of one of the nameless Guns who'd visited me during those long weeks before my trial, tapping brass knuckles against her palm. "Sure you don't want to change your story, Miss Vancour?"

I never had. It had done me no good at all.

A cold wind blew more snow across the road; it stung my cheeks. I shivered and stared at the woman's chocolate-brown fur coat, imagining its softness. If it were mine, I'd turn it inside out so that the luxurious fur was against my body, keeping me even warmer.

Anger at myself hit me – I was a lot better off than some here. I stopped Melody with a touch on her arm.

"Do you want to borrow my boots?" I said it in a rush, before I could change my mind.

She stared at me as if she didn't understand. Then she looked down at my heavy pilot's boots with their sturdy soles. "But why would you do that?" she gasped.

"Just until we get there." I glanced around. Most of the snowmobiles were ahead of us; we had a few seconds before they swooped back on another loop. I crouched down, fumbling to work my numbed fingers against the damp laces. Staggering and holding onto each other, Melody and I managed to swap boots.

Hers were as flimsy as they looked and pinched my feet. I felt my socks begin to dampen.

"Thank you," said Melody fervently. Her pretty cheeks were flushed. "I'll give them back to you as soon as we get to…to wherever we're going." She darted me a glance and hesitated.

"Amity, did you really do everything they said you did?"

The snowmobiles were heading back now, gliding and jumping over dips in the snow. We started walking again, my toes curling against the cold.

"It doesn't make any difference," I said.

She blanched. I'd been accused of treason. They'd downgraded it to murder: Gunnison being "lenient". "But…you were a *Peacefighter,*" she said.

I gave a terse shrug. "I'm a Discordant now, same as you."

Throughout my trial, I'd tried to say what happened over and over, sometimes almost shouting the words in frustration. There was no point repeating it now. Everything I'd said had been mangled; quotes attributed to me in the papers had borne no relation to reality. I was sure that only heavily-edited snippets of my trial had been shown on the telio.

Had Collie been watching?

My throat clutched. I thought of his smile, the feel of his arms around me. I could still hardly believe that the man I'd loved so much, trusted so totally, had turned out to be a stranger.

Unbidden, the memory came of the last time I'd seen him, when I was arrested in Topeka.

No. I was trembling, and not just with cold. I buried the memory somewhere deep and slammed a lid on it.

I focused instead on Madeline.

As the Guns sped past again, I let my hatred for the woman I used to admire so much stiffen my spine. Like Collie, she worked for Gunnison. Perhaps she always had.

I talked him into…I mean, I talked to *Truce…*

After Madeline had finished her testimony, she'd rushed from the courtroom, avoiding my eyes. I hadn't seen her again. But even now, struggling through the snow, I longed to confront her – to demand to know how she'd manipulated my father into turning his back on everything he believed in. Everything he'd made me believe in too. My need for answers was desperate.

Yet what did it matter now? I'd never know why he'd thrown the fight that put Gunnison in power. Nothing was going to change.

My toes throbbed in the too-small boots. A dull dread of whatever lay ahead was starting to fill me.

I had a feeling that Gunnison hadn't been "lenient" at all.

* * *

As near as I could tell it took us over another hour. The sun started dipping in the sky. My feet first stung as if on fire and then went numb. At last a massive enclosure came into view, enclosed in barbed wire. Watchtowers sat just inside, with buildings beyond.

John Gunnison was there.

I gasped in disbelief. In the distance, a moving-picture screen rose up from within the enclosure. A black-and-white Gunnison strode across a stage. His shouting voice echoed faintly: "...because I *care* about my citizens! I *care* about Harmony! I'll do whatever it takes, friends and neighbours..."

Several dozen strange, bulbous shapes sat perched on the chain-link fence amongst the barbed wire. At first I didn't really take them in – I was dazedly watching Gunnison.

Then, when we got closer, I realized.

I stopped short, my heart pounding. Beside me, Melody let out a whimper, her hand pressed against her mouth.

Heads. Some looked recent; others were so weather-battered that the skin was a sickly grey. They'd belonged to both men and women. Their eyes were open, glazed. All were topped with snow, glittering with frost.

Gunnison's image still shouted, but I hardly heard it now. Everyone came to an uncertain, shivering stop, staring at the heads. A few people almost hadn't made it this far – the older man had fallen more than once and stood breathing hard, supported by others.

A pair of Guns on the inside swung open the gates. The metal Harmony symbol at its centre divided into two. One of the Guns who'd escorted us got off his snowmobile.

"Welcome to Harmony Five," he called in a clear voice. He grinned and pointed at the fence. "That's what happens if you try to escape."

Chapter Three

The Guns herded us inside the gates. I huddled into my jacket, still staring at the heads. They'd all been people, once. Those eyes had seen things – those lips had laughed.

The men in our group were taken in one direction, the women in another. There didn't seem to be any couples, though a few people who'd talked together on the train looked over their shoulders as everyone was led away.

The screen disappeared when we turned a bend. Gunnison's voice boomed on. "…Harmony! The ruling force of all things! Without Lady Harmony's balance, we're *sunk*, folks…!"

"Faster," ordered one of the Guns, and our group somehow picked up its pace. The concrete buildings we passed looked defeated, in unending shades of grey. The sound of distant machinery battled against Gunnison's speech.

We reached a long building labelled *Induction*. I swallowed, wondering what this would involve. The Guns motioned with their pistols and we filed in.

Gunnison's voice faded. We were in a small room with a rough wooden floor. A sign on the wall read: OBEDIENCE IS HARMONY. Three female Guns stood, eyeing us with distaste.

"Clothes off," snapped one. "We have to disinfect everything you're wearing."

Like the rest, I glanced furtively at the six male Guns who'd brought us here. As they pulled off the scarves around their faces I saw their smirks and a dull anger filled me.

"Are you all deaf?" demanded the woman. She raised a pistol. "Clothes *off*, Discordant scum – now!"

Slowly, everyone began to obey.

I set my jaw. Then as I started to pull off my flight jacket, I suddenly remembered. Fear filled me. I touched the folded square of paper in my pocket. Would they search our clothes? They could take anything else, but I had to have this piece of paper.

My thoughts raced. As unobtrusively as I could, I gouged my fingernail through the pocket's worn inner lining. I pushed the paper through the tiny hole.

The female Guns watched narrowly as we undressed.

They ignored the men, who were laughing and making comments:

"Look, that one – how'd you like to get your hands on *those*?"

"*Touch* a Discordant?"

"Sure, that's all they're good for…as long as you disinfect yourself afterwards."

Raucous laughter. Beside me, Melody was silently crying. Her small body was thinner than mine, her breasts like tiny apples. She tried to cover herself as she took off her underwear, and staggered a little.

Don't let them see they're getting to you, I wanted to whisper to her. I tightened my mouth and looked away. I was naked now, trying not to shiver.

"All right, pick up your things and get moving," said one of the female Guns. She pointed to a door. "Line up in order of your sun signs. Now!"

I was an Aries. Once I'd had no idea where that fitted into the rest of the zodiac; now I knew it was the first sign. Reluctantly, clutching my bundle of clothes to my chest, I headed for the door with a few others. Whatever was going to happen, I wasn't eager to be one of the first.

They let us through into another room. This one had a small blaze going in a fireplace, though it clearly wasn't for us: a clerk sat behind a desk.

"Name?" he barked at the first woman.

She told him in a murmur; he wrote it down and noted a number beside it. He took her things from her and marked them all with the same number.

"You'll get these back when they're fit to wear again. And when *you're* clean enough to wear them. Next!" He tossed her clothes to one side.

A Gun motioned the woman through the next door. I hesitated as I moved forward. Melody's boots were on top of my things. My own boots were back where she was – she'd told me she was an Aquarius, the next-to-last sign.

"Put it all down," ordered the clerk. He was younger than I'd have thought, with glasses and thick brown hair.

I placed my clothes on the desk, angrily aware that he'd only wanted to deprive me of shielding myself. As I let go of my jacket I thought I could feel the small square of paper and prayed it would be safe.

"Name?"

"Amity Vancour," I said.

The man looked up with a sudden smirk. His gaze scanned my nakedness, lingering on my breasts. "Well, well," he said. "Welcome to Harmony Five, Miss Vancour – or should I call you Wildcat?"

I didn't answer. He had a large ledger in front of him; beside my name he entered a number. He reached for Melody's flimsy, fashionable boots and started to mark them.

"Wait," I blurted. He stopped, eyebrows up.

"Those aren't my boots," I said.

"Oh? Yet here they are with your things."

"I loaned my boots to someone further down the line. These are hers."

The clerk shrugged. "So you've traded."

"We didn't! Just ask her. She—"

One of the male Guns came over. "What's the hold-up?"

The clerk dangled Melody's boots as though they were dead rats. "Our esteemed prisoner thinks she's too good for these. She wants a different pair."

"That's not—" I started, and then sucked in a breath as the Gun put his pistol to my temple. The metal's chill seemed to burn against my skin.

"Shall I pull the trigger?" whispered the Gun. His hazel eyes were disconcertingly attractive, with long lashes. "I don't care if you live or die, you know."

"Don't do it in here," said the clerk. He'd marked the boots, and was now marking my other things, his pen scratching efficiently. "I don't need the mess."

"Ask me nicely not to kill you," said the Gun.

My pulse was frantic. "Please," I got out.

He flicked the safety off and I flinched.

He gave a harsh laugh. "You're not worth the bullet, you scum. Some day you'll wish you had been."

He yanked me up and shoved me into the next room. It had a long table in it; workers with ominous-looking instruments sat waiting. The woman who'd gone before me was in there already, grimacing at whatever was being done to her.

"Sit down," snapped a female worker. I was still shaky, trying not to show it. I sat gingerly, hating the feel of my bare buttocks against the rickety stool.

"Hand out," she said.

I hesitated and put out my right hand. Mouth pursed, she swiped at my grimy palm with a damp cloth. She didn't look at me as she started up a small drill-like machine and angled it at the base of my thumb.

I winced as a needle darted hotly in and out of my skin. Blood bubbled up in a thin line – and then I saw the ink that was following in the needle's wake.

A tattoo.

Coldness gripped me. The tattoo gun made a curving line, then went into a downward stroke. *No,* I thought, dazed. *It can't be.* But it was. The pattern continued upward, forming a stylized pair of ram's horns: the glyph for Aries.

Collie's Leo tattoo had been in this exact same spot.

"Do all prisoners have one of these?" I said without thinking.

The worker didn't look up. She put some finishing touches on the tattoo and then set the machine down.

"Next!" she barked.

I clenched my hand and started to ask again – then glanced at the Gun who'd put his pistol to my head. My mouth dried. Slowly, I got up from the stool and went into the next room.

It was unheated, with bare concete walls. Goose pimples scattered across my flesh. The woman who'd gone ahead of me stood in the corner hugging herself. A sign on the wall read: CLEANLINESS IS HARMONY.

"Now you get to wait until the others are done," said a female Gun with a smirk. "Aren't you glad you're an Aries? We know you fire signs love to wait."

I pressed against the cold wall and stared down at my red irritated palm – the curving symbol. I was marked for life, however long my life might be.

Collie's tattoo. I'd traced its swirl so many times, feeling the warmth of the firm skin beneath. Though I'd never have believed it, I now hated Collie almost as much as I still loved him. What did it mean that he'd had a tattoo in the same place?

I closed my hand tightly, unable to process this.

When Melody entered she came and stood beside me. I started to mention my boots and then saw the expression on her face. "Amity..." she whispered in a strangled voice. I swallowed as I saw the problem: a smudge of red on the inside of her thighs.

Melody looked agonized. A male guard lounged near the doorway; she shot him a frightened glance. "I – I don't have anything with me I can use."

None of us did, of course. "Wait," I murmured back. "They'll have to give you something to take care of it soon." I hoped it was true.

When the room was full of naked, shivering women, a group of Guns trooped in with buckets. We shrank backwards. Grinning, they glanced at each other and counted: "One...two..."

On "three" they heaved the liquid contents. I yelped in

shock at a slap of harsh-smelling disinfectant. It stung my eyes, drenched my skin.

The sound of pained sobs mixed with the guards' merriment. A fire hose lay coiled on the floor. A female Gun grabbed it, spun a dial, and a jet of icy water battered us.

Screams. Gasping, I tried to scramble away – so was everyone else. The Gun sprayed it in wild arcs, laughing as the men whooped and shouted. "Yeah, make 'em dance. Let's see 'em jiggle!"

Finally she turned it off, leaving us soaked and shuddering.

My chest heaved. I swiped at my eyes; they still burned from the chemicals.

"All right, Discordant scum – march!" ordered another Gun.

I wouldn't have believed it even of Guns. They made us go outside, naked and wet in the snow, and walk to the next building. Only a hundred feet, but the cold clenched my lungs. My skin felt shrivelled, too tight for my body. Spontaneously, we all broke into a run, desperate to get to warmth.

The Guns cheered. I guessed the ones who might have felt sorry for us wouldn't have lasted long.

We reached the next building panting and shaking. In it were two female Guns and clothes of a clumsily-sewn rough material. Trousers, blouses, rough-carved wooden shoes.

"Until your own filthy clothes are fit to wear," said the older Gun with a sneer.

We fell on the garments gratefully. My hands trembled as I yanked them on. Now that the show was apparently over the male Guns had drifted away, though the two women guarding us didn't look any friendlier.

I noticed that Melody had pulled on a shirt, but nothing else. Then I cringed when I saw why: the blood between her legs had been washed away by the hose but now it was back, worse than ever.

"Please, I…I've started my period," she stammered to the younger of the two Guns. "Do you have something I can use to—"

The woman recoiled at the sight. "Ugh!" she spat. "You'll get it all over the floor!"

"Discordants," muttered the older Gun. "Filthy animals." She took a rag from a drawer, but didn't hand it to Melody. "This isn't *free*, you know," she said snidely. "That's not how things work around here."

We'd all gone still. Melody's face was scorched a deep red. "I have some money with my clothes," she whispered. "I can pay you when I get them back."

The older Gun laughed. "Are you serious? No, you don't have any money. It's all ours, to help pay for your keep here."

Melody looked desperate. She squeezed her legs together, but her flow had become heavier, tracing down her skin as if she'd been in a terrible accident. "Then… then you can have my slip, or—"

"Payment now," interrupted the Gun. Slowly, deliberately, she rested the rag to one side.

I stood frozen with the others. The bright red blood twining down Melody's pale thighs was mesmerizing. I felt a shameful relief that my own period wasn't due to start for two more weeks.

"And you'd better figure out some way to pay for it fast," said the younger Gun. "If you stain that floor, you'll wish you hadn't."

She took out a stick and tapped it against her palm. I watched it fall: once, twice. I felt hot and tight inside.

Melody gave a half-sob. "But what am I supposed to pay for it with?"

The older Gun snorted. "Not very inventive, are you?"

"Honestly, they're all so stupid," said the other one, still tapping.

The older Gun smirked and nudged her colleague. "Okay, I'm in a generous mood," she announced. "Sing us something. If it's good, maybe I'll give you *two* rags."

Melody shot us a desperate glance and hugged herself. Finally, in a thin, quavering voice, she started to sing a Van Wheeler song.

The Guns hooted and laughed. "No, that's terrible!" broke in the younger one gleefully. "I know, I know – she could dance for us!"

"*Just give it to her!*" My voice rang around the room, surprising even me. I lunged for the desk and grabbed the folded rag. I thrust it at Melody.

Pain exploded across the side of my head. The world dimmed as I staggered and almost fell. Then the younger

Gun punched me square in the stomach. I went down, gasping, the breath knocked out of me.

One of them kicked me hard and I felt a rib crack. I cried out as I was hauled to my feet.

"You've got a lot to learn," hissed the older Gun. "Lesson one begins right now."

Chapter Four

July, 1941

PINK-VEINED MARBLE LINED THE CORRIDOR of the Pisces building. The plush carpet muffled Mac's footsteps. Outside, the Topeka summer burned. In here all was timeless, serene.

Reaching the meeting room door, Mac paused to quickly smooth his hair, wondering what the hell this was about.

Remember, pal, you're a loyalist all the way in there, he thought. These last few months had been disastrous. Screwing up was not an option.

"Don't worry, you look *very* sharp," a voice drawled.

Kay Pierce. Mac donned a relaxed smile as he turned.

"Hey, thanks." As they shook hands he kissed her cheek.

"You're not looking bad yourself, Kay."

Gunnison's Chief Astrologer was short, just about Mac's height, with pert features, light brown hair and freckles. *Freckles*, as if she were an innocent farm girl. She played up the wholesome act when it suited her.

She tucked her arm chummily through Mac's. "Glad you're here," she said with a squeeze. "There are some exciting things afoot. For *you* along with everyone else."

"Oh?" Mac arched an eyebrow and hid his apprehension. He doubted that he and Kay Pierce shared the same idea of "exciting".

"Intriguing," he said lightly. "What's going on?"

Kay giggled. "All in good time, Mackie."

She opened the conference room door and strolled in with Mac in tow. "Look who I found prowling around in the corridor," she announced.

At a long, gleaming table sat the two most powerful men in Can-Amer: President John Gunnison and his chief advisor Sandford Cain. A pair of bodyguards stood nearby. As always, the pat down when Mac had entered the building had been depressingly thorough.

A tired-looking Gunnison rose, smiling, and met Mac with an outstretched hand. "Good to see you, bud. You've been out there in the Western Quarter too long." The Can-Amer leader wasn't overly tall, but solid, with thick blond hair that was greying at the temples.

He and Mac shook hands with a hearty clasp. "It's all Mr Cain's fault, I'm afraid," Mac said with a grin, and his pale-eyed boss gave him a small, cold smile.

"Guilty as charged," said Cain. "If you weren't so competent, you wouldn't get sent out there so often."

The Western Quarter was formerly the Western Seaboard.

Near Angeles on the coast, nearly a quarter of a million pilots and other personnel were still being detained in the old Peacefighting complex.

At its heart, the international hub known as the Heat continued to be a seething, thriving city. Mac spent weeks at a time out there – ostensibly doing espionage for Cain. As far as most of Can-Amer was concerned, Mac was faceless. He used a series of aliases.

Mac took his seat. A folder waited at each place. On one wall there glinted a mosaic of two linked golden fishes. Through the window, three more Zodiac domes could be seen.

One was the Libra dome, where the World for Peace investigation was still ongoing – though Gunnison, who'd seemed distracted recently, had mostly passed it over to Cain now. Thankfully Mac hadn't had to be involved.

It had become known as "the purging". Forty-two officials had now been put to death.

Alaska had fallen only weeks after the Western Seaboard. Gunnison's illegal, mammoth army remained unchallenged. Other world leaders hadn't dared to confront him, though Mac suspected they were secretly building their own armed forces. They'd be fools not to.

But Johnny Gun had had a twelve-year head start.

The Day of Three Suns, Mac promised himself tautly. Somehow, the Resistance would still find a way to use it.

"...to go over the new work plan," Kay was saying, opening her folder.

Mac looked up quickly, keeping his expression merely curious.

"New work plan?" Cain echoed. "John, we haven't discussed this."

"Now, now, Ford," said Gunnison, patting the air in Sandford Cain's direction. "It was a matter for the stars, not you. Just listen to what Kiki has to say."

Kiki? Mac suddenly noticed just how close Kay and Gunnison were sitting: the president's arm was around her chair, his hand lightly caressing her shoulder. The warm look they exchanged was even more telling.

Warning bells went off in Mac's head. Exactly how much sway did Kay Pierce have with Gunnison now?

Quite a lot, if her faint air of triumph was anything to go by. She smiled prettily.

"Well, everyone, the Day of Three Suns will be coming up before we know it, bringing in the New Era. So in preparation, it seemed a good time to look at our working arrangements."

In February, a rare convergence of Venus and Jupiter would make the two planets visible at sunset. As Sephy, Mac's girlfriend, had guessed, Kay had judged this the most auspicious date for the Harmony Treaty, which would bring the entire continent under Gunnison's rule.

Appalachia – home to New Manhattan, Boston, Atlanta – was being coerced into signing by the threat of Gunnison's army and the false promise that they could keep some autonomy. Though Gunnison was already moving advisors into key roles, most Appalachians had no idea what awaited them. Until the Day of Three Suns their country remained technically free.

Despite their recent setbacks, the Resistance still fervently hoped to use the event as they'd planned.

What was going on now, though?

In a brisk voice Kay announced a series of new appointments. "And of course we'll need someone really excellent to be in charge of interrogations." She drew out another astrological chart and shot Mac a dimpled look. "That's you."

At first Mac thought he hadn't heard right. "Me?"

Gunnison nodded. "Effective immediately. You've been wasted doing reconnaissance out there in the Western Quarter for so long, bud. Now you get to play with the big boys."

"But I—" Mac bit back his protest: the only time in his career that he'd ever spoken without thinking. The look on his face must have passed for surprise.

"Now don't get me wrong, you've done a great job!" Gunnison went on. "Hell, Mac, those Resistance leaders are tricky to deal with and I've been damn glad you were out there. But the stars have spoken: it's time for you to move on." Though he seemed weary, he smiled.

"And I've spoken too. And what *I* say is, let's give a twenty-three-year-old man with everything going for him the chance to make his mark. Take some credit for his success for a change." He held up a hand. "This is how it's going to be. That's final."

Mac chuckled. "Well, it's very kind of you, Johnny. What can I say? I appreciate the vote of confidence."

His thoughts skidded on ice. His presence in the Heat was vital. He'd planned to propose spending even more time out there, "to keep an eye on things".

From Cain's frown – the equivalent of another man bellowing in rage – he hadn't known this was coming, either. He said merely, "An excellent idea. Mac will also continue to work with me, of course."

"Oh, of course," said Kay...and Gunnison didn't seem to notice or mind that Kay had just spoken for him.

Mac noticed, and was certain Cain had too – though, as of this moment, Kay's growing influence with the Can-Amer leader was the least of his troubles.

As the meeting continued, he managed to put a spark of excitement into his voice as plans for the New Era were discussed. He even managed to sound interested in his role, though just the word "interrogation" made his flesh crawl.

He tried to tell himself that all hope had not just died.

"You can get those files from Sandy," said Gunnison to

Mac, as the discussion turned to Appalachian officials who needed investigating.

Mac glanced up, feigning interest. "Oh, is Collis here?"

"He's working as one of my assistants." Gunnison had seemed preoccupied through much of the meeting, but now he winked. "He's too valuable to waste out there in the Western Quarter any longer, either."

After the meeting, in the usual shuffle of chairs and people rising, Cain shook hands with Gunnison and Kay in turn. "Excellent meeting," he said. "I feel we've made real progress."

Then he turned to Mac and added pleasantly, "May I see you in my office?"

Mac wasn't surprised by what his boss asked of him – he'd already decided the same thing for reasons of his own. He longed to be at home, discussing this with Sephy.

Instead he headed down the corridor to find "Sandy". A dozen assistants' offices adjoined Gunnison's; Collis Reed was in the one four offices over. Mac stuck his head in.

"Hey," he said.

Collis – or "Collie" or "Sandy", depending on who you were talking to – had been looking at something on his desk. He glanced up and quickly put it away in a drawer.

"Mac, hey," he said, crossing the room with his hand out:

an athletic-looking guy with sun-streaked hair and changeable blue-green eyes..

Mac had known Collis casually for a couple of years now. Reed was a small-time spy who'd somehow gotten catapulted into the big time – mostly by his work on the Western Seaboard Peacefighting base. Now Gunnison seemed to view the sandy-haired pilot as a kind of good-luck charm.

Collis's ready grin matched Mac's own. "Long time, no see," he said as they shook.

"Yeah, it's been a while," said Mac. He had no great love for Collis. The guy had always struck him as an operator through and through – too slick for his own good and not as smart as he thought he was.

"Remember training school?" Mac added, and they laughed. When needed back in the Heat, their cover story had been that they'd gone to Peacefighting training school together. They'd used it the last time Mac had seen Collis, in fact.

That had been the night Collis was out dancing with Amity Vancour.

Mac thought of her trial and the look that had been in her eyes when she'd said to tell Collis nothing. An ingrained habit to dig for the truth made him say, "Hey, you had everyone pretty worried for a while, you know, pal."

Collis sat down in one of two plush armchairs and motioned Mac to do the same. "What, the Vancour thing?" he said after a pause. "Hey, you want some coffee?"

"Thanks, why not?" said Mac, and waited until Collis had given the order through a small intercom on his desk. "And yes, I mean the Vancour thing," he went on. "I had Johnny asking me ten times a day if you'd checked in with us yet." He winked. "Everyone was starting to wonder if you'd become overly entranced by the lady's charms."

Collis sounded tetchy. "Oh, come on, not really."

"Of course, 'really'. You'd have thought the same."

"I couldn't check in any sooner; I was with her day and night. You know how tricky these things can get." Collis's gaze was direct, unblinking. It was, Mac noted with interest, the same straight-on gaze that he himself used when he was lying.

Mac grinned, defusing the tension. "Well, hey, she's an attractive girl. It can't have been much of a hardship. And you more than redeemed yourself."

Collis gave a small smile. "Sure, that's me…I always come through in the end."

The coffee came then. Once they were alone again, Mac settled back and said, "So what's Johnny got you doing now, anyway?"

If Collis was relieved at the change of subject, he hid it well. He described the administrative tasks Gunnison had set him on.

"Nothing too onerous then," said Mac.

Collis shrugged and rubbed his chin. "Yeah…I think mostly he just likes having me near. Which is great, of course," he added a touch too late. "Anything I can do is an honour."

You slipped, buddy, thought Mac with slight amusement. Or had Collis meant for him to hear the hesitation? He glanced at the tattoo on Collis's right palm that marked him as having once been a correction camp inmate. Collis saw him looking and closed his hand into a sudden fist.

"I hear she's in Harmony Five," said Mac pleasantly.

Collis froze. "Who?" he said after a beat.

"Vancour. Not doing too well, apparently."

Collis poured himself more coffee. He forgot to offer Mac any.

"Oh?" he said. Resting back in his chair he met Mac's gaze directly again, though his fingers around the mug were tight.

Mac shrugged and helped himself to more coffee. As Cain's assistant, he had easy access to this information. What he'd learned had saddened him, though he didn't show it.

"Fire sign," he said. "They never do well."

He didn't add that Leo – Collis's own tattoo – was also a fire sign, and so Collis should know. "Yeah, one of the reports said she got in trouble her first day, before she even made it through induction," Mac went on, stirring cream into his coffee. "They threw her in solitary for two weeks."

He knew Collis was aware what solitary was like, though he'd be surprised if Collis had ever experienced it.

He'd done a bit of digging once: Reed had apparently been one of those model prisoners who toed the line with excruciating care. Anything to get by, anything to survive.

Collis stared down at his coffee. "Shame," he said. He cleared his throat. "She wasn't bad, for a Discordant. Well...I guess that's what happens when you don't play by the rules."

"Exactly," said Mac cheerfully. "And you know what? From what I've heard, she *still* didn't learn. She's been in solitary twice since then. The last time finally broke her, though."

Collis's gaze flew to Mac's. His eyes looked pure green now, and for the first time, Mac saw raw emotion in them. Collis rose quickly.

"Hey, what time is it?" he said. "After four – great. I think that counts as happy hour, don't you?"

Mac watched as Collis went to a sideboard with a collection of liquor bottles clustered on it. Gunnison made certain that his assistants had the best, though in most offices this display was largely for show.

Here in Collis's little domain, the levels in the bottles were all low.

Collis poured himself a shot of whiskey and knocked it back. Then he added a slug to his coffee and returned bearing the bottle. "Come on, join me," he said jovially, and poured a shot into Mac's coffee before he could refuse. "Johnny won't care. We work hard; we should get some playtime too, right?"

"Right you are," said Mac, and clinked his doctored mug against Collis's.

For a few moments they drank without speaking. Mac was at ease with silence, but knew others weren't. Some of the most interesting revelations he'd ever learned had come from people rushing to fill a wordless space.

Sure enough, the atmosphere grew heavy quickly. Collis drained the rest of his coffee and then poured himself more, again adding a dollop of whiskey. Internally, Mac raised an eyebrow.

When Collis spoke again, his voice was slightly thick. "So…the last time broke her, huh? Well, good." He glanced up. "What…what happened?"

"I don't know much," said Mac. "Just that she kept getting into trouble…a dispute over a pair of boots, I think."

"Boots?" echoed Collis.

Mac shrugged. "Harmony Five." It was the harshest of all the work camps, set in the far north of the Yukon. A pair of boots could mean life or death there.

"Apparently you wouldn't even know she was the same woman these days," he added. He took another sip of his coffee, then leaned back, swirling the liquid in its mug. "Hey, this is good stuff, isn't it? Yeah, they say she's scared of her own shadow now, after all they've done to her. Not to mention physically weak, of course. I hear she may not last much longer. Well, solitary changes a person. Too bad it's necessary sometimes."

Collis didn't ask for details. He drained his drink, then looked down, rolling the mug between his palms. If Mac wasn't mistaken, his hands were shaking.

"You know, um...I've got a lot of work to do," he said. His smile had a taut look. "Let's catch up another time, hey, Mac?"

When Mac reached his apartment that night he felt wiped out. It had begun to truly hit him what his banishment from the Western Quarter would mean. *There has to be another way,* he told himself.

He could think of none.

Nearing his door, he heard the low sound of music: Van Wheeler's new hit, "For Ever and a Day".

She was home. Almost imperceptibly, his muscles relaxed.

Mac went inside. He closed the door behind him and stood leaning against it, gazing at the slim young woman who sat working at a desk in front of the bay window. She had skin the colour of rich, dark earth, and black hair coiled neatly atop her head. Her neck was long, aristocratic-looking.

"Sephy, will you marry me?" asked Mac in a low voice.

She didn't look up.

"No," she said.

Mac smiled and pulled off his overcoat. He went over and dropped to his knees beside her. "I love you," he said.

"Please, Sephy. Marry me and make me the happiest man in the—"

"Oh, get up."

Mac got up. He hefted himself onto the desk and Persephone gave him a pained look. "You're sitting on my ephemeris," she said.

Mac raised himself up with his hands and Sephy rescued the book of planetary charts. "How many times now have I asked you to marry me?" he said as she flipped through its pages.

"Seventeen. And we've only been together a year, and I only moved in eight weeks ago. It's kind of impressive."

"We've known each other since we were fourteen, and you've practically lived here from the second we got together," Mac countered. "Besides, you're keeping track. That's got to be good, right?"

Sephy was working on an astrological chart. After the events of the past few months, she was one of the only official state astrologers the Resistance had left. Whenever possible, she doctored information to save people. Mac saw the corner of her mouth twitch.

"It's more a kind of morbid fascination," she said as she carefully drew the symbol for Venus. "I ask myself, 'How many times will this fool try?'"

"That's easy. Until you say yes." Mac took the fountain pen from her fingers and laid it aside. He put his hands on her shoulders and kissed her. She smelled faintly of vanilla – her natural scent intoxicating to him.

"Mac, I'm trying to work."

"Go ahead, work," he murmured. "I'm not stopping you."

"I can't. You stole my pen, you…you pen-thief."

She was kissing him back now, her long, slim fingers stroking through his dark hair. Mac let his lips slide down her neck, shutting out everything that had happened, losing himself in the silkiness of her skin.

She pulled away and studied him carefully. Her brown eyes narrowed. "Something's wrong," she said, and laid her hand against his cheek.

Mac started to answer and stopped. He slid off the desk, wondering how to word it. Sephy rose too; she stood slightly taller than him. Her face reminded him of a doe's: long, narrow of chin, with softly angled cheekbones.

Now dread had come over it. "It's about the Day of Three Suns, isn't it?" she whispered.

Mac took a breath. "Yeah."

Mac had first been employed by Gunnison's regime as a message boy. Quick and able, he'd gradually worked his way up to Cain's assistant. It was all to benefit the Resistance – he'd been with them since he was sixteen. What had once been a fledgling, scattered movement had evolved into an organized network of thousands. They aided people found Discordant; produced underground newspapers; collected vital information.

Assassinating Gunnison had been their goal for years. Cain had to be taken out simultaneously or he'd seize power. It had long remained frustratingly out of reach. The Day of Three Suns had been exactly what the Resistance needed: both men up on a stage together for an event so massive that infiltration of the tight security was possible. Everything had been coming together: the snipers, the way in, all of it.

Then two months ago, a key man had been captured and their plan found out.

Mac had been blindsided, unable to tip anyone off. Crucial Appalachian contacts had been wiped out – the Western Quarter Resistance left gutted and gasping. Dozens were deemed Discordant by Kay Pierce and sent to correction camps. Though still largely functional in the former Central States, the Resistance's outer network was shattered.

The Day of Three Suns – originally scheduled for a conference centre in Philadelphia – had been relocated. The new city and venue were classified; Mac knew only that they'd be somewhere else in Appalachia. Madeline Bark was coordinating the event.

Mac didn't have a single contact now who stretched to her. Moving in and out of Appalachia from the closed Can-Amer was difficult. The international Heat had been their only real hope for reforging their Resistance "chains". And now, with Mac's relocation, his contacts there would think "Vince Griffin" – Mac's main Resistance alias – captured or dead.

Everyone would be cast adrift. Appalachia would fall, and Gunnison and Cain would continue to flourish.

Sephy's black hair had tumbled down around her shoulders. As they lay in bed hours later, Mac stroked its wavy length. "So that's how it is," he said roughly. "If they didn't search everyone who got close to the pair of them, I swear I'd assassinate them myself."

Sephy lay studying him, her dark eyes looking even larger than usual.

"You'd never make it out alive if you did," she said.

"So?"

She punched his arm, hard enough to hurt. "So I don't want you to die, you fool! Mac, there *must* be some way that we can still find out where the new venue is and put the plan back in place."

"We'll damn well try. But with half the Resistance wiped out..." Mac swiped a hand over his face. "No, the Harmony Treaty's pretty certain to go ahead, all right. And then we'll lose the eastern ports."

The Appalachian ports were vital, now that the Western Seaboard had fallen: they were the Resistance's only remaining route to get people and information out to the rest of the world.

Sephy swallowed and said nothing.

Mac added, "And if anyone encounters me doing interrogations, they'll think *they* were the ones I was double-crossing, not Gunnison." He stared up at the ceiling.

"Interrogations," he murmured. His muscles were tight.

Sephy stroked his arm. "This Miss Pierce must really have it in for you," she said bitterly.

Mac snorted. "Believe it or not, Kay Pierce likes me, as much as she likes anyone. I think she thought she was doing me a *favour*. Cain wants me to spy on her," he added.

Sephy straightened a little. "Really?"

"He pulled me aside after the meeting. It's why he didn't push harder for me to keep travelling to the Western Quarter; he wants me to find out how far her influence with Gunnison goes. I can sum it up in three words: she's screwing him."

Sephy frowned. "There must be more to it. Surely Gunnison's not some yokel who goes slack-jawed over sex."

"Sex plus his chief astrologer? Who he thinks holds the direct key to Harmony? Ha."

"Be careful," Sephy said. "I think our little Miss Kay is a dangerous woman. She's got a lot to win or lose."

"Don't we all?" Mac lay studying the ceiling's whorls and swirls. "'Interrogation' means torturing people, you know," he said, so softly Sephy hardly heard him. "I don't think I can do it, Seph. Not even if it's the only way I can stay close to Gunnison and Cain."

"Is it time to leave?" she said in a low voice.

Mac turned his head on the pillow to study her. "Would you come with me?"

She nodded, her eyes fixed on his face. Mac let out a breath and gripped her hand hard.

"All right," he said. "Just knowing that helps."

Sephy tugged playfully at his fingers. "Didn't you already know it?"

"You won't marry me, woman. How the hell should I know what goes on in that head of yours?"

She smiled.

"Okay. Let me check it out first," Mac said finally. "If I can manoeuvre myself into a role that I can deal with, I'll have to stay. I'm the only person we've got left on the inside."

Sephy leaned over and kissed him; her hair brushing his bare shoulder. "Whatever you decide," she said, "I'll be right there with you." She hesitated and touched his cheek. "And, Mac, listen – on a personal level…well, I'm pretty happy that you'll be around more."

"Yeah," he said in a soft voice. "Me too."

They lay in each other's arms. Mac could hear the sound of traffic outside, a noise he found soothing. The growls of autos and buses had been his first lullabies as a child. He was a city boy, through and through. He was aware of the warmth of Persephone's skin against his; the feel of the sheet against his legs.

"I saw Collis today," he said, remembering.

"Really?" Sephy stirred; the case had interested them both. "Did he mention Vancour?"

"I mentioned her," said Mac. "I wanted to see how he reacted."

"And?"

Mac shrugged, drifting off now. "I think he really cares about her," he said drowsily. "Whatever it was that happened, I don't think he planned it."

Chapter Five

November, 1941

In my mind I was flying.

I lay stiffly under the thin covers with my eyes shut. The concrete hut was icy. Around me, I could hear ragged breathing – a few coughs. From outside, as always, came John Gunnison's whisper and a distant, mechanical sound.

Machine oil, I thought. Its scent had been so rich, like perfume, every time I climbed into the cockpit. I imagined the stick in my hand, watched a billowing cloud grow larger as I flew towards it. I pulled back, soared high – then went into a roll and the world spun.

Sunshine. Clean, white clouds. The Dove, so responsive, like strapping on a pair of wings and stepping up into the sky.

I jumped as a siren wailed and the cabin's light came on. Gunnison's voice started booming: "…Because Lady Harmony has spoken, my friends! The way forward is clear! We…"

Five a.m.

A pair of grimy, sock-clad feet was pressed against my head. Wearily, I pushed them away and sat up. You'd think I'd be used to the smell here by now, but it still made my head throb: unwashed bodies, the too-full chamber pot. One of the windows had a crack in it. I both cursed it for the cold and blessed it for the fresh air.

At the other end of the bed, the owner of the grimy feet sat up too: a girl a little older than me named Fran, with hollow cheeks and dull hair. Every time I saw her, I wondered if I looked the same. My ribs had never been so prominent in my life.

"You were tossing and turning all night," she said. "I hardly slept."

I didn't answer. The bed was barely two feet wide – I'd have fallen off if I'd tossed and turned. As Gunnison's shouts echoed, I reached behind me for the bundle I'd been resting my head on: the pair of too-small boots with my flight jacket wrapped around them.

Around us, thirty-eight more women in nineteen other narrow beds were stirring. The wooden bunks lined the small, draughty hut. A pair of legs appeared in front of me as someone climbed down from the one above ours.

I sat on the side of our bed and struggled to pull on one

of the flimsy red boots. Familiar pain throbbed in my toes.

I stood up, trying not to wince. I knew I looked as scarecrow-like as the other women: my clothes hadn't survived "disinfecting" very well. They were practically falling off me now anyway.

"The Discordant elements *must* be rooted out, folks! And with the power of the stars, we..."

Fran took a makeshift wooden comb from somewhere under her clothes and ran it through her limp hair.

"Want to use it?" she asked, holding the comb out to me.

I didn't move. "How much?"

"Half your breakfast."

"No," I said shortly. We only got two meals a day and I worked in one of the mines. If I collapsed on the job, I'd get beaten. Or worse, sent to solitary again.

Fran shrugged and put the comb away. I didn't blame her for not offering it to me anyway. If I'd owned something so precious here, I wouldn't either. I thought of my pilot's boots and a hopeless resentment filled me. I still couldn't believe I'd been so stupid.

I went to stand by the door. We'd be called to the First Counting soon – you didn't want to be caught lagging behind, no matter what. From across the room, a girl named Natalie gave a low exclamation of dismay. "I've started!"

A woman named Claudia, not as thin as most here, puffed herself up slightly. She knew what was coming.

So did the rest of us; we shot her sideways glances of disgust and envy.

Natalie went over to her. Snatches of low conversation drifted over.

"Half my food for two days."

"Three."

"*Three?* Are you crazy? They're just rags!"

"Yes, but you need them, don't you?" Claudia sounded smug. She worked in the laundry and could steal scraps of cloth. The laundry was for the Guns, of course, not us. Claudia's hands were often raw and blistered from detergent, but any of us would have swapped places with her in a heartbeat.

Three days on half-rations…and Natalie's cheekbones were already growing so sharp. Nobody met her eyes. I had a tattered rag that I was saving, tied safely around my upper thigh. I gripped my elbows, glad no one knew about it.

"Fine," said Natalie tightly. "Three days."

Claudia passed over a rag. She kept them tucked close against her body, in some secret pouch. Natalie went off into the corner and turned her back to us as she fitted it in place in her underclothes.

A sign on the concrete wall read: GRATITUDE IS HARMONY.

Gunnison's voice blared on. Natalie came and stood next to me at the door, lips tight. "At least with three days of hardly any food, I might just stop having the damn things altogether," she muttered.

"Or you could get pregnant," said someone snidely. "One of the male Guns would probably help you out. You're still pretty enough. Just."

It wasn't really a joke. Some of the women did sleep with the Guns, for protection, for food. Once I'd thought I could never consider it. Now I understood. I'd been hungry too often myself.

I was hungry now, but doubted any Gun would appear to offer me a deal.

Natalie took in my thinness. In an undertone, she said, "Do *you* still have them? You've been here, what – five months?" It was a lifetime here.

"Six," I said. "And sometimes." I gazed straight ahead at the door's worn wood. Some of the women banded together, helped each other pay for necessities. I wanted none of it. Betrayal was too easy.

Natalie snorted. "You don't have to be so stand-offish. Everyone knows who *you* are...Wildcat."

She didn't say it as if she really cared. The world may have decided once that I was a crooked Peacefighter and a murderer, but what did that mean to anyone here?

I pulled my flight jacket tighter and touched its hem, feeling the square of paper that was still there, its edges worn now. *Ma. Hal.* Emotion threatened. I knew better than this. I dropped my hand.

We all stiffened as another siren blared. A Gun flung open our door. She looked almost unbelievably clean and warm: a long wool coat; a fur-lined hat.

"Outside, Discordant scum," she barked.

I filed out with the others into the harshly lit yard.

The sky was a glittering sweep of stars. The moving-picture screen rose up from beyond the other buildings. A huge black-and-white Gunnison waved his fist. "*Our Harmonic society depends on it! I will not falter, friends and neighbours!*"

His face was open, trustworthy. I barely glanced at it. I knew the cheering crowds, the waving flags, by heart.

Other prisoners had exited their own huts and waited shivering outside too, hundreds of us – and this was just the women's section. We formed a series of long lines. I could feel the grimy snow soaking through the thin boots already.

"Hands out," ordered a Gun. We all held out our right hands. I unfolded mine slowly, my fingers aching with cold. I didn't look down at the tattoo, or allow myself to think of the other one, on the hand of someone I'd once loved.

Flaps up, I thought. *Mixture control to rich...then flip the ignition switch and the engine starts up and you can hardly hear; it's your own little world...*

My hand gradually went numb. When a Gun got to me, she'd shown a flashlight at the tattoo, muttered, "Aries, number seven, hut twelve," and checked me off her list. She moved on and I slid my hand gratefully back in my pocket. It erupted into pins and needles as I rubbed my fingers together.

Abruptly, Gunnison's voice dropped to an urgent whisper. No one reacted. The non-stop footage changed volume at the whim of the Guns in the projection hut, sometimes blaring in the middle of the night.

At the rumble of an engine, all other thoughts vanished.

Awareness rippled down the line: the food truck was coming. I swallowed reflexively as its headlights appeared down the road, snow tyres rattling. With one hand I clutched the tin cup that I wore around my neck.

The truck stopped just past us. Snow covered its grille; a high arch of canvas protected the bed. The smell of food hit me and I felt faint.

A Gun sat in the back with a large black cauldron. I tensely studied his nondescript form.

"Who is it, can you tell?" muttered Rosie, standing beside me.

I stiffened and glanced at the guard still checking our group. We were supposed to stand silently. Someone else answered in a low whisper: "I think it's Fergus."

The name was muttered from person to person. I stayed motionless, wishing desperately they'd all shut up. The Guns weren't above punishing a whole group for the actions of a few. Half my group had never been beaten, never been in solitary. They didn't know – though they should. My gaze flicked to the heads just visible on the fence.

To my deep relief, the Guns didn't hear the whispers. When they finally let us go, those of us who'd been there longer hung back, letting the new people rush to the front of the line. Along with a few others, I manoeuvred my way to somewhere near the end, even though my stomach, now that it had been promised food, was alive and roaring.

We edged forward. Fergus stood in the open back of the truck, his movements rhythmical. One ladle of soup each. One small piece of bread. I kept my eyes locked on his hand, terrified that he'd chosen this day to change his routine.

But just like always, he skimmed the soup from the top of the cauldron. Those at the front had mostly watery broth. By the time I held up my cup, my hands trembling, he'd gotten to the soup's substance. I had two small chunks of potato, even a scrap of meat.

A few ravens flitted from roof to roof, watching our food with glittering black eyes. No one let a single crumb fall. In the distance Gunnison's face filled the screen, his voice an incessant murmur.

I leaned against the side of our hut and ate slowly, dipping the bread into the soup.

Natalie wolfed down her half-share. "You'd have done better to save it," said Claudia, standing nearby. She licked her spoon complacently.

I forced myself to hold back on a bite of bread. I tucked the stale crust in my pocket just as the siren went off again. I felt slightly stronger, though my stomach still complained. In between meals it grew dull and resigned; once it had tasted food, it wailed in protest.

As we got in line – one behind the other this time, ready to march through the gates – I saw Melody and stiffened.

She was getting in line with the group from her own hut, number four. As always, I glanced furtively at her feet. The boots I'd worn as a pilot were thick, brown leather, scuffed now, but no doubt just as warm and dry as the day I'd gotten them. My feet were damp already, the blisters throbbing.

It came back in a flash: the twist of stunned disbelief I'd felt when I got out of solitary that first time and Melody had claimed not to know what I was talking about. *No, there must be some mistake. These are my boots. They have my number.*

She hadn't been able to meet my eyes then, and she didn't now.

I studied her with sidelong looks, taking in every detail almost greedily. She was getting very thin – surely she couldn't last much longer? What would happen to my boots then? The old Amity would have been horrified by this thought. But it was only November – we hadn't even begun to reach the worst of the winter yet. If I couldn't walk, I'd be shot.

One of the Guns, a pretty blonde one, gave a sneering laugh. "Still thinking about those boots, Vancour?"

I tore my gaze away. "No, sir," I said. Guns were all "sir", no matter their sex.

"Want to go into solitary again, is that it?"

My mouth went dry at the thought of that small concrete room. Arguing with Melody, pleading with her, had landed me there twice more. "No, sir," I said softly. "I know the boots aren't mine, sir."

"That's right, and don't you forget it." The Gun glanced at a clipboard. Offhandedly, she said, "Oh, and we've changed the roster. You're in Mine Three now."

My pulse of alarm was deep, visceral. I'd worked in Mine Two for months. I had my niche there; I knew exactly how things worked. In Harmony Five, that could mean the difference between life and death.

Funny, but for some reason I still cared about that.

"Yes, sir," I said. "Mine Three."

"You don't sound very happy about it."

I stretched my lips into a smile, staring at the neck of the prisoner in front of me. "I'm very honoured, sir."

"March!" shouted another Gun from further up.

We started at a brisk pace as a band that clustered near the entrance struck up merry music: "Happy Days are Here Again". Gunnison had adopted it as his theme song ever since taking over the Western Seaboard.

We marched quick-step, his image behind us now, to show how happy we were to be working for him and the glory of Can-Amer. Once, I'd burned with hatred at the thought. Now I just concentrated on stepping fast enough not to get beaten.

I forced myself to look at the severed heads clear in the camp's lights. There were seven more on the fence than when I'd first arrived. Back then my gaze had flown to them each day with horror. Now I looked to remind myself what would happen if I wasn't careful.

The music played on jauntily. A gentle snowfall began as a pair of Guns swung open the main gates, dividing the Harmony symbol. Outside, more Guns waited on silver snowmobiles, revving their engines, shouting cheerfully to each other.

Under the dead eyes' scrutiny, we started the long walk.

Chapter Six

We trudged in silence, hunched into whatever clothes we had. The music faded. The snow was packed hard here – slippery, icy. The snowmobiles shot ahead, then skimmed back again, their headlamps and the moon our only light.

"Try to escape!" shouted a Gun. "Come on, I feel like target practice!"

The detested boots had wedge heels and hardly any grip, though I'd rubbed their soles over gravel. One heel was half-flopping off. I had to set my foot down too carefully, making me unsteady with every step.

The turn-off to the mines was a mile away. For the first time, I turned left with the group heading to Mine Three instead of continuing straight on. I felt a pang as the other group pulled away from us. Mine Two was reached from a road that passed through fields, and until the dark mornings had come, I'd always looked out for hawks flying overhead. If you showed too much interest in something the Guns made you pay for it, but I'd liked watching the hawks when I could. It was a tiny rebellion; the one thing I had that was my own – watching those birds soar through the air like Firedoves.

I was going to miss the hawks.

The new road went through woods. I'd seen them from the camp: a brooding tangle of dark branches. It was warmer than walking across the fields, but the trees made me feel oppressed, closed-in. I shivered and ducked my head.

I heard the mine long before we reached it. The air churned with the gnashing, crunching sound of machinery. We came out into the open and there it was: a hill with a gaping mouth and a road heading into it. Flames flickered from within.

Nearby, just like Mine Two, a broad clearing held mounds of crushed raw ore. Chemicals were dripped over them to extract some kind of metal – we weren't told what. Distantly, I could see the lights from the processing plant where other prisoners worked. Snow-trucks on giant caterpillar tracks trundled between the leach pads and the plant.

The Guns swept up to the mine's entrance on their snowmobiles, kicking up snow as they swerved to a stop. Our group kept going straight inside, over fifty of us, heads down.

We entered a cavernous space hewn from the rock. There were several metal drums with fires going. Guns with scarves wrapped around their mouths clustered around these, warming their hands. Overhead, holes in the ceiling let out the smoke and dust. Or tried to. The atmosphere was murky; the electric lights strung above could only dimly be seen.

Noise pounded incessantly. A rock crusher dominated the space like a prehistoric monster. A conveyor belt carried dusty chunks of rock up and up, thirty feet high. At the top they were dropped into a cradle where metal jaws churned; teeth ground them into rubble that spewed out the other side. Dust rose in billowing, choking clouds.

The sound was indescribable; it throbbed right through you. Workers tended to the crusher like acolytes. As miners emerged from the depths with full wheelbarrows, the workers helped them scatter the heavy rocks onto the conveyor belt. Then the miners trudged back again, wheelbarrows empty but shoulders just as tired as before.

The cavern bustled with dust and activity. I hesitated inside the entrance, unsure where to go. Most of our group headed straight for the picks and wheelbarrows piled against one wall. Guns with pistols accompanied them as they disappeared into the tunnels. If this was like Mine Two, the majority of miners would be men from the other section of the camp, who we seldom had contact with and weren't allowed to speak to – but women would help them with the lighter work.

A Gun came striding up, his voice muffled from his protective scarf. "You're on swing shift. Get to work on the crusher!"

My heart sank. Swing shift meant I did whatever job was needed each day. I'd never be able to make a niche for myself, never find a routine. That could be fatal in this place.

The crusher had been my old job at Mine Two. As the miners emerged and upended their barrow-loads, I stooped and grabbed rocks, then shoved them onto the conveyor belt. Sometimes I had to heft with both hands. The rocks were a dull brownish-grey, tinged with green.

When I'd first gotten here I'd wondered what we were mining. I didn't care much any more.

The hours passed. My throat burned with grainy dust. My rough hands got fresh cuts; a few old ones reopened. When I felt dizzy I ate the bite of bread I'd brought with me that morning, stuffing it in my mouth before one of the Guns could see.

Through the holes in the ceiling, snow flurried in. It battled briefly with the dust clouds, melting before it reached the fires. Miners exited the tunnels in a steady stream. Some had their shirts off, showing scrawny forms. The work made them too hot, then the cold up here chilled them again. Pneumonia was common. The incessant dust didn't help.

Running through the fields with Hal, I thought. *We're heading to the swimming hole and the sun is shining...*

But no, that memory was dangerous. We'd run through those fields to meet Dad landing one of his planes too many times.

I couldn't think very deeply about my father. Not here. Memories of him – the kind but distant dad I'd longed to know better – battled with the daily reality of what his thrown fight had led to. As always, my mind flinched from the thought.

I hastily discarded the memory. All right, a different one. I had dozens that I played to myself. I shuffled carefully through them in my mind, deciding. A shirtless miner passed close by, pushing a heavily-laden wheelbarrow, and I glanced at him.

I froze.

Even in profile, even with his dark curls shorn, I recognized him. He was tall and had been thin before he got here. Those long, angular features looked gaunt now, but his scowl was grim, stubborn.

Ingo.

Shock clutched my chest. I looked hastily away and spaced out the rocks on the moving belt so they wouldn't jam the churning jaws above. Finally I risked another look.

Ingo reached the front of the crusher and tipped out his heavy load. Black stubble showed through the greyish dust on his face. I could see his every rib. Leaning wearily over, he started throwing rocks onto the belt.

As Ingo straightened again, our eyes met and I saw him full-on. My constantly moving hands faltered.

The left half of his face was normal, if too thin. The right was a grotesque melted mask. A reddish burn scar puckered from forehead to chin. Part of his eyebrow was gone. The scar tugged downwards at one eye, pulled tightly at his mouth.

From the sudden flare of Ingo's nostrils, he recognized me too. As he stared at me, an expression I couldn't read sparked in his dark eyes. I quickly ducked my head, terrified of what might happen if the Guns realized we knew each other.

"What are you waiting for?" shouted a voice. "Get moving, you scum!"

Ingo's lip curled. After a beat, he grabbed the wheelbarrow's wooden handles and headed back into the mine.

I didn't see him again.

When it had been dark for hours, we women were marched back to camp. The Guns guarded us from their snowmobiles, headlights racing across the snow.

I buried my icy fists in my pockets. The heel of my left boot felt looser as I trudged along. I was used to losing myself in soothing daydreams, ignoring my aching limbs. Since seeing Ingo, the daydreams had shattered into dust. Unwanted memories of him raged like a storm in my head.

As we approached Harmony Five, its lights battled the stars. A raven sat on top of one of the severed heads, preening itself.

Sometimes I managed to save a little bread from my meal, in case I woke up too hungry in the night to go back to sleep. This evening it felt impossible. I ate fast, scraping the bowl. On the screen, Gunnison's solid-looking form was giving an interview, the volume soft.

"Well, Tom – mind if I call you Tom? It all started back when I was a child, growing up on the farm. You see…"

I went into the hut. Darkness encased me. When I groped my way to my bed, Fran was already there. I got in too and pulled some of the blanket over myself.

Neither of us spoke. Conversation happened in the morning; by this time of day everyone had shrunk into themselves, concerned only with hanging on for another night. I lay stiffly, not moving, as Gunnison whispered on.

They'd mentioned Ingo only briefly the first time they'd questioned me. The second time, in a cell before my trial, they'd harped on and on about him.

You're being very noble to protect Mr Manfred…but he certainly isn't protecting you.

Remembering it now, I saw with wonder how *clean* that cell had been. I hadn't noticed at the time – hadn't appreciated its warmth, or the fact that when I was hungry, food and hot coffee had arrived.

I hadn't thought about Ingo in months. Yet in that cell, the thought that he might have betrayed me had hurt keenly. The Gun had smirked as she'd tapped brass knuckles against her palm. "You might as well talk, Wildcat. He's told us everything."

Has he? I'd wondered in a daze. It hadn't seemed like something Ingo would do…but then, I'd hardly known him.

He was a former opponent, a pilot for the European Alliance. I'd trusted him because I had no choice. I'd had to break into the World for Peace building and Ingo had access to the keys – his girlfriend's father worked there. He'd seemed genuinely upset by the evidence of thrown Peacefights that we'd found in Madeline's office.

I hadn't thought about Madeline in months, either. Now dull hatred for her stirred. I remembered her fumble during my trial – her near-admission that she'd talked my father into throwing the civil war fight…with all that had led to.

Coldness clenched my gut. I pulled the thin blanket more tightly around myself. The papers Ingo and I had taken that night had proved that everything we'd believed in was a sham. What felt like an entire lifetime had taken place between those two events: stealing the evidence and my trial.

Madeline wasn't the only person I'd loved who had betrayed me.

I didn't want to think about Collie. I never wanted to think about him ever again.

But the thoughts wouldn't stop coming.

Chapter Seven

March, 1941

We drove for hours in the auto Collie bought from the farmer, heading towards the coast. By three o'clock in the morning we hadn't seen another auto in miles and we were both drooping.

I hadn't actually agreed to Collie's plan to catch a steamer somewhere...though I guess the fact that I hadn't argued about heading north-west maybe spoke for itself.

We found a forest road and took the auto deep into the woods. Then we crawled onto the back seat, and angled ourselves across it as best we could, curled in each other's arms.

Collie fell asleep in seconds. His breath ruffled my hair. Inch by inch my tension eased and I relaxed against his body. I'd been so sure he was dead – that they'd found out he knew about the corruption and had killed him.

Gently, I unbuttoned his shirt. I closed my eyes and stroked his warm skin, feeling the curve of his ribs, his muscles, the rise and fall of his chest.

It all seemed like a miracle.

When I opened my eyes again, sunlight was streaming into the car. Collie was still asleep. Stubble coated his jaw. I sat up stiffly. Condensation covered the windows; I swiped some away with my sleeve.

A morning mist wove through the dark trees. I stared out at the pale, wispy beauty and instead saw tanks rolling down a street.

What were Gunnison's troops doing right now?

"Morning," said Collie.

I turned just as he sat up. I tried to smile. "Morning to you, too."

He touched my forehead, gently stroking away its creases.

"Don't worry," he whispered. "We're together. Everything's going to be okay."

I sighed. Maybe he was right. Maybe to get away and be happy together was enough.

His hair looked a darker blond than usual, slightly greasy. I touched the thickened bridge of his nose: a childhood injury. My finger trailed down to his mouth, outlined his lips.

Collie's eyes stayed locked on mine. My pulse heated as I slid my hand slowly down his chest, his stomach, following the soft line of hair that arrowed towards his belt buckle.

"You know…I'm kind of glad you're still alive," I said huskily.

Collie looked pained. "Amity…" he whispered.

We moved at the same moment. He pulled me towards him and our lips met. The kiss deepened. Collie gave a rough groan, deep in the back of his throat. He fumbled with my buttons as I shrugged out of my shirt.

The auto was its own world, small and steamy. We slid down onto the seat, kissing fiercely. I ran my hands up and down his back, savouring his heat, his solid weight on me.

Collie reached for my flies. "Wait," I gasped. "Do you have a proph?"

His shoulders slumped. He let out a long breath and shook his head against my neck. "No."

Damn. Disappointment made my voice sharp. "We'd better stop then."

Collie didn't move. He kissed my neck, sending shivers through me; his hand caressed my breast in lazy circles.

"It doesn't matter," he murmured. "I don't care if you get pregnant."

I snorted out a laugh and pushed his hand away. "*I* care, you lummox."

"We want a large family, remember?"

"Not one started in the back of a...what kind of auto is this, anyway?"

I could feel him smiling as he laced more kisses across my skin. "It'll be a story to tell our grandchildren."

"You would, wouldn't you?"

"'Gather round, kids, and let Grandpa Collie tell you about how—'"

"Get *off.*" I heaved upwards and pushed him; he fell off me and lay sprawled on the floor of the auto, pressed against the backs of the front seats. He was laughing now, his bare shoulders shaking.

"You really know how to kill the mood," he said. "Has anyone ever told you that, you infuriating wench?"

I grinned and leaned down to kiss him. I whispered against his lips, "We can start our large family when we get to...Timbuktu, or wherever we're going."

Slowly, Collie got to his knees, his eyes locked on mine. "You mean it?" he said – and I knew he wasn't talking about children.

"Yeah," I said softly. "You're right. We'll leave Gunnison to whatever he's doing and get out while we still can. I guess..." I swallowed and touched his cheek. "I guess that's all we can do."

I traced my finger down his jaw to hide how much I hated the words – hated the thought of leaving Hal and Ma in such dire straits. But they were in enough danger already. They'd be safer if I went far away.

Collie closed his eyes. When he opened them again he looked like a man reborn.

"Thank you," he said. "We'll be happy, Amity. I promise."

When we finally reached the port city of Puget, it was almost evening and it was chaos. Thick traffic clogged the roads. The docks were a heaving mass of people – some struggling with suitcases, others waving signs that said, DISCORDANTS WILL FACE THEIR JUDGEMENT.

I gaped at the scene. Collie swore; we glanced at eachother. Through the slightly open window came a cacophony of shouts:

"*How* much? I can't afford that! No, please! I've got to have them—"

"Steamer tickets for sale! Get your tickets here!"

"If you weren't Discordant, you wouldn't want to leave! Gunnison's going to bring order and get rid of all you scum!"

A few ships in the harbour rose white and serene above the scene. Collie's mouth was hard; he angled the auto behind a bar attached to a seedy-looking restaurant. Dark shadows painted the area. "*Stay here*," he ordered.

"Where are you going?"

"To get tickets or die trying." He was already half-out, craning to scan the docks. "Don't worry – just stay out of sight." He ducked back in and kissed me, then closed the door. I watched his tall, sandy-haired form grow smaller;

he vanished into the seething crowd.

I rubbed my elbows, trying not to stare at the dashboard clock. I stiffened as the bar's back door opened. A pair of men came out carrying garbage cans. Neither glanced at the auto. They crossed to a large metal bin and hefted the dented cans upwards. Fragments of muttered conversation floated over:

"Why the hell doesn't Lopez *do* something?"

"What can he do against a goddamn army?"

"My sister said that troops have reached Riverside. Everyone lined up on the streets and cheered, she said."

"*Cheered?*"

"Well, it's better than being sent to one of those camps."

My spirits plummeted. *Hal.* What would it mean for him if Gunnison took over Sacrament where he was in hiding? What would it mean for Ma?

"See him on the telio just now?" said the first one. "He was waving some folder around. Says he's got evidence that the World for Peace is guilty as hell."

"Oh, so is that supposed to give him the right to…"

The back door opened and closed again. They were gone.

My thoughts were suddenly as chaotic as the docks. Had they meant *Gunnison*? What evidence? A desperate hope swept me. Before I could reconsider, I flipped up the collar of my jacket. I shoved my hair into the knit cap I'd been wearing and swung open the auto door. The shouts intensified. I could smell the reek of garbage, mixed with the ocean's salty tang.

I knew I shouldn't be doing this. At least the only person I was putting into danger was myself. Hands tense in my pockets, shoulders hunched, I went around to the front of the bar.

Smithies, read the lettering on the plate-glass window. It was packed shoulder to shoulder – a mix of seamen's blue wool jackets, double-breasted suits, fedora hats. Apparently everyone who wasn't trying to escape the Western Seaboard was drowning their sorrows.

I stood near the front door as if waiting for someone, occasionally glancing in the window. The telio set crouched on a shelf over the bar: a small round screen framed by curlicue speakers.

Gunnison was on it. He sat at a long table with four other official-looking people, motioning with a thick file. His silent image took out a small, battered notebook and pointed something out. When a woman leaned closer he put the notebook away, still talking.

I started as the bar door swung open and someone bumped into me. "Hey, sister, watch where you're standing!"

I didn't answer. I'd hardly moved. I still hardly moved even when the images on the screen vanished and the familiar black-and-white daisy came into view.

"There you are!" Collie appeared, relief battling fear. He grabbed my arm and hurried me back around the side of the building. "What the hell were you *doing*? I thought you'd been captured!"

Before I could respond, he said in a rush, "Listen, I got

tickets on one of the ships – the last two available, and it's a private room too. It's just about to start boarding. We'll keep you hidden somehow once we're there, and—"

"We can't go," I broke in.

"*What?*"

"*We can't go.*" I lowered my voice; my words tumbled over each other. "Collie – the evidence from Russ's house wasn't destroyed. I just saw it on the telio – Gunnison's pretending it says something it doesn't say, but it's still there; he has it! If we can get hold of it somehow, we can use it to bring him down!"

Collie gripped my arms. "Amity, the ship is boarding right this second. We can argue about this once we're on board."

"Didn't you hear me? I'm not going. I can't, not while there's a chance of saving Hal."

Looking frantic, Collie pushed his hands through his hair. He glanced over his shoulder at the ship. "Amity… please…you promised…"

My voice rose. "Don't you *get it*? This changes everything!"

Collie took my elbow and pulled me back to the auto; we got in and he slammed the door. In the sudden silence he said, "Even if you're right, *how* do you propose we get hold of this stuff? Just saunter up to Gunnison and ask nicely?"

"I don't know! But there must be a way. You're the one with contacts – wouldn't any of them be interested in this, help us get hold of it? The evidence proves Gunnison was in on the corruption up to his neck!"

"You probably saw something different – not the same file at all—"

"It is! I recognized Russ's date book!"

In a low, tight voice, Collie said, "We cannot get hold of it even if it still exists. And our ship is boarding *now.*" He clutched my hands, his expression raw. "Amity, please. You promised. This is our chance to get away, to have a new life—"

I jerked away. "And just leave Hal to rot when I can *do something* about it?"

"Amity—"

"We're the only ones who know what that evidence really says! We have to let the world know that the thrown Peacefights all led back to Gunnison. There must be thousands of people in hiding, just like Hal. This is the only thing that might save them!"

Shouts still came from the docks: *If you weren't Discordant, you wouldn't want to leave!* Collie scowled at the windscreen, bumping his fist against his mouth.

I sat staring at him. Suddenly it felt as if I'd never really known him. "Or don't you care about my brother?" I said finally.

He glared at me. "Of course I care," he snapped. Collie had grown up down the road from us; Hal was practically his brother too. "But, Amity…" He rubbed his forehead. "We're so close," he murmured. "We can still get away…"

Fury gripped me. I could see the bulge of his wallet in his back pocket; I reached behind him and yanked it out. I found the two steamer tickets, plucked them out and shoved them at him.

"Take yours and go," I hissed. "Sell the other one. And you'd better hurry – the ship's about to leave."

We slept in the auto that night, hidden behind a row of office buildings. We were hardly speaking. The ship had left hours ago. Silence draped over the docks like a cloak.

When I woke up, Collie was sitting with his shirt unbuttoned, gazing out the window at pink streaks of dawn. I sat up and he looked over at me. The corner of his mouth twisted.

"Still speaking to me?"

"Just about," I said warily.

He rubbed his temples with one hand. "You were right, okay?" he said at last.

I drew a startled breath. "Do you mean it?"

Collie let his hand fall. "Yeah. We can't leave if there's a chance of exposing this. I just…" He sighed, tapping a fist on his thigh. "I guess I panicked. The thought of escaping with you – of having the life we've always wanted together, for ever…" He trailed off.

I lunged at him and hugged him hard. He held me tightly. "I don't know if my contacts can help, but we'll try," he said against my hair. "It's worth a shot if it means we can save Hal and never have to worry about Gunnison again."

His steady heartbeat beneath my cheek felt a part of me. "Thank you," I whispered.

Collie took me by the shoulders, his expression as determined as when we were kids together, plotting some escapade. His eyes, pure blue now, locked onto mine.

"We *will* do this," he said. "I promise you. Then we'll have the only thing in the world I want: a life together."

"I want it too," I said softly. I traced the outline of his lips. "We'll have it."

Chapter Eight

November, 1941

"Faster!" shouted one of the Guns. They sat idling their snowmobiles, watching us trudge down the wooded path in the headlights. The Gun revved his motor with gloved hands.

"Lazy Discordant scum," he bellowed. "*March!*"

"I'll make them move," said another one. He raised his pistol and fired. My body flinched as the retort echoed. I felt only dull surprise when the bullet didn't tear through me, when no one in our group fell, staining the snow red.

"Next time I won't aim over your heads!" shouted the Gun to hooting laughter from his comrades.

Anger took too much energy. We emerged from the woods into a clear, icy night. I ached after a twelve-hour shift, struggling on my unsteady heel. Distantly, I recalled what it had been like to fly on such a night – to glide through the stars, in control of where I went. The idea seemed extraordinary.

It had been three days since I'd seen Ingo.

Had I only imagined the flash of recognition from the scarred miner's dark eyes? I prayed that I'd hallucinated the whole thing…and not just because I wouldn't wish this place on anyone. I resented the headspace I was giving Ingo. I couldn't afford it, not here.

Things I hadn't thought about in months kept crowding in on me: one of the Guns in my cell, holding a cigarette. *Let's talk about your father, Amity. Being a traitor runs in the family, doesn't it?* My trial: the moment when I'd finally broken down and the flashbulbs had gone crazy. *Wildcat Confesses,* screamed the headlines the guards had taunted me with.

More painful than any of it was my arrest.

No. No.

Shakily, I shoved the memory of Collie away. We were nearing the entrance to Harmony Five. The Guns shot past on their snowmobiles. Our group stood waiting, silently, not meeting anyone's eyes, as the gate slowly swung open.

At the first notes of "*Happy Days are Here Again*", I started to march forward with the others – and that's when I saw it.

Half-buried in the snow there glinted a thick shard of

glass about two inches long. My breath caught. Instinct shrieked at me to keep going. Instead I stopped short and crouched over my boot, pretending to tie its laces. My fingers scrabbled quickly in the snow; I grabbed the glass and tucked it up my sleeve.

A Gun kicked me in the shins so hard I almost fell over. "What's the hold-up?" he barked.

I rose, my leg throbbing. "I'm sorry, sir. I was just tying my boot." I stared straight ahead, sick with fear.

He glanced down and sneered at the state of my shoes. "Well, get inside!"

I hastened in, keeping my sleeve pressed against my side. I felt so agitated that I didn't pay attention to who was in charge of the food wagon, and found myself too far back in the line even though it was Darrow, a bottom-ladler.

Food in hand, I stood against our hut and ate quickly, dipping the bread into the watery soup and wolfing it down. A raven flapped at me and I jerked away. It snatched up a piece of bread that Rosie had let fall. She swore in tired dismay as it flew off.

"You found something," muttered Natalie. She'd finished paying her three days' half-rations to Claudia for the rags and had eaten her scanty meal even faster than I'd eaten mine.

"No, I didn't," I said.

But despite myself, I glanced furtively towards a shadowy corner of the camp. When we weren't working, the Guns didn't really care what we did – so long as it didn't seem suspicious and we were all present whenever they counted us. Everyone knew that area was the "marketplace" – if you had something to trade, that's where you went.

The shard pressed sharply against my wrist. Once I'd have seen it as garbage. Now its possibilities were endless. You could signal with it, start a fire with it, cut things with it…

It might even be enough to get a better pair of boots.

I licked the remaining soup from my cup, trying to hide the sudden shaking of my hands. The heel on my left boot was so loose now that I wasn't sure how it was hanging on. Worse, the too-tight fit had rubbed blisters upon blisters over the months – angry sores that I was terrified might become infected.

You did not want to be admitted to Medical in this place. You did not want to give the Guns the idea, ever, that you were unable to work.

On the screen, a smiling black-and-white Gunnison made his way down a line of soldiers, clasping their hands. The sound boomed abruptly: "…I'm sure proud to meet you, Ned! Lady Harmony is smiling on you…!"

I darted a look at the gates. The Guns stood talking in a bored cluster. A few people milled in the marketplace. The Guns didn't seem to know about it, though if too many people congregated there they broke it up… sometimes with gunshots.

Gunnison's voice bounced against my brain. Still over an hour till ten o'clock curfew – as long as I didn't attract any notice, I should be fine. I swallowed hard. I pushed away from the hut and started over.

As I passed the building that held the solitary confinement cells, I faltered. The door was opening. *Keep walking!* I screamed at myself. Standing and watching something, drawing attention to yourself, was the worst thing you could do. But I was frozen.

Two Guns emerged, carrying the limp body of a woman. Her eyes were open, dull. Her head hung to one side. She was so emaciated that one of the Guns could have carried her by himself.

"No, the honour's all mine!" boomed Gunnison. "Please, call me Johnny!"

I began to tremble, remembering the tiny, bare cells. Cold concrete and only four feet high, so that you could never stand up. No food. No sanitation. Water only once a day, and that foul-smelling. My first time had been for two weeks; by the time they let me out I could hardly stand and I'd been beaten for falling down.

Another stint at this point would kill me.

Head down, I hurried back to my hut. The reek of the overcrowded room felt like safety. I curled up on my bed as Gunnison shouted, grateful that Fran wasn't there yet. The shard pressed mockingly against my wrist. I was tempted to throw it away so I wouldn't be caught with it – but I couldn't be that craven.

I wanted to be, though, and I hated myself for it.

* * *

In the mine the next day I felt clammy with nerves. I was acutely aware of the piece of glass, which I'd tucked into my brassiere. It seemed incredible that the Guns didn't realize.

I bent and straightened, bent and straightened, feeding endless rocks to the conveyor belt. As I stooped to grasp one, a miner crouched down too, his face near mine. I stiffened at the angry crinkled scar.

In a low voice under the crusher's incessant noise, Ingo demanded, "Why did you betray me?"

My fingers fumbled as I grabbed at a rock. I glanced nervously at the Guns. We weren't allowed to talk.

Ingo grasped my wrist. "*Answer me.*"

I yanked away in a panic. "Shut up!" I whispered back. "Are you crazy? They'll hear you!"

"I don't give a damn. Tell me!"

"I did not betray you!"

Even stained with sweat and dust, Ingo's thin form held derision in its every movement. He straightened and hefted one of the largest rocks onto the conveyor belt. "Yes, and why should I believe you?" he said from between gritted teeth. "I'm *here*, you traitorous bitch."

Anger flared through me – the first I'd felt in months, dizzying in its power. As we stooped to the rock pile again, I shoved back one sleeve and showed Ingo my own scar: a cigarette-sized hole on my wrist, deep and puckered. It had been burned and re-burned in the same spot.

"This is what I got for *not* betraying you," I hissed.

"They knew everything – someone had told them – but I lied to cover for you anyway. And to hell with you if you don't believe me."

As Ingo stared at the mark, his lean face paled. Suddenly his own scar looked redder than before, his face more drawn and tired where the ruined skin tugged down at one eye. His gaze flew to mine again. He started to say something and stopped.

He rose abruptly and left, pushing the empty wheelbarrow before him. I could see every knob of his spine along his grimy shirtless back.

"What are you looking at?" shouted a Gun. "Get to work!"

On the second night after my whispered conversation with Ingo, it finally happened: a snowmobile swooped close, kicking up snow, and I stumbled. With a soft snapping noise, my left boot's heel broke off.

My pulse lurched. I stooped down and snatched it up in one motion, praying not to be noticed, and kept walking.

Immediately pain stabbed my foot: a nail, maybe, sticking up through the sole. It got worse with every step. I started to sweat despite the cold. I bit my lip and didn't stop walking, though I was limping badly now and could feel damp warmth in my shoe.

At the food truck I stood awkwardly in line. A group of Guns loitered near the fence. One was eating a sandwich.

He put it down on the hood of a truck as he laughed with another Gun, demonstrating a golf swing. A trio of ravens flapped overhead, black wings churning.

For once, pain took precedence over hunger and the sandwich barely registered. After I'd gulped down my bread and soup, I went into the hut and sat on my bed. Fran was already there, huddled under the thin blanket.

I hesitated, gazing down at the pinched boots that had once been a jaunty cherry colour. My blisters were so bad that I hadn't taken them off for days. I gritted my teeth and pulled off the left one.

Fresh pain flared. The stench of blood hit me. My sock was in tatters, stained dark brown. When I peeled it off, the skin of my foot was a damp-looking grey. The blisters oozed angrily. The wound from the nail was already a deep, red-black hole, stabbed in several places that had joined together.

I stared at it in dread. Unless I was lucky I knew what would come soon: red lines darting up my leg as infection set in.

Groping inside the damp boot, I found the offending nail. I took the fallen-off heel and used it as a hammer, reaching inside the boot to try to shove the nail out backwards, or bend it sideways. The heel's rubber fell to pieces in my hand. I flipped the boot over – the nail was half-buried in the sole. I clawed at it with my fingernails; for a panicked moment almost took to it with my teeth.

Fran had turned over and was watching me. Her blue

eyes held something like concern, though that wasn't it exactly…more dread that the problem existed and relief that it wasn't happening to her.

We didn't speak. I stood up and went into the corner where the chamber pot was. I ignored its stench and undid my trousers. I untied the rag that I'd hidden around one thigh. I'd been saving it for my next monthly; now I had no choice. I folded it in a small square and shoved it inside the boot, covering the nail.

When I gingerly tested it, I could feel pressure, but no sharpness. How long would it take before the nail ripped the cloth to shreds?

The temptation to just curl up in bed and black all this out was almost overwhelming. Instead I creaked open the hut's wooden door and went back out to the yard.

The Guns stood talking in a tightly-knit cluster that looked ominous. I shoved my hands in my pockets, trying to look as if I had nothing on my mind.

The ground had a fresh sheet of snow. I couldn't search for anything to blunt the nail without drawing attention. The spotlights on the fence blazed, almost drowning out Gunnison's image as he whispered about the Discordant problem, his eyes sorrowful. Melody stood at the doorway of her own hut with a few others, bunched together but not really speaking.

I gazed at her. Hatred throbbed.

Claudia drifted over. "What are you staring at?" she whispered. Her thin face was still fuller than most here.

It was rumoured that she was a spy for the Guns, that she did their dirty work for them.

"A thief," I answered without looking at her, and moved away.

Forget Melody. I had no choice. I waited until the Guns near the gate weren't looking...then hunched my shoulders and headed towards the "marketplace".

I'd rarely been there. It was just a corner between a few buildings, somewhat sheltered from the wind. Several other women stood half-hidden in shadow, talking in low voices. As I approached they looked up. I didn't know any of them, but their faces all looked similar: lean, big-eyed, hungry.

"What have you got?" whispered one.

I couldn't see the Guns from here and it made me nervous. I reached into my brassiere and drew out the shard. It glinted.

"This," I said.

Eyes widened. "What do you want for it?" someone asked in an urgent mutter.

I kept tight hold of the glass. "I need boots." I tried to keep the desperate hope from my voice.

Harsh laughter. "Are you crazy? We all need boots."

"Boots or nothing."

"...Unfortunately, Discordants can't be rehabilitated," Gunnison explained softly. "I hate it just like everyone else..."

The woman who seemed most interested in the shard inspected it carefully. "I can't get you boots," she said. She glanced at my feet. "What's wrong with those?"

"Nothing, except that they're going to get me shot soon," I said shortly.

She gave a tired, mocking smile. "We'll just get the glass off you then."

"Not if the Guns find it first."

"True. That would be a shame." She screwed up her forehead. "What if I could get you some cardboard, to thicken the soles?"

"That would only be temporary! I need something permanent."

"The only thing permanent here is *that*," she said wryly, and nodded towards the heads on the fence. "Do we have a deal?"

My heel throbbed. Thinking of trying to keep up with the others for over two miles the next day, I hesitated, tempted. But cardboard wouldn't even last a week. Then I'd be right back where I started.

I swallowed hard as I decided. I'd tear a strip off my already-tattered shirt to keep the nail at bay and come back tomorrow night – see if someone else was here that could get me what I needed.

"No deal." I tucked the glass back in my brassiere.

The woman shrugged reluctantly, but didn't improve her offer. She drifted away into the shadows. I watched her go, scared I'd made the wrong choice. If the cloth in my boot didn't hold out tomorrow then I'd pay for it with my life.

"Amity Vancour?" whispered a voice.

I flinched. Slowly, I turned, certain that I'd face a grinning Gun levelling a pistol at me.

The speaker was a gaunt, frowning woman, dressed in the same sort of rags as all of us. Before I knew what was happening, she pressed a scrap of paper into my hand and walked off.

"Wait!" I hissed.

She quickened her stride. "I've done all I said I'd do," she said over her shoulder.

I was hardly less alarmed than if it had been a Gun. Clutching the mysterious paper, I pressed against one of the buildings, trying to disappear in the shadows. As Gunnison murmured on, I glanced towards the main gates and unfolded it. Written in a hasty scrawl with what I guessed to be a piece of slate was:

Meet me. Midnight. Please.

Please was underlined twice. I crumpled the paper in a fearful reflex...then thought better of it and refolded it carefully; it could help battle the nail in my boot. It had to be from Ingo, of course. How had he gotten a note to me?

Sirens blared, pulsing through the air. I started, half thinking that my guilt in even having the note had been discovered. Everyone began moving to the outside of their huts. A surprise count, then.

I shoved the note into my jacket lining and hurried to my own hut. I got in line with the others, hand out.

"Aries seven..."

I stared straight ahead as the pretty blonde Gun checked me off her list. The note felt glowing, alive. Though I knew the meeting place Ingo must mean, to go there would be insane. We'd both be shot on sight if caught.

When it came Claudia's turn, I saw her whisper something to the Gun. I stiffened, but though the Gun's gaze narrowed, she didn't look at me. She strode on, her wool coat stirring around her ankles, and I let out a tiny breath.

Meet me. Midnight. Please.

Chapter Nine

"...AND THAT'S WHEN I KNEW that astrology held the key to all things..."

I lay tensely in bed. Gunnison's confiding voice was barely audible. Beside me, Fran's breathing sounded shallow and restless; from others came coughs and groans.

I'd be heard if I left – and several in here would be happy to go to the Guns with such information. Ingo and I hadn't been friends. We were barely acquaintances. We had nothing to say to each other.

So many good reasons not to go...and not a single one in favour.

The Guns changed shifts at midnight. When their trucks briefly drowned out Gunnison's voice, I shivered.

I didn't move for a long time after that. Yet I kept recalling Ingo grabbing my wrist, demanding answers despite the Guns; my own rush of anger.

I'd forgotten what it felt like.

Finally – I don't know why – I pushed back the blanket and got out of bed. Fran rose on one elbow, gazing at me.

I lifted my voice a little louder than I needed to. "I'm meeting with a Gun," I whispered.

I could sense her surprise though she was only a dark shape on the other side of the bed. "For extra food?"

"Why else?" I murmured back, lacing my tone with bitterness. I could almost feel the alert silence of a few of the others. If they thought I was meeting a Gun for a liaison, maybe they wouldn't report me. I hadn't done anything even remotely rebellious in months and everyone knew it. Why should I start now?

I prayed that would work in my favour – and cursed myself for giving in to the note's plea.

At the door I paused. A few times others had snuck out, and I'd seen how they did it. Harsh spotlights swept the yard at intervals. If you timed it just right, you could dart through the shadows that hugged each building.

"...now take my own sun sign, Sagittarius..." Gunnison murmured. Through the crack between door and wall I could see him looking earnestly into the camera. "You see, with Scorpio rising, that means..."

The spotlight lit up our hut. It dazzled my eyes even through the crack and I shivered, clutching the door jamb.

Who the hell was Ingo to me, anyway? He'd accused me of betrayal. Why was I doing this?

The spotlight passed. I was light-headed. I silently pushed open the door and slipped out into the night.

The place I knew Ingo must have meant was one I'd only heard about. Far behind the furthest hut, out of reach of the camp's lights, was a small storage shed. The men's section was just beyond: a fence bristling with barbed wire separated the two areas. The ground here was uneven, hilly. A slender gap showed underneath the fence, just large enough for a man to slither through, if he was thin… which described everyone here.

Couples met here sometimes. Mostly married couples, I supposed. We spent so little time with the men of the camp – who would risk everything for a random encounter? Though for some, maybe the momentary pleasure was worth it.

I was so late that I was sure Ingo wouldn't still be there. I kept my eyes on the shed's dark shape as I approached. Its shadows looked impenetrable and I paused, staring.

Anyone could be back there. A Gun could be lying in wait.

My muscles eased as a tall, thin form detached itself from the darkness. "You took long enough," said Ingo, his voice heavy with relief.

"You're lucky I came at all," I said. Neither of us

mentioned the time I'd waited on a gloomy street corner for him, hoping he'd appear with the key to the World for Peace building – though I was sure we were both thinking of it. The memory flashed past from another world.

Ingo came and took my arm. His puckered scar looked surreal in the moonlight, as if his face were made of wax and had half-melted.

"Come back here, where we're hidden," he whispered. He was Germanic but had hardly any accent, apart from sounding slightly too precise. I recalled him saying that he'd gone to school in New Manhattan, where his mother was from.

Behind the shed, cloaked in shadow, he let his hand fall. He wore tattered trousers and a jacket that hung loosely on his thin frame.

"Were you telling the truth?" he said.

I gasped out a disbelieving laugh. Was *that* why I'd risked my life to come meet him? "Ingo, what does it even matter? We're here now – we're both screwed."

His voice was taut. "Trust me, it matters. Tell me."

I sighed and stared out at the weathered concrete huts of the men's camp. From the distance came Gunnison's murmur, thankfully impossible to make out now.

"I didn't betray you," I said. "Whether you believe it or not, I wouldn't do that. But they knew everything anyway. Either you talked, or someone saw us." I studied him. "Which was it?" I asked finally.

Ingo's narrow shoulders had slumped as if he'd been

hoping for a different answer. "Neither." He cleared his throat. "All right…I believe you. And I wish to hell you were right that it doesn't matter any more."

"I have no idea why it would."

He snorted. "No, I suppose you wouldn't. Even during our brief previous acquaintance, I could tell that you have very little imagination."

It was the first thing I'd found even vaguely amusing in a long time. "Thanks," I said dryly. "Are you going to apologize for calling me a traitorous bitch?"

"No. I'm going to offer you a deal."

I stiffened. A searchlight moved past in the men's camp, and I pressed closer against the shed. "What kind of deal?" I whispered. "I don't want any trouble, Ingo."

My eyes had adjusted to the light enough to see his scathing glance. "Neither do I. But I have information. And you have skills."

"What skills?"

"Have you forgotten? You were keen to show off to me once before what a lock-picker extraordinaire you are."

I felt a flinch of alarm, as if a dozen Guns stood listening. "I'm not!" I said. "It was just kid stuff. Ingo, if you're thinking – if you're planning—"

"To escape?" he finished. "Yes, of course that's what I'm thinking! Aren't *you*?"

"We can't," I said faintly. "If they catch us—"

"If they catch us we die, and that's still a lot better than *this* place." He scanned my face; I saw his lip curl. "What's the matter, Wildcat? I thought *you'd* have an escape plan in place already. My information would just give you the final flourishing touches."

The spotlights swept across the men's camp again. I waited until they'd passed, as if the lights themselves had ears. "Well, you thought wrong," I said. "I take it you haven't been in solitary."

He grasped my arm. His fingers were thin, unrelenting. "Oh, is that it? We spent time in the box, and now we're too scared to piss until they tell us to grab a pot?"

I jerked away. "I've got to survive! That's all I know!"

"And you think anyone actually *survives* here?"

"What happened to your face?" I asked abruptly.

Ingo had been standing close; now he gave a humourless laugh and leaned against the shed. He jammed his hands in his pockets. "Let's just say that I found out for myself they're capable of sabotaging planes."

I went still, remembering how the wing of my own plane had exploded when I'd fired at my opponent. "So you had another Peacefight after we got the evidence from Madeline's office."

"Yes. I had to take it and go up, pretend I didn't know anything. Clearly they knew otherwise."

"And then they captured you?"

"And then they captured me." Ingo's voice was so flat that I knew it wasn't the entire truth. He stepped close, his eyes as dark as the shadows.

"We don't have time to waste on this," he said. "If we

escape, I'll tell you the whole sorry story in long, lingering detail. Are you in? Or not?"

"I don't know!" I backed away a step, panicked. "You don't realize what you're asking."

"The hell I don't, you coward." He gripped my arm again. "*Listen to me.* I am getting home to my family – that's all I know! And I need you to help me."

The worn square of paper in my jacket lining had never felt so precious, or so lost to me. Something in me snapped. "At least you have a family to get home to! I can't go near mine, not ever again! And if I escape, I'll be recaptured – everyone knows my face. So what's even *out* there for me, Ingo? What's even out there? Tell me that!"

"Maybe yourself," he said softly.

No. I was not going to cry. Not ever again.

I jerked from his grasp. "Fuck you," I said, and walked away as fast as my injured foot would let me.

Chapter Ten

August, 1941

Mac had never been on the former Western Seaboard Peacefighting base before, though to Collis, of course, it was familiar territory. Mac glanced at him as they were driven through the main gates, wondering what "Sandy" was thinking. In the front of the auto, their driver remained silent.

They were only in the Western Quarter for a few days. The World for Peace was still creaking along – Mac thought it suited Gunnison's regime to keep the venerable organization in place – but the Peacefighting bases were now slowly being disbanded.

When the Western Seaboard pilots had "attacked" Gunnison's invading troops, they'd been acting under direct orders from then-President Lopez. The former WS leader had been executed; the pilots were still being held under arrest. Cain had finally sent Mac to investigate them. Collis had been ordered along to help.

Mac gazed out the window at the eerily empty streets of the base. He'd have preferred to come alone; he had errands which he didn't want Collis to know about. But now wasn't the time to think about it. They'd reached their destination: a large hangar.

The driver pulled up to the kerb and Mac and Collis got out into the sunshine, resplendent in their Gun uniforms: pearly grey, with the red-and-black Harmony swirl above their hearts.

Collis looked pale. He said nothing. A World for Peace official came out and shook their hands.

"In here, sir," she said to Mac.

A few minutes later, Mac stood scanning the lines of former Western Seaboard Peacefighter pilots arrayed before him. He didn't care that every pilot here hated him and thought him Gunnison's lackey...but did care, deeply, that he'd have to sacrifice some to let others go.

It's all I can do, he told himself harshly. *And if I didn't do it, Cain would get someone else in and every last one of them would be sent to a correction camp, not just some of them.*

Maybe Sephy was right not to want to marry him.

The thoughts flashed past. Mac studied the clipboard of names in his hand. Collis stood beside him, facing his former colleagues without looking any of them in the eye.

When he and Collis had first entered, there'd been an audible intake of breath. Mac heard Collis's name being murmured; could feel that the animosity level in the hangar had ratcheted up by several notches. Every gaze was locked on Collis, who stood motionless, his cheeks tinged with red.

"Collie, you betraying bastard—" A burly brown-haired pilot lunged forward, only stopped when several of his friends held him back.

Mac inwardly begged the muscular pilot not to do anything that he, Mac, couldn't turn a blind eye to. The World for Peace security guard gave Mac a quick look. "Sir, would you like me to—"

Mac broke in smoothly with, "These are all the names?"

"Yes, sir." She nodded at the assembled pilots. "They're all here."

Mac went through the business of strolling through the lines, barking names now and then, questioning the pilots at random. He saw their fear of him, and understood in a sickened way how easy it would be to let this power go to your head.

"Harris?"

The pilot standing at attention didn't blink. "Yes, sir."

"Were you one of the pilots who engaged in an illegal attack on the former Central States on the morning of March 18th?"

The pilot's chin tightened; his gaze flicked disdainfully over Mac. *Levi Harris,* his full name on the clipboard read. "I was one of the pilots who defended my country, yes, sir."

Good for you, thought Mac, meaning both the action and the comeback. He raised an eyebrow and made a mark on his notes before moving on. In fact, he planned to make his selection almost at random, apart from a few "dangerous" birth charts that had been flagged. There was no other way he could choose, when they were all innocent.

No matter what, I'm only taking three dozen in, he told himself. The rest – a good seventy or so – could go free, officially adjudged by Mac as being of no danger to Can-Amer.

Finally Mac returned to the front of the room. Collis had been silent through all this, though he was here to help Mac with the process. Mac liked him better for staying quiet; these were Collis's former colleagues, after all. But now Mac made a show of angling his clipboard towards Collis and saying, "All right, make yourself useful. What do you think?"

"Do we have to do this here?" Collis muttered tightly.

Mac knew how he felt, but yes, they did, with those World for Peace security guards watching. "What better place?" he said mildly. "I hope you're not implying that this should be a secret process."

Collis stared down at the names...glanced through the parcel of birth charts with notes from Kay Pierce.

The hangar full of pilots stood watching him, their faces stone.

Collis's throat moved. "Not Taylor or Kelly," he said, softly.

Mac looked at the names Collis was indicating. *Harlan Taylor* and *Vera Kelly*. "They…weren't there during the attack," said Collis. He gave Mac a quick, pleading look. "They're no danger. They didn't even take part in it."

Harlan Taylor turned out to be the burly pilot who'd lunged for Collis earlier. He'd clearly overheard; he seemed to swell to twice his height and his broad face reddened. At first Mac thought he'd roar in indignation – then Harlan glanced at a female pilot with strawberry blonde hair beside him and kept quiet, fists clenched.

The female pilot – Vera, Mac assumed – was pale.

She looked ready to protest Collis's claim. Mac cut her off with a glare and said loudly to Collis, "Thanks for the information." To the armed guards, he said, "All right, I've heard enough. Take the following pilots into custody."

The hangar went deathly silent as Mac read thirty-six names at random. Though he read quickly, each name seemed to hang in the air. Mac kept his voice firm and tried not to think too hard about what he was doing – tried to think only of the seventy-two names that he wasn't reading. He was already taking in far fewer than would be expected. To save more could mean his own death.

Collis stood without moving as Mac read, his face very pale, and Mac wondered how many of the names Collis knew...and whether Collis was aware that Mac was putting his own neck on the line to protect so many of them.

Incongruously, Mac noticed that the sleek lines of the Gun uniform made Collis look older, more finished – less a boy and more of a man. Funny, thought Mac, how he always thought of Collis as a boy, even though he stood almost a head taller than Mac and was only three years younger.

Even funnier was how an outfit that meant only horror could make someone look a man.

After the thirty-six pilots had been cuffed and taken away, Mac addressed the rest. "You're officially cleared of any wrongdoing and are no longer being held. You have twenty-four hours to leave the complex. Thank you for your cooperation." *I'll call Sephy tonight,* he thought. The fleeting promise to himself felt like sanity.

Harlan's name hadn't been called. Nor had Vera's. Harlan looked grim; he put a muscular arm around Vera's slender shoulders. They approached, heading for the exit. Collis turned away from them, but not before Harlan met his eyes.

"Thanks, *bud,*" he said in a low voice. "We always knew Amity didn't do what they said – now I guess we know what happened to her. Did you work for them when they took our pal Clem away too?"

And he spat at Collis's feet.

* * *

Collis seemed in brittle high spirits as the auto took them back to the Heat. Mac half-suspected that he'd taken a swig or two from some hidden flask. He told raucous stories of his Peacefighting days and of his clever exploits, all the while with his odd, changeable eyes locked on Mac's, as if begging some response from him. What? Mac didn't know and didn't care.

The lobby staff at the hotel seemed to freeze when he and Collis walked in. The uniform always had that effect: mincing smiles, too-prompt service.

"Thank you, sir. Will there be anything else?" asked the front-desk clerk as Mac took their keys.

"No, that's all," said Mac. He handed one of the keys over to Collis, who gave him an ironic salute.

"Thanks," Collis said. "Any objection if I take a look around my old stomping grounds?"

"Feel free," said Mac, glad to be rid of him. Though the absent Cain might have seen things differently, Mac had no desire to babysit Collis and had his own pressing business to attend to.

"You might want to take that off, though," he added in an undertone, nodding at Collis's uniform as they headed for the elevator. "Your former teammates could still be around and I don't think you're very popular right now."

If anyone laid a finger on Collis while he wore that uniform, they'd be dead: that was what Mac really hoped to prevent. Collis winced a little at Mac's estimation of his popularity, but gave another fervent-looking grin.

"Oh, sure, good idea," he said heartily. "I don't like showing off in it anyway."

Alone in his room, Mac changed out of his own uniform. It was a relief to get back into his real clothes: tan trousers, a white shirt and brown sports jacket. Looking in the mirror, he tried unsuccessfully to tame his unruly hair, and glanced longingly at the phone. Sephy wouldn't be home yet. Mac craved the sound of her voice, to know that she still loved him no matter what he'd had to do that day.

He grabbed up his hat and went out.

Despite everything, the Heat was still going strong – this city where he'd once accomplished so much for the Resistance. Covertly, he'd spread leaflets exposing what was really happening in the Central States; gotten papers for people who'd escaped; made vital contacts – all under the cover of conducting business for Gunnison's regime.

Now he knew just where he was heading.

He walked with his hands jammed in his trouser pockets, fedora pulled low, casting a shadow over his face. The city seemed to throb around him. Flashing neon lights advertised bars and astrology shops. A couple stood necking in the same shadowy alleyway where Russ Avery, Amity Vancour's team leader, had been shot. Mac grimaced, recalling that night.

Nearby was a dance hall built over ruins from the long-ago Cataclysm, with stark grey rubble left in place for effect. Mac found himself wondering briefly about the ancients, whose destruction had given those in his own time a blueprint for how to live. Peacefighting: no more wars. No fear of another Cataclysm.

The new world's idealism sure hadn't lasted long, he thought wryly. Less than a hundred years.

He came to a run-down bar. *Harrigan's*, read the dully flashing green sign out front. Inside, an ancient telio set showed a boxing match. A large fan spun lazily near the ceiling.

Mac propped his forearms on the bar's worn, sticky surface as he ordered a beer. When he paid for it he gave the bartender a too-large tip and said, "Hey, is Frankie here?"

The bartender glanced down at the bill; his fingers closed over it. "I'll check. It's Vince Griffin, right?"

"That's right," said Mac easily. "Good memory, buddy."

A wall of ruins had been left in place here, too. Mac took a seat at the bar and contemplated them. Crumbling, reddish brick, with faint scraps of paint and a swirl with lettering on it: *Coca-*

Just then, the thought of a people who'd destroyed themselves felt ominous. Mac found himself wishing that someone had slapped some whitewash up over it.

The bartender had gone into a back room after giving Mac his drink. He returned quickly, but didn't come over. Mac didn't make eye contact. He drank his beer and watched the boxing. After a while the programme ended – Jimmy Darcy won; he always did. The Harmony symbol appeared and music started playing.

That new song by Van Wheeler again: "For Ever and a Day". Mac kind of hated Van Wheeler, but the tune was catchy and to his annoyance he knew the words.

If we had for ever, just we two,
Why, it still wouldn't be worth more
Than a single day with you…

The bartender appeared, drying a glass. "Want another one?"

"Sure, thanks," said Mac, and pushed more money at him.

The bartender palmed it. "Frankie's not here any more," he muttered as he pulled the new beer.

"Oh yeah?" Mac pushed his hat back a little and leaned forward on his elbows, keeping his voice casual. "Any idea where I can find him?"

The bartender shook his head and slid the new beer across to him. "No. Charlie said to tell you to give it up. Frankie's not in the game any more. No one knows where he is."

Mac had no better luck at the other places he tried, though he didn't dare hit too many in one night. But he went to the most important, and found that his abrupt absence last month had done exactly what he'd feared. His few remaining contacts had gone to ground.

Mac walked slowly back to the hotel. He'd been pinning more hopes on this brief visit than he liked to admit.

He had no idea now how they might infiltrate the plans of Madeline Bark, who was somewhere in Appalachia coordinating its takeover.

If the Harmony Treaty still went ahead on the Day of Three Suns – if they lost Appalachia and its ports – they were done for.

It was the same with all of their Resistance contacts now. The once-thriving, far-reaching network remained deeply compromised. Appalachia was only part of it. These last few months Mac had spent frustrating hours on a ham wireless set, trying to re-establish contact with operatives who monitored the airwaves up in the far north. He knew Gunnison was working on something big up in the Yukon area. He'd felt on the verge of figuring it out when the spate of arrests happened – shutting down the contacts who'd known the operatives' check-in times and wireless frequencies.

The far north was now adrift like so much of the Resistance. In hundreds of static-y transmissions so far, Mac had never heard the code words. His own use of them was ignored.

Meanwhile Gunnison had been keeping an uncharacteristically low profile, hardly appearing on the telio. Once he'd prowled the Zodiac's corridors incessantly, throwing his ready grin in every direction. Now when Mac occasionally saw him in passing, he was always talking intently with Kay Pierce, so that Mac could only nod and keep going.

Despite Gunnison's hearty persona, the man was close to very few people. Mac, lower down the chain than Pierce, wasn't one of them.

He wondered tensely what was going on…and if it could help the Resistance.

When Mac had encountered Gunnison on his own a week ago, his pulse had spiked. *Finally.* "Morning, Johnny," he said, pausing in the corridor.

At first Gunnison had frowned as if he didn't recognize him. "Mac. Hello. How's it going?"

"Fine." Mac had been hyper-aware of the bodyguard nearby. He hesitated and drew his eyebrows together. "Listen, I hope I'm not speaking out of turn, but…is everything all right, sir? You seem tired."

"Of course," Gunnison said shortly. He rubbed his temples. More gently, he said, "It's just the ups and downs, Mac. We have to make sure that certain elements stay down, for everyone's good."

He headed off along the hallway, leaving Mac bewildered and unenlightened. *Ups and downs?*

Mac's office was close to Kay Pierce's. He'd gotten into the habit of dropping in on her, offering coffee, joking around and getting her to smile.

It wasn't just so that he could report back to Cain on her movements. Mac's instinct was that Kay – close to him in age and suddenly propelled into one of the most powerful roles in the country – was lonely, a bit frightened. And he'd bet money that she knew where the Day of Three Suns was being held, and what was going on with Johnny Gun and his "ups and downs".

Maybe. But though she was as friendly as ever, she'd become much more closed-off of late. The Zodiac air felt thick with secrets.

"Hi," Mac said softly on the phone to Sephy later. As he sank onto his hotel bed and heard her warm voice in his ear, something in him eased.

"Hey, stranger," she said. "What have you been up to?"

"Not much," he said. "Will you marry me?"

"No. Oh good, we've gotten number eighteen out of the way already. Now, what's new over there?"

Mac laughed, though he'd rarely felt less like it. "Let me think," he said after a pause. "Hey, do you remember that little place we used to go to, the Italian with the great linguini? It's closed down. The owner died or something."

That was the completely banal combination of words that they'd decided would be the code for Mac not being able to get in touch with any contacts. He could almost feel Sephy's bitter disappointment through the phone line.

"Oh, that's too bad," she said finally. "Giuseppe, was that his name? Nice old guy."

He grimaced. "Yeah. Too bad."

"But you know what, Mac, there's a new place I've found around here that I think is almost as nice."

Mac straightened, his heart suddenly pounding. This wasn't part of the script. "There is?" he said.

"Yeah, we'll go there when you get home. I think you'll really like it; it's almost as good as the old one. Great bread rolls. Maybe we can take Walter along."

Walter, their fellow Resistance member. Sephy seemed to be saying that their hopes to destroy Gunnison's regime weren't completely gone. *Almost as good as the old one.* Not ideal, then. But something.

"Hey, that sounds great. I'll look forward to it," Mac said, and wished desperately that they could talk freely. But if Gunnison hadn't arranged for someone to listen in on his calls, Cain probably had – *trust no one* was both men's creed.

Thoughts whirring, Mac had to let it go for now. He lay down on the bed and stretched out, feeling the tiredness of his muscles.

"Help me take my mind off things, gorgeous," he said.

"Long day?"

"The longest," he said, and saw again the vast hangar and the thirty-six pilots he'd arrested.

"You're doing a good job, Mac," said Sephy's voice softly in his ear. "Don't you ever doubt it." Mac exhaled. She knew what kind of choices he had to make. If she were here, she'd tell him to think of the seventy-two, not the thirty-six.

"Where are you now?" he asked after a pause. "I want to picture you."

"Bedroom."

"What are you wearing?"

Sephy's voice turned sultry, rich with humour. "Ooh, is this turning into one of those dirty phone calls I've heard tell about?"

Mac grinned and twined the phone cord around his hand. "Want it to be?"

"Well, I—"

A volley of knocks came at Mac's door. He jerked up, irritation prickling over him. "Hold on, sorry," he said, and scrambled off the bed. He swung open the door.

The man who stood there had the hotel emblem on his tie pin and looked deeply uncomfortable. "Mr Jones? I'm the hotel manager; I'm very sorry to disturb you. There's a…situation with your colleague in the downstairs bar."

Collis. With an inward curse, Mac said a hurried goodbye to Sephy and threw on his sports jacket and shoes. As he accompanied the manager down the corridor and then into an elevator which whirred them downwards, the man kept up an apologetic chatter.

"Most irregular…if he were just a customer off the street, we'd call the police, but of course with one of our valued guests…and, well, especially in your case…" The manager cleared his throat and gave Mac a sideways look.

Translation: *your fellow Gun is roaring drunk*. The elevator had mirrors with golden-black streaks. Mac gazed at his reflection and marvelled at how calm he looked, when all he wanted to do was throttle Collis Reed.

The elevator door slid open and they stepped out into the lobby. Mac's skin tingled with sudden apprehension. He could hear someone bellowing obscenities, and then a crash – the sharp tinkle of breaking glass. A knot of anxious-looking people stood outside the bar, peering inside and murmuring.

Mac broke into a run.

Collis stood alone in the middle of the vacated bar, surrounded by overturned tables, broken glass. He was swinging a chair around as if he were a lion tamer. "*It wasn't my fault*!" he yelled into the empty space, and then let fly with the chair. It crashed against a table.

As Mac closed in Collis staggered backwards, almost fell. He spun on Mac, his eyes wide with fury. "Leave me alone! Why can't all you bastards just—"

"*Collis!*" Mac ducked the wild swing Collis threw at him and then gripped him by the arms. "It's me, Mac!" he shouted. "Calm down, all right? Just calm down!"

Collis blinked. His face was damp. "Mac?" he whispered. All at once his wild mood seemed to leave him. Staring around them at the shattered bar, he swayed unsteadily. Mac's grip on his arms tightened.

"I didn't have a choice," Collis murmured.

He wiped his eyes, and Mac realized, startled, that it wasn't perspiration dampening Collis's cheeks. He gave a choking laugh and looked back at Mac. His glassy gaze was dark blue in the dim lights. "You never get a choice, do you, Mac?" His voice was thick, hard to make out.

"Come on, back to my room." Mac put his arm around Collis's shoulders and led him out. He kicked aside a broken martini glass as they crossed the room. When they reached the manager, who stood anxiously by the door, Mac tucked a bill into the man's jacket pocket.

"This didn't happen," he said in an undertone. "My office will pay for the damages."

The man looked relieved. "Yes, sir, of course." He glanced at Collis, now slumped inertly against Mac's side. "Do you, ah…need some help?" he added.

"Thanks, I've got him," said Mac grimly. He had an idea what Collis had been bellowing about. The fewer people who heard him, the better.

Collis was a head taller than Mac and more solidly built. Mac doubted once or twice that he was going to get the staggering ex-pilot all the way to his room.

"Come *on*," he said through gritted teeth. "Collis, if you pass out on me, I'll murder you."

Finally the pair stumbled through Mac's hotel room door. Mac slammed it shut and shoved Collis in the general direction of the sofa. He was damned if the guy was going to take his bed.

He crossed to the phone. He could hear Collis groaning as he called room service. "Coffee," he said. "Lots of it. And you'd better send some food too."

When Mac had finished placing the order, he hung up and turned around. Collis sat on the sofa with his head slumped in his hands. His hair glinted golden in the light of the desk lamp, reminding Mac why Gunnison called him "Sandy".

"Food's coming," said Mac. He pulled off his jacket and threw it onto the bed. "You'd better eat something, if you can keep it down."

Collis didn't seem to hear him. "I fucked up," he whispered. He raised his head. His face was streaked with tears. "Oh, Mac…it was the only thing I ever wanted. I fucked it up so bad."

"Here," said Mac.

It was eight hours later; he'd just given Collis's inert form on the sofa a rough jostle. When Collis gazed blearily up at him, Mac put a cup of fresh coffee on the table – less an act of kindness than the fastest way to get him moving. "We've got a plane to catch soon," he said shortly.

He'd already had a shower and was wearing only his trousers. He went into the bathroom and filled the sink with hot water. As he was scraping a razor over his cheeks, he saw Collis appear in the mirror, wan and red-eyed, his clothes rumpled.

"You look like hell," said Mac.

"Feel it." Collis leaned against the doorway and rubbed his eyes. After claiming to have "fucked up" the night before he'd said little. For once, Mac hadn't had the heart to try probing someone for information when they were down.

Scrape, scrape, went the razor. Mac dipped it into the

water and gave it a quick swirl. "Want to explain?" he said. "I bet you did a grand's worth of damage down there. I don't have that big of an expense account, pal. It's coming out of your pocket."

Collis winced and stared at the floor.

Mac studied him in the mirror. "You were yelling some pretty strange things, you know," he said conversationally. "All about how it wasn't your fault; it wasn't your fault. You seemed pretty worked up."

Collis's jaw tensed. Finally he looked up.

"You're with the Resistance, aren't you?" he said softly.

Mac's hand stilled. After a moment it started moving again. His gaze met Collis's in the mirror. "I could have you shot for that."

"I wish you would."

Mac finished shaving and swiped his face with a towel, his thoughts racing. He turned. "Collis, I'll tell you frankly, I'm worried about you. First last night and now this. I think when we get back, you'd better—"

"No." Collis was beside Mac in a moment. He grabbed his wrist, almost trembling. "Mac, *please*. I know none of us are ever honest, but please be honest with me now."

Mac pulled away. "You're still drunk."

"You are, aren't you? I've suspected it for months."

"You're losing it, buddy." Mac's amused snort gave no hint of tension. "What the holy hell gave you that idea?"

Collis hesitated. "It was that night in The Ivy Room… look, it doesn't matter! Please, Mac. I've got to know."

Shit, of course, thought Mac, remembering. He'd tried to hint that Russ Avery was in danger, hoping Collis might tip him off. It hadn't happened. Avery had been killed for demanding more money.

Now surprise stirred. Collis had suspected since March and hadn't acted?

Mac leaned against the sink and shrugged. "Well, you're wrong, but you've got me curious now," he said mildly. "Okay, fine, let's say I'm a double agent and I really work for the Resistance. What exactly do you want? Think carefully, pal," he added before Collis could answer. "I might go straight to Cain and report every word of this."

The same wild, agonized look as from the night before flashed in Collis's eyes. "Fine, tell Cain! If I'm shot, I don't care. I can't do it any more. I've got to get out."

"Out?"

"Of this. Of what we do." Collis pressed a fist to his mouth and closed his eyes. Finally he spoke again.

"It's too late for some things," he said. "I know that; I'll always know it. But maybe not for everything. Mac, I'll do whatever you say. Just let me join you. Please."

Chapter Eleven

November, 1941

THE DAY AFTER I MET with Ingo I stepped on my inflamed heel as seldom as possible. At the mine I was grimly unsurprised when they put me to work outside on the ore mounds: a whole day of walking in a half-tiptoeing tread, of needing to balance as I upended the wheelbarrow.

At least I didn't encounter Ingo. The day was grey, brooding. Nearby, workers dripped chemicals onto the heaps of raw ore. Smoke from the processing plant rose in the distance. As I limped from the mine with another load, I wondered wearily why my heel-less boot hadn't occurred to me the night before. Escape was impossible even if there *was* something on the outside for me – I wouldn't last a day on the run.

Yet somehow the reason I'd given Ingo had felt like the only true one.

I managed to steal a small rock from the mounds. That night back in the hut I sank onto my bed and closed my eyes for a moment, almost too tired to hope. The cloth in my boot was tattered now; the scrap of paper from Ingo's note ripped to useless shreds. Finally I wrestled the boot off. With the small stone I shoved at the nail, trying to push it backwards or blunt it.

"*Work*, damn you," I muttered.

The nail bent sideways. My pulse leaped...but when I felt the nail I realized I'd just locked it into place, its sharp tip angled upwards.

In a sudden frenzy, I scraped at the nail again and again. Finally I had to give up. When I gingerly put the boot back on and tested my weight, the nail still bit at my heel.

Fleetingly, I thought of asking one of the others for help, but we all knew each other's possessions as well as our own. No one had anything that would help for long – and when I went to the marketplace again later that evening and held whispered consultations in the shadows, showing the shard of glass, no one there did either.

"I can still get you some cardboard for it," said the same woman as before, her gaze knowing as she took in my awkward stance.

I felt cold as I rubbed the glass. I'd risk it for one more day, I decided. Tomorrow night someone with boots might come to the marketplace. Meanwhile I'd refold the cloth against the nail and pray that it held.

I put the shard in my pocket, trying to hide my apprehension. "Will you be here tomorrow?" I asked her.

She shrugged. "Maybe. If you want to be sure of the cardboard, you'd better let me have the glass now."

"No...I need boots," I said softly.

That night I woke up from a restless sleep, my heel throbbing. I lay awake, almost too scared to move. When the morning sirens finally went, I struggled the boots off and stumbled outside, my feet numb in the cold. On the screen, Gunnison was shouting, "*We WILL prevail! The Discordant elements will not hold us back!*"

In the camp's floodlights, I saw that my heel was angry and swollen. But my ankle had no red lines shooting up it, and I exhaled in relief. I scooped up a handful of snow and tried to clean the wound.

I gritted my teeth as I stood in line for food later, trying not to touch my heel to the ground. At least Melody was nowhere in sight. Seeing my boots on her feet that morning would have been more than I could bear.

I made it to the mine, though I was the last one in and struggling. When they put me on the ore mounds again I was tempted to let them shoot me.

Twelve whole hours of trundling back and forth between the ore mounds and the crusher. Somehow I did it. On the way back to the camp, dizzy and limping badly, I realized I'd almost been better off pushing a wheelbarrow – it had taken some of the weight off my foot.

It was nearly a replay of when I'd broken my boot's heel. Suddenly a Gun roared past on his snowmobile, and I flinched. My heel slammed the ground. I yelped and stumbled.

I fell. I must have blacked out. The next thing I knew I was lying in the snow. It was oddly peaceful...but then, as if from a great distance, I realized a Gun was shouting at me. It took a second for the words to coalesce into meaning.

"Get up, you worthless scum! *Get up!*"

The peacefulness vanished. I cried out as he kicked me in the ribs – and then I saw the pistol pointed at my head, stark black against the snow.

A sharp *click* as the safety catch was taken off. From some reserve I hadn't known existed, I staggered to my hands and knees. I paused, head hanging, breathing hard.

He kicked me again. Clutching my side, I managed to rise, the world reeling in a blur of trees and barbed-wire fence. The Gun shoved me hard. "Get going!" I did...but not before fingering the glass in my pocket.

I could drag its sharpness down my wrist and end all of this.

I'm not sure why I didn't, or how I made it back to camp. I almost didn't stand in line for food. All I wanted was to curl up in bed and not move. Some small stubborn instinct wouldn't allow it.

Slumped against the hut to eat, I realized that I had no choice now. I had to hope that the woman from last night would be at the marketplace again, so I could barter the glass for the cardboard. And then in a few days, the nail would have worked through the cardboard. Only maybe this time, I wouldn't be able to get up when the Gun was shouting at me.

A shard of glass for a few days of life. It was almost funny.

The film's volume throbbed at the air. I watched blindly as Gunnison leaned back in an armchair, solid and pleasant-looking: "...just a poor farm boy, held back through no fault of my own. But Lady Harmony was smiling, Tom! And with the help of the stars, I..."

I started as the sound went off completely. Gunnison's mouth kept moving.

The sirens began.

It was the short double wail that we all dreaded more than anything. My blood chilled. As the sirens faded, the camp fell perfectly still. Along with everyone else, I looked at the high wooden platform near the gates.

A Gun was climbing the floodlit stairs, with another pair of Guns behind him. Between them was a prisoner, head bowed, wrists bound behind her thin back.

Claudia sidled up next to me. I smelled soup and realized with a wave of longing that she still had some left. She slowly licked her spoon, gazing at the scene unfolding in front of us.

"I know where you went the other night," she whispered.

My pulse stuttered. Did she?

She glanced at me, and I saw the smirk in her eyes. "But I got there with the information first." She nodded towards the execution platform. "Thanks for letting me know. Double rations for a week."

The Guns had reached the top of the platform now, and I could see who their prisoner was.

Melody.

I froze. Then my heart went crazy; my gaze flew to her feet. She still wore my boots.

"Move, Discordant scum!" shouted a Gun, and I didn't hesitate – as if in a dream, I limped along with the others towards the platform, staring at Melody.

I know where you went the other night. Claudia had whispered something to a Gun after the surprise counting that same night, before I'd gone to meet Ingo. What information was she talking about? What had she done?

Does it matter? I thought wildly. My boots were about to be up for grabs. I edged to the front of the crowd.

On the platform, Melody stood motionless, the expression on her bruised face dull. The Gun read out from a piece of paper:

"Two days ago, this prisoner stole a sandwich from one of President Gunnison's esteemed representatives here at Harmony Five. She has confessed to it. The crime of thievery is contrary to the precepts of Harmony and is punishable by death..."

I stood rooted at a sudden memory. Three ravens, so notorious for stealing food, had been flapping overhead when the Gun put his sandwich down.

Soon after, I'd told Claudia that Melody was a thief. She must have heard about the missing sandwich and thought I'd seen Melody take it.

This was happening because of me.

The Gun's declaration went on and on. No one stirred. A crescent moon hung in the sky, oddly beautiful behind the faded grey wood of the platform. My fists were rigid. Would a word from me save Melody…or just get me shot too, for interfering?

I didn't know. The Guns might even find it amusing to free one prisoner at the last moment and shoot another – their boredom up here was legendary. But no matter what she'd done to me, Melody hadn't committed this crime.

Then my gaze dropped to her feet. In the harsh floodlights, I could see my boots so clearly. The scuffed brown leather was still thick and solid. The soles were firmly in place. Melody had tied the laces in neat bows.

I studied the boots for a long moment. I didn't shake. I didn't move.

Finally I lifted my eyes to Melody's face again…and I didn't say a word.

The Gun finished his proclamation. He motioned to the band, who had been standing shivering nearby. They roused themselves and started to play "Happy Days are

Here Again". The tune bounced on the cold air.

"Do you repent your crime?" barked out the Gun.

Melody whispered something inaudible.

The Gun raised his arm. The other two snapped their rifles to chest level. They flicked the safeties off and paused, with the head Gun's arm still raised. Melody started to shake.

It seemed to spiral endlessly. I watched Melody close her eyes and twist her head away, her mouth trembling. And I felt again the Gun kicking me when I'd fallen in the snow...recalled the moment when I'd wanted to drag the glass down my wrist and let myself bleed to death. My mouth felt carved in stone.

The rifles went off. Melody's body jerked backwards and fell. One of her legs twitched convulsively. A Gun strode over to her and shot again. The rifle's retort battled briefly with the music.

Her leg went still.

I swallowed, suddenly feeling colder. The head Gun gazed out at us and smirked. He motioned to the band and they stopped playing.

Silence, apart from the slight rustle of the wind through the trees beyond the gate. Around me, the crowd had perked up a little, expectant now, those in the front staring at Melody's body.

I was too.

The Gun grinned. Very deliberately, he prodded Melody's inert form with his boot. She rolled, bloodying the already-stained platform. He prodded her again, until she lay on her side just on the edge.

My heart racketed in my chest. I'd never been involved in this before – but nothing would stop me this time. Nothing.

"Enjoy yourselves, Discordant scum," called the Gun. He shoved Melody's body hard with his boot. She rolled off the platform and fell with a lifeless *thud* onto the snowy ground.

Adrenalin surged. I bolted from the crowd, sprinting towards her. Suddenly I was in a chaos of screaming and shouting – of flailing fists and kicks.

I battled my way to Melody's body. Mine. *Mine.* Someone else was near her boots and I shoved her roughly away; I got to the boots first and fell bodily across them, clutching them to my chest even as they were still on Melody's feet.

I held on grimly. I was jostled from all sides as others pulled and tugged, taking her other clothes. Somewhere overhead, the Guns were laughing. The band started up again, obviously at the Guns' direction, playing a rollicking tune you might hear at a sporting event.

I crouched there, rigid, hanging on with all I had. At long last others began drifting away. A hot, swelling silence descended, full of my own heartbeat and nothing else. I realized I was the only one left. I sat up cautiously. My upper arm throbbed where I'd been punched; another bruise was forming on my kicked thigh. It didn't matter.

My boots.

My cold fingers fumbled feverishly with the damp, knotted laces. I got them loosened and tugged the boots off Melody's unresisting feet. Her socks were grimy, but far more intact than mine. I took them too. Her bare feet looked pale, the toes relaxed as if she were only sleeping.

Right there and then, I yanked off Melody's hated boots from my own feet, wincing at the pain. Their once cherry-red leather was cracked and peeling. I quickly bathed my injured heel with some snow, then dabbed it as dry as I could with the disintegrating scrap of rag. It was in tatters now. I wouldn't have lasted another day.

I pulled on the socks and my flight boots. I'd lost so much weight that the boots were slightly loose, but they were *real*. I let out a quick, fierce breath. These boots had been made to last for years. I could walk in them for miles if need be. They wouldn't injure me.

I was going to survive.

The adrenalin was fading, leaving me trembling and drained. I staggered as I stood up, clutching Melody's ruined boots with one hand. The scavengers had left her nothing. She lay exposed to the elements, blue eyes glazed.

On the platform above, I could still hear the Guns laughing. The music had stopped. "Better than horse races," one said. "Told you the Vancour bitch would get the boots – now pay up."

The words sounded distant. I felt hot; my heel gave a fierce throb. I stood staring down at Melody's lifeless body…and had an overwhelming urge to kick it as hard as I could.

My jaw clenched with the effort of not doing it. I started to tremble, staring down at her. As the severed heads on the fence watched, I stiffly tossed Melody's boots to the ground beside her. They landed in an untidy tangle near her bound wrists.

"These are yours," I said hoarsely.

The next morning as we waited in line for food I deliberately didn't look up at the fence. I knew what I would see. But when the sprightly music started up and we all marched out the front gates, I was able to keep up with the others. My injured heel already felt a little better.

Over the next few days, the difference the boots made to my life gave me new sympathy for Melody, though I hated her no less. My first day here, I'd been thrown in solitary for two weeks. By the time I'd gotten out, Melody had lived half a month in this place – she knew survival could hinge on the most basic things. My boots had been technically hers, according to the records. Would I have been able to resist keeping them, had our positions been reversed?

Back then, I probably would have. More fool me.

At the mine I was put alternately to work on the ore mounds, the crusher or deep in the mine itself. Though the work was still bone-aching, though I was still weary and hungry, at least my feet could keep going now for as long as I did.

Yet I felt numb inside. I kept thinking of that moment when I'd had to stop myself from kicking Melody's lifeless body. I wanted to feel horrified.

I didn't.

The worst thing was that if her body were in front of me right now, I'd be just as tempted.

Four days after Melody's death I saw Ingo at the mine. He was heading for the front of the crusher, pushing a loaded wheelbarrow. I was pushing an empty one, about to get another load of gravel for the ore mounds.

I stiffened as our eyes met. His were dark; I saw a scornful flash in them despite his weariness.

We both kept going through the dusty mine with its slanting light that never quite pierced the gloom. Neither of us spoke, but my skin tingled with awareness of him. Not as a man – the thought was ludicrous these days – but as what he'd always been to me: an opponent.

In our Peacefighting days, Ingo had been my favourite person to fight against, even before I knew his name. His flying kept me guessing, challenged me to do better. When we'd met by chance one night in a club, I'd liked talking to him just as much – but we'd never lost that faint adversarial edge.

I grabbed a shovel and started loading my empty

wheelbarrow with gravel, my shoulders aching. I wished that I'd never seen Ingo here, that I could have relegated him to being a footnote in my past: the guy who'd helped me break into the World for Peace building and was then never heard of again.

But Ingo was here. Still challenging me.

My spirits hardened. As Ingo passed me on his way back into the mine I didn't look up. Our eyes didn't meet again.

Later, as the moon rose, Claudia stood beside me in front of our hut as we all ate. On the screen, Gunnison greeted the troops. Stray snowflakes cast fluttering moths across his image. "Call me Johnny!" he whispered.

Claudia had double portions just like she'd said: her tin cup was brimming full.

She saw me looking and dipped her bread in the soup. She offered it to me. "Want some?"

Her pointed smile said that it was because of me that she had it. I accepted the soup-drenched bread without speaking. I'd learned months ago that an extra mouthful could mean the difference between staying on your feet and collapsing.

After I'd swallowed it and then licked the inside of my own cup, catching every last scrap of soup, I finally did what I'd avoided doing these past days. I looked at the fence.

Melody's head was still pristine and unmarked, her long blonde hair stirring in the breeze. I gazed at it for a long time, wishing I felt more than I did. Wishing I could feel something – anything at all.

That evening I did something I hadn't done in months. Long before curfew, I lay down on the narrow bed I shared with Fran, and dug my fingers into the lining of my jacket. I took out the folded square of paper. I could have traded it for food dozens of times over – paper was precious here, for lining clothes against the cold. I'd never even considered it.

I unfolded the paper carefully. It had been drenched and weakened by the disinfection; I'd known that looking at it too often would destroy it. But as the months passed, that hadn't been the main reason I'd avoided taking it out.

The smudged ink was still legible, showing my mother's pretty, looping handwriting.

Dear Amity,

Darling, I've tried so hard to get to see you but they say it's impossible. I'm frightened to try any more in case they arrest me too, which they've threatened me with, and as you know I have responsibilities which mean I must avoid this at all costs. I hope very much to be at your trial, though, even if it's just in the gallery so that you can see me there, but it seems they're trying to make things as unpleasant as they can for you and so they might not allow that, either. But, darling, you're NOT alone. Even if I'm not there in person, I'll be there in spirit, thinking of you every moment. I know you didn't do what they say you did, so don't give that another thought. Just stay strong and be my good girl and everything will somehow be all right.

I don't have any news of Hal, but I hope that wherever he is, he's keeping strong and well too. I hope this letter reaches you. I will try very hard to make sure it does, no matter what.

With love from,

Ma

Though my throat felt tight, my eyes stayed dry as I read the familiar words. I knew that she'd tried to be there. I knew it with everything I had. My mother and I hadn't always gotten along, but I'd never doubted for a second how much she loved me.

My fingers tightened on the paper as my gaze lingered on the last paragraph, the words Ma had underlined. *Keeping strong and well.*

When Ma had written this letter my brother Hal had been all right – though still in hiding in that tiny room under the floorboards. I wouldn't allow myself to even consider that his situation might have changed since then. No, Hal was still all right – please, please, he had to be, and so did Ma. The "responsibilities" Ma mentioned were taking care of him, of course. Her friend Madame Josephine would hopefully be protecting him – it was her house Hal was sheltering in – but Hal needed our mother now.

I needed her too, even if for most of my life I'd prided myself on being too grown-up for that. "Ma," I murmured, my voice inaudible. Even if I escaped, I couldn't go near her.

She and my brother were lost to me for good.

Though I tried never to think about Collie, a long-ago conversation came back: he'd told me how a girl on his street in the Central States had been arrested, and he'd stood by and done nothing.

"Don't blame yourself," I'd told him.

"No," he said. "I don't blame myself. That's the part I hate most."

In the cramped hut with its heavy smells, I slowly refolded the letter and tucked it away again. I knew that I didn't blame myself for my inaction, either. I'd do the same thing again in a heartbeat.

What's out there for me? I'd asked Ingo.

Maybe yourself, he'd said.

Feeling hollow, I stared down at my boots: the thick unbeautiful pieces of leather that had saved my life – at least physically. What about the rest of me?

And I knew I only had one option.

Chapter Twelve

December, 1941

At the mine they kept me outside on the ore mounds, with the grey smokestacks of the processing plant rising up in the distance. Snow-trucks rumbled between the two. Over a week passed when I didn't encounter Ingo – I was terrified that they'd make me permanent on the mounds and that I'd never get a chance to speak to him again.

In the evenings I skirted the marketplace and kept an eye out for the woman who'd passed his note to me – she must know him, surely? I never saw her. She'd melted away into the nameless, faceless women who kept to their own groups and huts. To show too much interest in another group was to ask for trouble. I couldn't risk it, not now that I'd decided.

Had I decided? The thought filled me with dread.

But finally one morning in early December I arrived at the mine and the Gun in charge jerked his head towards the tunnels.

"In there today. Help out whatever miner needs you."

It felt like lightning had struck. I kept my face expressionless. "Yes, sir," I said, and headed into the mines, choosing the tunnel I'd seen Ingo emerge from most often.

The mines were a mazelike series of rough tunnels with electric lights strung along the ceiling. The ringing of metal against stone filled the air. Guns patrolled, looking bored, as male prisoners swung pickaxes at the stone walls, prising rocks from them. Women prisoners helped wrest stubborn rocks free and pile them into the wheelbarrows.

I made my way down the tunnel, my heart thumping as I kept an eye out, but I didn't see Ingo. Soon I came to a miner working on his own; a Gun stood nearby, watching. With an inner curse, I stopped and started to help. The miner looked stooped and old, though probably wasn't much more than thirty.

We weren't supposed to talk. We barely even met each other's eyes. Finally, when the Gun had wandered away a little, I leaned close. "Do you know Ingo Manfred?" I whispered. "Is he in this mine today?"

The miner looked startled. His gaze darted worriedly to the Gun. "Around that bend," he murmured, jerking his head further down the mine.

We worked in silence for some time longer. The rocks I wrested from the wall came out in small cascades of pebbles; my calloused hands were grimy with dust. The pickaxes rang through the air, along with the sound of grunts and thuds. The Gun hummed tunelessly, looking bored.

An alarmed shout came from up near the mine's entrance. "Keep working!" our Gun barked at us, and strode towards the noise. Another Gun from further down the mine followed.

Further down – where Ingo was. It felt like the ocean was roaring through my senses. I put down my pickaxe and walked away. After a startled pause, I heard my miner start up work again more feverishly than before, as if trying to cover my absence.

I turned the bend. I saw Ingo instantly – he was the third miner down, shirtless and sweat-streaked like the others, his burned face clear under the harsh lights. The woman working with him was older, not someone I'd seen before. I hurried to them and drew out a scrap of bread I'd saved from my breakfast.

"Trade places with me," I hissed urgently, pressing it into her hand. "I'm working just around the bend."

She stared at the food. I saw her throat move.

"*Hurry!*" I urged. "The Guns'll be back in a minute!"

She clasped her fingers around the bread and darted off. Without looking at Ingo – who'd paused, staring at me – I grabbed hold of a loose-looking rock in the wall and started gouging at it with the small spade she'd left behind.

"Keep working," I said in a feverish undertone. After a

moment he swung the pickaxe again, sending pebbles and dust skittering down the wall.

I didn't breathe again until the Gun guarding Ingo's section was back in place. Like the other Gun, he seemed bored, patrolling the long area with lazy strides. He didn't appear to notice that one of the drab, faceless workers had changed.

No alarm came. After several minutes my shoulders eased. I risked a glance at Ingo. He was frowning, not looking at me. When the Gun had taken a dozen steps in the other direction, he muttered, "Pissing without permission for a change?"

"I had to talk to you," I whispered back.

He pulled a rock from the wall with a grunt. "So talk."

I helped him heft it into the wheelbarrow; our heads were side by side. My heart was beating so hard that I hardly heard myself speak. "I think I've changed my mind."

His dark eyes raked over me. "You *think*?"

I started to answer. Nothing came out.

Ingo turned away, the scarred half of his face a crinkled mask beneath the dust. The Gun was heading back again. Ingo swung the pickaxe viciously, as if he wished he were levelling it at the guard. When the man had passed, he hissed, "Thinking is no good to me. You have to be sure."

When I'd first met Ingo, a lifetime ago, his hair had been a riot of crisp black curls. Now it was shorn so short that I could see his scalp through the dark hair. It made his lean face look too exposed, his nose and chin too prominent.

My throat felt tight. "I'm sure."

Ingo sagged slightly. He didn't look at me, but a humourless smile touched his thin lips.

"You time your decisions well, don't you?" he whispered.

"What?"

I could hardly hear what he said next. "It has to be tomorrow night. There is no other time."

Tomorrow night. I went still and Ingo nudged me sharply; the Gun was returning. I crouched down and started gouging at a loose stone. Ingo went back to swinging the pickaxe.

For half an hour, maybe, the Gun stayed near us, rocking back and forth on his heels and occasionally shouting jokey banter to the guard further down. From what they were saying, the cry we'd heard earlier had been a miner hurt in a small rockfall. They seemed to think it a big joke that the man had been sent to Medical...probably never to return, if he didn't heal fast enough.

Ingo and I kept working. His hands were large, but with narrow wrists; his fingers were long and dusty. I glimpsed the tattoo on his palm – the swirl for Leo – and almost gave a humourless laugh.

The same tattoo as Collie. If I believed in omens, I'd take this as a bad one.

Finally the Gun wandered down the tunnel to stand nearer the bend and talk to the other guard. Ingo dropped quickly to his haunches and reached to help me pull out a rock.

"Meet me tonight," he muttered. "The same place. Midnight."

I started to nod, then remembered. "It's difficult. There's an informer in my hut."

"There's an informer in every hut. Be there."

I swallowed hard. "All right."

Ingo's eyes were ink-dark; his right eyelid drooped, pulled tightly by the scar. "You're sure?"

I nodded without looking at him. "Yes," I said shortly, and wondered how I was going to manage it.

The changing of the guard had occurred only moments ago now searchlights swept across the yard in a long arc. They licked hungrily at my toes, then moved on.

I darted through the shadows, timing my progress from hut to hut. Finally I got away from the main compound and relaxed a fraction. It was darker here, with fewer Guns.

Getting out of the hut hadn't been as hard as I'd expected. For a change it had been relatively silent, its dark forms asleep or disinterested. Maybe it was about time that I had a little luck.

When I reached the storage hut Ingo wasn't there yet. I hid in the blackest part of the gloom behind the small building. It was colder when you weren't moving, and soon I was shivering.

Even after so many months, I couldn't get used to how thin I was. Before, I'd had firm curves on the generous side that I'd always taken for granted. Now I had no padding, hardly any breasts. Even just standing here, rubbing my legs against each other, I could feel the hard knobbliness of my knees.

I stiffened as two Guns on patrol passed close by, their footsteps solid.

"Tomorrow night should be good," said one.

The other laughed. "Anything that's different is good… man, I can hardly wait to finish my term and get out of this place."

My skin prickled. Tomorrow night – when Ingo had said we had to escape.

Their voices receded. Gunnison's indecipherable murmur rustled against the silence. After an eternity a dark figure appeared on the fence's other side. Ingo. He hesitated, looking around him, and then squirmed under the opening.

"Move over," he panted.

I exhaled and did. Ingo slipped into the shadowy space and leaned against the building next to me. In the faint moonlight I saw him rubbing his hands under his arms. His angular face looked haggard, but he gave a dry smile.

"You're on time tonight," he whispered. "I thought you would be."

I glanced out towards the other huts. "I saw two Guns not long ago. They were on patrol."

"All right, we'll have to hurry. Why did you change your mind about escaping?"

"Does it matter?"

"If I'm going to trust you with my life, it matters very much. Tell me."

"You see these boots?" I asked finally. Ingo glanced at my feet. "They…made me realize something," I said. "I've got to get out of here or die trying."

It was true, yet I felt bleak inside. There was still nothing out there for me.

"So you betrayed someone to get them." Ingo's voice was expressionless.

"In a way. She betrayed me first. Do we have to talk about this?"

"Yes. If we're going to do this thing, we have to trust each other."

"That goes both ways."

"It does. Do you trust me?"

I fell silent. The crazy thing was that I had always trusted Ingo, even when I had very little reason. "I think I do," I said at last. And briefly, I told him about Melody – about not speaking up when the Guns had read out the crime she didn't do, and then sprinting to wrest the boots from her body.

"I don't regret it," I said in a low voice. "I'd do it again. But…"

"But much more of that, and you won't be human any more," finished Ingo. His hands were buried in his pockets, his thin shoulders hunched as he glared out at the men's camp. "I know…oh, I know," he said softly. "All right. I understand now. I'd feel the same."

We were standing close, our arms touching, our voices barely whispers. It was the first confidence I'd exchanged with anyone in months. Part of me felt panicked. I wanted to snatch the words back.

"The Guns said they were looking forward to tomorrow night," I said. "Does that have anything to do with your plan?"

The shadow that was Ingo nodded. "Tomorrow's Gunnison's birthday. There's a big party planned for tomorrow night. The Guns will all be celebrating – distracted."

From far away in the woods, an owl called. I pictured the always-bored Guns with something to do for a change. With luck, their focus would be entirely elsewhere.

"You're right, it's a good time to try it," I said. "What's your plan?"

Ingo leaned his head close and told me. I felt the blood leave my face. "You're serious," I said.

He straightened. "It's the only way. People who try for the train are found in no time. Have you got a better idea?"

"No," I said after a pause.

I'd heard whispers of other escape plans. All had involved trying to reach the train and hide on it, to be taken away from this place. The Guns knew it was our only way out of this barren wasteland. Finding escapees was child's play.

If you were caught, you got thrown in solitary for days of "interrogation". Then the Guns put what was left of you up on that platform near the gates and had their fun with you, for hours sometimes, before finally releasing you with a bullet.

Ingo's tone was faintly mocking. "Still want to try?"

"Yes. Of course." Though there was no other answer, the sense of despair in me grew.

"We could both be killed, you know," said Ingo. "Our heads could end up on that fence next to your betraying friend's. I suppose she was the blonde? She must have been pretty, once."

"Yes, I know we could both be killed – that's not exactly a newsflash! It doesn't matter."

"Speak for yourself. I very much want to live." Ingo fell silent, his dark eyes studying me. He looked away and let out a breath. "Look...there may not be time to talk about 'what next' tomorrow. You said before that there was nothing out there for you."

"There isn't."

"I have information that might change that."

Surprise and wariness stirred. "Go on."

"A few months ago, I got a new bunkmate from another hut. He'd been with the Resistance. He was sick; he died not long after we met."

The word *Resistance* made me think of Collie and his "contacts". I stiffened.

"Who?" I said finally.

"His name was Miguel. He knew people who worked for a conference centre in Appalachia."

"What does that—"

"Listen! He said Gunnison's planning a coup in February: he's going to force President Weir to sign a treaty that annexes Appalachia to Can-Amer. Weir will still be in charge, but in name only. They're calling it the Day of Three Suns – Gunnison and all his top people will be there."

So now my father's thrown Peacefight would lead to Gunnison taking over the entire continent. Deep down, pain stirred in my gut.

I gave a harsh, whispered laugh. "Are you suggesting we could try to stop it? This conversation's insane, Ingo! We're still in *here*."

"I realize that! When the hell do *you* propose we discuss it? Look, Miguel knew he was dying. He gave me a message about the Day of Three Suns for someone named Vince Griffin, in case I escaped. He said it's vital if they're going to bring down Gunnison."

I hated the urge that stirred in me to try. I'd tried before, with everything I had, and no one had cared. I started to protest...and then my trial flashed into my mind.

Madeline.

She'd somehow talked my father into betraying the world's trust. She knew why he'd done it. And she worked for Gunnison now.

If his top people were all going to be there, then so would she.

Electricity touched my scalp. Slowly, I said, "This Day of Three Suns...do you know where in Appalachia it's happening?"

Ingo wrapped his thin coat more tightly around himself. "No. Miguel didn't tell me everything in case I was captured. He said Vince Griffin would know the details from the message."

"You could have told me this before."

"Why should I give you such valuable information before you'd committed yourself?" Ingo gave me a sharp look. "It makes a difference to you, I take it?"

From nowhere, I saw my father at our kitchen table again – heard my own voice.

"*Dad...you can tell me anything.*"

"*Maybe someday. When you're a Peacefighter, too. It's the only thing worth being, Amity...I always knew that.*"

I stared blindly at the barbed wire of the men's camp. The pain of my father's thrown fight – my daily knowledge of exactly what it had led to – never left me, though ever since I'd gotten here I couldn't bear to look at it too closely.

I couldn't now either. I shivered and shut it away somewhere deep. But I could confront Madeline – I could finally get answers. The thought was dizzying.

I cleared my throat. "Yes," I said. "It makes a difference."

"To me, too," said Ingo. "Miguel said the Resistance would help me if I gave Vince Griffin the message. I think he hoped I might join them. Well, I have no interest in doing that. But I *do* have interest in getting their help."

"For what?"

"To get home again," Ingo said shortly. I remembered him saying that he was from the Germanic Counties, down near the Med – thousands of miles away.

In the men's camp the spotlights swung in their relentless arcs. The world was very still, full of defeated concrete buildings and jagged shadows.

"So it's agreed," Ingo whispered after a pause. "If we make it out, we'll go to Calgary. That's where Miguel told me to go and ask for Vince."

I glanced at his profile. Calgary had to be at least a thousand miles south. "Ingo, are you sure you want to travel with me? Everyone knows who I am – I'll put you in danger."

He snorted slightly. "I don't want to insult you…"

"That's never stopped you before."

"Fine, so I won't bother attempting tactfulness now. No one would ever recognize you from your photos these days, Amity. You look like shit."

And for some strange reason, this was the funniest thing I'd heard in a long time. I slumped against the side of the building, laughing weakly. Finally I straightened and swiped my eyes with the back of my hand.

"You look like shit, too," I said.

"I know. Shit with half its face burned off. If anyone sees us, they'll just think a pair of fiends from a telio play have appeared." Ingo studied me. His tone grew more sombre. "If we're really going to do this, then I propose a pact. Total trust. No matter what."

Remembering the last time I'd trusted someone so completely, I went taut. My fist clenched, hiding the tattoo even though it was too dark to see it.

"Half the time I don't even like you," I said.

"So? I don't like you, either. But I trust you – and that matters a lot more right now. Have we got a pact?"

I shivered. I knew if I made this vow, I'd keep it. Would Ingo? It was ridiculous to be so afraid – so angry at even the thought of trusting someone that way again.

But if we were doing this, then that was the way it had to be.

I put my hand out to him. "All right. Total trust. I swear it."

"And so do I," said Ingo quietly.

We shook.

When we let go Ingo shoved his hands back in his pockets. "We've got to find something for you to pick the lock with tomorrow night. What do you need?"

"Something long and thin. Remember, I used a letter opener before?"

"I can't get you that. But there's a sort of marketplace in the men's camp. A guy there had some thick wire earlier tonight that he wasn't able to trade."

"That would do, if it's thick enough."

"Good. Do you have anything to trade? I have an extra shoelace, but that won't be enough."

I thought of Claudia and her rags and smiled wryly. "You could always promise him half your meals for the next week."

The dark silhouette that was Ingo gave a bitter laugh. "If he'd cheated me like your Melody, I'd do it. Come on, have you got anything?"

I fingered the shard of glass in my pocket. It would get us whatever we needed. But tucked deep in my jacket's lining, I could also feel the letter from Ma. I'd held onto it for so long, despite paper being so precious here – I'd resisted trading it even when desperate with hunger.

I thought of Madeline and my spine tightened. *I talked him into...I mean, I talked* to *Truce...*

I traced the glass's lethal sharpness. Then I reached past it and pulled out the letter. Its paper felt soft to the touch. I handed it to Ingo.

"Use this," I said levelly.

Chapter Thirteen

March, 1941

COLLIE HELPED ME OUT OF the back of the auto. My muscles had turned to cotton.

"All right?" he whispered.

It was three a.m. We were in an underground parking garage in Topeka, John Gunnison's capital city. Autos crouched in pools of light, their long, rounded lines gleaming.

"Just about," I murmured back.

The garage belonged to the Royal Archer Hotel. When Collie had gotten our room it had been too early for me to risk going up without being seen. We'd agreed that I'd stay hidden until it was safe.

I put on the hat that he'd bought for me in the Western

Quarter: a small, dainty thing with stylish black net that covered half my face. I smoothed my hands over my skirt. Collie had bought second-hand clothes for us both. I'd teased him when he brought them back to the motel room that he'd chosen tight-fitting blouses for me on purpose.

"I'm really sorry you had to wait so long." Collie grabbed up our cases and glanced at the stairwell. "Saturday night – I guess no one ever sleeps in this city. I kept hearing doors opening and closing in the corridor."

I caught a whiff of his breath and my eyebrows rose. "You've been drinking?"

He nodded, his second-hand fedora shadowing his face. "Just a couple of beers. There was a message for me to get in touch with the Resistance guy. It seemed a good time to meet, so that we could get things going faster."

I started to answer and stopped. He'd met with the Resistance while I'd been hidden in the auto? I shook my disquiet away. Collie was right – it had been practical to start things moving.

"Has anything been arranged?" I asked in an undertone as we headed towards the stairwell.

"No, not yet." Collie's grip on our bags looked tense. "I have to meet someone else tomorrow who might be able to help us get the documents. I don't even have any names… I think they're trying to make sure I can still be trusted."

Before coming to Topeka, we'd spent several days near Angeles. Collie had liaised with contacts there, trying to get entry papers to the former Central States. The region was still guarded by checkpoints.

He hadn't told me who he'd met, but I assumed it wasn't Mac Jones. Collie had gone to Mac before, when we'd been trying to find out how deep the corruption went. While we'd waited in vain to hear from Mac, our friend Clem, a fellow Peacefighter, had been taken away.

But this time, whoever he'd gone to had come through. Yesterday, we'd gotten past the checkpoint more smoothly than we'd dared hope, with me hidden in the trunk and Collie showing his false papers.

I knew how much Collie must hate being back in the Central States, where he'd lived in fear for years. But in a way it made no difference. We were all under Gunnison's rule already.

The Western Seaboard had fallen. I wondered what the outside world thought, but there was no news of it any more. All we'd seen on the cheap, battered telio set in the Angeles motel room were images of crowds lining the streets, cheering as tanks rolled past.

I thought of the restaurant workers I'd heard talking. Would the rest of the world realize that people were just scared? Or believe whatever lies Gunnison was spouting?

We went through the stairwell door and started up the winding steps. Our echoing treads were the only sound.

One floor. Two.

We both heard it at the same time: someone coming down. Collie moved all at once; he dropped the suitcases and shoved me up against the wall. He started kissing me. Despite everything, desire leaped through me.

I wove my fingers through his hair. His hat fell to the floor. We kissed as if we were drowning and the other was air. I heard the footsteps pass and a low, masculine chuckle.

Somewhere below, the stairwell door closed.

We kept kissing, more slowly now, deep and lingering. When we finally pulled apart, I ached with wanting him. I touched his cheek, our eyes locked on each other.

He grabbed up our things. "Come on," he said, his voice husky. "Or I'll start ripping your clothes off right here."

We were in room 303; when we got inside, we didn't even make it to the bed. The hotel room had a soft rug with a pattern of swirling blues and greens. As we moved together on it, I let my hands roam his warm skin. Hope surged through me.

We were here. We would do what we'd come to do. It would all be okay, somehow.

In the bathroom afterwards, I noticed how nice the hotel room was. The taps were gleaming silver – the countertop black marble. A soft bathrobe hung on the door with "Royal Archer" embroidered on its pocket. I put it on.

When I came out, Collie was putting down the phone, wearing only his trousers. "I got us room service," he said. "Just one meal so they won't guess, but we can share it."

"Good." I was starving suddenly. I went to him and hugged his bare waist; he turned and held me tightly.

"I really needed that," he murmured, pressing his face against my neck. I knew he didn't mean the hug. I pulled back and rumpled his tousled hair.

"I was sending you crazed with lust?" I teased.

He grinned. "You always do, you temptress." He touched my cheek. "No...I just meant I needed to feel close to you."

I kissed his jaw. The window was right behind him, its silvery-grey curtains long and stiff-looking.

I hesitated and then pulled one aside.

Downtown Topeka lay below. The Zodiac complex was only a few blocks away. I stared at the familiar white domes I'd seen in so many newsreels, stark against the night sky.

Collie's arms encircled me from behind. His faint stubble prickled against the side of my forehead.

"Don't look," he said, his voice bitter. "It's a terrible view."

But I did look. I looked for a long time, wondering whether my father had ever been here. Whether he'd been to secret meetings in that very building. Was it here that he'd agreed to throw the civil war Peacefight to ensure Gunnison's win?

My heart felt like thick glass: hard and breakable. Finally I let the curtain drop and gazed around us. The bed had a carved headboard. There was a walk-in closet, and a white dressing table with lights around the mirror like a telio star might use.

My eyebrows knitted together. "We don't really need to be throwing money around, do we?"

Collie shrugged. "It's where the Resistance guy back in the WS said we should stay, so we don't have much choice. With luck we won't be here long."

When the food arrived we hid my things and I stayed in the bathroom. We ate the burger and fries in bed, though I didn't have much appetite after all. I kept picking up my half of the burger and then putting it down again. I couldn't stop thinking of what lay just beyond the window.

"Why would the Resistance want us to stay here?" I asked finally. "Wouldn't we have been safer in a place that wasn't so central?"

Collie didn't look at me. He ate his last piece of burger before replying.

"I don't think we're safe anywhere," he said. "But at least we're close to where the documents are. That's got to help." Abruptly, he leaned over me to put the plate on the floor. I felt the stretch of his stomach muscles.

I noticed that he hadn't really answered the question. "Collie?" I asked, and then stopped, unsure what I wanted to say. Something about the way he was acting bothered me, though I couldn't put my finger on it. But if he was acting slightly off-kilter, no wonder, when he was back in this place that he hated.

He hefted himself upright again and kissed me. "It'll be all right," he whispered against my lips. "I promise."

He stroked my hair. "Are you ready to sleep? I've got to meet this guy in just a few hours."

"Yes, fine," I said after a pause. He snapped out the light; the room fell into gloom. He pulled me close and I lay against his chest.

I deliberately hadn't asked Collie what the plan was, and could sense his relief. In a way it was insane that I'd come here – but we'd had no choice. The only place we could escape to once we had the documents was further east, to Appalachia. It was still a free country.

I lay tensely awake, listening to the occasional auto passing down below. It sounded like traffic anywhere. Yet we were in the Central States. *Can-Amer*, I corrected myself. All I cared about was getting what we'd come for and then getting the hell out of this place.

"Amity?" whispered Collie, and I started. I'd thought he was asleep.

"What?" I murmured back.

He hesitated. "Nothing."

I raised up on one elbow and studied him in the faint light from the partially-open curtains. I stroked his arm. "What's wrong?"

He gave a short laugh. "What *isn't* wrong, being back here?" He rubbed his forehead. "Look…I love you, okay? No matter what. Do you believe me?"

"Of course I do," I said in bewilderment. "I love you, too. Collie, what…"

The sheets rustled as he rolled onto his side, facing me.

He took my hand and played with my fingers. "I just… I wanted to tell you…"

He faltered and fell silent. I heard a milk truck pass down below, bottles clinking. It faded. "Tell me what?" I said.

"Nothing," he repeated finally.

I gripped his fingers. "No, it's *not* nothing. Collie, tell me."

In a low voice, he said, "You know…I think about my father sometimes."

At first I thought I hadn't heard him right. Collie's father was a fast-talking man who smiled too much and had hard, calculating eyes. The few times I'd met him, back when Collie and I were both children, I'd wanted to stay far away.

"Is he here?" I asked uneasily. Collie had told me once that his parents were still in the Central States – that he didn't know what had happened to them.

He rolled onto his back again. "I don't know," he said, sounding tired. "I don't want to know. Amity, the thing is…he loved Goldie."

At the mention of Collie's mother, I went still, remembering the pretty, drunken woman who'd danced in their shabby parlour while her young son lay feverish in the next room.

"You probably don't believe that," Collie said into the darkness. "But he did. And he made her unhappy anyway. He couldn't help it. He wasn't good enough for her. Eventually he dragged her down to his level and—"

I moved quickly, straddling him. Collie gave an *oof* of surprise.

"*Stop it,*" I snapped.

"Stop what?"

"You're making some kind of analogy between you and your father! Well, knock it off. You are *not him*, Collis Reed."

He started to speak; I gently shook his shoulders. "Are you listening? You're a good person! You make me the opposite of unhappy. Don't you know that, you big jerk?"

I'd wanted to make him laugh. I heard him swallow. He took my wrists. "There's…a lot you don't know, Amity."

My skin chilled. "Like what?"

When he didn't answer, I slid off him and pressed close against his side. I touched his cheek. My heart hurt with all I wanted to say. "Collie, please," I whispered. "Isn't it time for me to know exactly what happened to you here?"

He gave a sort of choking laugh and wiped his eyes. "Yeah, probably. But not while we're still in this place. I just can't. Once we're safely away, I'll tell you everything."

I squeezed his hand hard. "Promise?"

He nodded. His fingers felt strong against mine. Yet when he spoke, I could hardly hear him: "Yes. I promise."

Chapter Fourteen

December, 1941

When the morning sirens went off I'd been awake for hours, thinking about what was going to happen that night. I rose with the others and went through my usual routine, trying to act like nothing was different.

"Well, that's a good question, Tom," boomed Gunnison's voice. "And you know, I think the best way to answer it is to ask a question myself: have *you* known the joy of Harmony in your life?"

"I hope so, Mr President."

"Of course you have! You're a Libra, aren't you?" A chuckle. "Oh, yes, I checked. So you see, for *you*, Harmony is going to be all about balance. The power of astrology can—"

The volume dropped to an intimate whisper. As I retied my boots I froze and looked up: outside, the band had started playing "Happy Birthday".

We glanced at each other. Anything different here was to be feared.

"Happy birthday to *who*?" muttered Claudia, her eyes wide.

I let someone else volunteer the information. "Gunnison, I think," Natalie said in a small voice. "December 8th..." She trailed off.

We all jumped – someone was outside our hut banging on a garbage can lid. "Get out here, Discordant scum! Sing!"

It was five minutes before the counting. We scrambled for the door. Some of the women hadn't finished dressing yet and stumbled to yank on shoes and coats. Trepidation filled me. Ingo and I had assumed that this would be the perfect day to escape. Instead it suddenly felt like a wild card.

We gathered in rows, like for the counting. The Guns hooted. "No, no! We need a choir! Who can sing?" Randomly, they started pulling people from the ranks. My heart pounded. Was it better to volunteer or not?

Before I could decide a Gun grabbed me. The pretty blonde one. Laughing, she shoved me in place with the others. She stood in front of us and pretended to conduct, waving a stick in the air. "All right, all together now...sing!"

"*Happy birthday to you,*

Happy birthday to you,

Happy birthday, dear…"

Our voices sounded ragged in the cold air. The Gun stopped us with a slice of her stick. "No, louder!" she cried. "Is that the best you can do?" She took out her pistol and pointed it at us. "Show me how much you love President Gunnison! Now SING!"

We started again. I sang with all my might, belting out the words. I've never been able to sing; it didn't matter. The Gun levelled her pistol and flicked off the safety. I flinched, but kept looking straight ahead, kept singing even as she fired.

The shot thundered in my ears. The Guns were all laughing, singing along.

Finally the song ended. I stood motionless with the others, trembling, staring blindly at Gunnison's murmuring screen image as he sat relaxed in an armchair. But from the corner of my eye, I saw a huddled shape on the ground and recognized Natalie's hair. Red stained the snow and the hair. The hunched figure didn't move.

The Gun grinned and put her pistol away. "One less to count. Get in line!"

We did.

At the mine it was the same. I was put onto the crusher – much too near the Guns, who stood around their flaming oil drum all day, warming their hands. Today they were also passing around a brown bottle. Their cheeks were ruddy, their eyes too bright. I kept my head down and prayed none of them would notice me.

They noticed others. That day I heard more infractions, made-up or real, than I'd ever imagined. Hardly a half hour went by without one of the Guns pouncing on someone. "You there! Stand straight! I'll teach you to be proud to work for President Gunnison!"

Tonight, I thought fervently. No matter what, Ingo and I would try to get out of this place.

Then unease stirred. I dared a glance towards the tunnels. Where *was* Ingo? I'd been here for hours and hadn't seen him. I squelched the thought and redoubled my efforts, stooping to grasp rocks and then shove them onto the conveyor belt.

Finally Ingo appeared. I was so intent on avoiding attention that I didn't see him until he had almost reached me. Then I gasped out loud.

He was hunched over. A purpling bruise spread across his ribs, with an ugly, dusty wound at its centre. The wheelbarrow wobbled in his grip as he struggled to keep it steady, his jaw rigid. I froze; my gaze flew to his in horrified dismay.

What had happened? But it hardly mattered – I could guess. I turned back to the crusher. My skin felt too tight for my body. *Our plan tonight.* How could Ingo escape like this?

He couldn't.

With a dull scraping sound, Ingo upended his load of

rocks next to the crusher. As he crouched to help me, he touched my wrist fleetingly, asking me to look at him.

Imperceptibly, he nodded: *I will still be there tonight.*

A Gun strode over in his long wool coat, carrying a switch. Ingo looked away again; I did too. Not fast enough.

"Stop dawdling!" barked the Gun. He raised the switch and fire licked across my back. I cried out and stumbled, falling against the mound of rocks. The switch whistled again as he brought it down hard across Ingo's shoulders.

The Gun laughed and tucked the switch away. He kicked at Ingo's bruised ribs and Ingo sucked in a hissing breath, abruptly paling.

"Ha! That'll teach you to work harder." The Gun strolled back to the others.

A tide roared in my ears. Gritting my teeth against the pain, I kept grasping rocks, kept pushing them onto the endless, eager tongue of the crusher.

Ingo got to his feet. His movements were tight, steely. He gripped the wheelbarrow's handles and headed back into the mine, slower and more hunched-over than before. A trickle of blood coursed down his thin back.

He didn't appear again.

That night there was a party for the Guns at the camp director's house. Those who had been left to guard us were thin on the ground but making their presence known.

"Ready, steady, go!" I heard one yell distantly, somewhere outside our hut. Cheers rang out. I cringed as I realized: they were forcing prisoners to run races, and betting on who would win.

The camp felt abandoned. Everyone who'd so far escaped the Guns' notice was hiding inside their hut. It was where I wanted to stay too. Instead, once the food truck had been gone for two repetitions of the films, I braced myself and stepped outside.

Bedraggled-looking red bunting framed the moving-picture screen. Gunnison's solid, suit-clad image shouted faintly to a cheering crowd: "*...I'll stop at nothing! I WILL rid the Discordant elements from our Harmonic society!*"

"Where are you going?" Claudia's thin face seemed to swim at me from nowhere. A searchlight swept by, flashing briefly across us.

I tensed. I'd thought she was in bed. "I've got something to trade."

"Tonight?"

"Yes. Tonight."

Her gaze flicked to my boots. Everyone knew how much I'd needed them – and now I had them. Her unspoken words seemed to hang between us: *what do you need so badly that it can't wait?*

"I've got rags," she said, as though fishing for the answer.

"Thanks, but no." My mind ticked desperately. Claudia was an informer. Tonight of all nights the Guns would love to be informed of something. She'd be more eager to sell me out if she suspected where I was really going.

On impulse, I clutched her arm. "Would you come too?" I whispered. "Please! Two of us would be less likely to attract attention."

She recoiled. "No! Go on your own, if you're that stupid."

After a show of hesitation, I set off towards the marketplace. From the direction of the races I could hear the Guns laughing. I slunk through the shadows, avoiding the searchlight.

When I glanced back, Claudia still stood in front of our hut, watching. Then to my relief she went inside.

I veered off between two huts, leaving the marketplace behind. Finally I reached where I was going. I pressed into the shadows and stared out at a large, square building that stood on its own at a crossroads, its windows dark.

Claudia's domain: the laundry.

I licked my lips, taking in how exposed it was. I hadn't seen a Gun in a while, but those still around were swarming in packs tonight, bored and resentful at being kept from the party.

"Lady Harmony has spoken!" cried Gunnison's fervent whisper.

I grabbed my courage with both hands and darted for the laundry, veering for its rear door. It was shadowy back here, with a gate across the nearby road – a dead end if I was caught.

As I pressed against the dark doorway, the cut on my back throbbed. This was insane. Ingo wasn't going to come; he couldn't.

Yet even as I thought it, I heard footsteps.

When Ingo's lean form appeared I let out a shaky breath. In the dim light I could see him moving more stiffly than before, hunched over and clutching at his side.

Our eyes met. His were ablaze, as if hanging on by sheer force of will. He seemed to be daring me to protest.

"I was afraid you might not make it," I whispered. "Are you all right?"

"I said I'd be here, so I'm here." Ingo pressed a piece of thick wire into my hand and glanced over his shoulder. "Do it," he hissed. "Hurry."

As Gunnison whispered on, I took the wire apprehensively and crouched down. I hadn't picked a lock since that time in the World for Peace building. This one was more basic, even with my hands half-numb from cold. With a few well-placed prods, I felt the tumblers click into place. The door opened and I drooped in relief.

Ingo exhaled, and I realized he'd been scared that I might fail too. We hurried inside and shut the door behind us. Gunnison's voice faded.

We were in a back room full of sinks and boxes. A delicious warmth embraced us. A furnace sat in the corner with embers still glowing through its door.

"In here." Ingo motioned to the main room.

Its only windows were small, high up. Ambient light

from the camp slanted in. Industrial-sized washers lined one wall.

Ingo went quickly to a rack of clothes and started scraping through them. "These are the women's, I think. What size are you?"

I told him, then stopped short. "No – better make it a few sizes smaller."

Ingo's laugh held no humour. "The Harmony diet. It works wonders."

He thrust a Gun's uniform at me. We found one for him as well, and clean underclothes for us both. There were even gloves; fur-lined hats; long woollen coats, with thick fleece linings. We'd broken into a treasure trove. I felt light-headed as I pulled a coat off the rack and handed another to Ingo.

"What do we do with our old things?" I said. "Burn them?"

"Perfect."

We rushed back into the small utility room. Ingo started stripping off with no hesitation – I did the same. For a second it was like being a Peacefighter back in the mixed-sex locker room, except that no Peacefighters had ever looked as scrawny as the pair of us.

Ingo winced as he shrugged out of his tattered shirt. I winced too, to see the extent of the wound that gashed across his ribs. It was gaping, grimy with dust. The bruise looked worse now, a mottled stain on his skin.

I glanced around and found a rag – grimly reflected that

this was where Claudia must steal them from. I turned on a tap in one of the sinks. "We've got to clean it, or it might get infected."

Ingo looked at himself and then me, more carefully. "We've both got to get cleaned up, in case we're challenged."

The possibility filled me with dread, but he was right. I wet the cloth and found some soap; I hastily cleaned Ingo's wound for him. Grime ran in rivulets down his skin. He stood motionless, gritting his teeth.

"It needs stitches," I said as I wrung the rag out in the sink.

"I know. Forget it."

"Do you really think you can make it, even if we escape? Ingo, you can hardly walk! I think you've probably broken a rib."

"I'll make it." His tone was low, deadly. He grabbed the rag from me and finished mopping himself off, swiping it over his face and arms.

"What happened, anyway?" I asked.

Ingo shook his head shortly. "One of the Guns in the mine today. A stupid contest, ho ho, how amusing... another miner swung badly and got me with his pick. I wish he'd gotten the Gun in his head." He thrust the rag at me.

I got myself cleaned off. We helped each other with the shallow cuts on our backs, then quickly fashioned a bandage for Ingo's wound from a torn-up shirt.

We got dressed in the glow from the furnace. Our stolen uniforms were too big, but with belts they weren't bad.

I still had my leather jacket. I put it on over my uniform for extra padding with the long coat over it.

We shoved our old clothes – twin piles of filthy rags – into the furnace.

"Good riddance," murmured Ingo, his jaw tight as we watched them burn. I knew just how he felt.

We searched the room hastily, grabbing anything that might be of use: a ball of twine, some rags. There wasn't much; the cabinets were all locked. As an afterthought, I swiped my hand across a high shelf and my fingers closed on a prize.

"Look," I said with a small smile, holding up a half-full pack of matches.

Ingo nodded. "Good. Keep them dry."

The coats came with scarves tucked under their lapels. We wound them around our necks and mouths the way the Guns did.

"All right, listen," said Ingo, his voice slightly muffled. "Remember, the Resistance leader's name is Vince Griffin. We ask for him in a Calgary bar called the Mayflower. The message is this: *The caterers can smuggle in what you need.* There are three names." He gave them.

I stared at him. "Why are you telling me this?"

"Because if one of us falls, the other keeps going. No heroics. Agreed?"

He meant him. He was afraid he wouldn't make it.

Once I would have protested. Now I thought of getting to Madeline and nodded. "Don't worry, I'm not heroic.

And the same goes for you." I adjusted his scarf a little, covering more of his scar.

"Do we pass muster?" Ingo asked tautly.

"You do, I think." I pulled on a hat and bundled my filthy hair up into it, tense with fear. "What about me?"

"Yes, I think you'll do..." Ingo broke off. His dark eyes flew to mine as we both heard it.

Footsteps, approaching down the path.

My pulse spiked. Ingo grabbed me; we flattened ourselves against the wall in the shadows. My eyes stayed riveted on the door. I'd locked it after us, hadn't I?

The footsteps drew closer and stopped. The doorknob rattled as someone tried it.

A hesitant knock.

"Excuse me?" called a voice. "Is...is somebody in there?"

Claudia. I caught my breath. Ingo and I didn't move. I stared at the window, sickly aware that the stove's flames were bathing the room in a warm orange glow.

A long shadow fell across the floor as she peered in. I'd thought we were hidden. We weren't. Claudia gaped at the scene – at Ingo, at me, at both of us wearing Guns' uniforms – and then turned and ran.

Chapter Fifteen

INGO LUNGED TO OPEN THE door. I shoved past him after Claudia, bursting out into the cold slap of night. The stars were a million icy pinpoints – Claudia a dark, running shadow ahead.

"Escape...escape..." she panted.

Hatred and fear surged. I somehow put on a burst of speed. I brushed her tattered coat with my fingers; I yanked hard and she stumbled and I tackled her, taking us both down in a flurry of gravel and snow.

She shrieked, tried to scramble to get away. One of her flailing fists hit the side of my head and the world dimmed. Her mouth was wide open; she was about to scream for the Guns – *no!*

With a frenzied lunge, I slammed her head against the ground – then again. Claudia slumped and went still.

"I'm glad you asked that, Tom," murmured Gunnison in the sudden silence. "Growing up on the farm, I thought a lot about justice…"

For a second I wondered if I'd killed her, but her chest gently rose and fell. I sat up shakily and shoved away from her. We'd been lying as close as two lovers, and the feel of her skin sickened me.

Only seconds had passed. Ingo appeared, clutching his side. His expression as he stared down at Claudia was wild, fevered.

Our eyes met. I knew he was thinking the same thing I was: our plan depended on getting away undetected hours before the morning counting. There was only one thing that could guarantee Claudia's silence.

"Come, we have to get her inside," said Ingo finally.

Even in the dim light, I could see his wince, his sudden paleness as he crouched down and took Claudia's arms, and I cursed her even more. We carried her into the laundry. Sprawled on the floor in the furnace's glow, she looked more like a rat than ever: brown hair, sharp face and elbows.

Ingo stared down at her grimly. He prodded her with his foot. "Your informer?"

"Yes."

He snorted. "I can tell. She looks better fed than most."

The shard of glass lay in my flight jacket's pocket along with the matches. I reached in and touched its razor sharpness. "She was curious about where I was going tonight," I said. "I thought I threw her off my track, but… obviously I didn't."

A heavy pause. Ingo and I looked at each other, weighing what we had to do. In a flash I saw Melody's limp body again as it dropped from the platform.

I swallowed and let go of the glass, hating Claudia all the more. "I can't do it," I said softly.

Ingo rubbed his scar as if it bothered him. "No, me neither," he said finally. "More fool us."

We had to use the twine we'd found to bind Claudia's ankles and wrists – then we gagged her with a rag that she'd probably sell for extra food when she finally got free. We dragged her into a storage closet and jammed the door shut with a chair.

"That won't hold for long," muttered Ingo. "A few good thumps from the inside and she'll be out. I can think of a hundred ways she might attract the Guns' attention from in here."

So could I. "Maybe she'll stay passed out until morning," I said.

"I wish that even the tiniest part of you believed that."

The plan had been risky enough before; now I felt almost sick with dread. "If only there were some other night we could try it," I murmured. "We could go back, pretend she was making it all up…"

"Don't be stupid; it's tonight or nothing," said Ingo bitterly. "Did you forget? We burned our other clothes."

The enormity of this fact hit me like a lead weight.

"That's that then," I said finally. "I guess we'd better take our chances."

The camp director's house sat on a hill, lit up as if on fire. Music throbbed faintly from it. Apart from distant, raucous shouts, quiet lay over the camp. Gunnison's voice had faded – though when I glanced back, his screen image stood laughing with a soldier.

Whether we lived or died, soon I'd never have to see those films again.

As we neared the gate that led to the Guns' quarters, dread filled me. "You're sure there's no other way?" I asked in a low voice.

"Yes," Ingo said shortly. I couldn't see his mouth under the scarf, but his eyes had a darkly reckless glint, as if we'd passed the point of no return. I supposed we had.

"It'll be fun," he said.

"You're crazy."

"Yes, why not? Everyone should be crazy once in their lives."

He gasped as he said it, and I realized to my alarm that he was fading fast. His forehead looked clammy below his fur-lined hat; he walked hunched, holding his side. My gaze flew to his coat. I wondered uneasily if the wound was bleeding through.

"Are you all right?" I asked in an undertone.

"Stop asking me that. I'm fine."

Another whooping shout came from the distance, and inspiration struck. "No, you're drunk! Like half the Guns here." I put my arm around Ingo's waist. "Lean on me," I said urgently.

He pulled sharply away. "If I can't make it, you'll leave me. That was the deal."

"There was no deal that said I couldn't help you."

"I told you, I can walk! Amity, you're skin and bones; you're hardly any stronger than I am."

"We'll support each other then," I hissed. "Don't be an idiot! If you're captured, they'll take me too."

Ingo gave me a quick glance and succumbed then, putting his arm around my shoulders. I could feel the relief in his muscles as we walked in a shambling duo towards the open gate.

Two Guns stood nearby, guarding. I saw the red glow of a cigarette and heard their laughter as we approached. Somehow our feet didn't hesitate as we walked through the open gate.

"Evening," called out one of the Guns. She strode loosely towards us. I stiffened – it was the blonde Gun who'd shot Natalie that morning. She nodded at Ingo, her expression friendly. "What's with him?"

We stood in half-shadow that felt hideously bright. Surely she'd recognize me, even with the scarf? I shrugged. Ingo was tense against my side. He'd dropped his cheek against my shoulder, hiding his scar.

"He's fine." The words were muffled and she looked at my scarf. My blood cold, I slowly tugged it down a little. She didn't react.

"Too...too much happy juice, that's all," I said.

The Gun gave a guffawing laugh and I realized how drunk she was. "No such thing! Especially tonight, eh? Here, let's see if you can catch up with your friend." She grinned and handed me an open flask.

I managed a smile back and took a quick gulp, turning my head away. Whisky burned down my throat.

"Thanks," I gasped out as I handed the flask back.

"Been to the party?" she said cheerfully. "Listen, it's in full swing now, you can sneak in and they'll never know if you're off duty."

I longed to pull the scarf back up. I swallowed. "No, we've just been having our own party...but maybe we'll sneak in later."

The other Gun approached through the shadows, even drunker than she was. "Elsie, come on, I thought we were having a target contest!" He spun suddenly and shot at a tree. He missed wildly, staggering, and whooped with glee. "Hey, we should get some prisoners over here to aim at!"

Elsie rolled her eyes. "You know I'm already in trouble for that. Bit of fun this morning," she added to me with a conspirator's smile. "But honestly, you should have heard her sing!" She and the other Gun collapsed into giggles.

"That bad?" I said after a pause.

I couldn't laugh, couldn't even sound as if I were smiling.

I stared at the Gun's pistol and imagined the warm weight of it in my grip. He was so close. I could grab the pistol and hold it at them both. Shout at them to sing, no, louder – SING!

Ingo's arm tightened warningly. "Time for bed," he mumbled.

The Guns laughed. I tried to smile.

"Goodnight," said Elsie, steering the other guard away. "Hope you make it to the party after you get your friend home. We'd better get back to 'guarding'." She said the word in quotes. She sounded *nice.*

Nice.

When Ingo and I were far enough away, he sagged out a breath and studied me briefly. "I suppose I shouldn't be surprised at your nerve, after fighting you so often."

I was still shaking. "What nerve?" I snapped. "I didn't do anything! I wanted to grab that pistol from him and..." I trailed off. "That woman killed one of my hut-mates this morning," I said. "Just shot her, for no reason."

Ingo's look was laced with bitter understanding. Our footsteps mingled with the distant music from the party.

"We'll get away or die trying," he said. "That's all that counts. And you got us through the gate."

He straightened a little and dropped his arm from my shoulders. "I think I can walk now," he added. "It was a cramp...thank you."

Neither of us spoke for a while, apart from quick, whispered consultations about direction. We steered our way through the Guns' enclosure by the stars and the dark outline of the nearby woods, until we were walking down a long road that we hoped backed onto the fence near the mines.

The rest of Ingo's information had to do with the processing plant beyond the mines. Whatever it produced was packed into canisters, then loaded onto a small fleet of snow-trucks by the male prisoners. Ingo had been recruited to help many times – and at the end of each day he'd seen the fully-loaded snow-trucks drive off across the snowy fields towards what he knew must be the Guns' section of camp, to be stored overnight.

Strangely, the Guns often spoke freely around us. They seemed to literally see us as sub-human. One afternoon, straining to help lift one of the heavy canisters, Ingo had overheard a driver complain about how early the trucks left each morning, to get to wherever they were going – and how much of a pain it was to have to stop halfway and shift over from snow-runners to tyres.

"They leave before the first counting," Ingo had whispered to me when he'd first told me the plan. "And the only way to get to the trucks is through the Guns' section. They don't search there when someone escapes; I'm sure of it. If we can be hidden on one of those trucks when they leave, we'll be taken away from here."

"To where?" I'd asked, and Ingo had shrugged.

"Somewhere warmer, with roads," he said. "We can steal an auto, maybe."

I'd stared at the barbed wire of the men's section for a long moment before saying, "Should I state the obvious?"

"State away," Ingo had replied curtly. "It's a risk we have to take. Either come, or don't come."

I hadn't said it. And here I was now. But we both knew that there was a chance the snow-trucks were simply transferring the canisters to another prison camp: Harmony One, Two, Three or Four.

The music had faded behind us, yet I was taut, certain that our every footfall would attract Guns who'd discovered Claudia. Finally we rounded a bend and saw a lit area ahead of us, illuminating large, boxy buildings with huge doors.

For a fleeting second I thought of aircraft hangars, but no: these were garages for snow-trucks.

Our steps slowed. Ingo had that do-or-die glitter in his dark eyes again. "Second thoughts, Wildcat?" he said pointedly.

"No. It's a bit late for that." I glanced at him, irritated. "I wish they'd given *you* a nickname in the press, since you keep harping on mine."

He turned back to the enclosure. "Well, no prizes for guessing what it would've been."

My gaze flicked to the burned half of his face, wrinkled and mask-like in the shadows. *Scarface.* I didn't say it.

A high chain-link gate stretched across the road. We'd had no fresh snow in days, and to my relief, the enclosure was trampled with footprints. Our own wouldn't give us away.

We pressed against a tree and watched. No movement.

"Shall we try it?" I said finally.

Before Ingo could answer, a monotonous drone wailed through the air. We froze; my veins turned to ice.

"A counting," I breathed. Why were they doing a counting *now*?

Claudia.

Ingo swore in Germanic. "Come on!"

He lurched towards the gate and I followed. I'd been hoping to pick the padlock; there was no time. The fence shook as we scrambled over it, digging our toes into the chain-link diamonds.

I staggered a little as we dropped onto the snow-covered pavement. Ingo was already propelling himself towards the nearest garage. It wasn't locked. We rattled the massive door open and ducked inside.

We pulled the door closed. Darkness. Ingo fumbled at the wall and the garage burst into light. A snow-truck towered over us: a giant metal insect with a huge grilled mouth and curved feelers that would skim over the snow. The cab sat high off the ground.

Outside, the sirens had stopped. I felt like throwing up. Everyone in the camp was lining up to be counted now, palms out.

Ingo clutched at his rib, his face a sickly greenish hue. "Quick, under here," he gasped.

He ducked under the snow-truck into the shadows. Tall caterpillar runners crouched to each side. Above was the floor of the truck's bed.

Ingo muttered feverishly in Germanic, sweeping his hands over the metal overhead.

"What are you saying?" I cried in frustration.

He banged the "ceiling" with his fist. "I'm saying, where the hell *is* it?" Then he saw something nearer the cab and darted over. "Here, here – see? There's a compartment."

His long fingers prised at a trapdoor. It swung open, revealing a dark space. I joined him and peered upwards. A tyre almost as large as we were was attached by bolts.

"It opens from inside the truck's bed too," said Ingo. I heard him swallow. "I checked once when I was loading the canisters. There's space above the tyre; we'll both fit if we squeeze together."

I gripped the edge of the trapdoor. "Isn't this one of the tyres that they'll swap for the runners halfway?"

"No. Those are in compartments on the side, easier to get to. This is the spare. Come on, climb up."

"You'd better go first," I said, glancing tensely out at the garage. I could see snowsuits hanging limply on the wall, with goggles drooping over them like dead eyes. "I'll turn off the lights. Then once I'm in, I can stretch back down and shut the trapdoor."

"I'll do it. I have longer arms than you."

"I know, but you're hurt."

"Pot, meet kettle."

My patience, never great, snapped. "For crying out loud, Ingo, will you stop arguing?"

Unexpectedly, he flashed a quick one-sided smile. "You sounded just like my sister then. All right, fine. You're right."

With a grunt of pain Ingo hefted himself up onto the tyre; his long legs disappeared in a flurry of wool coat. I ducked out and turned off the lights, then groped my way back to the truck.

I scrambled up into the compartment, then managed to dangle down and shut the trapdoor. I lay flat on the tyre beside Ingo, breathing hard. The ceiling – some part of the truck-bed – was almost touching my nose. If either of us had been a normal weight, we could never have fitted in here.

The darkness was total. I could feel Ingo pressed beside me, hear his shallow, uneven breathing.

"Are you all right?" I asked finally.

"Yes. But I wish you'd quit asking me that." To my surprise, Ingo sighed and added, "Sorry about calling you Wildcat before. I can be a dick when I'm nervous."

"Accepted," I said after a pause. I craned to hear outside. Still only silence. "Is that why you've been a dick nearly every time we've met?"

"*You* don't make me nervous, if that's what you're implying. But being in this place, finding a man murdered, breaking into the World for Peace building…"

"Point taken," I said. "I haven't been at my best for a long time either." The understatement was so vast that I almost wanted to laugh.

The dark shadow that was Ingo shifted. I felt his wince of pain. "Anyway, look," he said hoarsely. "My sister has a...kind of code phrase that she uses to let me know when I'm out of line. You could always use it too."

"Go on."

"She says, 'Fuck off, Ingo.'"

Despite everything, I gave a small chuckle. "I think I like your sister."

Ingo started to respond. He fell silent as another siren started up: the quick, pulsing one that meant prisoners were missing.

Neither of us spoke.

"I like her too," he said finally. "I hope I'll get to hear her tell me that again."

We lay in the cramped darkness for what seemed like hours, staying mostly silent. I clutched the shard of glass. It wouldn't help much if we were caught, but I was glad to have it anyway.

Finally we heard footsteps outside. I stiffened, gripping the glass. The garage door rattled open. "...so what do you know, the bunch of bored idiots got lucky, for a change."

I flinched at a sudden loud clanging: the back of the snow-truck being opened. Footsteps came from above; another voice floated down: "Three gone though. Bet that shocked them."

"Ah, the scum probably waltzed out the front gates

under their drunken noses… Yeah, everything looks good."

My bones seemed to melt. Almost inaudibly, I heard Ingo's release of breath. *Three gone.* They hadn't found Claudia yet. The counting had been random; the Guns didn't know that we might have breached their domain.

The first voice lifted to a shout. "Hey, Joe! We ready to roll?"

The cab doors slammed shut with twin echoes. The world erupted into noise; the spare tyre shuddered as we started to move. I caught my breath, blood pounding.

Before we'd gone very far, the truck slowed and stopped. I lay without moving, listening wildly – but then we started up again and I realized we must have passed through the gates.

We were out.

Ingo touched my arm. His breath tickled at my ear as he leaned close to whisper, "Just like flying a Firedove."

He sounded as tensely hyped-up as I felt. And I knew he meant not just the steady drone of machinery, but the freedom. Exultation burst through me. We would do this. We *would.*

I would get to Madeline and find answers.

"It's even better," I muttered back.

Chapter Sixteen

September, 1941

THE SUDDEN ROAR CRASHED THROUGH Topeka's Harmony stadium like thunder. Belatedly, Mac surged to his feet with the cheering crowd as Sechelski knocked a home run out of the park with two men on base.

He'd never cared so little about such a great play. Everyone sank to the benches again, talking excitedly. As the food vendors' shouts filled the air, Walter leaned towards him and Sephy again. As always, the *Topeka Times* editor resembled a large, dishevelled lion.

"All right, you were saying?" Walter murmured.

"A comet's due to arrive," Sephy said, without looking away from the playing field. At Walter's slight frown, she leaned towards Mac for more popcorn and expanded:

"A periodic one. I found a reference to it in an astronomy journal. It'll be in the night sky from early February, for over a month."

"Keep talking."

"It interferes with DOTS," said Mac.

Walter's bushy eyebrows shot up at the acronym for the Day of Three Suns. "Really?" he muttered urgently.

Sephy nodded. "The whole rationale for it, according to our lovely Miss Pierce, is that the positions of Venus and Jupiter will dominate the sky that evening and make it the astrologically perfect moment to annex Appalachia. But comets are historically portents of doom. Bad news, as far as Gunnison is concerned."

"If we use this right, it'll be the end of DOTS," Mac put in. "He'll want to delay the signing until another astrologically significant date. Sephy says there's not another big one till summer."

"So why doesn't Pierce know about this comet?" asked Walter.

Sephy shrugged tensely. She wore a red beret; a tendril of black hair graced her cheek. "Guess she's not an astronomy buff. It's only a minor one – hardly visible without a telescope. But it'll be there, all right."

Mac propped his elbows on his knees. Under the buzz of the crowd, he said, "Walt, listen, we could even spin it so that he should hold the signing here, instead of in Appalachia. Say that the comet means President Weir should come to us."

His voice was tight with hope. If the historic event happened here, where the Resistance was still largely intact, with luck they could locate the venue – they could still take out Gunnison and Cain.

Walter looked doubtful. "But he's not going to listen to *you* about astrological interpretations. Even if he's tipped off about the comet, Pierce'll just shoot down anything she doesn't like."

Mac sighed, tapping his thigh with a fist as he watched the playing field. "I need to persuade her to put Sephy on her staff."

Walter winced. "Really?"

"It's the only way," said Sephy steadily. "Then I can get Gunnison's ear about the comet and explain why the stars say the signing needs to happen here."

From Walter's expression, he was remembering that Kay Pierce had sent almost all of Gunnison's former astrologers to correction camps. Mac himself hadn't been able to forget it even once since he and Sephy had started discussing this plan. He didn't want her anywhere near Pierce.

But Sephy was the only official state astrologer they had left with enough experience to even be considered for such a post.

Baxter struck out; the crowd groaned. "So *can* you persuade Pierce to hire her?" Walter asked Mac finally.

Mac took some popcorn and then found he wasn't hungry. He jiggled it in his hand, looking down. "I'm working on it," he said. "No dice yet."

"Well, easy does it," said Walter grimly. "Don't push it and spook her."

Mac didn't need the warning: Kay Pierce was wary enough these days. So was Mac. He'd finally gotten some information on Gunnison, but didn't understand it – and had a feeling it could be vital.

The day before, he'd been summoned to John Gunnison's private office, which was part of a comfortable but not-too-lavish apartment deep in the Sagittarius dome, complete with bedroom and kitchen.

Mac had never been asked there before and was surprised to be now, when he'd hardly seen Gunnison for weeks. One of the ever-present bodyguards let him in, eyeing him suspiciously – and Mac's fleeting hope that security might be lax here died.

At first there was no sign of Gunnison. Instead, Mac found Kay sitting at the kitchen table wearing only a short bathrobe, her hair loose and tousled. She was peeling an apple, her expression wan.

When Kay heard him she looked up, startled. Then she smiled and pulled the robe round herself more tightly. "Mac. Hello."

"Hi." He'd slid onto the chair next to her and nodded at the apple. "Got a piece there for me?"

She'd sliced him one. "What are you doing here?" She glanced over her shoulder at the bedroom door.

"The boss asked me," he said.

Kay frowned. "He did? I don't remember him saying…

Oh well." She gave a shaky laugh and pushed her hair back with both hands.

In Mac's reports to Cain, he'd told his boss that, yes, Kay seemed close to Gunnison, but he didn't think she was influencing Johnny in any way. Mac hoped Cain believed him; he needed Kay Pierce to stay right where she was. Surely at some point, she'd open up to him?

Sitting there at the kitchen table, she'd seemed more vulnerable than Mac had ever seen her. He fleetingly touched her hand.

"Hey," he said. "You okay?"

Kay pulled quickly away. "Don't."

"I'm your friend, remember?"

"I know. Sorry. He just...depends on me so much," she said, and bit a nail. "If I get something wrong..."

"You won't," Mac assured her. "You're great at what you do." And she was, that was the hell of it. She had an uncanny grasp of astrology; she could find the interpretation she wanted in the most innocuous chart.

Kay made a face. Mac added casually, "You know, seems to me you could use a little more assistance, though." He helped himself to another slice of apple. "You got rid of almost the whole astrology staff when you came in. What were you trying to prove, Kay?"

She started to respond and then broke off as a muffled noise came from the bedroom. "Wait here," she said, and hurried to the door. She slipped inside. "Johnny, what is it?" Mac heard her say.

Mac rose and moved closer, searching for a glass in the nearby kitchen so that he could claim he'd only wanted some water. Voices floated out from behind the partly-closed door.

"They haven't called yet," said Gunnison's voice. "Kiki! Why haven't they called?"

Kay sounded soothing. "They will. There's still time."

"I need it *now.*"

Mac glanced over. In the slice of room visible to him, he glimpsed Gunnison pacing. Kay stood watching, gripping her elbows.

The phone on Gunnison's desk rang; Mac heard him grab it up. "Hello?"

Mac took a glass from a cabinet, straining to listen.

"Four thousand seventy-two," muttered Gunnison, sounding as if he were writing it down. "That's two less than yesterday." There was a pause. "You're sure? Those are the correct names? All right. Thank you."

A receiver being set down. "No change," said Gunnison.

"It's all right, Johnny."

"Of course it's not all right!" His voice lifted to a near-shout.

As Mac poured himself some water he risked another glance. Kay had gone to Gunnison, was stroking his arm. "If you'd just let me get more details…I'm sure it's absolutely fine. It's going exactly the way we want."

Gunnison let out a long breath. Finally he gripped Kay's hand. He was holding a piece of paper; he shoved it into a folder on his desk. "No," he said. "Just let it play out. We can't interfere. *Mac!*"

Mac jumped, but hid it. He went and poked his head around the door. "Hi, Johnny. I've got those reports you wanted."

Kay let herself out; she gave Mac a brittle smile.

"All right, how are the interrogations going?" Gunnison barked.

Mac, startled, saw that the usually-impeccable leader was unshaven, and had a stain on his shirt.

He instinctively kept his voice calming. "Very well, Johnny. Excellent, in fact."

Gunnison snapped his fingers, motioning for the reports, and Mac handed them over. "Stay here while I read them through," he ordered.

The Can-Amer president slouched in an armchair and started flipping through the pages. Mac stood beside the desk. The interrogations were the standard ones to seek out Discordants. He despised doing them, but saved as many people as he could.

"Good…good…but damn it, these don't even matter," Gunnison murmured. He rubbed his unkempt jaw, staring at the pages. "It's still the ups and downs I've got to worry about…how it's all going to play out…"

Ups and downs. That phrase again. Mac's arms prickled. He hesitated, taking in Gunnison's distraction.

Silently, he opened the file on the desk.

An astrology chart – not one he recognized. Sun in Aries,

and at its centre a symbol like a cross in a square. A scrawled note read: *The dark mirror taunts me I am in despair.*

The handwriting wasn't Gunnison's. Mac closed the file and leaned against the desk. When Gunnison looked up, Mac had his arms crossed over his chest, his expression concerned and helpful.

Under cover of the baseball game, Mac had told Walter about it. Now, as the three of them left the stadium together, lost in a crowd of thousands, Sephy repeated what she'd said to Mac the night before: she thought the symbol sounded like a Grand Cross.

"They're pretty rare," she said, her forehead creasing. "Interesting…"

"*Dark mirror*," murmured Walter. "Not Gunnison's handwriting, you say?"

"Didn't look like it," said Mac. "But the man was as agitated as I've ever seen him. Kay must know what it's about. I'll keep working on her."

Sephy glanced at him and slipped her arm through his. Mac drew her close.

"I wonder if those 'ups and downs' are to do with whatever's going on up north," mused Walter. "Any luck with those airwave operatives?"

Mac grimaced. "No. It's worse than a pin in a haystack."

It was Walter who'd first realized Gunnison was up to something in the Yukon area, from a chance interview with a worker who'd helped build a factory up there – though what the factory was for, the man had had no idea. Mac was still working with a ham wireless set, trying to re-establish contact with their lost operatives. So far, he'd yet to stumble on the right frequencies and times – the code words were never spoken or acknowledged. He could only hope that their northern spies were still monitoring the airwaves, so that whatever Johnny Gun was up to could at some point be uncovered.

"I'll keep trying," Mac said grimly.

Walter nodded. "All right, what about Collis? Are you still meeting him later?"

Mac checked his watch. "Yeah, I should head over there now. It's across town."

They were standing at a busy intersection under a billboard for Capricorn cigarettes; traffic grumbled past. "Made up your mind about him yet?" asked Walter.

"Not yet."

Walter looked unsurprised. Even now, no one was certain about Collis Reed. "Well, we all trust your judgement." He gave a small salute and headed off.

Mac and Sephy kept walking down Central with its flashing neon signs and moving-picture houses. Sephy had her hands in the pocket of her tan overcoat. She hesitated. "Listen, hasn't this Collis guy proved himself by now? You know, we need everyone who's willing."

Mac made a face. "Gut feeling? I'm just not sure about him."

Sephy was right though, and he knew it. The Resistance as a whole remained scattered, broken. He sighed.

Sephy stopped walking and studied him. She pulled Mac into a doorway. Her lips on his were gentle but insistent. Mac wrapped his arms around her. This, with Sephy, was what was real. Sometimes it felt like the only thing that was.

When they drew apart he touched her face.

"Number nineteen," he said. "Will you? Please?"

Sephy put her hand over his. "No. But I love you," she said. "And I hate seeing you so worried. If Collis joins us, maybe he could really help. Just listen to what he has to say, all right?"

After that moment in the hotel bathroom when Collis asked Mac if he could join, there'd been silence. Finally, his face expressionless, Mac had said, "You know, if I *were* with the Resistance, I'd tell you to shut the hell up right about now."

Collis had.

Back in Topeka, Mac had discussed it with Walter and a few others. Mac had never thought much of Reed and didn't trust him. But Collis Reed could be damn useful, if sincere: another man on the inside.

"Test him like we've never tested anyone," Walter had said tersely.

Mac had an anonymous note delivered to Collis's

apartment, directing him to be at a particular street corner in an hour and to tell no one. A few of the guys had tailed Collis, then covertly watched as he waited.

He hadn't been followed. A switchboard operator who worked with them confirmed that he'd made no phone calls before leaving.

Collis had waited for over six hours before he finally made his way home.

Similar episodes had led to Collis being ordered to locations with hidden envelopes to deliver them elsewhere. These contained false information about Discordants needing aid. The info wasn't betrayed. Collis hadn't even looked inside the envelopes.

They'd allowed him to think he'd been accepted. A few of the guys put themselves on the line for this, meeting with him and giving false names – congratulating him. After several weeks of minor missions he'd been asked to a meeting in an abandoned warehouse.

"Guns" had invaded. They'd shot several of the members with blanks; fake blood had made it grisly and realistic. Collis had been taken into custody.

They told him Gunnison wouldn't protect him. They kept him all night, shouting at him, demanding names. When he wouldn't give them, they roughed him up – probably pretty good, Mac knew. Collis still hadn't cracked.

Finally they let him go, telling him to say he'd been in an auto wreck. Collis – bruised and in pain – had apparently realized it was a test then. Though shaken, he'd nodded and left.

Grady, one of their best, had been the head Gun. "I'm pretty sure he believed it up until that point," he'd reported to Mac. "He was pale – kept rubbing his tattoo. But all he'd say was, 'You've got the wrong guy. I don't know anything.'"

As Mac had taken this in, thinking, Grady had hesitated. "I'll tell you what, Mac…when the fellows had to rough him up, I admired him. He's tough."

On the surface, at least, Collis Reed was a perfect candidate.

Mac met Collis in a run-down joint called Joe's Place. They ordered beers and sat at the bar. A boxing match was playing on the telio, sitting high on a shelf. The crowded room erupted in delighted *oohs* as Leadfist Maguire plastered a solid right hook on Jimmy Donovan.

Mac hadn't told Collis why he wanted to meet. He'd hardly spoken to him since that morning six weeks ago. Now he kept his eyes on the swinging black-and-white figures and said, "So I hear you've been having an interesting time."

After a beat, Collis's gaze cut to Mac's. His face was still faintly bruised. "Not sure what you mean," he said.

"Oh, you do, buddy. I want to know everything about your past, Collis. *Everything*. And I'm very good at sniffing out lies. If I'm really with the Resistance, then I promise you: a lie will see you dead in some mysterious way in a few days."

Mac watched Collis suddenly realize: *this* was the real test.

Collis's gaze stayed level. "And if you're not?"

Mac took a swig of beer and joined the bar in a vicarious *oof!* as Maguire took a hit. "Then I've been putting together quite the dossier on you for Cain, pal," he said in an undertone. "You're dead either way in that case – might as well tell the truth. Start talking."

"How far back do I go?"

"Amity Vancour," said Mac.

"That's...pretty far back." Collis's jaw tightened, but he didn't hesitate. "All right. The first thing you should know is that I love her. I've been in love with her for years."

"Go on."

"We grew up together. Her family had a farm up in Gloversdale, a few hours north of Sacrament. I lived next door to her. Her parents kind of...took me in. Amity and I were best friends."

Looking down, Collis pushed his beer mug around in a circle of condensation. "See, I was one of *those Reeds.* I guess every small town has a family like that. My mother was a drunk; my father and uncles were in on every shady deal going. Amity's family meant everything to me. They treated me like..." Collis paused, clearly searching for words.

"Like you weren't one of *those Reeds*?" said Mac.

"Yeah. Exactly. You've heard that her father, Tru, was a Peacefighter. By the time I knew him he still taught pilots to fight but he worked mostly for the World for Peace. He was like a dad to me. He taught me to fly. He..."

To Mac's amazement, Collis's eyes filled. It didn't seem an act. Collis took a long swig of beer.

"Sorry," he said roughly. "I haven't thought about Tru in a long time."

He collected himself and glanced at Mac. "He really did throw the civil war fight, you know," he said. "I didn't meet him until the year after that, when I was seven, but...I'm sure of it. I have no idea why he did it. I just know that it broke him."

"What do you mean, 'broke' him?"

Collis let out a breath and gazed at the telio. "Like I said, my dad was into some shady stuff. Back during the Big Dry, he used to bootleg liquor. He made a lot of money at it. That's when he married Goldie."

"Goldie?"

"My mother. She was only seventeen when they got together. Anyway, when the Repeal came in, he had to look for something else to do. And he got into selling dope. Coke, hop-leafs, all of that."

Collis looked down, his shoulders tense. "People used to come to the house," he said. "I wasn't there much – I was usually at Amity's – but sometimes when I was, Dad would have me take money from them and give them these little packets in return. I didn't know what they were. I was...pretty innocent back then."

Mac drained his beer and signalled the barman for two more. "Keep talking," he said.

Collis waited until the new beers had arrived. "All right, well...the thing is, I guess Tru was looking for a way to blot everything out. See, he drank sometimes. Sometimes I'd stay over at Amity's, and in the mornings I'd find an empty glass in their kitchen that smelled like Goldie's bottles at home. I remember once Amity started to use one, and then she smelled it – and I felt so tense; like I knew a secret about Tru that I didn't want her to find out. She washed the glass out without saying anything – and Amity was someone who always said what she was thinking. But that time she didn't, and I saw that, on some level, she knew too. Neither of us mentioned it. We just went out to play or something, but...I knew just how she felt."

Mac sat silently, watching him.

"Looking back now, it seems like...Tru was a man in constant torment. And apparently he went to my dad a few times to buy whatever crap he was peddling." Collis grimaced. "I didn't know any of this then; my father told me later. He said that the last time Tru was there he'd been drinking, and...he said some stuff."

"What?" asked Mac.

"I'm not sure exactly. Whatever it was, it made my father suspicious about the civil war fight. By then, it was getting harder for Dad to get hold of stuff to sell – laws were tightening up, he owed money to too many people… and so…he started blackmailing Tru."

Mac's eyebrows rose. Collis looked bitter, angry.

"He was pretty smart about it, I guess," he said in a low voice. "He didn't try to bleed Tru dry. He just got a nice little payment from him, once a month – and then gambled it all away, of course, but those payments just kept on coming until Tru died."

Collis looked down. "You know…ever since I found out…I've been even more grateful to Tru. Because if it were me, and my daughter was best friends with the son of the bastard who was blackmailing me, I don't think I'd have even wanted to see the kid's face, much less be like a father to him. But Tru never treated me any differently. Not once."

"What about Amity's mother?" asked Mac.

"Rose?" Collis's tension seemed to ease a little; he smiled. "She's wonderful. She never knew any of this, I don't think. She and Amity didn't always get along, but I loved her. She raised me, basically. And Hal, Amity's little brother…he was my brother too. They were my family, all of them."

Collis gazed at the bar and took another sip of beer. "Amity was always asking me to move in with them for real. I couldn't. My dad didn't give a shit about me, but he would have put a stop to *that* in a hurry." He gave a crooked smile. "So I had this…half-and-half childhood. Amity's place was like a fantasy, like…like I could be the

Collis I really wanted to be. And then I'd get home, and it was just…squalor. Cold. Not enough to eat. And it felt like *that* was the real me and always would be, no matter what I did."

Collis glanced up suddenly. His eyes were blue-green, full of self-doubt. "Sorry," he said. "Is this the kind of…? I mean, I feel like I'm talking too much."

Mac pushed a bowl of peanuts at him. "You're doing fine, buddy. Keep going." On the telio, the fight had ended and music had started to play: one of the jaunty songs they'd made Van Wheeler do in praise of Gunnison. The Harmony symbol was on the screen.

Collis took a peanut and shelled it slowly. "When I was younger, none of this bothered me as much," he said at last. "But by the time I was thirteen or fourteen, it bothered me all right. I knew what everyone in that town thought of my family. And I knew how impossible it all was. Being in love with Amity. Not having anything to offer her."

He let out a breath, playing with the peanut shells. "Then Tru died when I was fourteen. His plane crashed. After that, none of it really mattered any more. It took a few months, but without Tru's payments the money dried up, and my family had to take off. My dad owed too many people. Leaving Amity was…"

Collis fell silent. He gazed unseeingly at the Harmony symbol. Finally he said, "Anyway. Dad acted like he had a plan, but he didn't. We just drifted for a while. And then one day he found out that I knew how to fly a plane."

Collis's jaw was steel as he added, "The next day he moved us again…to the Central States."

Mac helped himself to a peanut. "Let me guess. So that he could make the right contacts and then pimp you out as a crooked Peacefighter?"

"You got it," said Collis sourly. "I didn't know at first. But I guess it turned out to be a lot harder than he'd thought – you can't just go up to someone in charge, hint that you know that Peacefights have been thrown, and be met with open arms."

Collis went on, explaining that he'd had to go to work at fifteen; his father, failing in his grand plans, had had to go to work also, in the same factory. Collis had tried to fit in, despite this new world of Shadowcars and whispers of correction camps. He'd always been good at making people like him, but he was terrified. All he wanted was to go home, to Amity and her family.

Then when he was seventeen, he was found Discordant.

"My father was furious," Collis said tonelessly. "It was like he blamed me. And Goldie cried. She was…oh, hell… she was such a drunk by then. But she got sober enough to try to stop the Guns when they took me. They hit her. And dragged me away, and…and I was sent to Harmony Three."

Mac saw Collis's throat move as he swallowed. Finally he said, "This next part isn't easy to talk about."

Mac said nothing.

Collie rubbed a knuckle across his chin. "Once I got

there, I did whatever I thought I had to, to survive." He looked down and cleared his throat. "If you've never been in one of those places, you can't really understand… Anyway, there's always a prisoner who turns informer. Betrays others to save himself. That – that was me."

Mac felt a stirring of respect for Collis for admitting it. If he'd had doubts before, he had none now: he was hearing the truth. He took another sip of beer, letting the silence do its work.

Collis's hands were tight around his own beer mug; he stared down at them. "Whatever you're thinking, Mac, however much disgust you have for me, it's nothing compared to what I feel for myself," he said in a low voice. "I justified it – I told myself I had no choice. The truth was that I hated the world by then. I thought everyone was out for themselves and that I'd be a fool not to put myself first."

Collis's voice hardened as he went on: "So, yeah, I survived all right. I finally got given a job in one of the offices. I was known by the Guns as the guy who could get information. And I guess they found me pretty useful. Word of me got all the way to Gunnison. He needed information about one of the prisoners, someone who hadn't buckled yet. And…I got it for him."

He didn't go into details and Mac didn't ask. Collis stared down at the mug, stroking the rim. Finally he went on.

"So Gunnison got interested in me and checked out

my chart. He had his best astrologers go over it, and they decided, hey, what do you know, there'd been a mistake – just, like, a fraction of a degree point, but enough – and that I wasn't Discordant after all. And they set me free so that I could work for Gunnison."

"So that's how it happened," murmured Mac. He'd often wondered.

Collis gave a strangled laugh. "Oh, hell, what a joke," he said. "You're Discordant if he doesn't like you, and then magically *not* Discordant if he changes his mind. The hypocrisy is just…and he doesn't *see* it, that's the thing, isn't it? He honestly believes all this stuff."

The bar was full now, rollicking and noisy, though even the laughter had a restraint not found in bars in other countries: you never knew when you might get reported. Collis sat hunched over, playing with a peanut shell. Mac slid off the bar stool suddenly and grabbed his fedora. He clapped Collis on the shoulder.

"Come on, pal, let's get some fresh air," he said.

Collis looked relieved. He drained the rest of his beer and rose too.

They headed for the graceful, arching structure of the Bradford Bridge. They stopped halfway across it, leaning on their elbows and looking down at the tumbling, moonlit water.

"I think he sees me as a kind of good luck charm," Collis said. He added bitterly, "He calls me 'Sandy', you know. They called me that in high school too. Once, when

Amity and I had gotten together, she called me Sandy and I almost jumped out of my skin."

"So she never knew," said Mac.

"No," whispered Collis. "No. Not about any of this."

"All right," said Mac finally. "I already know how you became a Peacefighter. Gunnison needed a pilot he could plant in the Western Seaboard base to throw fights and spy on Commander Hendrix. Right?"

"That's it." Collis scraped a hand over his face. "In training school, everyone else was there because they believed in Peacefighting. I knew it was a lie, but I pushed myself to be a better pilot so that I could move up the ranks fast, make more money on the thrown fights. But then I got to the base, and…Amity was there."

Collis stared down at the water as he described the rush of joy at seeing her again – followed closely by shame as he realized what she'd think of him if she knew what he was doing.

"Part of me wanted out then, but…but if I'm honest, Mac, part of me didn't; I wanted all the money I could possibly get. Because I was still one of *those Reeds.* If I wanted to be with Amity, how else could I ever have anything to offer her?"

"So she's one of those dames who cares a lot about money?" asked Mac mildly.

Collis snorted out a laugh. "Oh, hell, no. She never even thinks about it. She's always *had* it, you see. No, it was me…all me."

He stared at his hands as he described how he knew he should keep away from Amity but hadn't been able to. Finally, a month after he arrived at the base, the two of them had gotten together. Collis had kept his covert activities totally secret from her.

"Most of my fights were actually legit, you know." Collis rubbed his temples with one hand. "I'm not trying to make light of what I did. I threw seven fights altogether, and every time I did, I betrayed the Western Seaboard. I just mean…I was able to forget about it a lot. Being with Amity made me so happy that…"

He trailed off. "But she was so idealistic. She believed in it all so damn much. And I knew about Tru, and what he had done, and I thought I'd give anything for her to never find out about that – or about me."

"She wouldn't have understood?"

"Why I was throwing fights?" Collis gave a wan smile. "No. Absolutely not."

Mac shrugged. "I'm not excusing you, boyo. But you'd been through a hell of a lot. Sounds like you'd gotten yourself into a tough spot. I mean, what were you going to do – say *no* to our lord and master?"

Collis stared at him, clearly startled, as if a more charitable explanation of his actions had never occurred to him. "Of course I couldn't say no," he said finally. "But I wanted the money too."

"So you're human. You grew up poor and money's pretty nice to have. Doesn't mean you weren't scared shitless about what might happen to you if you refused. Which I'm sure you were, since you're not a *complete* idiot."

Collis's smile was tight. He pushed his hat back slightly. His hair was washed-out gold in the street lights.

"There's more," he said. "Don't get too forgiving of me just yet, Mac."

They started walking again, their hands in their trouser pockets, their footsteps echoing. Collis said, "When I trashed that bar, you said I was shouting that it wasn't my fault. Remember? Well...I was lying to myself. It was. All of it."

"All right, tell me," said Mac.

Collis did.

A long time later, they were sitting on a park bench. Collis had just finished speaking.

Mac was silent for some time, taking it all in. Collis's explanation of what had happened on the Western Seaboard base hadn't surprised him; he'd already guessed a lot of it. Vancour had started to uncover the corruption and Collis had panicked. He'd known Hendrix was corrupt, and Amity had been talking about showing him the evidence she'd found in her team leader's house. If she did, Collis had known she'd be killed. Yet if Collis told Amity the truth, he'd lose her.

He'd tried stalling her instead, telling her he was checking everything out with Mac. When she'd taken the evidence to Madeline Bark at the World for Peace, Collis hadn't known whose side Madeline was on – he'd realized it could all explode at any moment. He'd been tempted to run but had stayed to try to protect Amity if he could.

Mac recalled that time himself: after Vancour went to Madeline Bark for help, Bark had called Cain in a panic. It was decided that Vancour would have to be taken out.

No one in Gunnison's camp had been sure at that point whether Collis could still be trusted. To take no chances, he'd been drugged to prevent him from tipping off Vancour before her sabotaged Tier One fight.

When he'd ended up in the sickbay, Collis said that he'd gotten a promise from Amity not to fly. He knew she was likely being set up, but hadn't told her the truth even then – though he swore to Mac that he would have if he'd known she still planned to take the fight. Mac believed him: it was clear that Collis was crazy about the woman.

Anyway, most of it wasn't too admirable but none of it was surprising. What Collis had done in the Central States though, after he and Vancour escaped together...now *that* had rocked Mac. He felt like puking – or, better yet, taking a swing at the guy's already-bruised face.

So close. And now gone for ever.

The park's trees rustled in the breeze, their shapes large and dark.

Collis sat leaning forward, staring at his clenched hands. "Now she's in that place and it's my fault," he said in a low voice. "I've been in hell, Mac. There's nothing

I can do. I've tried. If I could take her place there I would, even if she never spoke to me again."

He gave a short, humourless laugh. "I've tried dope a few times, you know. Anything to block out the look on her face… It doesn't work. Nothing does. That's why I've got to do something, got to be someone I can look at in the mirror again, or I swear I'll pitch myself off the nearest bridge. I can't live like this any more."

Mac sat quietly, thinking. He still hadn't spoken.

Collis gazed tensely at him. Finally he said, "Mac, please…say something. Get it over with."

Mac pinched the bridge of his nose.

"All right, look," he said tonelessly. "I'm not in the business of absolution. But since you seem to want my opinion, yes, I think you acted like a cowardly bastard, and what happened to Vancour was just the least of it. I'd be failing at my job if I didn't have severe doubts now as to whether you'd protect us, if enough pressure was put on you."

Collis went still. "Us?"

Mac fixed him with a look. "Yes. Us."

Collis let out a long, shuddering breath. "I knew it," he whispered. He rubbed both hands over his face and then let them fall. "Mac…I know there's nothing I can say to convince you. But I'd give anything to undo what I did. Put me through whatever other tests you want. I wouldn't betray you."

"You know what, pal? I'm inclined to believe you."

Collis looked up. His throat worked; he gazed quickly back down at his fists.

"Thank you," he said roughly.

Mac stood up. "I'm going to take a chance on you, because I think you've told me the truth and I believe that you want to make up for what you've done. But the Resistance is no more in the business of absolution than I am. We don't give a damn about your conscience, buddy-boy. That's for you to wrestle with. We care about your loyalty and your silence."

"You've got it," said Collis. He stood up too; they shook. Mac didn't think it was his imagination that Collis seemed straighter now – taller.

They started walking again. "Listen," said Collis. "I don't have any right to ask for anything; I know that. But—"

"Lay off the martyrdom, Reed," Mac broke in. "You've told me your story and now I've forgotten it. Clean slate; you're one of us. Spill it."

Collis's smile looked sincere for the first time since Mac had known him. "Thanks," he said softly. "All right, look – there's something I need help with. People I need to try to save. It's the most important thing in the world to me. Will you help?"

Chapter Seventeen

December, 1941

The spare tyre's constant vibration shook my bones. Before the first hour had passed I felt sick and battered, my wounds constantly prodded. However much I hurt, I knew Ingo had it worse. I kept speaking to him, terrified that he might pass out and not be able to move quickly when we needed to.

"Talk to me," I said for the dozenth time under the drone of the engine. For a long moment he didn't answer, and I shook his arm. "Ingo! Talk!"

"And say what, you harridan?" he mumbled.

"That'll do. I just needed to know you're still alive."

"Please shut up and stop jostling me," he said shortly, his voice tight with pain. "You don't die of a broken rib, Amity."

No, but you could die of blood poisoning from an infected wound, or if your rib pierced a lung. I managed not to say it...but as I lay there I listened to his breathing, and remembered with unease my promise to leave him behind if he couldn't make it.

It seemed as if we'd spent days in this dark, cramped tyre compartment, though I knew it was only hours. How many now? Eight? Ten? At first I'd tried to guess how fast we were travelling and how far we'd come, but it was impossible to tell. At least a few hundred miles, I hoped. Far enough south that we were nearly out of the snow.

The truck stopped.

I gasped out loud at the shock of the sudden silence. The dark, tiny space felt claustrophobic suddenly. I strained to hear what was happening. To my relief, I could feel Ingo alert beside me.

"Maybe they're changing the runners for tyres now," he muttered in my ear.

"Hopefully not much further then," I whispered back.

We both cringed as the snow-truck's back doors clanged open. Ingo had said the tyres they used were stored on the truck's side.

Footsteps echoed above. A long scraping noise, like a canister being moved. At the same time I heard a compartment door being opened on the side of the truck. It banged shut again. Another one opened.

An irritable voice called out, "This is stupid. We're gonna get behind schedule."

"Ours not to reason why, pal. Whole convoy's in the same fix," shouted back someone else. I flinched, my pulse battering; the speaker was right over our head.

"Can't we just pretend we didn't understand them on the talkie?"

"No. Keep searching. All compartments."

Another slow scraping noise…this time directly above us.

Ingo shoved my arm vehemently. I didn't need coaxing. I lunged wildly off the tyre, fumbling downwards for the trapdoor. I got it open – saw a patch of snow. I propelled myself out in a wild scramble.

The snow was deep, breaking my fall with hardly a sound. Ingo was right behind me. When he landed he surged upwards, scattering snow as he hastened to close the trapdoor again. I was feverishly thankful for the clangs and bangs happening all around.

A pair of snowshoe-clad feet appeared to one side, circling the truck. "Want me to check underneath?" their owner called.

Before he'd finished talking we were burrowing into the snow. A foot of soft powder lay over an icy crust; acting on panicked instinct, I wriggled deep under its surface. Ingo followed, kicking upwards to make it fall on top of us.

Neither of us moved. My cheeks went as prickly as if I'd burned them, then numb. I lay shivering, expecting hands to burst through at any moment and grab us.

There was only a grey, heavy silence.

As the minutes passed my shivering became convulsive. Beside me, Ingo was trembling just as badly. What if they'd already left and we didn't know? We could be trapped here until we froze.

All at once, the ground shook. A distant thunder came. Our dim, snowy cave lightened: the snow-truck had moved away. I lay fighting against the primal urge to claw my way out. *A convoy*. How many more?

A low rumbling. Another shadow.

Abruptly, the snow crunched in on us. Hard, smothering. I tried to scream – snow choked me. I struggled, panicked; was dimly aware of Ingo clutching my arms. It went on and on, until the snow was packed so tightly I could hardly move.

After a long time, there was silence again.

I knew we should try to dig ourselves out. The idea seemed to come from very far away. I was starting to feel warm, almost comfortable. *Sleep,* I thought. Just for a little while.

An eruption came next to me – a violent churning. *Ingo.* Alarm filtered through my brain. Somehow I forced myself into action, kicking, flailing. My gloved hands became claws, tearing at the smothering whiteness.

With a strangely gentle sound, our roof crumbled. Suddenly I was blinking up at a grey sky, my chest heaving. Next to me, Ingo gave a ragged gasp, his head and shoulders covered with snow.

We crawled out and collapsed onto the ground. I couldn't

stop shaking. For long minutes neither of us spoke.

Finally I forced myself to sit up. I looked around us.

The ground was packed hard from the caterpillar tracks. They headed away into the distance, twin rutted roads in the snow. Faintly, I could still hear the snow-trucks' rumble.

Apart from that, there was nothing. We were on a hill. In every direction there lay only snow, fir trees, more hills. Heavy-looking clouds hung above, with the afternoon sun just a faint lightening to the west.

As I took this in, the sound of the vehicles faded. The silence was immense.

Ingo sat up too. His face was greyish with cold, apart from the red, wrinkled mass of his scar. I saw him swallow.

We looked at each other.

"I have a little food," he said.

I fervently agreed with his choice not to discuss this just yet. Our muscles still sluggish, we put what food we had together. It amounted to a few scraps of bread, a tiny morsel of meat. We each took a bite of bread – one bite – and then Ingo put the food away in his pocket.

I chewed the bread slowly, trying to make it last. We had no water. I looked at the snow, remembered it choking me, and shuddered at the idea of putting any in my mouth.

Finally Ingo grimaced. "We're alive, at least," he said. "No thanks to your informer."

I felt a dull stab of hatred for Claudia. She'd told the

Guns about our stolen uniforms, of course, or else they wouldn't have searched the snow-trucks.

"We should have killed her," I said tiredly.

"That thought's crossed my mind, yes. Well, what now?"

"Any idea where we are?"

Ingo sighed. "Two, three hundred miles from Harmony Five, maybe? But in exactly what direction…" He shrugged.

I licked my lips, thinking of the maps I'd loved to study as a child – the thousands of square miles of wilderness surrounding us.

"We'll have to follow their tracks," I said.

"Yes. And if this is their regular route, they'll probably see our footprints. They're already looking for us."

Far above, a hawk wheeled through the air. There was no other movement, not for as far as the eye could see. Even as large as the snow-trucks were, they had to be going at least forty miles an hour. It might be hours more before they reached their destination.

"Do we have a choice?" I said finally. It wasn't a challenge. I was hoping beyond hope that he'd say yes, we did, and present me with some new, shiny idea.

Ingo wrapped his arms around his thin frame and studied the snow-swollen sky.

"No," he said. "I don't think we do."

* * *

The treads' deep ruts were spaced too awkwardly to walk on. We moved far to one side and quickly learned to tread lightly on this mix of old and new snow – or else break through into cold wetness up to our knees. Over and over, I misjudged and had to flounder my way out. Despite the long fleece-lined coat, my trousers were soon soaked. I couldn't stop shivering. Ingo's face was set and grim; he walked hunched over, not speaking.

Night came all too soon. There were no stars. Before it became too dark to see, we took refuge in a copse of fir trees.

We didn't speak much. We fashioned a crude shelter out of branches and collapsed into it. I had never been more exhausted. I couldn't imagine how Ingo felt.

We slept pressed together for warmth, our coats wrapped tightly around us. It didn't help much. I closed my eyes fully expecting not to open them again…yet in the morning I awakened to a greyish dawn.

I looked over at Ingo. His gaunt face was as grimy as I knew mine must be. Black stubble coated his jaw, except for the barren wrinkles of his scar. But his eyes met mine.

"Still alive," I said hoarsely.

He nodded. "Still alive."

We each had a bite of bread and kept on. The wind picked up. Soon it was a knife that sliced through me. It skittered fresh snow over the trucks' tracks, so that we had to move closer to keep them in sight. As the sun moved slowly across the sky we both began to fall through the snow more and more. My muscles quivered with cold, with fatigue.

I lost count of how many times I fell that day. Finally I went down and couldn't make myself move again. Ingo battled over and grabbed my arm.

"Get up!" he yelled over the wind.

I was almost crying. "Ingo, please, just let me—"

"*Up*, you coward!"

Anger lashed through me. I gritted my teeth and managed to rise with his help, my legs churning against the snow. For a fierce, hot second I hated him for not letting me lie there.

But he was struggling too. Soon after, he stumbled over a half-exposed rock and just lay there, his face a sickly grey. As the wind howled, I put my arm around his shoulders; panting, I hauled him up.

"You have to keep on if I do, you bastard!" I shouted in his ear. "Move!"

Somehow we dragged each other on with curses, insults, long after it seemed there was no point. Overhead the sky was a smooth, ominous grey.

The first snowflakes were as gentle as kisses. More followed until they came thick and fast.

Before long the tracks had vanished. Earlier, we'd seen trees in the distance. Spurred by the thought of shelter, we trudged on, sinking to our knees with almost every step now.

Time slowed as the snow whined around us, measured

footstep by flailing footstep. I wasn't sure what direction we were heading in any more – was certain we'd gotten turned around.

Ingo staggered to a stop. "Look at the ground in front of us!" he called. He put his head close to mine, shouting in my ear: "Tell me what that looks like to you – think about flying over the base!"

The thought of flying was a sharp pain. I looked at the ground, trying to imagine it…and saw a faint ridge in the snow to the west. It continued on straight, for as far as I could see, and suddenly I recalled faint, ancient lines sketching the earth.

"A road!" I shouted.

"Yes, I think so!"

My pulse skipped. We battled our way up a hill, following the road, heads down. The snow was howling now, an attack of white bees.

When we finally reached the top, at first I could see only whiteness. Then shapes emerged: a dozen small mounds at regular intervals. The snow faltered momentarily and a piece of machinery appeared – a familiar, hulking mass.

"Ingo!" I grabbed his arm and pointed.

He was panting, clutching his side. "A rock crusher," he breathed.

For a sickening moment I thought we'd travelled in a circle and arrived back at Harmony Five. But this crusher was rusting, falling to pieces.

An abandoned mine. Were the snowy mounds buildings?

Please, please, I thought. We started down the hill. Snow hid the road now, its ridges evening out into a blinding whiteness.

The way down became steeper. Too steep. I knew we'd lost the road, but it was snowing too hard to go back. I could barely see where I was placing my feet. Struggling beside me, Ingo's shoulders were thick with snow – his eyebrows beneath his hat looked half-frozen.

"We'll lose each other in this!" I yelled, the wind whipping my words away.

"Keep hold of me!" Ingo held out his gloved hand.

I half-turned to take it; suddenly the world jerked sideways and I screamed. Snow and rocks seemed to explode around me. Sky and ground spun – I was tumbling, falling down the hill.

Abruptly, the world stilled. I lay motionless, panting. My head hurt. The snow kept falling, swirling towards me. Getting up seemed heartbreakingly difficult. I thought how nice it would be to just close my eyes and never bother to move again.

It's the only thing worth being Amity...I always knew that.

The pain spurred me. I still needed answers. I struggled up in a skitter of gravel and snow.

"Ingo!" I shouted, cupping my hands around my mouth – and then saw the grey mound of his coat a few feet away. I stumbled over. Before I reached him he'd managed to get up, but stood hunched, chest heaving. He gave me a grin that was more like a baring of teeth.

"That's…that's one way to get down the hill!" he shouted.

Our fall had carved a long, gravelly ribbon against the white slope. The wind shrieked, whipping us with snow.

The nearest mound was one of the largest. We fought our way to it. Beneath the snowy covering was a building of weathered grey wood.

The door was stiff with ice but opened inward when we tried it. We got inside and shut it behind us. I gasped in relief at the sudden lessening of sound. We were in an old office; there was a desk. My knees felt made of water. I sank onto the floor with my back against the desk, breathing hard.

I never wanted to move again.

Chapter Eighteen

At last my numb fingers and feet started coming alive with painful prickling. Wearily, I roused myself, took off my gloves and swiped off the hat. I gazed around us.

Junk filled the small office. Newspapers were scattered everywhere, yellow with age. The smell of dust hung in the air.

Ingo was sitting on the floor with his bare head against the wall, eyes shut. The unscarred half of his face had more colour now; the burned side blazed a crinkled red. His hair was damp.

"What happened to leaving each other behind if we couldn't make it?" I said.

He gave a tired shrug. "You're obviously as idiotic as I am."

"That's pretty idiotic then."

Ingo laughed without opening his eyes. "Did you just make a joke?"

"I do make jokes sometimes," I said. "Or I used to."

"I don't believe you."

"It's true. It's just that no one ever got them."

"All right, *that* I believe..." Ingo sighed and opened his eyes. He had one hand pressed against his side. I glanced at his torso, wondering if his wound had opened up again.

"You know what I'm going to ask," I said after a pause.

Ingo got to his feet. I had the impression he was standing upright through willpower alone.

"I'll live," he said. "What about you? Your head's bleeding."

I touched my forehead, suddenly aware as he said it of a warm stickiness. My hand came away bloody. "Look at that," I said shakily. "I still work."

Ingo came over. "Two jokes in two minutes...don't wear yourself out." He inspected my head briefly. "I think you'll live too. It's just a scratch. They bleed a lot, on the head."

"I know," I said. "My brother got a scratch on his forehead once..." I trailed off, not really wanting to think about Hal, hopefully still hidden in that tiny cell under the floorboards. I shook my head. "It'll stop bleeding soon," I said shortly.

The wind howled at the windows. Already, the cabin felt scarcely warmer than outside. Suddenly I recalled the matches in my flight jacket pocket. I groped hastily for them.

"Where's the best place to build a fire?" I said in a rush. "Maybe if we crack open a window, so that we have ventilation—"

Ingo was scanning the shadowy walls. "No, here!"

He hurried to a dark, cluttered corner; a black pipe snaked up one wall. I helped him heft aside the trash: a rusted metal bed frame, old packing crates. Hidden behind them was an ancient pot-bellied stove, covered in cobwebs.

We crouched before it reverently. Ingo creaked open its slatted door. The ashy remnants of the last fire were still there.

"Do you think it works?" I asked, almost in a whisper.

Ingo nodded tensely. "We've got one like it at home. It'll work, if the matches still do." He glanced at the small pack in my hand. It was the flimsy cardboard kind you find in bars.

"They look damp," he said.

I winced, remembering all the times I'd fallen in the snow. I took off my gloves. "They feel a little damp," I admitted.

There was a pause. "Well, fingers crossed," said Ingo finally.

He quickly cleaned out the stove with a piece of board. We made kindling from breaking up old boxes; Ingo arranged them in a careful tepee inside the stove's mouth and added some twisted-up scraps of newspaper.

We took turns trying. One after another, the matches failed. Finally, with only two left, one caught. Ingo hastily shielded the tiny blaze and touched it to a piece of newspaper. Neither of us breathed again until the wooden tepee was in flames.

Ingo's shoulders slumped. "There," he said softly.

We gathered up the firewood – bits of crates, a broken chair. Looking through the desk, we found an old timetable. "The manager's name was Dave," I said, reading it. "We're in the New Hope Mine."

"Last Hope, more like…" Ingo pulled open the bottom drawer and gave a bark of triumph. He held up a half-full whiskey bottle, its label grey with age. "Look, Dave forgot something. Lucky for us."

We fed the fire and watched it grow. Faster than I would have believed, the little room lost its icy edge. I rubbed my fingers with relief.

Ingo nodded towards a bucket in a corner. "Look, we even have a chamber pot."

Over six months in Harmony Five had made me immune to embarrassment. "Agreed," I said. "I'm not going out there again."

The wind whistled. All I could see through the window was a white blur, casting the cabin into a greyish gloom.

I took in Ingo, still too pale, and frowned. I went and got the bottle of whiskey. "Take your shirt off," I said.

His normal eyebrow flew up. He gave a bitter laugh. "My scarred mug must be an improvement. Usually the alcohol is consumed *before* I hear that."

"Very funny." I sat down beside him. "I want to see if your wound's infected. We can clean it with this." I held up the bottle.

"You're insane," said Ingo flatly. "We're not wasting good alcohol on that." He took the bottle from me and pulled out the cork. He took a swig.

"How is it a waste?"

His dark eyes glinted dangerously; I wondered if he could possibly be drunk already. "Because if I'm on the road to gangrene, sloshing whiskey on it at this stage won't help. What the hell are you going to do, start hacking at me to dig out the infection and then watch me bleed to death?"

I started to answer; he broke in: "Leave it, Amity. If it's infected I don't want to know. Have a drink and shut up." He pushed the bottle into my hand.

I was silent for a long moment. I took a drink; the fiery warmth was more welcome than I would have believed. "If you die from some horrible blood infection, don't blame me," I said finally.

"You'd feel exactly the same, so don't bother with the plaintive noises. Here." Ingo brought our food out of his inner pocket and laid it carefully on the floor. There was pitifully little, but at the sight of the few scraps of bread my stomach woke up. Suddenly I felt faint with hunger.

"Put it away," I said roughly. "There's not enough to help."

"Some is better than none. Eat." Ingo handed me a crust, his fingers as grimy as mine. "Think of it as a picnic."

I wanted to protest but didn't. I ate the crust. Ingo put the rest of the food away again.

Neither of us spoke for a while; occasionally we took sips from the bottle. The wind rushed past outside. Through the tiny window we could see the snow still falling. Yet inside it was warm. It seemed a miracle. Despite everything, I felt myself relax a little for the first time in days – months.

"Is it crazy to feel slightly hopeful, even with no food and hundreds of miles of snow around us?" I said.

"No. That's what the whiskey's for. We can be despairing again tomorrow." Ingo used his gloves to open the hot stove door; he angled another stick of firewood through.

"So you have a brother?" he asked.

"We don't want to do small talk, do we?" I said, deadpan. It was what he'd said to me the night we'd first met.

Ingo snorted and closed the stove door. "Memory like a steel trap, I see. Is it really small talk now? I think we've moved beyond being casual acquaintances."

I gave a tired smile, watching the flames dance. There was nothing better than being warm, nothing in the world. The sensation was as luxurious as satin sheets.

"Yes, I have a brother," I said. "Younger than me. Fourteen."

Ingo stretched his long legs out. "Name?"

"Hal. Halcyon."

I wondered if I wanted to talk about this. I decided I did. "He's in hiding," I said. My voice came out more brusquely than I'd intended.

Ingo's black eyebrows drew together. After a pause, he said, "I'd ask for a translation, but I have a feeling I know."

"Your English is perfect. It means exactly what you think. He's in hiding – the last time I saw him was in a tiny room under a closet in a neighbour's house. He was found Discordant."

There was a twist of metal on the floor – a half-melted lump. I picked it up and shifted it from hand to hand, looking down. All I could see was Hal's face when we'd closed the trapdoor over him, slowly slicing him from view.

"I'm sorry," said Ingo quietly.

I wished I hadn't mentioned this. I rested the metal to one side. "Well, we both know that being in hiding is nothing compared to what could happen to him. I just hope he's all right – he was the last time I heard from Ma. That was months ago though."

I was aware of Ingo's dark, steady gaze, and remembered then the letter I'd given to him. I wondered if he'd read it. I watched the fire, thinking of Madeline, of what she knew. I wasn't sorry that I'd chosen the shard of glass instead – I could still feel it in my pocket, undamaged by my fall – yet felt somewhat lost and lonely anyway.

I cleared my throat. "Anyway. His name's Hal, he likes

Peacefighting comics and stickball, and he could give even you a run for your money in arguing. Tell me about your sister."

Ingo kept looking at me for a moment, then he took a drink and shrugged. "Angelina," he said. "We call her Lena. She and I are almost the same age. When we were little, everyone thought we were twins."

"How old is she?"

"Twenty. A year younger than me. I have a brother too. Erich. He's older."

"Three of you?"

"Yes. I'm the difficult middle child."

"I can believe it."

Ingo was gazing at the fire. The corner of his mouth lifted. "Actually, though you *won't* believe it, I'm the super-responsible one...Lena's always telling me not to be so boring. She's a little wildcat." Then he realized what he'd said and gave me a tired grin. "Sorry. Not trying to annoy you that time."

Sitting talking before a fire, sharing a drink, felt surreal after Harmony Five. I smiled. "All right, so she's a wildcat, only not the kind who gets called that in the national press. What else about her?"

"She's tall, almost as tall as me. She likes to dance. She has a lovely singing voice." Ingo looked down, rolling the bottle of whiskey between his palms.

"Do you want the truth?" he said finally.

"If you want to tell it to me," I said.

"What the hell. Total trust, right? The truth, Amity, is that Lena is one of my best friends. I miss her very much. She and Erich both."

I hesitated. "Have you…heard from them, since any of this?"

"No. I haven't heard from anyone back home since my arrest."

"Which was?"

"Three days after our jolly little World for Peace escapade. I haven't been able to get in touch with my family." He snorted. "I have no idea what they were told – maybe that I was killed in a crash, for all I know. My trial only lasted two days, and then I was found guilty and thrown on a train. I didn't even have a representative from my country there."

It sounded all too familiar. There was a long pause.

"So your family don't know about…" I bit the words back, but not fast enough. Ingo gave me a dark look.

"About this?" he said pointedly. He ran a finger down the burned half of his face, pulling at the ruined skin. "No, of course not. But it's all right. When I see them again, I'll just keep my good side to them at all times."

It would have been funny, if he hadn't said it with such bitterness. "It won't matter to them," I said.

"Don't worry, I know that. They'll just be thankful I'm alive." He let out a breath. "Just like us, right? Filled with the joy of life for evermore."

I didn't answer, but knew what he meant. What we'd

been through had changed us. Just at this moment, it felt as if pure joy might never be possible again.

For several long moments the only sound was the fire crackling. "You know, growing up, Lena and I almost had our own language," Ingo said finally. "Nobody else could understand us. We drove everyone crazy, especially Erich." He smiled slightly. "Our poor brother. He felt so left out. He's a good guy, Erich. Very solid. Dependable."

I stretched my legs out. "What about your parents?"

"My father got married late; he just turned seventy last year. He's very…proper, in a way, but funny too. Dry sense of humour."

"Is that where you get it from?"

Ingo's mouth quirked; he shot me a look of real amusement. "Is that what I have? I thought I was just an ass. Anyway, Dad's very sharp. You can't put anything past him. We own a vineyard. Just a small one, we'll never get rich from it, but it's his life. He loves it. Loves the land. So do I, actually. The sun on the fields…" Ingo shrugged and looked down.

"And my mother is a music teacher," he said after a pause. "She's from New Manhattan, a lot younger than him, but they're crazy about each other. She made us all take piano lessons when we were children. She sings when she cooks."

"They sound like a nice family," I said.

"They are. I love them all very much." He said it simply, with no edge.

I contemplated the fire. "My family's very different," I said. "We're all sort of...closed off from each other. Even when my father was alive." I glanced at him, suddenly wary. "How much do you know about my father?"

Ingo shrugged. "Nothing at all about Truce Vancour, the man. I just know what everyone knows: he allegedly threw the Peacefight that put Gunnison in power."

"Thanks for saying 'allegedly', but it's true. He did it," I said curtly.

There was a silence. "How long have you known?" Ingo asked.

"Only since March. Before that I...always thought of him as a hero."

A piece of wood settled in the stove with a shower of sparks. "He died when I was thirteen," I said, fiddling with the twist of metal. "He wasn't a Peacefighter any more by then, but he still flew. He had two planes, a Dove and a Gauntlet, and...and he crashed the Gaunt in our field. I was there. I couldn't save him."

In a vivid flash I recalled kneeling beside my father, frantically pressing my hands against the wound at his throat – feeling the warm slickness of his blood, the feeble pulsing of the torn artery.

Ingo didn't move. "Of course you couldn't," he said quietly. "You were thirteen. But I'd bet money that you did more than most kids your age would have managed."

I stared at him. "Why do you say that?"

"I used to be your opponent, remember? You're

resourceful, cool under pressure. You don't lose your head. You act."

"Are you actually giving me compliments?"

"No. I'm just telling you facts."

I gazed into the flames and wondered at the fact that my eyes were dry. Though it felt as if a lump of steel was wedged inside me, my eyes were as dry as if I'd never cry again.

"I doubt I was very cool that day," I said.

"Who would be?"

Somehow it helped that he sounded matter-of-fact. I sighed and hugged my knees. "Thanks. But the thing is, even before Dad died, I always felt like...I never really knew him. I wanted to. A lot."

I hesitated, my chest suddenly tight. No – this was all far too close to Dad's thrown fight, with its consequences that I still couldn't bear to think about. I shoved it away and straightened. "Anyway...my family's very different from yours."

"What about your mother?"

"More small talk?"

"Why not?" Ingo took a pull from the bottle and handed it to me. "Have you got a more pressing engagement?"

I shrugged out of the stolen greatcoat, wincing at my bruises but marvelling that I felt too warm with it on now. Then I took a drink and smiled slightly, thinking of my mother's perfect hairdos and small, veiled hats.

"I love my mother. I really do. But we're from different planets. After I became a Peacefighter, I always used to dread going home, and then I'd feel so guilty. I know she loves me, but...well, I guess I've never been sure whether she actually *likes* me."

I realized then that I was a little drunk...and that I'd never voiced this thought out loud before. Certainly not to Collie, who had adored my mother. Who had also adored him.

Ingo gave a bitter smile. "Yes, loving and liking are different things, aren't they?" He rose to his knees and shoved another piece of wood on the fire: a quick, angry motion. "I've certainly found out that you can love someone and not like them."

I wondered whether he was thinking of Miriam – the "blonde witch" who, nine months ago, he'd claimed had his heart. I covertly studied the puckered scar that defined his face now. I wondered exactly how it had happened... and whether Miriam knew about it.

"Anyone else would have told me not to worry, that of course my mother likes me," I said after a pause.

Pain winced across Ingo's features as he settled on the floor again; he touched his side. "Do you want pretty words?" he said testily. "Sorry, I'm not very good at them. How the hell should I know whether your mother likes you? I've never met the woman."

"No, I don't want pretty words. I'm glad you didn't say it. I hate it when people offer phoney reassurance."

"Well, spouting platitudes is one thing I've never been accused of, at least. Rude bastard, yes. Platitudes, no." After a pause, Ingo looked at me. "Anyone else would have told me I'm not a rude bastard."

I shrugged. "I'm not much on platitudes, either. You're not a bastard," I added. "Just rude enough to pass for one sometimes."

Ingo laughed. "*Touché*."

The wind whistled; I listened to it rattle the windowpane. It felt as if we were in the Arctic, in the only warm spot for a thousand miles.

Ingo stretched for the bottle and took a long swig. The corner of his mouth tugged upwards. "Lena used to give me hell for it," he said finally. "Being rude, I mean. So did Erich. Growing up, he had the tiresome chore of beating up the other kids to keep them from flattening me. I was always the short, annoying one who couldn't help piping up with an unwanted comment to save his life."

"Short?" I glanced at Ingo's long, lanky form.

"I shot up when I was fifteen. Erich was relieved; he was tired of getting into fights on his stupid brother's behalf. Of course, by then I'd learned to keep my mouth shut occasionally." Ingo smiled slightly and glanced at me. "How did Hal hurt his head?"

"What?"

He touched his forehead. "You said…"

"Oh, right." I laughed as the memory came back. "He fell off his bike. He was trying to ride it with no hands, and—" I stopped suddenly, the hairs on the back of my neck prickling. "Do you hear something?"

Ingo frowned, listening. "Aside from the wind? No."

"No, there *is* something," I insisted. "I heard a noise in that corner, I'm sure of it." I sat up, craning to listen. It came again: a scratching, rustling sound from the pile of junk. I sucked in a breath. My gaze went instinctively to the floor.

"Maybe you're right," said Ingo in an undertone. "Do we have a guest, do you think?"

"Not a very welcome one," I managed to get out.

I felt almost nauseous. Staring at the cluttered corner, I groped one-handed for the twist of metal. Despite growing up on a farm, despite my months in Harmony Five, I had never, ever, lost my fear of rats.

Ingo raised his good eyebrow. "You've gone quite pale," he informed me wryly. "Could this really be my stalwart former opponent?"

"Shut up! I can still hear it."

"Amity, relax. It's only—"

I stifled a shriek as a large brown blur shot from the corner; at the same moment I scrambled backwards, flinging the twist of metal as hard as I could. More by luck than skill, I got it. There was a squeal; the rat went head over heels. The metal knot clattered to a stop.

Ingo straightened abruptly.

"I don't believe it," he muttered. "Remind me never to startle you." He went over and inspected the rat, his lean face screwed up with distaste. "Good shot, but not good enough. The thing's still twitching. Do you want to come over here and finish it off?"

I was shaking. "No!" I couldn't take my eyes off the rat. It lay with its legs moving feebly. Part of me was terrified that it might get up and run at me again.

I hugged myself. "Can't we just...throw it outside or something?"

Ingo shot me a dark look; he muttered something in Germanic. "By *we*, you mean *me*... I really would not have taken you for the helpless maiden type."

"Fuck off! You know I'm not."

Ingo blew out an irritated breath. He picked up a piece of our firewood – a chair leg. "Fine. Avert your eyes, fair maiden, while I bludgeon the vicious, terrified rat for you."

I did avert my eyes. I covered my ears too, but still heard a dull, welcome *thump*. When I looked again, Ingo was standing over the rat with the firewood still in his hand. There was a strange look on his face.

I swallowed hard. "Please tell me it's dead."

"Yes, it's dead...Amity, the thing's almost as big as a cat."

"I don't need the details! Throw it outside."

"Do we really want to?"

"What do you..." I started, and then realized. "You *can't* be serious. They're vermin!"

"So are rabbits, and they're edible." Ingo looked over at me then. The hunger that neither of us had allowed ourselves to unleash was alive on his face now. He looked taut, slightly glassy-eyed.

I hesitated. Slowly, I got to my feet and went over.

We stood side by side, staring down at the rat. It was lying on its side. Its head was caved in. I felt a shudder of loathing even though it was, most certainly, dead.

But I also felt my stomach growl.

"We don't have anything to cook it in," I said finally.

"We could make a skewer from a piece of metal and hold it over the fire," Ingo said. "Just like toasting marshmallows."

The image was so horrible, so unlikely, that I snickered. Ingo's mouth twitched too; he shot me a glittering, almost feverish look. Suddenly this seemed hilarious, in a wild, upside down way.

"We can pretend we're sitting around a campfire," I said.

"Exactly. We'll sing songs and tell ghost stories…" Ingo swallowed and sank to his knees. So did I. Neither of us had stopped gazing at the rat.

"We just need to skin it," said Ingo. "And gut it. Is there anything we can use?"

I nodded. I was still wearing my leather flight jacket; almost in a dream, I reached into the pocket and drew out the shard of glass.

"This," I said.

Chapter Nineteen

THE THICK SHARD OF GLASS worked as well as a knife. Handling raw rat with my fingers, peeling the meat off its small ribcage, should have disgusted me – but by then my stomach was alive and roaring and I would have roasted my own boot if we hadn't had the rat. In fact, I was starting to wonder if we really had to cook it, if we couldn't just gobble the rat down right now.

We started eating before we'd cooked all of it. "Screw it, I can't wait any more," Ingo muttered. His hands were trembling as he plucked hot, cooked meat from the skewer; he dropped it onto a piece of newspaper. "We'll cook the rest later, yes?"

"*Yes,*" I said fervently. The cabin had filled with the

aroma of cooking; it smelled rich and gamey and utterly delicious.

Neither of us would have won prizes for table manners. We wolfed down the small portions, licking our fingers. The meat tasted faintly greasy, but not bad. Wonderful, in fact.

"More," I gasped when I'd finished. Ingo was already loading up the skewer.

I took it from him when he'd finished and held it over the fire, rotating it carefully. I watched as the pink meat shrivelled slightly, dropping grease onto the flames, making them sizzle and flare up. Already, the desperate hunger was receding a fraction. I could feel my body responding to the food with a whisper of strength.

I grinned with pure joy. "It really is just like roasting marshmallows."

The taut look on Ingo's face – the look that had been so ingrained that I hadn't even noticed it; the look that all the prisoners shared – had relaxed slightly. It made his long, angular features appear younger, less forbidding. He lay propped on one elbow, gazing dreamily at the fire.

"No songs though," he said.

"I'm not up to songs yet."

"Good, me neither. Is it done?"

"Almost."

"You look different," Ingo said abruptly. When I glanced at him, he was studying me. He shrugged. "Less haglike. More human. It's a compliment this time."

I laughed. "Well, 'less haglike' is definitely the nicest compliment I've ever gotten."

"Yes, I've been told I have a way with words. It's true though," he added. "Your face is softer, or something. You look better."

"So do you," I said after a pause. "Look marginally more human, I mean. Amazing what a good home-made meal of cooked rat can do, isn't it?"

"Yes, if one actually gets to eat it." Ingo was gazing impatiently at the fire. He sat up and plucked the skewer from my hands. "Come on! It *must* be ready by now."

When we'd both had enough, there was still a little meat left. We slept in front of the stove, wrapped in our coats. It was the first night in months that I'd gone to sleep feeling warm and well fed. If I'd had a soft bed as well, it would almost have been too much. This was just right.

This, I could believe in.

I woke up slowly, blinking and gazing at the stove. The fire had burned down to embers but still gave off a friendly heat. Through the window, the pearly light of dawn shone. Snow still fell, gently now, just a few drifting flakes.

Yawning, I pushed the coat aside and got to my feet. Ingo and I had put the remaining meat on the window sill where it was cold – under an empty coffee can with a brick over it, just in case the rat's friends had no scruples.

Ingo was still asleep, half-hidden under his coat. I went

over and lifted the coffee can. The night before, we'd divided the meat into two piles. I selected a small piece from my own pile and ate it slowly, savouring the sensation of food – the taste of it, the feel of it. More than that: food at a time when I'd chosen to have it. Food that I could have *just because*, that I hadn't had to wait in a line for, shivering and clutching a tin cup.

I rested the coffee can back in place and studied the abandoned rock crusher outside. I smiled. No matter what happened, I would never have to be near one that worked ever again.

I started to turn away from the window and then paused. A crease touched my forehead. Very faintly, I could see a shape moving in the grey sky. No, more than one. Hawks, maybe?

Then I heard it: the dull *thump, thump* of rotors.

My heart lurched. "*Get the fire out!*" I shouted. I ran back to the stove and yanked the metal door open, yelping as it burned my fingers. I grabbed a stick of firewood and jabbed frantically at the glowing embers, scattering them.

Ingo awoke with a jolt. "What, what?"

"Choppers!" I cried. "The smoke – we've got to get the fire out, *now!*"

Ingo swore and lunged to his feet. The choppers' vibrating beat was closer. He rushed for the pile of ash he'd cleaned from the stove. I scrambled to help; we flung handfuls over the still-red embers. They slowly winked and went out.

I swallowed and backed away a step, staring at the window. Ingo stood breathing hard, his eyes locked on it too. I'd knocked over the pail we'd used as a chamber pot when I raced to the stove – the smell of urine hung in the air.

The choppers kept coming. The sound filled my senses. One swooped across our field of vision and I flinched; as one, we darted for the wall and pressed against it, trying to flatten ourselves into nothing.

My gaze flicked to the door. We'd bolted it the night before, though it had felt as if we were the only people in the world.

"What do you think?" muttered Ingo. "Did they see?"

"I – I don't know. It's still snowing a little."

"Good, so maybe they didn't notice the smoke. Maybe they're just…" Ingo trailed off as a chopper grew louder. Its vibrating thuds beat through me. I caught my breath – it was right outside.

It was landing.

I burst away from the wall and snatched up our coats from the floor; kicked the bony remains of our dinner away into the corner. The floor was damp beside the overturned bucket – in a panic I flung old newspapers over it.

"Here, here!" hissed Ingo. He was clawing a space in the pile of clutter. I bolted over and we crawled into it, between the rusting hulk of the bedsprings and sheets of corrugated metal.

The chopper's blades stopped. Ingo and I huddled together, hardly breathing. I could smell the sharp sourness of his unwashed body, knew mine was the same – and thought feverishly that if they got close enough, they'd smell us.

I had a peephole through a corner of the bed frame, though I didn't want one. I stared at the cabin's small window, craning to hear. It sounded as if they were fanning out, searching the area.

I was just daring to hope that they might pass us by, when two Guns in their long wool coats came into view, heading straight towards us. The Harmony symbol was stamped over their hearts.

I started to shake. *No, they'll see!* I closed my eyes and pressed against Ingo, trying to still my body's tremors. I felt a jolt of pure hatred towards them that I'd been reduced to this.

"Do you still have that piece of glass?" murmured Ingo against my ear. I could feel his heart beating: a wild, caged thing.

"Yes," I said. "I've got it here."

"I will not let myself be taken," he said.

I licked my lips. "Me neither."

We exchanged a look. We both knew exactly what we meant. "Another pact," I said softly, and Ingo nodded.

The Guns' steady tread drew closer. One appeared at the window, peering in with cupped hands.

Neither of us breathed as the man slowly scanned the

room. Everything looked incriminating: the angle of the chair, the open drawers. My mouth felt like parchment. If they entered, they'd smell the urine. They'd search – they'd find us in seconds.

Someone tried the door. "Locked," a disgusted voice said, then a dull thump as he kicked it. "Should we break in? Wood's half rotted."

"Yeah, we'd better. They said check all buildings." The man at the window turned away, glancing over his shoulder. "Look's like the captain's in a bad mood."

"Who the hell isn't?"

A moment later rhythmic *thuds* started echoing through the room.

Ingo swallowed. "Get the glass ready."

I was already drawing it from my pocket. I felt hyper-alert – oddly calm despite my heart's frenzied beat.

"I'll break it in half," I whispered.

"Yes, good."

As the door shuddered with each blow, I struggled frantically with the glass. "I can't break it, it's too thick!"

Ingo was already groping at the floor, his hands scrabbling like spiders. He held up a lethal-looking scrap of metal. "All right?" he gasped out.

I nodded. Flashes of light showed with each blow now.

"Right here," Ingo muttered, and touched the pulse point of his throat. "We'll do each other at the same time."

"On three when they get in," I whispered. "Do it quick."

"You too," he said hoarsely.

A faint splintering sound came from the door frame.

We were both shaking. Our eyes stayed locked – Ingo's were as dark as night. Sweat glinted through the grime of his face.

Gently, I pressed the glass's sharp point to the vulnerable spot on his neck. He did the same to me. The strange thought hit me that I wouldn't have wanted to die alone… and that Ingo wasn't a bad person to die with. His fingers groped for mine; our free hands squeezed each other hard.

A distant voice shouted something.

The thudding stopped.

"What?" called back one of the Guns.

We froze; I gasped out loud. My pulse was hammering so hard I was certain the Guns would hear it.

The voice drew closer. "Come on, we're leaving."

"What about 'search all the buildings'?"

"Nah. No one's been in this shithole for decades. Captain's orders, there's another storm coming. This is nuts anyway – they've already frozen to death somewhere."

A fed-up snort. "I bet we'll still be looking after the storm, though."

"Yeah, Sector Six. Man, at this rate we'll be looking for the scum till we're dead ourselves…"

Through the peephole, the Guns' grey backs had appeared. Their three wool coats grew smaller, stirring around their heels with each receding *crunch, crunch* of their footsteps. A smudge stained the window where the first one's hands had been.

The murmur of voices – even some laughter. Soon the choppers exploded into life again. The motorised hums grew louder and louder, until I thought the roof of the office would blow off.

They faded.

Neither of us had moved. It was as if we'd forgotten how. At last Ingo let out a gasp; the metal dropped from his fingers with a clatter. He slumped against the wall, eyes closed, breathing hard.

I was trembling. I crawled out of our hiding space and got up, stumbling; my knees felt as if they were made of water. I crept to the window, keeping flat to the wall, in case it was a trap. Finally I risked a peek.

Snow. The rock crusher. That was all.

I clutched the sill with both hands. "They're gone!" I cried. "Ingo, they're really gone!"

He appeared beside me. We stared out at the snowy emptiness.

Ingo wiped an unsteady hand over his face. Without speaking, he went and found the whiskey bottle and came back. He took a quick gulp and then handed it to me.

I took a swig too. The whiskey blazed through me, made my hands stop shaking. False courage, but I'd take any courage I could get just then.

"They're still looking for us," I murmured, gazing at the rock crusher's skeletal form. "It sounds like they're not going to stop."

Ingo was sitting on the floor against the desk now,

his head tipped back and his eyes closed.

"Concise," he said. "Depressing. But concise."

I went and sat beside him and gave him the whiskey again. He took another pull and then looked at me, rolling the bottle between his hands. His normal colour was coming back. I felt as if mine might be too.

"Would you have done it?" he asked finally. His dark eyes were unwavering.

"Yes," I said without hesitation.

He gave a slight smile. "Thank you," he said softly. "I'd have done it too."

"I know," I said…and realized to my faint surprise that I did know.

Outside, it had started to snow again, thick and hard. It made the light in the room seem greyish and streaky.

We sat in silence, finishing the bottle, passing it back and forth.

Chapter Twenty

December, 1941

"It won't be easy," said Mac with a frown.

He and Collis sat in a Topeka diner; Mac was studying a map Collis had given him, hidden in a newspaper. It showed a neighbourhood in the Western Quarter with a few houses marked.

Collis sat tensely, leaning on his forearms, watching Mac's reaction. Since he'd joined the Resistance three months ago, Mac had used Collis in many missions: he'd escorted people to the border; delivered crucial maps and papers; planted false birth charts in the Records Office. In every instance, Mac had found him cool-headed, reliable. A good man to have on your side.

Finally Mac folded up the newspaper and passed it back

to Collis. He signalled the waitress for more coffee.

"What if I say no?" he said.

Collis's fist clenched but his voice stayed level. "Then I'll accept that and keep working for you."

The waitress appeared and refilled their mugs. "Catch the game last night?" Mac asked Collis, stretching an arm out along the top of the booth.

"Oh, man – *Mitchell*, boy," said Collis, and chuckled. "Wish I could have seen that touchdown in person."

When the waitress had left, Mac motioned to the newspaper. "Destroy that," he said.

Collis nodded and drew it silently towards him. He looked down, his broad shoulders slumped, stirring cream into his coffee.

Mac said, "If you can find a reason to travel out there, I won't stop you. We'll help in any way we can."

Collis went still; his head snapped up. A beat later, shocked joy flowered over his face. "Really?"

"Yep." Mac stirred cream into his own coffee. "It's risky, but we don't want to abandon them any more than you do. And I think you'll be more useful to us if you can get this off your mind."

Collis sat grinning, jubilant. "Have I told you lately that I love you, Mac?" he said. "I'm serious, pal. The way I feel right now, I could lean across the table and kiss you."

Mac laughed. "Please don't. I've got a girlfriend, remember? Things might get confusing." After a pause, he added, "Hope you can pull it off. It'd be nice as hell for something to go right for a change."

Collis's happiness visibly dimmed. "Still no luck with Pierce?"

Mac shook his head. Kay Pierce had so far resisted his hints about hiring Sephy. He thought he was making progress, but to be too obvious could be fatal.

Easy does it, Walter had said. *Don't push it and spook her*.

Mac had to remind himself of that daily, so great was the urgency. The official annexing of Appalachia was going ahead in February – and without Sephy, Gunnison remained ignorant of the comet that might make him rethink the Day of Three Suns.

If they lost those eastern ports, the entire continent would go dark.

The diner bustled around them. Finally Mac sighed and said, "Listen, don't get caught, buddy. I'd hate to lose you."

The next day, Mac went to Kay's office bearing home-made cookies. Her secretary just waved him past now; he and Kay talked daily.

Mac started to knock at Kay's door and then paused, listening. She was on the phone, her voice a low hiss.

"Don't give me that! This is your fault – your people let Vancour escape! Don't you dare let on to him, or it'll be *your* head on a fence – do you understand?"

A pause. "All right. Good. *Yes,* of course you should keep searching!" A slam as she hung up.

Vancour. For a moment Mac stood where he was, his mind ticking. Then he knocked and opened the door. He stuck his head around it.

"Hey," he said.

Kay was sitting at her desk with her hands over her face. She looked up quickly, trying to compose herself. She was pale as they gazed at each other.

"Come in and shut the door," she said finally. "Lock it."

Mac did. He went and sat across from her. He placed the cookies on her desk and Kay stared down at them as if not recognizing what they were.

"You heard, didn't you?" she said.

"It doesn't matter," Mac said softly. "Listen, pal, I'm on your side. Whatever's going on, you can trust me."

Kay gave a half-sob. "I wish I could really believe that. Mac, look – we *are* friends, aren't we? A little bit?"

Mac felt a twinge of guilt and squelched it. Kay Pierce was directly responsible for the deaths of some of his friends in the Resistance. Their severed heads now perched on those same fences that she'd mentioned.

He reached across the desk and took her hand. "Yes," he said simply.

Kay's eyes filled. She held his hand between both of hers and dropped her head onto it, her slim shoulders trembling. Mac gently stroked her hair.

Finally Kay straightened. She sniffed, and Mac reached for his handkerchief. He handed it to her.

"Thanks," she said. She blew her nose, dabbed at her eyes. "Oh, look at me, charming..."

He gently jostled her arm. "Come on, have a cookie. They work wonders."

Kay reached obediently for one but didn't bite into it. She turned it over in her hands. "Sephy?"

"Me, actually."

She gave a wan smile. "Really?"

He brushed a stray tear from her cheek and shrugged. "What can I say? I like to bake." It was true; it relaxed him. Two o'clock in the morning often found Mac messing around in the kitchen while his brain refused to turn off.

"Sephy's a lucky woman." Kay put the cookie down. She cleared her throat. "So...I suppose you're wondering about what you just heard."

Mac leaned back and studied her. "I'll tell you, kid, I'm a little concerned. It sounded like Vancour's escaped...and that you were telling someone to keep it from Johnny."

Kay took a quick breath. She rose, hugging herself, and went to the window. Finally she turned and faced him. "I had to," she said. "Mac, I promise...it's for the best. Our Harmonic society depends on it."

Kay sat across from him, the two armchairs in her office drawn close together. She huddled in her seat as words spilled out from her.

It had all started nine months previously, she said.

Vancour had been on the run, with evidence proving Gunnison had orchestrated the thrown Peacefights. Kay had found herself in disgrace for not flagging Vancour as a danger to start with. Then Kay had "discovered" that Amity Vancour's birth chart shared a karmic link with Gunnison's.

"There's a *karmic link* between her and Johnny?" Mac's stunned look wasn't an act. What a ballsy move.

Kay pressed her fingers to her forehead. "Yes, but I – I think I overestimated the importance of it," she said faintly. "And Johnny...well, once he started thinking about it, he really latched onto the idea. You know: how can the two of them be karmically linked, when he's a force for Harmonic good, and she's a traitor? Does that mean *he* could be a traitor? Or that she really isn't? And so on. And on. He..." She trailed off, hugging herself.

Mac sat staring at her, taking in the implications of what sounded like Gunnison in the grips of an obsession. Remembering that he was being supportive, he rose and squeezed her shoulder. He started to pour two glasses of water from the jug on her sideboard.

Kay smiled weakly. "Something stronger?"

He poured them both a swig of Scotch, though he had no intentions of losing his wits just now. Kay took a quick, tense gulp. It was the first time since he'd known her that she'd drunk anything stronger than champagne.

"So how long has this been going on?" Mac asked.

Kay grimaced. "Since I told him, I think. But I only

knew about it after Vancour was found guilty. That's when it really seemed to hit him – remember, he stopped presiding over the World for Peace trials back in June? The thought of their karmic link just kept preying on him, worse and worse. So I looked at the charts again. And I realized that their karmic link was a kind of…inverse one."

"Inverse," repeated Mac.

Kay gave him a quick look. "When his luck is up, hers is down. So the fact that she was in a correction camp actually meant that Johnny's luck was on the upswing."

Ups and downs. Holy hell, thought Mac. Gunnison had been talking about his supposed link with Vancour – the need to keep her "down". This has been preying on the man's mind for *months.*

He cleared his throat. "So…let me get my head around this. If Vancour were to die…"

"Oh, that would be wonderful!" gasped Kay. "But she *hasn't.* She just keeps hanging on, and now Johnny's latched onto *that* as well. He's convinced that so long as she's still alive, even if she's in dire straits, his own fate can never achieve its true glory."

The dark mirror taunts me I am in despair. It had been Gunnison's handwriting after all on the strange birth chart Mac had seen on his desk. The man had to be completely breaking down.

Mac pushed the electric thought away and kept his expression concerned. He leaned forward. "Listen, kid, have you never thought of…well, I don't know, hastening

Vancour's demise? If it would ease Johnny's mind?"

"I can't! Johnny's determined that no one should interfere, that fate has to speak for itself. He told the directors of Harmony Five not to treat Vancour differently to any other prisoner. I've tried to get past them, but..." Kay shook her head miserably.

Mac had known there was a reason. Otherwise Kay would have ensured that Vancour didn't last a day. *How can I use this?* he was thinking frantically.

Kay took another quick sip. "Anyway, I've been hoping that the Day of Three Suns will jolt Johnny back to his old self. Oh, Mac, it *has* to! Thousands of people cheering him, taking another country into the Harmonic fold..."

"But now Vancour's escaped," said Mac intently. "Which means...what? That the dame's on an *upswing*?"

"Yes." Kay gave Mac a wretched glance. "He doesn't know yet. The call came through to me. I told the Harmony Five director that he was dead if Johnny found out Vancour was gone. So for now, he's still telling Johnny that the numbers haven't changed – but it's been almost a week and I don't know how much longer I can keep it quiet before Vancour maybe surfaces somewhere and—"

"Wait. Numbers?"

"Johnny doesn't want them to know he's especially interested in Vancour, in case it affects how they treat her. So he waits for the call from Harmony Five every day, after they count the prisoners. Mac, if he finds out she's gone..."

"What?" Mac leaned forward. "What do you think

he'd do?" *If she thinks he'd commit suicide, I'd tell him right now – even with Cain poised to take power.*

Kay slowly shook her head. "I don't know," she whispered. "I think he could become violent – lash out, try anything to restore the balance. It wouldn't be good, not for any of us."

Mac sat motionless. No. That didn't sound good at all.

"If Vancour's alive, she has *got* to be recaptured," went on Kay. "And then it'll be all right, because they'll put her to death just like any other runaway. I'll have proof I can show to Johnny."

"What can I do?" said Mac urgently.

"Be a pal and cover for me?" asked Kay. At his quizzical expression, she said, "I'm travelling to Harmony Five tomorrow to make sure they're doing everything possible to find her. I've told Johnny I'm checking on something else in the area."

"Something else?"

Kay shrugged dismissively. "Just an industrial site nearby. I'll stop there on my way home. But if I need you to back me up, will you do it?"

What industrial site? Was this the major thing his lost airwave spies had caught hints of?

Mac's expression didn't change. "Of course I will," he told Kay softly. "You can count on me, kid. You go get Vancour back so we can all rest easy again."

Kay let out a breath. She kissed his cheek. "Thank you. Now what do *you* want?"

"Me?"

"You're doing me a pretty big favour, Mackie – keeping quiet. So let me do something for you too."

"Not necessary. We're friends, remember?"

She playfully shook his arm. "Please? If there's nothing *you* want, what about Sephy?"

"What about her?"

Settling back more easily in the armchair, Kay reached for the cookie and bit into it. "Mmm – I'm impressed. She's a state astrologer? Is she any good?"

"Well, of course." Mac offered his relaxed grin. "I'm only attracted to women who are smart as sin, you know."

Kay smirked as if the compliment had been meant for her. "All right, how would she like a pretty big promotion?"

Here it was, what he'd been so carefully angling for. Mac felt both despairing and grimly jubilant. He and Sephy had at times discussed this for hours: argued about it, shouted about it. Protecting her couldn't be a factor.

"She'd like it," he said.

When Mac finished work, he made sure he wasn't being followed and then went to Walter's. Sephy was already there. Opera played on the phonoplayer, the disc scratching slightly against the soaring voices.

When Mac explained what had happened, Sephy gave a relieved gasp. "Oh, finally! When do I start?"

"Tomorrow." Mac looked down at his iced tea. "And

Pierce is away for at least a week. With luck, you can work on Gunnison about how the comet affects the Day of Three Suns." His tone was flat.

Sephy rubbed his arm. "Mac, don't worry. I'll be fine."

He gripped her hand hard. "She has already gotten rid of almost all the astrology staff," he said. "Once you're in, I can't help you; that department has nothing to do with me. *Be careful.* Come off like you're a threat and you'll be killed."

"I know, baby," Sephy murmured. She slipped her arm around his waist and pressed close. No one spoke for a moment as the music warbled on.

In his armchair, Walter was frowning at the ceiling, contemplating all of this. "What about the Vancour information?" he said. "Is it time for me to blow my cover? Let the *Times* announce to the world that Wildcat's on the loose?"

Sephy's head snapped up. "No! That puts Mac in too much danger. The Pierce woman would know it came from him."

"I'd say it came from Harmony Five, or that she'd been spotted somewhere up there."

"And then you'd be shot and that would be the end of it!" Mac raked both hands through his hair. "We don't know how Gunnison would react, Walter. From what Kay said, it could make things worse."

"How the hell could they be *worse*?"

Mac's voice rose. "Are you kidding? We're sitting here

listening to opera and drinking iced tea! Imagine the city in total lockdown – tanks everywhere, people being beaten in the streets—"

"You're being a little hyperbolic there, boy."

"Oh, you *think*? I've seen the footage from the Western Seaboard attack! I know what Johnny Gun's capable of when his back is up."

"So have I, and—"

"Stop!" cried Sephy. "Both of you, stop. Walter, Mac's right. Gunnison's a maniac; putting this information out there could backfire. Let me try to get the Day of Three Suns changed. Maybe we can still get rid of him and Cain at the same time."

The disc reached its end and the needle bounced gently back and forth, whispering static. Finally Walter lumbered to his feet. He changed the disc and put on a string quartet.

"Something more soothing," he said gruffly. "You're both right. I just hate not being able to act yet."

Sephy went and hugged him. Walter clasped her to him briefly. "All right, what about this mysterious industrial site?" he said, releasing her.

"Somewhere near Harmony Five," said Mac. "Mining, I'd bet, since it's the Yukon. What, though?"

"I've got an atlas in the library – wait a minute."

Walter left the room. Mac heard Walter's wife letting someone in. A moment later Collis appeared, still in his double-breasted suit from work. His cheeks were rosy from the cold.

"Hey, Mac, Sephy," he said.

"Hey there, yourself," said Sephy. She liked Collis. She said he seemed sweet and shy and a little lost – all adjectives that Mac would never have applied to the guy before, but he knew what Sephy meant. Collis was less brash now; much more genuine.

The liquor levels in the bottles in his office hadn't changed since he'd joined the Resistance.

"Just thought I'd stop by in case you were here." Collis shoved a hand through his wind-tousled hair. "Mac, listen, I've worked out a cover story for why I should go to the Western Quarter—" He stopped and glanced at Sephy.

She waved him on. "Oh, I already know. The man has no secrets from me."

"It's true," said Mac with a grin. "Go on, Collis, what have you got?"

Walter shambled back into the room, gazing down at a large, open book he was carrying. "You know, if Vancour really *has* escaped, she's probably dead by now. Hell of a place to—"

Mac spoke quickly over him: "Walter, Collis just dropped by to give me some information. Would you excuse us?"

Walter looked up and saw Collis. He winced.

Collis's face had slackened. He stood motionless. "Amity's escaped?" he whispered.

The room had gone silent, apart from the soaring notes of the string quartet. Sephy stood stricken. Collis spun towards Mac, fists clenched. "Mac, *tell* me!" he cried. "I have to know!"

"This way, Collis." Mac took him by the arm and led him into the library. He shut the door behind them. The music faded.

Collis stood stock-still. "Is it true? Has she really gotten out of that place?"

Mac sighed and rubbed his forehead. "Yes," he said. "Whether she's still alive, I don't know. Pierce is looking for her."

Collis was practically quivering, as if electricity was coursing through him. "Weren't you going to *tell* me?"

"No."

"*No?*"

"Absolutely not. And whatever you're thinking—"

"I have to go up there," broke in Collis. He started to pace. "I have to try to find her – to help her—"

"Oh no you don't," said Mac. "Sorry, but that's the last place you're going, buddy-boy."

Collis whirled towards him. "*Are you crazy?* Mac, I love her! It's my fault she was in that place! Imagine if it were Sephy; would you just—"

"Will you shut up and start talking sense?" snapped Mac. "She's probably already dead and if she's not, you couldn't find her without a small army."

"I have to help her!"

"You can't! It's a thousand square miles of snow! And how would you explain it if Pierce found out? This is deeply classified info, pal. You're with us now, and you will *not* do anything to endanger us."

The ex-pilot stood glaring, looking ready to take a swing at Mac. "You can't stop me," he said hoarsely. "To hell with this. I quit."

Collis started for the door. Mac was a head shorter, but grabbed him and slammed him up against the wall. Collis's eyes flashed; he started to struggle. The look on Mac's face stopped him.

"Make one more move and I'll tell Cain you can't be trusted," Mac said in a low voice. "Then you can travel up to the camps by train like everyone else." He shoved him hard and stepped back. "Don't test me, Collis. Too much is at stake. Think about it for more than two seconds and you'll agree."

The fight seemed to sag out of Collis. He started to speak, then stopped.

Slowly, he slid down the wall to the floor and put his hands over his face.

Mac sat beside him. Distantly, he could still hear the music – Sephy and Walter talking. "And you can't quit, by the way," he said, only half-joking. "Your soul belongs to us now, buddy."

Collis let his hands fall and dropped his head back against the bookshelf. He stared at the ceiling. His eyes were red. "I'm not quitting," he said finally. "Sorry. I just..."

"Skip it."

Collis swallowed and looked at his hands. "If she's still alive…isn't there anything we can do to help her?"

"Not really. I'm sorry." Mac thought it better not to mention the cut-off northern airwave spies – the only ones who might be able to do something, if Vancour was alive to be helped. He prayed that they might get word of her.

Mac cleared his throat. "Listen…I understand how you feel," he told Collis. "And to answer your question, if it were Sephy, you'd have had to restrain me too. But you'd have done it."

"I know." Collis rubbed his eyes. He gave a hollow laugh. "I'm probably the last person she'd want to see anyway."

Mac looped his arm around Collis's neck and squeezed roughly. He scrambled to his feet. "Come on, tell me about your Western Quarter plan, pal. Let's save those two, at least."

Chapter Twenty-one

December, 1941

I woke up and there was sunshine.

I straightened slowly, blinking. The mining-office window, not quite covered by snow, showed a stripe of blue at its top. Light angled in, revealing the room's barrenness. By then we'd burned almost everything. Only the metal had survived.

I nudged Ingo's still-sleeping form. "Hey," I said weakly.

He prised his eyes open, looking bleary. Then he saw the sun and sat up too. We glanced at each other.

If we planned to get out of this place, this was our chance. Yet if another snowstorm came like the one that had chased the Guns away, we'd be caught in the open. We wouldn't find a shelter like this twice.

Ingo staggered as he got to his feet. His dark eyes burned. "Onwards," he said.

"Onwards," I agreed.

When we swung the door open, a mound of snow blocked the doorway. We angled the desk against it and crawled out; we emerged shivering into a sparkling world of white. Even the rock crusher was a thing of glory, crusted with icy diamonds.

The storm had lasted four days – our fuel only two. No other rat had appeared to feed us. We'd talked little, hunched into our heavy coats on the floor. Having had one good meal made the hunger even harder. It felt as if my stomach was my enemy, determined to destroy me.

I refuse to die, I'd told myself over and over. *I have to get to Madeline and find out the truth.*

Though weak and famished, Ingo and I broke into all the buildings we could. Most held nothing of use. Then in a long, low building we found abandoned tables stacked against one wall and a kitchen behind a door.

A kitchen.

We rushed into it. Ingo started feverishly opening cupboards while I rifled through drawers.

"Anything to eat?" he gasped.

"No, nothing...there are some knives though."

"Good. Next time we need to kill each other, we can do it in style..." Ingo banged a cupboard door closed. "Come *on,* Cook! Dave left his precious whiskey! What did *you* leave?"

I pulled open another door, exposing a small room lined with shelves. "Here! The pantry!"

Ingo was at my side in a moment. Tucked away in a corner was a mouldy cardboard box that fell to pieces when we tore it open.

Inside were a dozen tin cans, their labels faded and discoloured. I grabbed one up; I squinted to make out the wording.

"Beef stew, I think," I said, my voice trembling.

Ingo was back at the drawers, searching them in a frenzy. "I don't give a shit *what* it is, so long as it's edible. Bring it here."

There was no can opener. We hacked into one of the cans with a knife, producing jagged metal edges that could have sliced a finger off.

Chunks of beef – potatoes and carrots in a congealed sauce. The rich smell of it wafted out, making me feel faint. We took turns with a wooden ladle, wolfing it down. Then we prised open another can and ate that one too.

Finally Ingo slumped against the counter. "So we won't starve to death at least," he said in an undertone. He rubbed a hand over his face.

"We've got ten cans left." I gently stroked their discoloured tops. "We'll share one a day. Agreed?"

"Agreed." Ingo hesitated. "There's something we haven't thought of, you know."

I was looking for something to put the cans in. "What?"

"The choppers. Where did they come from?"

I froze mid-motion and stared at him. Choppers were short-range flight vehicles. As near as we could guess, we'd travelled several hundred miles from Harmony Five. Those choppers couldn't have come from there.

"Some sort of landing pad," I murmured. "Somewhere to refuel."

"Exactly."

I leaned against the counter next to Ingo, my thoughts tumbling. The landing area could be a pump and a shed in the middle of nowhere…or, if we were lucky, something more developed, with roads and trucks.

"It could be at another Harmony," I said after a pause. "Just like wherever the snow-trucks are heading."

"It could be. But maybe it isn't."

It was another chance, at least. "Let's still follow the trucks for now, like our original plan," I said. "At least we know they're heading directly to a place where it's warmer, maybe with autos."

"Yes – but we'll keep an eye out for the choppers, and see if we can tell where they're coming from." Ingo's smile was grim. "Just as well they're still looking for us, I guess."

We both knew this intensive search was because I was Wildcat. Ingo would have been safer on his own, if he could have managed it.

I found a burlap bag and we loaded the cans into it.

"Sorry you asked me to join you?" I said finally.

He shrugged. "I couldn't have escaped without you."

"You know that's not what I meant."

Ingo started making cardboard sheaths for the knives. At first I thought he wasn't going to respond, and then he glanced at me.

"No. I'm not sorry," he said. "We've eaten a rat together and are willing to shove deadly implements into each other's throats. I think that means we're bonded for life, in some strange way." He handed me one of the blades. "Do you want to carry the bag first, or shall I?"

We hiked up the road that led to the top of the ridge where we'd fallen, then hid in the copse of trees we'd glimpsed before the first storm. The snow-trucks arrived less than an hour later, trundling across the landscape, their tracks leaving a straight line across the whiteness.

We started to walk.

We spotted the choppers often – always in the distance, buzzing over the terrain like malignant flies. I craved seeing them as much as I dreaded it.

We couldn't tell where they came from, though we kept a careful watch. But the snow-trucks were heading roughly southeast. Others returned by the same route. As the days passed, we kept following their tracks, looking out for them on the horizon so we could get out of sight.

Half a can of cold stew a day was barely enough to keep us going. Hunger gnawed constantly. We took turns carrying the bag, which grew progressively lighter.

The scenery was sweeping, the sky huge. One night, the

northern lights appeared, shifting like weird green smoke across the stars. Sometimes in the day, we saw herds of moose, their legs long and ungainly – once a grizzly bear in the distance.

We slept in crude lean-tos of branches hacked from trees, scattering them into nothing each morning. The cold turned bitter after dark and we slept curled together for warmth. Night after night, so tired there was no conversation, I lay pressed against Ingo's thin form and felt his breathing as if it were my own.

From the stiffness of his movements, his side still bothered him. There seemed no point in mentioning it – there was nothing we could do.

As we journeyed, the weather gradually became warmer, until finally we reached a snow-dusted road – and, from the trucks' tracks, the point where they changed the runners for tyres. Ingo and I stood studying it. "We're getting somewhere, at least," he said.

"Somewhere," I agreed.

But where?

When there were no choppers or trucks in sight, the world felt empty. We trudged on, too tired to talk much. Occasionally Ingo mentioned his siblings, or I'd talk about my childhood with Hal.

I never brought up Collie or my father. Ingo never mentioned Miriam. When I'd known him before, he hadn't been able to *stop* mentioning her – even when it was clear she'd hurt him.

Finally, when we'd been following the snow-trucks' tracks for over a week, we heard the choppers' distant drone and saw what we'd been praying for – they were landing. We watched with taut hope as one by one, they disappeared down into the trees in the distance.

"A fuelling point?" murmured Ingo, not taking his eyes from the horizon. His thin shoulders were slumped. We were both bone-weary, muscles aching. "Or are they just getting a closer look at something?"

We glanced at each other. There was only one way to find out.

We stood on a wooded rise, gazing down at a huge compound.

"What *is* it?" I breathed.

Whatever it was, it was laid out below us: dull grey buildings, gridlike streets. A few autos were moving about. Roads stretched away to the south and north, arrow-straight. In a strange way it reminded me of the Peacefighting complex.

Ingo's face had gone slack. "There must be hundreds of people working there. What the hell? Is there a *town* nearby?"

"None of this should exist," I said in a daze. An auto crawled along a road: a distant moving dot. "Ingo, I mean it! I used to love maps, growing up – I'd pore over them for hours. This whole area should have *nothing*."

"Yes, I was just the same. And you're right." Ingo snorted, still staring downwards. "Well. It looks like Gunnison's been quite the busy bee these past twelve years."

Just then it hardly registered that Ingo had shared my childhood passion. "Some kind of foundry maybe," I ventured tensely, studying the northern road. "For whatever metal we were mining."

"Must be, though it's about ten times larger than I'd have thought any foundry needed to be. I wonder—" Ingo stopped short and grabbed my arm. "*Look.*"

I followed the line of his pointing finger. The similarity to the Peacefighting complex increased tenfold. "An *airfield?*" I gasped.

"Only one runway – but yes." Ingo barked out a disbelieving laugh. "I think we've just discovered where the choppers refuel."

We glanced at each other. Neither of us had dared hope for this. A runway meant airplanes. *Airplanes.*

Ingo and I were both pilots.

He gave me a grim, wolfish smile. "Are we thinking the same thing?"

The feverish light in his eyes probably matched my own. The idea was insane. Yet there was no fence…and with luck, our stolen uniforms would be the same as those worn by the guards.

"We are," I said softly.

* * *

Hours later, we'd made our way down the hill without being seen and were hiding among the bushes at the edge of the airfield, watching to see if there was a routine we could use to our advantage. So far, we hadn't noticed one.

We saw a few overall-clad workers, but the hangars remained closed, no planes in view. Whenever I was about to suggest that we risk checking them out, a worker would stroll past.

The sun crept across the sky. The small airport was just a few hangars. What appeared to be an office – glass-walled and sleek, with a reception desk inside – fronted onto a larger building. Above, a red-and-black Harmony flag rustled in the breeze.

Ingo and I shared the last can of stew. Neither of us commented on the fact that our food was now gone.

"Do you know what I like about you?" said Ingo suddenly.

I glanced at his weary, angular profile. "I wasn't aware that you liked *anything* about me," I said.

Ingo shot me a wry look and for a split second I was startled by the burned half of his face. I'd actually forgotten about it.

"Don't be idiotic," he said. "We've eaten a rat together, remember?"

"True. That does things to you, all right. Fine, what do you like about me?"

"I like," said Ingo, "that you're not one of those annoying people who's constantly saying things like, 'Do you think we'll get a chance soon? Ingo, do you think there are any planes in those hangars?' When you know perfectly well that I don't know, but you just have to chatter to hear yourself talk."

"I hate that too," I said. Then I glanced at him. "Who are we talking about?"

"Most people. But Lena, sometimes."

"And my mother," I said.

"And Miriam," said Ingo after a pause.

His expression was complicated, bitter. Just like the first night I'd met him, when he'd studied Miriam's laughing face from across the dance club and I'd commented how beautiful she was.

I was abysmal at this kind of thing. I hesitated. "Do you want to tell me about...?"

"No," said Ingo. "Forget I mentioned her."

"All right," I said. I cleared my throat. "Okay, I think we need to make a decision. The next time we see a worker pass, should we just take a chance and head over?"

Ingo let out a bark of laughter, and my eyebrows rose.

"What?" I said.

The relieved grin he gave me made him look about sixteen. "Add that to the list," he said. "You're capable of actually dropping a subject when asked."

Before I could respond, he looked back at the airfield. Surprise flashed across his face.

"No, look!" he hissed. "There's someone in the office."

Chapter Twenty-two

We peered tensely through the branches. The office lay across the airstrip. Through its glass windows, I could see that a cluster of people had arrived: several Guns, and men in double-breasted suits.

Two Guns carried a placard on a tripod outside. They set it up. I could read only the top words: *Welcome to AHD!*

"AHD?" muttered Ingo.

"No idea," I murmured back, gazing at the Guns. Their uniforms were the same as ours, only cleaner. Then I noticed the glances they were casting at the sky. My skin prickled; my eyes flew upwards too.

"Ingo, I think..." I started, and then broke off as we both heard the vibrating roar of a Merlin engine.

There's nothing like it in the world: a deep, primal noise that goes right through you. "There!" Ingo said, pointing a grimy finger. Through the bush's branches I saw the familiar shape approaching.

The small plane was at about two thousand feet. It came in at an angle as the pilot viewed the runway, then straightened out, its nose lifting for the landing.

"A two-seater," I murmured as the plane touched down and taxied to a halt. The propeller slowly stopped. A worker darted over to shove chocks under the front wheels and the gang from the office swarmed forward, smiles ready.

The cockpit slid open. A young woman with coiffed, light brown hair climbed out as her pilot emerged from the other side. She wore a stylish flight suit with a fur coat over it. She smiled prettily as one of the men hastened to bring a small set of stairs over and helped her down them.

I stared at her. "I don't *believe* it."

Ingo glanced over. "You know her?"

"That's Kay Pierce! Gunnison's Chief Astrologer. She was at my trial." Sourly, I recalled her sitting at the prosecution table, whispering with my attorney.

Ingo gave a soft snort. "I guess she's up here dispensing astrological wisdom to AHD, whoever they are. How nice for them."

Someone helped Pierce take off her parachute and the group headed for the glass-walled office. One of the suited men held the door open for her; she swept inside with a ripple of fur coat. They all passed through some inner door, leaving the office empty again.

My chest clutched. Suddenly the airfield was quiet. The workers had vanished into a hangar. The Merlin sat crouched on the pavement, its nose pointing towards the sky.

"We can't think," Ingo gasped. "We just have to go."

We scrambled from the bushes and started walking towards the airfield as if we belonged there. My heart battered coldly at my ribs. I kept my eyes on the office, certain that any moment it would fill with people again.

We reached the asphalt. Our steps echoed as we started down the airstrip in quick unison. I forced my arms to swing loosely at my sides, though I was so frightened I could hardly breathe.

"We look like Guns," I muttered out loud. "We're Guns, Guns."

"If no one looks too close," Ingo said in an undertone. His face was as dirty as mine; our hair under our hats a greasy mess. He scanned the plane with fervent desperation – that wild, almost-euphoria I'd seen in him before.

"I'll get the chocks while you start it up," he said.

"No, I'll do it – I can move faster than you with your injured rib."

"All right. Just grab them and hop in; don't waste any time."

"Are you actually not arguing for a change?" I joked feebly, and he gave me a quick one-sided grin.

"I'm too shit-scared. I can put up a token resistance, if it makes you feel better."

We'd almost reached the office by then, with the plane just ahead. I glanced at the placard...and froze.

"Ingo!" I gasped, grabbing his arm.

"*What?* We don't have..." Ingo stopped as he saw it too.

Welcome to AHD! And then below, in smaller letters, the sign read: *Atomic Harmony Devices: the hope for a new era.* A logo underneath showed a laurel wreath. Its stylized leaves encircled an item that looked archaic, ominous, belonging only in history books.

A bomb.

"What...what is this place?" I got out. My spine was ice.

"*Atomic Harmony Devices?*" said Ingo, his voice rising. "No. No, this can't mean what we..."

He trailed off. He was pale. I stared at the office. The inner door was glass too. Beyond it, I could see a vast, high-ceilinged space.

I couldn't help myself.

Feeling unreal I went over to the empty office and slipped inside. The only sound was my footsteps. I crept to the inner door and peered through the glass, distantly aware that Ingo had followed.

Kay Pierce and the group of men stood in the middle of what appeared to be an old hangar. Next to them was a large bomb. It lay lengthways on wooden trestles, its metallic surface glinting silver.

Pierce smiled and nodded as one of the men motioned enthusiastically to the weapon. I eased open the door.

"...of course, only a model for visitors, but it's all to scale. If you were here longer, we could give you the grand tour and show you the actual production process..."

"Amity, look!" hissed Ingo. Still stunned, I closed the door silently and turned.

He was beside a bulletin board. *Welcome, Miss Pierce!* said a sign at the top. The board was covered in glossy black-and-white photos.

I went and stood beside him. I couldn't speak.

One photo showed a bomb like the one I'd just seen – a real one this time, I assumed. It was about twelve feet long and easily that much around: a fat, bloated thing with fins on one end. Four men in lab coats stood smiling in front of it.

Other photos showed a production line; two bombs side by side; a snowy region with a mushroom cloud rising up, stark white against the pale sky. A circular graph was titled, "Bomb Blast Effects on a Typical City of Ten Million People".

I gaped at the display, almost literally unable to believe it.

I stammered, "But this – this goes against all..."

"Atomic weapons," Ingo breathed. "That's what destroyed the ancients." He quickly read the text below the graph. "*Uranium.* That's what we were mining – it mentions Harmony Five's mine! Uranium's needed to create them."

Uranium, that we'd mined at the point of a pistol. Atomic

weapons, built for no other reason than to kill millions.

This, too, was because of what Dad had done.

I couldn't breathe. Evidence. We had to have evidence. I started ripping the photos off the board. Ingo did the same, wincing as he strained for the top ones. The rattle of a hangar door came from somewhere in the distance and we both started.

"Come on!" Ingo gasped, jamming the photos in his coat pocket. He pushed through the door and raced for the Merlin. I paused to snatch the graph. As I shoved it in my pocket I glanced up.

Kay Pierce and the others were heading back. Through the inner glass door, her eyes met mine. Her gaze widened abruptly.

I turned and ran. Outside, Ingo was grabbing up the chocks from the Merlin's front tyres, flinging them away.

"*Get in!*" I shouted, pounding towards the plane. The pilot's side was closest to me. I clambered onto the wing and shoved open the hood.

"*Stop her!*" screamed a voice.

I felt as if I'd been punched – a split second later I heard the gunshot. The impact slammed me against the side of the Merlin. Another shot whined past overhead. Panting, I clutched the hood and swung myself in, half-falling into the cockpit.

Its dials and levers were all so familiar, yet this had to be a dream. I stared blankly at my left thigh.

So much blood.

Ingo flung himself in next to me and slid shut the hood. They were running towards us – shouts – the world dimmed in and out of focus.

No. I would not die before I had answers. Suddenly furious, I gritted my teeth. With trembling hands I hit the ignition, eased back on the throttle. The plane started to move, picking up speed.

"Are you—" Ingo broke off. I heard his startled swear – felt his hands on my leg, putting pressure on the wound. "Keep going!" he cried over the roar of the engine. "Pull back; you can do it!"

The pain was fire-bright with black teeth. We hurtled down the runway, the Merlin shuddering. My skin was clammy. I struggled to focus, sweat stinging my eyes.

I pulled back on the stick. The rugged horizon slanted as we took off. The massive complex drifted past our port wing, growing smaller as we left it behind.

"Just a little bit longer! You're doing fine," Ingo kept saying. I knew he must be desperate to take over the controls, but the pressure of his hands on my wound didn't falter. "*Hang on!* Just level it out, Amity; then I'll take over. You can do it."

I did, though I don't know how. I kept hold of his voice like a lifeline. I got us to five thousand feet, above the clouds, and then levelled it out and put it on autopilot. My fingers slipped from the controls.

"Please – take over—" I gasped.

An arm around my shoulders. I heard Ingo's own grunt

of pain as he hauled me from the pilot's side. Somehow we changed places. I slumped back in the passenger seat, half-sobbing.

Ingo quickly checked the controls, then pulled his scarf off and leaned over me. I felt him fumble at my leg, then yelped as sudden pressure cinched. I gazed down in a daze. My left thigh was a darkly mangled mess; Ingo's scarf was tied tightly just above the worst of it.

He tugged my own scarf from my neck and lashed it snugly around the wound itself. "I don't know a damn thing about first aid," he muttered. His hands had my blood on them – his face shone with sweat. "But if we're lucky maybe you won't bleed to death now."

"Thank you," I mumbled. "Ingo…thanks." I was so tired; pain throbbed through me. I closed my eyes.

I felt him touch my shoulder. "That was some amazing flying, my friend," he said softly. "It would have been a good take-off even if you *hadn't* just been shot."

I tried to answer, but darkness was claiming me. The last thing I was aware of was the plane turning smoothly on its starboard wing as Ingo took over the controls and steered us away from this place.

My father stood in a doorway, dressed in his old flying gear. My heart skipped. He wasn't dead after all. Yet the knowledge I could never bear to face – what his thrown fight had led to – brought waves of despair.

"Dad?" I whispered. "Please...tell me why. I need to understand."

"This is for the best, Amity," he said. He levelled a pistol at me and shot.

I jerked awake, breathing hard. The roar of a Merlin engine surrounded me; I was in the vibrating cocoon of a cockpit. Pain pulsed. For a confused moment I thought it hadn't been a dream: that my father had shot me and was now flying me somewhere.

Then it all came back. I looked over at Ingo in the pilot's seat. The normal side of his face was to me – the same face I'd occasionally glimpsed during Peacefights. "How...how long was I out?" I said.

He glanced at me, and I saw his tension. "A few hours," he said shortly. "How are you?"

The words seemed to swim past with little meaning. "Are we near Calgary?" I had a dim memory that it was where we were heading.

"Not near enough."

"Ingo, what's..."

"Nothing. Go back to sleep."

I struggled to sit up a little, gritting my teeth. My leg was a useless, throbbing weight.

"Tell me," I snapped. "Total trust, remember?"

Ingo's fingers on the stick stayed light; his voice sharpened. "It's not that I don't *trust* you, I'm trying to spare you! Fine. We're almost out of fuel."

My gaze flew to the fuel gauge. The needle hovered just

above the "E". Maybe another twenty minutes, if we were lucky. Then I remembered that the Merlin was bigger than a Firedove. We had even less time than that.

"We'll have to bail—" I started.

"No parachutes. Total trust, or else I'd be making reassuring noises."

No parachutes? "But—" I gasped, then fell silent at a terrible memory: when Kay Pierce and her pilot had gotten out, the workers had helped them take off their parachutes. Apparently the workers had kept them, to help the esteemed guests back into their chutes when they left.

"Shit," I whispered.

"Exactly. If you want to pass out again, I won't blame you."

I tried to heft myself still further to look out the window; pain gripped me and I fell back in my seat. "What's...what's the terrain like?"

Ingo shook his head. "Rocks and trees, mostly. At least there are some roads below now."

"Think you can get it down?"

"With luck. I'm hoping for a field somewhere..." He glanced in one of the mirrors; his eyes widened and he swore.

"Hang on!" he shouted.

He pointed the plane's nose into a screaming climb. The Gs slammed me against the seat as we arrowed upwards; I yelped in pain. The world turned grey as we entered the clouds, then spun as Ingo rolled us and peeled off to the west. The engine roared.

"How many?" I gasped out.

Ingo half-stood in his seat, clutching his rib and twisting behind to see. He sank down again. His face was as wild, as borderline violent, as it had been when we discovered Claudia.

"Three choppers. We've gained some distance but they're still following." He dipped back into the clouds and opened the throttle. "Those didn't come from the bomb factory!" he said over the engine. "Their range isn't far enough."

He was right. "How did they find us?" I cried, and then it hit me as the clouds whipped past. "A tracker," I whispered. "There's a tracker on this plane."

"Yes, and they knew from the pilot exactly how much fuel we had. All they had to do was bide their time and then show up for the kill." He opened the throttle still more, keeping an eye on the fuel gauge. At this speed it seemed to be plummeting by the second.

So did the daylight.

I noticed now what I hadn't before: it was late sunset. All too soon, the last of the sun's rays would wink from view and we'd be flying blind. Struggling not to pass out, I twisted in my seat too and gazed behind us. The three choppers were a loose, shifting triangle in the distance, keeping pace with us. Ingo was right: they were waiting for the kill.

Several times he hurtled us back into the clouds to lose them, choosing different directions; each time he emerged again, they were still there. With each shrieking manoeuvre the red-black pain chewed me harder, until my face was clammy with sweat.

"Are you all right?" called Ingo.

"No," I got out. "But keep going."

He shot a glance behind us. "Why the hell doesn't this thing have a firing button?" he muttered.

"At least...at least they don't seem to have one either."

Things had started to take on a dreamlike cast. The engine coughed, then sputtered: a rasping, feeble noise. The needle lay far below the "E" now.

The engine stopped.

This should have been alarming, yet it just felt peaceful. In the sudden silence, I could hear the choppers in the distance. Slowly, our propeller ceased turning. The four blades stood out starkly against the sky.

Ingo flipped a few levers. Though I could see the tension in his jaw, his fingers on the stick stayed light and sure. He got us down below the clouds and we glided like a large, ghostly bat.

"You really are an excellent pilot, you know," I murmured. "I used to love fighting you."

"We'll see if you're still saying that in a minute... Amity, there's nowhere good; I'm going to try it here. *Hang on!*"

A chaos of trees rushed up to us. The plane jounced as branches snapped past, whipping at the cockpit – a wing tore off with a wrenching jolt. I screamed. Distantly, I could hear Ingo shouting. The plane slammed to a vicious halt – dark trees lurched sideways—

Crack.

Pain.

A red, velvet darkness...fading away into nothing.

"Amity! *Amity!*"

Someone was jostling my arms. "No, stop," I murmured.

"*Get up!*"

"Please let me sleep." My mouth was sore; it was hard to say the words. Then I cried out as fresh, sharp pain burst across my cheek. I opened my eyes.

The world was sideways. In the moonlit gloom I saw dazedly that I was lying across the starboard cockpit window. The control panel was at my head and the port window above, showing branches and stars. Ingo crouched beside me.

"You *slapped* me," I realized.

"Amity, *get up!* The Guns will be here any minute!"

I tried to shake my head; the motion brought a fresh wave of pain that almost made me vomit. "Ingo, I..."

His half-burned face was a twisted mask of fury. "*Up!*"

He hauled me bodily to a sitting position – held me in place with a trembling, wiry arm as he battled the mangled cockpit hood. I was shuddering. Our plane's crumpled nose slid in and out of focus. Why were we in the trees?

"Ingo, no...I can't go fast enough..."

He had the hood about halfway open; even the fresh air seemed to hurt, invading the cocoon of the cockpit. "You'll damn well try," he said.

My mouth tasted salty, too warm. "We have a pact. Remember? If one of us can't go on—"

"*To hell with that!* Shut up and move!"

He dragged me from the cockpit. We dropped to the ground in a tangled heap; I sobbed in pain and almost blacked out again. The plane hung sideways in the trees above us. I stared at it, half-stunned.

"Come on. We have to hurry." Ingo's voice was surprisingly gentle now. He helped me up and put his arm around me, supporting me as we staggered away through the trees.

"Faster," he whispered. "Come on. Faster."

Darkness – our panting breaths – our stumbling footsteps. I couldn't put my injured leg to the ground; each hop brought fresh waves of pain. Dimly, I took in that Ingo was injured too. He was limping badly, his breathing even rougher than mine.

"Do you have the photos?" I gasped out.

"In my coat pocket."

The world was swaying around me. "Then, Ingo, *please!* Take the photos from my pocket too and go on without me. You have to get them to the…to the…"

I couldn't think of the word and almost wept in frustration; my knees buckled and Ingo pulled me upright again.

We froze at the sound of choppers thundering overhead. A streak of light raced towards us through the trees. Ingo swore and lunged into the undergrowth; he tugged us both to the ground.

We crouched in bushes until the lights had passed. I felt sleepy again, detached. Ingo's arm was still around me. I rested my head against his shoulder and closed my eyes, letting the world drift away.

"They'll see where we crashed in the trees…it must look like a strip taken out by a lawnmower…" He lapsed into Germanic, beating a fist against his thigh.

"What did you just say?" I murmured drowsily.

"I said they'll find a place to land soon, and start combing the woods. Come on!"

"Where though? Ingo…"

"*Get up!*"

He hauled me for what felt like miles, though was probably less, given the state we were both in. One of the giros kept cruising overhead, back and forth; we hid from its lights a dozen times. Yet by the time I heard shouts behind us, they seemed far away.

Finally we skidded down a small hill to a dirt road. There was a sort of overhang between road and woods: a carved-out half-tunnel of roots and dirt. Ingo sank to the ground and pulled us into it, clutching at his side. In the faint twilight I saw the sheen of sweat on his face. His dark eyes scanned the road feverishly.

"This…this isn't a bad place to hide," he murmured.

"Maybe...maybe we can flag down a passing auto."

It felt so good to stop moving that I wanted to weep. I slumped against Ingo's side, struggling to focus. The rough dirt road curved beside us. It didn't look very used.

"Will one pass by?" I whispered, and then added, "Sorry. I know you hate that kind of question."

"It's your first one in over two weeks," said Ingo. "I think you should get a medal for that." He shifted and put his arm around me. I didn't like the sound of his breathing. It was so uneven, as if every intake hurt him.

"You wouldn't have made it much further even without me," I realized.

"No. Probably not."

I swallowed hard, suspecting that he'd stopped because he couldn't go on. Nothing hurt any more. The velvety blackness kept tugging at me. I wanted to sink into it, but I was so afraid. What if I didn't die? I could hear faint shouts behind us, through the trees.

"Ingo...they're going to find us..." I got out. "Our other pact...please..."

His arm tightened around my shoulders. "Not yet," he said.

"Please. You have to. I don't want them to find us... I can't go back there..."

"Listen to me," he whispered. He touched my face. "Amity. Open your eyes and listen."

I struggled to focus. Ingo's face was half-ruined but at the sight of it I relaxed a little: his dark eyes were so direct.

"It's not time yet," he said softly. "I have my knife right here. If it's time, I'll do it. I promise. They won't take either of us." He let his hand fall from my face. "All right?"

I sagged. It felt as if a weight had tumbled from me. I nodded blearily and he drew me against him. I could trust Ingo; I knew that. He always meant exactly what he said.

I closed my eyes, feeling strangely at peace. The shouts grew closer. Very distantly, I felt Ingo's heartbeat against my cheek.

Still alive…and so was I.

I let the darkness carry me away.

Chapter Twenty-Three

December, 1941

Joe's Place again. There was no boxing match on this time; the telio showed the last of the World for Peace trials. Sandford Cain was sentencing the final few "traitors" to death. Mac kept his eyes fixed avidly on the screen, forcing himself to look gratified.

Collis slipped into the booth across from him.

"Cheer me up and tell me how it went," said Mac.

Collis had returned from the Western Quarter that morning; he was almost visibly fizzing with excitement. He shrugged out of his jacket. "Great," he said. "Mac, it all went perfectly."

Mac glanced at him. He had news of Vancour but couldn't bring himself to say it yet, with Collis looking so jubilant.

"They're all right?" he asked instead. "How's the kid?"

"They're both fine." Collis hesitated; he took a gulp of his beer. "Listen, Mac, I know this is a little out of the blue, but…he and I were talking on the way back, and…well, what would you say to letting him join us?" Collie's smile was rueful. "I'm assuming you don't beat up *everyone* who does."

Mac smiled slightly, too. "No, you were a pretty special case, buddy." He looked back at the screen. "Bitch deserved it," he said raising his voice as a murmur went through the bar at Cain's announced sentence.

"Got what was coming to her, all right," said Collis clearly.

A few beats later, Mac looked at him. "Where is he now?"

"I've got him at a safe house not far from here. Sephy and I have got it all worked out. But if—"

"Wait, whoa, back up." Mac raised an eyebrow and surveyed Collis with faint amusement. "You've been colluding with my girlfriend?"

"It's in a good cause, pal. Sephy said we use kids not much older than him as messengers sometimes. But if you don't agree, that's that."

Mac considered. "How old is he?"

"Almost fifteen."

"That's young. We're not babysitters, Reed."

"He's damn competent, or I wouldn't ask. And he wants to help. He's desperate to, in fact."

"Dangerous business for a kid." On the screen the gallows was showing. Mac's mouth hardened. "You'd be better off telling him to get the hell out to Nova Scotia while he can."

"He says it's his fight too. I can't really argue with him."

Mac forced himself to watch the execution. A half-hearted cheer went through the bar as the woman dropped. The black-and-white swirl of the Harmony symbol appeared on the screen and music started: one of Van Wheeler's ditties praising Gunnison.

Mac had preferred the inanity of "For Ever and a Day".

He turned to Collis. "All right, let me meet him later. We might be able to use him, at that."

Collis's fist had tightened as he'd watched the screen. Now he turned to Mac and his eyebrows rose. "Really?"

"Sure. I trust your judgement, Collis. But you know, if he's ever captured, he'll suffer the same fate as the rest of us."

Collis gave a troubled smile and gazed down at his beer. "I think I was hoping you'd say no."

"I can't turn away warm bodies who want to help. We're past that now."

Collis looked up. His eyes were dark blue in this light – steady and concerned. "That bad?"

"That bad. But also that close, if we're lucky."

The Day of Three Suns was still going ahead at the end of February, somewhere in Appalachia. Beyond that, Madeline Bark's plans remained secret.

Yet fear of Sephy's comet might even now persuade Gunnison to delay the treaty signing and relocate it here.

Sephy had made progress these past ten days…of a sort. Johnny Gun had declined to discuss her "serious concern" privately. But he'd scheduled a meeting with both Sephy and his Chief Astrologer. Pierce returned this evening: the meeting was tomorrow afternoon.

Tomorrow Sephy, too, might be sentenced to death, if she played this wrong.

Mac shoved the thought violently away. He studied Collis. He didn't relish what he was about to say.

"Listen, pal," he said finally. "I've got some news for you. I'm afraid it's not good."

Collis froze. "Amity?" he whispered.

Mac glanced around them at the bar. "I need you to stay relaxed, buddy. Should we leave?"

"Just tell me," Collis said tautly.

"Pierce called me this morning. Vancour and her accomplice have been recaptured."

Collis's lips went pale. He didn't move. His fingers around the beer mug became so tight Mac was surprised it didn't shatter.

"I'm sorry," said Mac after a pause. "I wouldn't have told you, but I was afraid you might hear it at work and not be able to control your reaction. You've got to be able to, if that happens."

Collis shivered convulsively and swiped a hand over his face. "Not everything is about the fucking *Resistance*, Mac."

Mac thought of Sephy. His voice sharpened. "You don't need to tell me that. But you do need to tell me that you can control yourself."

Collis drained his beer in a quick, angry motion. Around them, the bouncy Van Wheeler tune entwined with the rise and fall of conversation.

Collis put his mug down and sat staring at the empty glass. His red-rimmed gaze was hollow.

"So that's it, isn't it?" he murmured.

Mac sighed. "Yeah. I'm sorry." They both knew what was done to prisoners who were recaptured. Vancour would wish for death long before it came.

Collis rose suddenly, grabbing up his jacket. "I've got to get out of here."

Mac started up too. "I'll come with you, pal."

"*No.* Don't." Collis closed his eyes and then gave Mac a steady look. "Don't worry," he said flatly. "I'll control myself if anyone mentions it to me at work. But right now, I've got to be alone."

Mac nodded. He didn't really blame him. "You'll bring the kid around later, right?"

At the mention of the boy he'd rescued, Collis let out a long breath. "Yeah," he said softly. He rubbed his hand over his eyes. "Yeah," he repeated, more strongly.

Mac rose and offered his hand. "You did a good thing, you know. Getting them out."

Collis grasped his hand; his throat worked. "Aw, hell, Mac," he whispered.

Mac gripped his shoulder. "You go on," he said. "Find someplace where you're alone and cry or scream or whatever you've got to do. And then we'll keep on fighting... because, buddy, I'm afraid we ain't got much choice."

When Kay had called Mac that morning, she'd sounded gleeful. "Vancour's been recaptured; they took her back to H5 this morning," she said. "There was another one with her. They got him too." She giggled. "Apparently they put up quite a fight, for two scrawny half-starved things."

Mac had winced, thinking of Collis. "Hey, congrats!" he'd said. "That's a real relief, kid. So everything can go ahead as planned, right?"

"Yes, exactly as planned," said Kay Pierce, her voice jubilant even through the crackly, long-distance connection. "See you tomorrow, Mackie."

Mac had slowly hung up. They'd both been referring to the Day of Three Suns, even if one of them had fervently been hoping the answer was no.

He thought dully that he could ease up now on trying to reach the airwave spies in the far north. If the northern Resistance was still operating, it didn't matter any more whether they'd overheard news of Vancour and her accomplice on the private airwaves.

Mac was wearing his Gun uniform: he had to interrogate a few suspected Discordants. An oak tree grew near his window that he often gazed at before these sessions. Taking in its rhythmic, curving lines was a reminder of sanity. Of who he really was. Today the tree was just a tree.

Mac's fist clenched. He rose and grabbed his hat. Out in the corridor, he stiffened. John Gunnison was heading towards him. Mac hadn't encountered him in weeks. The once smiling and hearty leader looked thinner now, frowning. He strode ahead of a few subordinates.

Mac almost thought Gunnison wouldn't recognize him – the man looked distracted enough by "the dark mirror" not to – but his gaze fell on Mac and he stopped short.

"Interrogating Discordants?" he barked.

Mac managed a helpful expression. "That's right, Johnny."

Gunnison scanned him coldly. He leaned close. "*Get them,*" he hissed.

He walked on. Mac swallowed, shaken. *I wish to hell you were a thousand miles away, Sephy...but tomorrow it's all up to you.*

"I'm about to put you in check," said Collis the next evening. A chessboard sat between him and Mac.

"Have at it." Mac glanced at the clock. Almost eight. Where was she? He rubbed a fist across his palm.

Collis's expression was troubled. "Stop thinking about it, pal." He poured Mac another drink.

Mac ignored it. He rose and went to the window again. Very carefully, he peered out. The street below his apartment looked exactly the way it had for the past three hours, apart from being darker.

"I should have stayed," Mac muttered. "I should have figured out some excuse..."

"You couldn't; it had to be business as normal," said Collis quietly. Mac didn't answer, willing Sephy's straight, slim figure in its tan overcoat to appear around the corner.

Collis put another disc on the phonoplayer. Trumpets wailed through the room, with a brisk drumbeat underneath. He jammed his hands in his trouser pockets and leaned against the sideboard.

"Hey, um...how about some gin rummy instead?" he said.

Mac let the curtain drop and moved away from the window. He went to the coffee table where the chessboard was set up and picked up the drink, swirling the liquid in the glass.

"Mac?"

Collis still looked pale and flattened after the news of the day before, but the guy was here, trying his best. Mac blew out a breath. He started to put the drink down and then took a gulp.

"No," he said. "But thanks." He glanced at Collis. "Hey, I liked the kid," he said.

Collis nodded. "He's a good guy."

"He's settling in okay?" asked Mac.

"I think so. I'll check in on him later."

The boy Collis had rescued had now been installed in a

more permanent safe house, with false papers showing he was seventeen. Sephy was going to give him lessons so that if needed, he could take a state astrologer's post. Meanwhile the kid would be valuable as a messenger.

Mac put the drink down again and studied Collis more carefully. "So you didn't tell him," he realized.

Collis looked at the rug. "No," he said finally. "I didn't tell him that she'd escaped in the first place, so there was no need to…stir everything up for him."

Good call, thought Mac. He started to say it and then the restlessness overcame him again. Eight fifteen.

He went to the sofa and perched on its edge. He flipped through a magazine. All he could see was Sephy, sitting at a table with Pierce and Gunnison. In his mind's eye, Gunnison's face darkened at what Sephy had just told him – Pierce was glittering, devious.

Mac realized he'd been staring at the same page for several minutes. As part of his job, he sometimes had to look at photos of what had been done to prisoners.

If some future photo showed him Sephy, he would lose his mind.

The sofa cushion shifted as Collis sat beside him. "Hey, buddy, come on. Don't do this. Cards, okay?" He held up the deck and then shuffled. "Something brainless. Tick Tock, or—"

The disc went briefly silent between songs and Mac's head snapped up at the sound of footsteps outside. He jumped to his feet. Collis rose too, staring at the door.

The next song started: a wild rumba, pulsing through the air.

Was it Guns out there? *If they've caught her I don't even care any more whether they've come for me,* Mac thought.

The door opened and Sephy walked in. When she saw Mac, she stopped short. Her skin looked ashen.

She put her hands over her face and started to cry.

Mac rushed to her, banging his calf against the coffee table. Her purse had dropped to the floor. She was trembling. "Are you all right?" he asked urgently, smoothing her hair back with both hands.

"Yes…but, oh, Mac…"

The corridor was empty. Mac closed the door, got Sephy to the sofa. He drew her onto his lap and held her as she cried. "It doesn't matter, baby," he whispered against her warm neck, his eyes tightly shut. "Whatever happened doesn't matter; I don't care. You're all right, you're all right…"

Distantly, Mac felt Collis clasp his shoulder. The door shut as he let himself out.

At last Sephy raised her head. She just gazed at Mac. He stroked away her tears with his thumb.

"Mac…I've made it worse," she said hoarsely. "Kay Pierce took what I said and ran with it. The coup's now called the Day of Fire. It's still in Appalachia…and it's in just over five weeks."

Chapter Twenty-four

December, 1941

I woke up in a bed. I blinked groggily at the ceiling. Vague memories came of furtive voices – of being carried – of the low hum of an auto and the sight of dark trees whipping past.

I started at the sound of a door opening. A sturdy-looking guy with skin as olive as my own appeared at the side of my bed. He had surprising green eyes.

"You're awake," he said. He looked relieved, but there was a nervous energy about him; a sort of twitchiness just under the surface.

I swallowed hard. "I…yes."

"Don't worry, you're safe. You can call me Arvin. How are you doing? We got a doctor in. She said you'd be okay."

He spoke so quickly that it took me a moment to realize there'd been a question.

It was an effort to speak. "I'm not sure. Fuzzy."

"We've been giving you pills for the pain. You had a bad blow to the head, not to mention your gunshot wound. You've been out for almost two days. Do you need the doctor again?" He bit a fingernail. "That wouldn't be easy, but we could do it."

I had no idea if I needed the doctor again. The pain felt distant, held at bay. What bothered me more was the bed's softness. It seemed almost scary, as if I might sink too deeply into it and be smothered. To try to explain this felt exhausting, so I didn't try.

I could see that I was in a bedroom, not a hospital room. The photos on the walls showed a smiling family that looked nothing like Arvin.

He tapped a fist against one denim-clad thigh. "Don't tell me who you are," he said. "No names! We don't want to know. We've sent someone to put the word out that there's a message for Griffin, but things are difficult now. We're not sure if...well, we're trying our best."

The words were a flow of confusion that made my head hurt. "Who's we?" I asked in a mumble.

"You don't need to know any details. Just call me 'Arvin'." He shoved a hand through his hair and sighed, studying me.

"You better rest," he said. "I've got to go now. Someone will check on you later and bring some food."

I was drifting away again. "Wait," I got out. "How's Ingo? Where is he?"

But Arvin was gone.

I slept, but had fitful dreams, so that I felt harried and frightened even in my sleep. Heads stuck on a chain-link fence, sparkling with frost. Ingo's voice: *Hurry! Faster!* Hunger clawing at my stomach. A rat that lay half-eaten while Guns battered in the door.

I woke up with a gasp, breathing hard.

"You too?" murmured a voice.

I caught my breath fearfully – but the voice had been Ingo's. A small lamp was on; in its light I saw him in an armchair near the bed. He looked as if he'd been sleeping there. I stared at him, taking in his cleanliness – the freshness of his clothes. It seemed almost unbelievable.

"You didn't keep your promise," I said finally.

Ingo came over and sat beside me. "Yes, I did," he said. "I said I'd do it if it was time. It wasn't time. How are you?"

I licked dry lips. "Is there any water?"

"Here."

There was a full glass by my bedside. I drank almost all of it. When I sank against the pillows again, I studied Ingo's face. Apart from the cleanliness, there was something strange about it, and then it hit me: he'd shaved. At the same moment, I realized that my own hair was clean.

The sensation was overwhelmingly luxurious. Yet

somehow it was too much. I plucked at the sheets. I wanted to hide, to cry.

"Where are we?" I whispered.

"Above the Mayflower – the bar in Calgary that Miguel told me to find."

My eyes flew to his. "How?"

"The Resistance has spies up here; they listen in on the Guns' private talkie-waves. They knew escaped prisoners had stolen a plane. One of them saw us crash – they found us and picked us up. We were still seventy miles from Calgary; they brought us here when I asked."

The fear was deep, automatic. "Is it safe here? Are you positive?"

Ingo didn't hesitate. "No. I'm not positive. But I'm fairly sure. They got us medical care. Clothes. If they're really on Gunnison's side, it's the most roundabout way of turning us in imaginable." He offered a twisted smile. "Guns aren't known for subtlety."

I sat up a little; my leg gave an angry throb through the haze of pills. I lifted the covers and gazed down at myself. I had on a nightgown: an impossibly soft thing of pale blue. My left thigh was bandaged.

"Apparently the tourniquet was a good idea," said Ingo quietly. He gave a humourless laugh. "Just as well, since I had no fucking clue what else to do...you scared me, you know."

"I scared myself."

"The bullet went right through. The doctor said it

didn't hit the bone, though. You'll be okay, she said. You might have a limp."

I glanced at him as I pulled the covers back into place. "Were you there when she bandaged me up?"

Ingo nodded. "I wanted to know you were okay. You'd have done the same for me."

He was right.

Somewhere in the room a clock ticked, measuring out the seconds. "What's going on?" I asked apprehensively. "The guy I spoke to – Arvin – said things were difficult now, but that they'd sent someone to get word to Vince Griffin."

"Arvin? I haven't met him yet. I've hardly spoken to anyone. They seem scared; they don't want details."

"That's what Arvin was like."

Ingo rubbed tensely at his scar. "From what I can make out, this part of the Resistance has been cut adrift. They're scrambling a bit now. At least we're safe for the moment."

"Safe" seemed an alien concept. I could hear the faint sound of traffic. That seemed alien too. I gently touched the sheet, feeling its smooth softness.

"Did you show them the photos?" I said finally.

"No, I wanted to talk to you first. I think we should wait and show them to this Vince Griffin person – what about you?"

Recalling Arvin's fear, I nodded. "Yes, I agree." Dull despair stirred as I thought of the bomb factory...the smiling scientists...my father's actions to blame.

I talked him into… I mean, I talked to *Truce…*

My spine steeled. "A limp," I murmured, wondering if this would affect my ability to get to Madeline.

I glanced at Ingo. "But I'll walk, right? Did the doctor say when?"

He gave a small smile. "Knowing you, as soon as you decide to."

My gaze lingered on him. "You're so *clean*," I said. Ingo's dark eyebrows stood out starkly against his skin.

"So are you. Strange, isn't it?"

"And your clothes…" He had on tan trousers cinched with a belt around his too-thin waist; a white shirt as pristine as fresh paper. The fact that someone could wear a white shirt – could expect it not to get filthy, could actually *change* it every day – boggled the mind.

Ingo shrugged and gazed down at his large, thin hands. "One of them gave me pyjamas," he said. "They were too comfortable; I couldn't wear them. That sounds idiotic, doesn't it?"

"No. Are you all right?"

He gave a short laugh then, and I saw that he was feeling as disoriented as I was. "Oh, fine," he said. "My broken ribs didn't puncture a lung. My wound had reopened, but it's all stitched up now. I'm fine."

"You're not," I said softly.

The bed was a double. Ingo sighed and stretched out beside me, his movements halting, stiff.

"No. I'm not." He scraped a hand over his face. "That's

why I came in here. I couldn't sleep. Every time I closed my eyes..." He didn't finish.

"I needed to hear you breathing," he said, gazing at the ceiling. "I guess I've gotten used to it. These last few weeks, whenever I'd wake up and hear you breathing...I knew that at least we were both alive."

"I know," I murmured. "Me too." I was drifting off again.

"Do you want me to leave?"

"No. Stay. I'll sleep better too."

I closed my eyes. As I slipped away I was conscious of Ingo's lean form lying beside me. We weren't touching, but I could hear the rise and fall of his breath, and knew when it turned softly rhythmic.

This time there were no dreams.

My leg throbbed. I put the crutches aside and lowered myself gingerly to the rim of the tub. I gazed down at my body.

A basin of warm water and a sponge sat on a chair beside me. In the days that Ingo and I had been here, this was the first time I'd managed to bathe on my own, without one of the Resistance women helping me.

I'd gained a little weight and felt stronger, but my body still had no curves. My thighs were strange, skinny things. The left one had two dark, round holes that wept: one on the lower part of my inner thigh and the other just above the back of my knee. I could count my every rib. Apart from when Ingo and I had hastily changed our clothes, it was the first time I'd been wholly undressed since my induction at the camp.

Induction. Melody, with blood coursing down her thighs. Then months later, her wasted body rolling off the platform. The feel of her unresisting limbs as I'd lain over them to protect the boots from the other scavengers.

With a start, I realized the water in the basin had grown cold.

Little things struck me the most. Like the lampshade on my bedside table. It was yellow, with tassels hanging from it. Tassels. Such extravagance, just for a lampshade. And a delicate ballet dancer figurine, poised on eternal tiptoe. I spent long minutes gazing at it, marvelling at a life so safe that such things could exist.

I'd constantly dreamed of my old world while at Harmony Five, so why did everything feel so off-kilter now?

Arvin and the others assured us tensely that "wheels had been put in motion" about us. Ingo and I couldn't doubt their sincerity. They fed us and hid us – and seemed desperate for Vince Griffin to respond and take us off their hands.

We stayed in the small apartment, with the noise from the bar downstairs drifting up. We learned it was a

Resistance safe house. The door to the apartment stayed locked and no one entered who wasn't supposed to. Even depleted, the Resistance seemed more organized than I'd imagined.

I realized now that my wariness when Ingo first mentioned them was because Collie had made them sound so unreliable. But Collie was a liar. Maybe the Resistance's plan to bring down Gunnison was a good one. Maybe Ingo's message from Miguel about the Day of Three Suns – the names he'd been given, the information about the caterers being the way in – would mean they could really do it, if we reached Vince Griffin in time.

The hope was painful. Our information *had* to be successful.

The bed still felt too soft. I took painkillers and my bandages got changed and slowly the seeping red-black holes wept less. I tried to read but couldn't concentrate. How could Harmony Five and this cosy apartment exist in the same universe? Nothing seemed real.

The nuclear weapons haunted me. If Gunnison wasn't stopped, *millions* could be killed…and Dad had made it possible. At the thought, the thing I had refused to face since Harmony Five struggled to be heard.

My guts chilled. I buried it deep. *No.* I couldn't go there.

But Madeline had talked Dad into throwing that fight. And she'd be at the Day of Three Suns.

Two weeks after we'd arrived, I'd found a pistol in one

of the drawers in my bedroom. I'd stared down at it, leaning heavily on my crutches. Finally I'd picked the weapon up and weighed it in my hand. A box of cartridges lay beside it.

I'd stood holding the pistol for a long time before putting it away again.

A week later, as I sat in the green armchair with my leg propped up, trying to read, the moment came back. A tremor of disquiet went through me. I looked up as Ingo came in, relieved to see him.

"Look what Arvin brought," he said, holding up a guitar.

I mentally shut everything away and put the book aside. "Does he play?"

"No idea." Ingo sat on the floor near the bookcase and started to tune it, twiddling with the knobs. Twangy notes floated out as he plucked at the strings, testing. He looked better now – still too thin, but his face had lost its gaunt look.

It had been raining for days. Drops pattered against the windowpanes. "Do you actually know how to play that thing?" I asked.

"No, not really…how's the book?"

I shrugged. "Same as the others. I keep reading one page over and over."

"Try poetry."

"What?"

Ingo stopped tuning the guitar and studied the bookshelf. He selected a thin volume and tossed it to me. "Here," he said. "When I can't read anything else, I read poetry."

I flipped through the pages, reading snatches here and there. I'd only encountered poetry in school. I'd always preferred adventure stories and non-fiction books about flying.

"There's a poem about April," I said.

"See? April happens everywhere," said Ingo. "Even in Harmony Five." He glanced at me with a rueful smile. "That kept me going sometimes, thinking that," he said. "Maybe they could take away everything else, but they couldn't keep the world from bursting into spring… Okay, that sounds incredibly stupid, saying it out loud."

I thought of the hawk I used to watch. "No, it doesn't… this is nice," I said, scanning the poem. "Thanks," I added, looking up. "I think I might be able to read these."

Ingo struck a chord then and started to play. Under his long fingers, a tune drifted out from the guitar's strings. It reminded me of spring too. It was lightness and hope, with a plaintive undercurrent. I sat up a little, listening.

"Is that your idea of not being able to play?" I said when he'd finished. "When people ask, do you tell them you can't really fly airplanes, either?"

Ingo smiled and kept strumming, coaxing out another song. "You're not very musical, are you?" he said without rancour. "Seriously, I'm not that good. My brother Erich is the musician. Him and our mother."

"Well, Erich must be a genius then."

"Don't tell him that if you ever meet him. He's conceited enough already."

I hugged my good leg hard, remembering everything Ingo had said about his family. I knew I'd never see my own family again – I hoped Vince Griffin could help Ingo get home to his.

"Tell me more about them," I said softly. "Erich and the others."

He glanced up. "Like what?"

"Anything. Erich is a musician and so's your mother. You said your sister Lena can sing… What about you, actually? What do you do?"

He smiled slightly. "You mean apart from flying Firedoves and playing guitar very badly?"

"Yes. Apart from flying Firedoves and playing guitar very badly."

I thought he wasn't going to answer at first. He studied the guitar, his fingers still moving across the strings. "The vineyard," he said. "I help out on it…well, we all do; it's a family thing. But I'm the one who actually likes it. I think…" Ingo trailed off. He stopped playing.

Tapping the side of the guitar, he said, "I think Dad hoped that I'd run it someday. Erich has no interest; he's studying to be a lawyer. And Lena would never want to stay in one place long enough."

"But you would?"

"Yes. I love the vineyard," he said. "I love our home there. My idea of heaven would be to just watch the seasons shift over those fields for the next fifty years...ah, hell."

He started playing again, something quick, almost angry, and I knew he was remembering that his family probably thought him dead.

"Why did you become a Peacefighter?" I asked finally. "I mean, why did you leave?"

"I've been asking myself that question for the last three years." Ingo put the guitar aside; he dropped his head back against the wall. "It was Lena," he said wryly. "My sister hates being bored. She was always getting me into trouble, growing up. And our village..."

My thigh throbbed; I shifted on the chair. "What's it called?"

"Calliposa. About forty miles from Florence. It's tiny; a bread van comes twice a week and that's the most exciting thing ever. It's up on a hill. Lots of olive trees. You can see vineyards in every direction...on a clear day, the Med to the west."

"It sounds beautiful," I said wistfully, imagining it.

"It is. Well, *I* think so. Lena always wanted to travel, though – to see the world. Our whole area is actually a big Peacefighting place. Lots of EA pilots are from there." Ingo snorted slightly. "Even our name. Manfred. It means 'peace warrior' in Germanic."

"Really?" My smile felt bitter. "That's my name too. Amity for peace, and Louise for warrior."

There was a silence. I looked down, thinking of the World for Peace flag in the Western Seaboard base. How it had made me feel to gaze upon it each morning and know that I was protecting the world from war.

I felt like such a fool.

Finally Ingo shrugged. "It meant something once. Maybe it still will, someday. Shall I go on?"

"Yes, I want to hear."

"All right, so Lena got a bug in her ear about becoming a Peacefighter, and she got me and a few of our friends to apply with her. I don't actually know what I was thinking, to be honest. I was barely eighteen and had just spent four years in boarding school, only coming home for holidays—"

"New Manhattan," I said.

Ingo's good eyebrow shot up. "How did you know?"

"Memory like a steel trap, remember? At The Ivy Room that time, you told me your mother was from New Manhattan and that you'd gone to school there."

"Ah, yes." He gave me an evil smile. "You'd commented on my excellent English for a foreigner."

The Heat was neutral territory. I'd felt like an idiot the moment I'd said it.

"You knew exactly what I meant, you louse," I said. "How was I supposed to know that you've been speaking it your whole life?"

"I'll forgive you. Anyway, all I wanted was to stay at

home and help with the vineyard, but Lena kept asking, and…I got swept away. It felt like a lark, an adventure."

"So what happened?"

Ingo made a face. "Guess. None of the others got into training school. Lena and our friends all went home, and I stayed – the only one who hadn't wanted to do it in the first place. But to admit to that felt too feeble for words, so I ended up going on and making it as a pilot. I've been homesick every day since."

He plucked a discordant note on the guitar; it hovered in the air. "So there you have it: my youthful stupidity."

"You love flying though," I said. "I mean, you must, the way you fly."

"Yes, I do love it," Ingo admitted. "And…I believed that Peacefighting was important. Noble, even. The problem is, I'm not particularly noble."

I understood now why he'd been so upset to learn about the corruption. "You're fairly noble," I said after a pause. "You saved my life, if you don't remember."

"Against your will."

"That probably makes it even more noble, doesn't it? Hauling my resisting carcass across however many miles?"

"Knock it off with the 'noble', Amity. It was entirely selfish; you're my only friend for about ten thousand miles and I like your company. All right, your turn. The Peacefighting story, please."

Stalling, I said, "Small talk again?" The night we'd first met, I'd asked him how he became a Peacefighter, and he'd fielded the question by saying we didn't want to have small talk.

"Only it's not small talk at all, which is why neither of us wanted to tell it before." Ingo picked up the guitar again and strummed a dramatic chord. "Go on. Amity Vancour became a Peacefighter because..."

I felt myself go tense. I played with the cane that sat propped beside the chair – I found it easier to use than crutches now.

"Maybe later," I said. "You're right, it's not small talk. I'm not really in the mood."

Ingo glanced up quickly. "I've upset you," he said. "I'm sorry."

I cleared my throat. "No, it's not your fault. If I told anyone, it'd be you. But...not right now, okay?"

He nodded. As he started playing again, I thought of the reasons I had longed to become a Peacefighter, and wondered dully why I couldn't cry any more.

I reached for the cane and got up from the chair. I stumped my way over to Ingo, wincing, and settled on the floor beside him, lowering myself awkwardly with one hand.

"No need to rupture yourself. I'm fine with you not telling me," said Ingo dryly.

"I know." We sat in silence as he played. "Am I really your only friend for ten thousand miles?" I asked.

"Who the hell told you that?"

"In the Heat you seemed to have dozens of friends. All those EA pilots you palled around with."

Ingo shrugged and plucked out another tune. "Do *you* have dozens of people you consider real friends?"

I saw his point. "No. Okay, you're right."

"Call me old-fashioned, but to me a friend is someone you're willing to half-carry for over a mile with Guns after you…so, by that definition, you're the only one on the continent, sweetheart."

Though he weighed the endearment heavily with irony, his use of it made me think of Miriam. Apparently I wasn't alone. Ingo looked down, his fingers growing still on the chords.

"This isn't a come-on in any way," he said finally. "But I'm starting to think that being friends with someone should be a prerequisite to…everything else." He glanced up, his dark gaze level. "You've never asked me exactly how it happened. My face, I mean."

I swallowed, wondering how that was connected to Miriam, and managed not to flick a glance at his ruined skin. "I guess I thought you'd tell me if you ever wanted me to know."

Ingo put the guitar aside but was silent for so long that I thought he'd changed his mind. Finally he said, "Three days after you and I broke into the World for Peace building, I had a Peacefight against Oceania. At first everything was normal. It was above the Holy Hills."

I winced, and he saw. "What?" he said sharply.

"That's where mine was," I said. "When my plane was sabotaged."

"Oh, wonderful." He gave a short laugh. "Nice and isolated, I guess… Oh, *fuck*, why does that make it worse somehow?"

"Go on," I said.

His shoulders were tense. "How did yours happen? Amity, please don't tell me that a wing blew off when you—"

"When I tried to fire. Yes." I cleared my throat. "So they knew you'd been with me then. They'd seen us together in the Heat that night."

"Yes, they knew."

"The only reason I survived was that I took the wrong parachute – the straps of my own had been cut. What about yours?"

Ingo shook his head. "My chute was fine. I don't think they wanted to kill me. It was a warning – a show of power. What they wanted was information about *you*. I didn't know that until later, though. I…"

He took a deep breath. In a monotone, he said, "My plane went into a spin. I bailed. The other Dove just…flew away. What was left of my plane crashed on the ground, right in the middle of that ancient arena – you know where I mean?"

I nodded. Oh, I knew.

"I tried to steer the chute away, but there was a strong wind. I landed too close, and then the plane exploded." He fell silent, his fists tight. "My, um…my helmet had a loose strap," he said finally. "I'd been meaning to get it fixed for days. It came right off my head in the blast. Then something hit me; I was knocked out. When I came to, I could smell myself burning."

Silence settled. There was only the rain, and the faint sound of the bar downstairs. I wanted to touch him, squeeze his fingers, but felt frozen.

"My face," Ingo finished. "I'd been hit by a burning piece of engine. My hair was on fire. My skin smelled like meat cooking." He swallowed. "It didn't hurt, that was the strange thing. I panicked. I rolled on the grass, got the fire out – all I could think of was that they knew. I could hear more planes approaching, so I ran."

He explained that he'd hidden on the road near the arena for hours, his face hurting now, but not so badly that he'd thought he was seriously injured. Finally a truck had passed by; he'd taken a chance and swung himself onto the back of it. He'd crouched unseen between some crates. The truck took him right into the Heat.

"I think I was half-crazy by then," Ingo said softly. "All I could think of was getting to Miriam. If she knew that I'd stolen the keys to the World for Peace building from her father, I had to try to explain it to her. I didn't want her to think that I'd betray her family on a whim..."

Ingo looked down. "My family is very important to me," he said finally.

I swallowed. "I know."

"I missed them a lot when I first got to the base. I still do. Then Miri and I met at a party one night and started seeing each other...and her family were good to me, you know? Always having me round for dinner. Her father and I would debate politics, and she had a little brother who I'd play chess with..." Ingo sighed. "Remember we talked that time about loving and liking? I'm starting to realize that Miri's family was the only thing I really *liked* about her."

He tipped his head back against the wall, studying the ceiling. "But I loved her. No, I was *besotted* by her. I'd had girlfriends before, but I'd never fallen so hard for anyone. I'm not even sure why, now. I thought she was beautiful, of course, and exciting... I don't know. She was all I could think about. Even when she was making my life hell, I couldn't walk away."

"You didn't seem very happy with her," I ventured. I was remembering Miriam ignoring Ingo the night of his peak day celebration, when he'd just completed half his three-year Peacefighting term. He'd told me later that she'd done it because she liked playing games.

"No. I wasn't. But I was *in love,* you see, so that was all right. Maybe I thought all the agony was purifying." His mouth twitched. "You called her a bitch once, remember? The second time we met. Lena thought the same."

I hugged my good knee to my chest. "She met her?"

"No. It was from things I said in my letters home. Or rather, things I didn't say. Lena would mention meeting Miri someday and I'd never respond." He looked down at the guitar and plucked a string.

"The thought of ever introducing Miri to my family gave me cold shudders," he said. "They know when I'm really happy and when I'm just putting on a front. And Miri was always making these little barbs that were supposed to be jokes..." He gave a quick, angry grimace.

"Anyway. Lena called me up on base and made me tell her the truth. I've never been able to lie very convincingly to my sister. She told me that Miriam was a spoiled, bored little rich girl who was just playing with me, and I should dump her. I told her to go to hell. Very enjoyable."

"I like the sound of Lena more and more," I said. "She was just worried about you."

"I think you two would get on very well, actually. And yes, I know. We made it up later. But I was still angry that she didn't see how perfect Miri was for me, despite everything."

Ingo gave a short, bitter laugh. He rubbed his forehead. "You know, I'm sitting here and I'm saying these words to you," he said in an undertone, "and part of me still can't believe that I ever thought them. But I did."

I hesitated. "What happened after your crash?"

"I went to Miri's house. It was dark by then; I don't think anyone saw me. There was a broken latch on her bedroom window. She left it broken so that I could get in without waking her parents late at night." He went quiet.

Finally he said, "My face still didn't really hurt much. But I felt very strange. Once I got into Miri's room, I didn't look in the mirror. Maybe I was afraid to. I could hear her in the bathroom, getting ready for bed. And when she came into the room…and saw me…" He stopped.

I sat tensely silent. Ingo took a breath.

"She screamed," he said. "I went to her. I tried to explain about the keys, the corruption…I told her I loved her. She backed away. She was horrified."

I hated having to defend Miriam, but said softly, "Anyone might have been startled at first, Ingo."

He sat with his wrists dangling loosely over his knees, gazing at the ceiling. "No, it was more than that. She was…revolted. I saw it in her eyes. She told me to leave."

I stared at his melted-wax profile, trying to picture what his injury must have looked like only hours after it had happened – how desperately he must have needed medical attention. "She told you to *leave*?"

"Yes. I was so stunned that I did. The World for Peace security picked me up not long after that. They took me in for questioning. They knew about the keys. They told me that they had you – that you'd blamed everything on me."

"They told me the same thing about you," I said.

"Standard ploy, I guess. I believed it then, because the alternative…" He grimaced. "But then at Harmony Five, I knew you weren't lying. You hadn't talked. I guess on some level I'd realized it all along. Even if someone saw us breaking in, they couldn't have known all the details the Guns came out with. Miri must have told them everything."

Ingo picked up the guitar again, but didn't play it.

"You know, when I saw the disgust in her eyes, it killed

whatever I'd felt for her," he said at last. "I never would have believed it, but it's true. It just ended, like turning off a tap. Maybe it was never really love. But at the camp...it still hurt to realize that she'd turned me in."

Pain stirred. I nodded. I knew exactly how he'd felt.

After a pause, Ingo glanced at me. "Did you believe it? What they told you about me?"

"Not really," I said. "I wasn't sure, but I didn't think you'd betray me."

"You hardly knew me at that point. Do you make a habit of trusting strange men who give you champagne in clubs?"

"No. But I thought I could trust you."

"Why?"

I considered for a moment. "Because of the way you fight," I said finally. "And because of the time when you shot me down and then cared about whether or not I bailed. We seemed to...feel the same way about Peacefighting."

Ingo had listened intently; now he gave a soft, bitter laugh. "So a stranger who I'd known for about five hours had me pegged better than my girlfriend of ten months. Why does this not surprise me?"

I studied him. "Do you think that's why she talked? Because she thought you'd betrayed the World for Peace?"

"I'm sure that's what she told herself," said Ingo curtly. "But no – I think she talked because half my face had been burned to a crisp."

At my expression, he gave a bitter shrug. "Look, maybe I wasn't a male model before, but some women found me attractive. Miri was one of them. If I'd emerged from that crash unscathed, she'd have listened. She liked drama. It excited her. We'd probably have ended up in bed before I'd even finished the story. But a half-burned horror who made her recoil in revulsion? No."

I didn't speak. After a moment Ingo glanced at me. "Thank you for not denying what I look like," he said in a low voice.

When we'd first met, I'd have said Ingo was "offbeat" rather than handsome. For me, his long face was too angular, his mouth too thin and wry, to be really good-looking. But there'd been something appealing about his lean, mobile features – the way his dark eyes lit up as he talked. They still did sometimes, despite the broad, puckered scar that pulled so harshly at his skin.

"I'm used to what you look like," I said softly.

"Really? I'm not." Ingo strummed the guitar for a few moments, not really playing, just teasing at chords. "You know, I've been looking in the mirror a lot since we got here," he said finally. "I hadn't really seen my face since just after it happened. Horrific, isn't it?"

He said it matter-of-factly. I winced but tried not to show it.

"When you first see it, maybe," I said. "I hardly think about it now." I hesitated. "Does it hurt?"

"No. I don't feel much of anything from here to here."

As he spoke, Ingo pointed first at his forehead and then his jaw. He kept strumming, his dark head down. "Well, I'll get used to it too, at some point," he said. "I haven't got much choice, unless I want to be depressed every time I look in a mirror."

"I'm sorry," I said.

Ingo's head snapped up; his almost-black eyes flashed with irritation. "Oh, to hell with that. I don't need your pity, Amity."

"I know you don't. I mean, I'm sorry because it's partly my fault, isn't it? If I hadn't asked you to help me, it wouldn't have happened."

"Ah, and then I could still be wallowing in happy ignorance, is that it? Please give me some credit. I knew it was dangerous when I said yes."

"I didn't tell you *how* dangerous," I said in a low voice. "I deliberately didn't tell you that they'd just tried to kill me, so that you'd help."

Ingo already knew this. He shrugged. "All right. Thanks for the apology," he said finally. He was playing something light now, jazzy. "But there's no need. You wouldn't have done anything differently if you'd known and neither would I, probably. I had to know the truth, even if I hated it." His mouth quirked ruefully. "I've always been irritating that way."

I studied him, remembering that he was one of the few Peacefighters I'd ever met who had read the papers. Who, like me, had wanted to know what he was fighting for.

"Well, there's a bright side," I said. "You're not stuck with Miriam the bitch any more."

To my relief, Ingo gave a bark of laughter. He shot me a grin.

"Amazing," he said. "Every cloud really *does* have a silver lining."

It had stopped raining and sunlight was angling in through the window. I fiddled with my cane. "You know," I said, "when we were at the mining office...and the Guns were about to break in..."

Ingo stopped playing, watching me.

The words came haltingly. "I thought...that you'd be a good person to die with. It felt so lonely, thinking of it happening alone. Sometimes even with other people around, I still feel lonely. Not with you."

"Irritated sometimes," said Ingo after a pause. "Wanting to kick me sometimes."

"Yes to both. But never lonely."

Ingo smiled. "Thanks," he said quietly. "You too, for me." He kept plucking at the strings, the same jazzy tune as before – light, but with discordant elements, like sunshine and shadow.

"That's nice," I said. "What is it?"

"Nothing; I'm just making it up. Can I ask you another intrusive question, since the Peacefighting story is off limits?"

I tensed, suddenly apprehensive. "Collie?"

Ingo's fingers kept strumming. "Don't tell me if you

don't want. Total trust doesn't mean you have to tell me things that are none of my damn business."

"It's okay," I said. I tried to smile. "You told me yours, I'll tell you mine."

Chapter Twenty-five

March, 1941

COLLIE HAD BEEN GONE FOR over ten hours.

I paced our Topeka hotel room, rubbing my arms and telling myself over and over that everything was fine. Of course it was. It had to be.

I crossed to the window again and stared out at the city streets. The stark white domes of the Zodiac dominated the view. Shadowcars occasionally cruised past. I stood watching out for their high, rounded lines, as sickly mesmerized as if they'd been sharks.

Collie, where are you?

This morning he'd checked to make sure the *Do Not Disturb* sign was still hooked onto the outside of our door. "The maids shouldn't come in," he said. "But keep the security bolt on anyway. Don't open the door unless it's me."

I'd nodded tensely. "How long will you be?"

"I don't know. I'm supposed to meet the Resistance contact at a coffee shop to discuss the next move... hopefully it won't take very long." He was wearing the blue second-hand suit he'd bought in the Western Seaboard. I watched as he gazed at himself in the mirror, knotting his tie with fingers that didn't falter.

Collie was the best friend of my childhood – and now, for months, we'd been as intimate as it was possible for two people to be. Yet there was still so much of his history that I didn't know. *Soon,* I told myself. He'd promised to tell me everything as soon as we escaped this place.

Still at the window, I started at a knock. I froze, alert as a deer. I wanted to sprint to the door; I forced myself to tiptoe. I pressed my cheek against the smooth wood and gazed out of the peephole.

"It's me," whispered Collie, just as I saw his face.

Relief rushed through me. I threw open the door; he hurried in and I flung myself into his arms. He lifted me off the floor.

"I'm sorry!" he gasped. "It took for ever – they drove me to a little town out in the middle of nowhere to meet this other guy, and at first he didn't show up—"

"Are you all right?"

"Yes, fine."

"What did they say?"

Collie took off his fedora and jacket; he threw them onto the bed and sank into the plush armchair. I sat on his lap and he hugged me close, burrowing his face against my neck.

"They're going to help us," he murmured.

Yes. I let out a ragged breath. "When?"

"Tonight. Late. I'm to go to the Zodiac to meet one of them, and they'll have the documents for me. There's a party or something."

I stared at him. "Just like that?"

He shrugged tensely. "I didn't ask for details, Amity. That's a good way to get killed with these people. One of them must be a high-up with Gunnison, or have access to someone who is."

I didn't glance out at those pure white domes again, crowding out the rest of the skyline – but could almost feel them behind me, as if they were watching us. "Do you trust these people?" I said.

"Kind of late not to." At my expression, Collie rubbed my arm. "Don't worry. Yes, I think so. If they were with Gunnison, I'd have been arrested last night when I told them what we know. Guns don't bother to play coy."

At the reminder of his meeting the night before, disquiet filled me again. Before I could say anything, he went on: "Listen – the Resistance had no idea what those documents Gunnison's been waving around really said. Now we're offering to smuggle them out of the country and release them to the world. Don't worry, they'll come through tonight. They'd do anything to overthrow him."

I wanted to feel wholly relieved, but couldn't, not while we were still here. "What about Hal?" I said after a moment.

Appalachia was the only place we could escape to once we had the documents – but my brother would still be in hiding in the Western Quarter. I was desperate for Collie's contacts to help him, too, if they could.

Collie was taking off his tie; he paused. "Hal?"

"Can they do anything? Get him out somehow?"

An expression very like guilt flickered through Collie's blue-green eyes.

I slid off his lap. "You didn't even *ask*? Collie—"

"I *did* ask!" He jumped up and gripped my shoulders. "It's just…they're not sure. They'll do what they can. But, Amity, if they can't help him, we still have to go. You realize that, don't you?" He studied my face anxiously.

My throat felt full of sand. "Yes," I said at last.

He put his arms around me. I stood stiffly, heartsick at the thought of Hal. But no matter what, we'd be helping him by releasing those documents. I sighed and relaxed against Collie. His embrace tightened: warm, familiar.

"We'll be all right," he whispered against my hair. "It's almost over…just a few more hours."

* * *

We spent the rest of the evening not talking about what lay ahead. We took a bath together, with music from the telio playing in the background. Van Wheeler had a new song out, "For Ever and a Day". Like his others, I didn't like it, exactly – but once you'd heard it you couldn't stop humming it. I lay in Collie's arms in the warm, soapy water and longed for it to be the next day, when with luck we'd be in Appalachia.

Darkness fell. Finally, near midnight, it was time. Collie got dressed again and combed his hair back. He took my hands tightly in his. "I hope this won't take long, but try not to worry if it does," he said. "Get packed while I'm gone, all right? The second I'm back, we're making a run for it."

"Thank you for doing this," I said in a low voice.

"Hey, I already told you—"

"No, I *do* have to thank you," I broke in. "Collie, this means everything to me. It's not just about getting those documents out to the world. It's...it's to do with Dad."

Collie went still, his eyes locked on mine.

I spoke haltingly, struggling to articulate what I hadn't put into words before, not even to myself. "I'd give anything to understand why he threw that fight," I said. "I'll never know. But...maybe I can undo some of what he did. I feel like I'll never be able to think about him again without part of me hating him until I do. Never find any peace."

I touched Collie's face. "So thank you," I whispered. "I need this."

For a flicker, Collie's expression turned complicated: pity, anger, something else I couldn't define.

Then he smiled slightly, though it didn't reach his eyes. He picked up his fedora from the dresser. "I know you do," he said. "I love you. I'll be back as soon as I can."

After Collie left, the hotel room felt twice as large, yet claustrophobic, its silent walls pressing in on me. Glad of something to do, I moved quickly around it, picking up our things. Collie had mostly packed already, but one of his shirts was on the bed, and a pair of his cufflinks lay on the dresser.

Our second-hand cases sat on a stand, Collie's on top. I undid the clasps. He was a lot tidier than I was. Inside, his shirts and trousers were arranged as neatly as if they were in a shop. I hastily folded the stray shirt and added it.

The cufflinks had a box; I remembered seeing it. There was no sign of it in the room. I delved into the suitcase, holding the folded clothes to one side. I could feel a piece of paper, but no box.

My spine stiffened at a rustling noise. I spun where I stood. A letter had appeared, slid under the bedroom door.

I gazed at the unmarked envelope in apprehension, listening to footsteps retreat back down the corridor. I pushed my fear away and quickly went over and picked it up.

When I drew out the folded sheet of paper, its letterhead

read, "Royal Archer Hotel". It was just a receipt for the room, made out to Mr Collis Reed. I sagged and started to put it in the suitcase – and then stiffened.

Underneath the amount we owed for the night before was written, *Charged to Zodiac expense account as requested.*

I stared at the receipt. The words made no sense. The management had made a mistake – confused Collie's bill with someone else's.

I remembered my hand brushing that other piece of paper in his suitcase. Slowly, an emotion I didn't yet understand stirring through me, I found it and pulled it out. Another receipt for the first night we'd stayed, identical to this one.

At the bottom, another note saying the same thing.

A Zodiac expense account. It wasn't possible. My gaze flew to the bulging envelope in Collie's case where he kept the money he'd been paid for the fixed Tier One fight.

"No," I whispered. Collie wouldn't throw a fight.

Would he?

My hands were cold. Suddenly I knew exactly why his meeting yesterday had bothered me so much. I'd been hiding in the car. Would Collie really have chosen an initial meeting with the Resistance then, when it might have been a trap? He would never have left me in such a vulnerable position.

He hadn't been worried.

Whoever he'd met with, he'd had no concerns about doing so. In fact, the only time he'd seemed really tense was when he smuggled me up the stairwell. He was *unhappy*, yes – but nothing like a man who'd barely escaped this region and now feared for his life.

Had he been meeting with the Resistance at all?

Only a few minutes had passed since he left. I went to the window, pushed the curtain aside.

The twelve white domes of the Zodiac shone against the stars. Below, the sidewalk was lit from flashing signs – regular pools of street lights.

As I watched, Collie walked through one, heading for the Zodiac. I recognized him even from above. He had his hands in his pockets, head slightly down. He was nearly at the complex now. Just before he faded from view, he turned down a side street and was gone.

Amity...there's a lot you don't know.

It felt as if I could barely breathe. I'd thought he meant the things that had happened to him while he lived here. Things to do with the fact that he was Discordant.

The money. Hal. The look of guilt I'd seen flickering in his gaze.

The documents.

I dropped the curtain and flung off my hotel bathrobe. I dressed in a quick scramble, throwing on my trousers and leather flight jacket; they were both dark colours. There was a woollen cap in my jacket pocket. I shoved my hair up under it.

I went to the hotel room door and listened. Silence. I undid the lock and slipped out into the corridor. I made for the stairwell and ran down the steps. When I emerged outside I took the same street I'd seen Collie on, my hands painful fists in my pockets.

Collie, please, this cannot be true.

The city at night throbbed in a blur of neon and blinking lights. Up ahead, the closest domes of the Zodiac loomed in my vision. I started to jog, dodging pedestrians. My footsteps chopped through me, until suddenly the domes were right there, across the street.

I stopped, breathing hard, and glanced to my right. Was this the cross-street Collie had taken? It was shadowy, leading to offices that were dark now.

Part of the Zodiac stretched right across a street: a graceful bridge called the Ascendant, enclosed in glass, connecting two domes. Gunnison often gave press statements from there; I'd seen it on the telio. Now the bridge was gently lit…and as two figures appeared within it, my sudden gasp caught in my throat.

Collie. He was walking with Gunnison; I could see them both clearly. They stopped halfway across. Collie had a thick folder under his arm; Gunnison motioned to it and seemed to be asking a question. Collie nodded as he replied, his expression earnest. Then he raised an eyebrow and grinned – the same easy smile I'd seen a thousand times.

Gunnison threw his head back and laughed. He clapped Collie on the shoulder, then turned and retraced his steps into the capitol. He looked as if he were whistling. Collie continued across the bridge, his smile gone now.

The night air prickled coldly as I watched. It felt as if the world had just shifted on its axis and I'd never be warm again.

Up above, Collie vanished from view. I waited, but he didn't appear at street level. He had to be still inside the complex somewhere. I darted to the side door of the building that the bridge connected to. It opened. I edged inside and shut the door softly after me.

I was in a long ornate corridor lined with windows. A curving staircase with wrought-iron banisters led upwards; another led down. A small light shone over an oil painting of Gunnison that hung on the wall.

Footsteps.

I tensed, then realized they were coming from the downwards staircase, already fading from my hearing. *Collie.*

I slipped quickly down the stairs: broad grey marble, each worn gently at the centre. At the bottom was another long corridor, this one more utilitarian. Doors. Which one?

I crept down the hallway, listening hard – and then saw a door partly open at the end. As I neared it I saw an orange glow reflected on its surface.

I reached the doorway and looked inside. A furnace room. A rabbit-warren of pipes led upwards from the furnace's broad iron belly. Its door was open and a fire burned within.

Collie stood beside it, prodding at the flames with a poker. An empty folder lay on the floor.

"*No!*" The word tore out of me.

He spun round, his face a mask of surprise. With a cry I raced to the furnace, but the papers were already gone: red, fragmented ghosts, wavering with heat. Briefly, I could make out Russ's datebook, with all its incriminating comments. Then it too collapsed into the flames and melted into nothing.

Collie stood motionless, his expression slack, the poker held limply at his side. The only sound was the crackling of the flames. Their light played on his cheekbones.

"What have you done?" I whispered raggedly. "Who *are* you?"

His face was grey. "Amity…please, listen…"

I turned and ran, because if I'd stayed I might have killed him. Down the hallway, up the stairs. He caught up with me before I reached the door, grabbing my arm and spinning me towards him.

"Let *go* of me!" I cried.

"No! You have to listen!" He pulled me into an empty room and clutched my shoulders. "We couldn't have won anyway!" he said fiercely. "You never got that, you never *would* get that! This was the only way I could make sure we'd ever have a future—"

"A *future?*" I jerked away. "What about Hal? What about *his* future? You threw that Tier One fight, didn't you?"

Collie's eyes were wide, startled. He started to speak and stopped.

"Why aren't you denying it?" I spat. "You can't, can you? You threw the fight that gave Gunnison extradition rights! You put my brother into hiding!"

He threw his hat onto a table. His voice rose to a whispered shout. "*I had to!* They'd have shot me like Russ otherwise! But, Amity, I swear to you, I didn't know what the fight was for."

"You knew it was a Tier One! You knew its outcome would affect millions of people! *Why?* Why would you help Gunnison, after—"

"If I hadn't thrown it, someone else would have," he broke in tightly.

I stood staring at the man I'd thought I knew better than myself. "All that time you spent stalling me, telling me that Mac was checking on things…nothing was happening, was it?"

His cheeks reddened.

"*Was it?*" I shouted. "You just didn't want me to find out what was really going on! People were being taken into custody. *Clem* was taken. And now you've left my brother to rot!"

"Don't you dare judge me, Amity – Hal's practically my brother too. Do you think I don't care? I was trying to *protect* you!"

My heart was shattered glass. All those thousands of people in hiding, in correction camps. The world's only chance to get rid of Gunnison, burned away to ash. Just as painful was Collie pretending to help and lying to me all along. He'd thrown a *Tier One.*

Just like my father.

"I saw you with Gunnison," I said finally, my voice dead. "You're more than just a crooked pilot – you're the high-up who was able to get the documents. Who exactly are you, Collis?"

He slumped against a table and rubbed his forehead. "There's no time," he whispered. "Look, let's…let's go get the auto and get away from here, and then—"

I gasped out a laugh. "Do you actually still think I'm going to *leave* with you?"

"Yes! You need me, if you're going to escape this country." He gripped my hands; his fingers felt hot, fervent. "Listen to me. No matter what I've done, *I love you*. I can explain everything. We can still—"

I pulled slowly away, staring at him.

I turned and walked from the room.

CHAPTER TWENTY-SIX

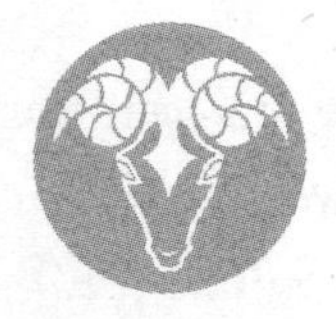

JANUARY, 1942

AFTER ALMOST FIVE WEEKS IN the Resistance safe house, Ingo and I had become very used to the noises from the bar below. Our time was measured by its opening hours. Mornings were quiet, with no one downstairs except Arvin and Katrina, his wife. It was all right then for us to move around, for Ingo to play his guitar, for us to talk and flush the toilet and not worry about the scrape of furniture on the floor.

At noon, that all stopped. The first customers started arriving, wanting lunch and beer. The bar wasn't noisy enough then to cover our own noise, so afternoons were our quiet times. Ingo and I played games a lot, for want of anything else to do. He taught me chess and I taught him poker, though it wasn't any good with only two people.

"You can use it later," I told him. "Poker is a life skill."

"Yes, if we ever get out of here and have a life," Ingo said.

Both of us were restless, sick of waiting. It didn't help that I was so frustrated with my leg.

Even with the cane, walking sent jolts of weakness and pain through me – two major muscles had been damaged. I was supposed to exercise and did so grimly, promising myself that I'd become fully mobile again.

And soon. I had to be. Vince Griffin would know where the Day of Three Suns was being held from Ingo's information.

Wherever it was, Madeline would be there.

"You won't make your leg better by sheer force of will, you know," said Ingo, playing guitar as I limped up and down the small room, wincing.

"I refuse to believe that," I said. I wasn't sure whether I was kidding.

"Refuse away," Ingo said without looking up. "But if you collapse, I'm not carrying you this time."

"Of course you will. I'm your only friend for ten thousand miles."

"Don't push it," he said.

Ingo was frustrated too. Each night, when the bar was finally in full swing below, he played angry-sounding songs on the guitar, his tension clear with every chord. His music suited my mood. If Gunnison took over the entire continent...

No. We *had to* reach Vince Griffin in time to bring Gunnison down.

The hope hurt. I swung from thinking that ending the regime would be all that mattered, to needing Madeline's answers more desperately than ever.

Harmony Five never left me. It's barbed wire and too-thin inmates haunted my dreams. I knew it must be the same for Ingo, though we rarely discussed it. Somewhere deep down, my pain over Dad – the fact I could never bear to face about his thrown fight – felt even larger, colder than before.

The photos from the bomb factory were seared on my brain.

Madeline taunted me. She'd somehow convinced my father to put that man in power. Occasionally I found myself opening the drawer with the pistol in it, checking that it was still there – that it still had cartridges.

I told myself I had no idea why I wanted to know this.

We'd done it – we'd escaped. Yet a deep bitterness had taken hold of me. I wasn't sure whether the catalyst was discovering the nuclear weapons, or revisiting what had happened with Collie.

I'd told Ingo everything...including what Collie did when I was arrested.

After I'd finished talking, there'd been silence. We were still sitting against the wall. I'd gazed at the window opposite, not wanting to see whatever was in Ingo's eyes. There was a birch tree, and a street light. One of the tree's pale branches had kept brushing gently against the top of the street light, as if trying to catch its attention.

Finally I looked at Ingo, sitting beside me with his long legs stretched out. He seemed shocked, staring out the window.

He glanced over. A rueful smile creased the good half of his face. "Congratulations," he said. "Your ex sounds even worse than mine."

I gave a short laugh of surprise. "Why doesn't winning that particular competition make me feel any better?"

"Sorry. Just a statement of fact. I could try for some reassuring words instead, if you'd prefer."

"Don't bother. I don't think any words exist that could be reassuring enough."

Ingo dropped his head back against the wall. "I can't believe he destroyed the evidence." He murmured something in Germanic, then added, "He never had any intention of releasing it, did he?"

"No." I gazed out at the birch again. I cleared my throat. "One thing that's confused me since Harmony Five…Collie had a tattoo." I touched the Aries glyph on my palm. "Right here. The sign for Leo, just like yours."

Ingo's spine straightened. "He was in a *camp*?"

"I don't know. I suppose so. He never mentioned it." Bitterly, I added, "He never mentioned all kinds of things."

"But if he was in a camp, he was Discordant. How did he—"

"I don't know," I repeated. I shook my head tiredly. "I don't know any of it, Ingo. All I know is what I told you."

"We should get him and Miri together," said Ingo finally. "They sound like each other's type."

The awful thing was, they did. I made a face. "At least this proves astrology is a crock, if we needed it proved," I said. "You're a Leo too. The two of you couldn't be more different."

"I'll take that as a compliment."

"It's meant as one."

Ingo picked up the guitar again and started to strum. The tune was soft, contemplative. "Well, it's just like I said the first time we met."

"You said a lot of things."

He gave me a dry look. "In particular, on the subject of your boyfriend and my girlfriend, I suggested that there might be something wrong with us – remember?"

"With *us*?"

"Yes, us, lady. And now I know exactly what it is. We have terrible taste in the opposite sex."

I snorted; it turned into a grudging laugh. "All right, you have a point."

"Next time we'll know better." Ingo hit a wrong chord, started again. Then he grimaced. "Though if I find someone who doesn't mind this mug of mine, she'd have to be insane. So it doesn't bode well right from the start."

"You're not so bad," I said after a pause. "And there's more to life than looks."

"Ah, immortal words," he murmured. "True, there's always my devastating wit. And my terrible guitar playing."

"Stop it," I said softly, and he gave me a surprised look and did.

A silence fell, filled only by his playing. I sat listening, my good leg pulled to my chest. The tree's branches moved outside as the music wound around us, not perfect, but sad and pretty, suiting my mood.

"I like that," I said.

His head was down as his fingers moved across the strings. "I thought you would."

We'd slept pressed together nightly for warmth; we'd supported each other when we could barely walk. Yet I'd never once felt aware of him as a man.

Now, sitting beside him on the floor with at least two feet of space between us, I was suddenly conscious of his closeness. As he coaxed music from the guitar, I gazed at the back of his neck: at his black hair, slightly curling, the way it looked so crisp against his skin.

A wistfulness that I didn't understand stirred through me. I swallowed hard and had to look away. I felt so empty inside.

At least he'll be all right, I thought. *Once he's back with his family, he'll be fine.*

I was glad one of us would be.

* * *

"All right, we finally have some movement," Arvin said a week later.

He'd just brought our dinner up to the small apartment. He put a tray on the battered wooden table in the front room. Ingo had been sitting on the sofa plucking softly at the guitar; he scrambled up.

"What does movement mean?" he said at the same time that I rose clumsily from my chair and said, "What are you talking about?"

Arvin sank down onto one of the dining chairs. His face looked different, and I realized he was almost giddy with relief. He motioned to the plates of pork chops and potatoes.

"Come on, eat and I'll tell you," he said. Then he smiled. "You know, I think this is the first time that I've brought you two food and you haven't fallen on it like rabid hyenas."

It was true: we were still both somewhat obsessed with food, even though we hadn't been hungry in weeks – which in itself felt like a miracle. I'd gained fifteen pounds and just looked skinny now, instead of half-starved. Ingo looked a lot better too: much more like the lean opposition pilot who I'd met that fateful night in The Ivy Room.

We sat down. I winced as I lowered myself into the chair again, keeping my weight on the cane.

"All right, here it is," said Arvin as we started to eat. "We've managed to find Vince Griffin, finally. I just spoke to him. See, our contacts were all captured last year; that's why it took so long – we had to send someone to try to locate him, without raising any suspicion. We've got to get you to a rendezvous point near Topeka. Vince will meet you there."

I chilled, remembering gazing out at downtown Topeka from the hotel room. The domes of the Zodiac, and seeing Collie in the bridge.

"How do we get there?" Ingo asked.

"Vince has been trying to put links back into place. There aren't many of us, but enough. I'll start you on the first leg in a few hours – drive you to Whiteknife, and then someone else will take you from there."

A few hours. Ingo and I glanced at each other, startled. After all the time we'd spent waiting, it felt unbelievable. I let out a breath. "And then what?"

Arvin shrugged. "Then, I don't know. Things are bad; Appalachia's about to fall. But Vince will take care of everything. He always does."

We spent the next few days travelling south, being taken from one remote Resistance meeting point to another. Shadows and whispers; furtive figures who didn't give us their names. The mountains of the north gave way to plains and sweeping skies.

Neither Ingo nor I had been outside in over four weeks. It was nearly February now. As we moved from strange auto to safe house to strange auto again I found myself breathing deeply, drinking in a smell of leaves and growing things that made my blood tingle.

"Spring's coming," I murmured to Ingo once, and he nodded.

"See?" he said. "The Guns couldn't stop it."

Finally, in the middle of the night on the third day of travelling, we neared Topeka. Our Resistance contact, a woman with prematurely white hair piled up in a bun, was driving. She'd told us her name was Greta.

I sat in the back seat with my cane propped between my legs, twisting it back and forth. I could sometimes walk without it now, but only for a few steps before the pain and weakness got to be too much. Even with the cane, I wasn't very mobile yet.

Ingo sat in the front; occasionally he and Greta spoke in low murmurs. I could hear his anxiety, and knew he was worried about getting home to his family. If Appalachia was about to fall, what would happen to the eastern ports?

We'll be in time for our information to stop it, I thought. *We will.*

We headed down a wooded lane. The trees shone in the headlights, ghostly browns and greens.

"What's the rendezvous point?" I asked, leaning forward.

"The ruins of an old house. It's just around this next bend." Greta's hands on the steering wheel looked tight.

A few moments later, we pulled up beside a falling-down house, its clapboards a weathered grey. When Greta turned the auto off, I could still see it. There was a full moon, coating the world in silver.

We got out. We were the only ones there. Greta glanced at her watch: a quick, tense motion. "We're a little early."

"You don't have to wait," Ingo said.

"Yes, I do," she said shortly.

Silence descended. Greta was a pacer, it turned out. She walked up and down the short drive, peering along the forest road each time she reached it. Ingo and I stood propped against the auto. He let out a breath and rubbed his scar.

"I hate it being so close, but not here yet," he murmured.

"I know," I said. I tapped my cane on the ground, as restless as Greta. Ingo put his hand briefly over mine, halting the motion.

"Stop that, please," he said.

"Sorry." I twisted the cane from side to side instead.

Ingo was in the tan trousers and white shirt he'd been wearing when I first woke up. They fitted him much better now; his belt was no longer on the lowest hole. I wore a plain skirt and sweater. Flat-soled shoes. Our battered suitcases held the other clothes the Resistance had found for us – and the photos that we'd taken from Gunnison's bomb factory.

I gazed blindly at my case, recalling the images…and my father's despair the night before he died. Pain and a stonier emotion stirred within me. Soon, with luck, I'd have the answers I craved.

There was something else in my case, too. I hadn't told

Ingo about it and I hoped he wouldn't find out.

He started to speak, then we both straightened abruptly as a sound floated to us through the trees.

Autos. More than one.

Greta came and stood with us. "All right, I think this is it," she murmured.

Their headlights swept through the dark trees as they approached: pure white beams angling through the black. The sound of the engines slowed.

Two autos rocked into the drive, one after the other. I winced in the harsh glare of the headlights – and the night of my arrest flashed back. Sudden fear iced my spine. What if someone had betrayed us and this was a trap? I couldn't run now.

Ingo seemed to be thinking the same thing. He put his arm around my shoulders. "If anything happens, get behind me," he whispered, watching the autos.

My lips were dry. I could feel his tension. "I thought you weren't noble," I murmured back.

His hand tightened on my shoulder. "I'm not, just stupid...shut up, can't you?"

The headlights switched off as the autos came to a stop, one with an inexpert lurch. Its driver burst out, slamming the door behind them. A figure came racing towards us in the moonlight, all long legs and pumping arms.

"Amity!" called a familiar voice. "*Amity!*"

My pulse leaped. I slowly straightened, staring.

"Hal?" I whispered.

My brother threw himself into my arms. My cane fell to the ground and pain rocked through me; I hardly noticed. With a gasp, I hugged him. He was taller than me now.

"*Hal!* But how..."

My question faded. All that mattered was holding onto him. I buried my face against his warm neck, smelling his familiar scent – the silkiness of his dark hair, so like mine.

Finally we pulled apart. Hal's cheeks were damp; he was grinning widely. "It's you, it's really you! Holy moley, I couldn't *believe* it when I saw you – we didn't know who we were coming for—" He glanced at Ingo then and faltered; from his expression I remembered how Ingo looked when you first saw him.

I swallowed. "This is my friend Ingo. He escaped with me. Ingo, this is...this is my brother." My voice caught on the word.

Ingo must have hated the look that had flinched across Hal's face. He didn't show it. "I've heard a lot about you," he said, putting his hand out. "But I didn't hear that you were with the Resistance."

Hal seemed to grow taller; I saw him push back his dread of Ingo as they shook. "I am," he said. He wiped his cheeks and turned back to me. He shook his head with a wondering smile. "We thought you must be dead, Sis. But you escaped!"

My brother's face wasn't a boy's any more. Its lines were stark in the moonlight, his round cheeks gone. I licked my lips and nodded. "So did you."

He grinned and glanced back at the other auto. "Well, I had some help."

In a daze, I looked over at it too. The driver had gotten out but hadn't moved towards us. He stood staring at me, his face frozen as if he were seeing a ghost.

Collie.

Chapter Twenty-seven

I STOOD LOCKED IN PLACE. As our eyes met, a tumult of emotions almost robbed me of speech. Dread – shock – a terrible longing. In a rush I remembered the feel of his arms around me, the taste of his lips.

I had loved him so much. Maybe, despite everything, part of me still did.

I shoved it all away and turned urgently to Greta. "It's a trap – he's with Gunnison!"

Hal clutched my arm. "Amity, no! It's all right, Collie helped me escape. He's with the Resistance."

"Hal, *listen* to me—"

"*You* listen! I know what he did, okay? He told me! But he really is with the Resistance."

"You know?" I said. I gave a trembling laugh and felt Ingo touch my back. "So you know he destroyed the evidence. You know he's in cahoots with Gunnison. You know that he threw the Tier One fight that put you into hiding, and that he—"

"Yes! So does the Resistance. They know everything and they trust him."

Collie looked pale even in the moonlight. He hesitated, then started over.

I groped for my cane. Ingo grabbed it from the ground and handed it to me, gazing over at Collie. Our eyes met and I knew he was as unsure as I was.

Collie reached us. He stood behind Hal and put his hands on his shoulders as if he needed someone to hang on to. I saw him swallow. His eyes never once left my face.

"Amity," he said.

"Hold it right there," said Greta. Her expression was taut, fearful. "You're not Vince Griffin. Do you have anything to tell me?"

Collie dragged his gaze from me. "It's…it's Greta, right?" he said. "I'm supposed to tell you that the show ran late and there was a lot of traffic."

Greta sagged. "He's okay," she said to me and Ingo.

"You're sure?" said Ingo sharply.

"Griffin gave me that code himself, just this morning."

Hal touched my arm. "It's true. I promise, Amity. It's fine."

I started to answer and stopped. The world had turned upside down.

"So what's your plan?" Greta said to Collie. She stood jingling her auto keys. "Are you taking them back with you, or what?"

Collie was still staring at me; a beat later, he apparently realized Greta had asked a question. He glanced at Ingo beside me. Recognition dawned. Collie and Ingo had met once, almost a year ago.

"Manfred," Collie said finally.

Ingo returned his gaze levelly. "Reed."

"We were told someone has a message."

"Then you were also told the message is for Vince Griffin, and no one else."

Collie glanced at me again; he seemed to be trying to steady himself. "Yeah, fine," he said, his voice rough. "Why don't we…we'd better get moving then."

Greta let out a breath and took a step towards her auto. "The best of luck to you both," she said to Ingo and me.

Wait, I wanted to say. Things were moving too fast. But Greta hardly stayed long enough after that for Ingo and me to thank her for having sheltered us. A few moments later, the sound of her auto was fading away through the night.

The four of us stood beside the abandoned house. Its windows were dark, lifeless eyes in the moonlight.

Collie looked the same as always, that was the strange thing. He looked exactly the same.

"Were you with the Resistance when I was arrested?" I asked in a low voice. "Were there people you were protecting? Is *that* why you—" I broke off.

Collie's eyes flew to mine. He was holding a set of auto keys. They made a scraping noise as his fist clenched.

"No," he said softly.

"But he is *now*, Amity, and that's what counts!" burst out Hal.

Collie rubbed his forehead. "We should get going...we, um..." He trailed off. He looked at me again. When he spoke next, I almost didn't hear him. "We were told you'd been recaptured," he said.

"*What?*"

"Recaptured. Kay Pierce told us that they'd brought you in. We thought you'd been killed."

"That's not true," said Ingo. "We escaped over seven weeks ago. We've been on the run ever since."

Collie exhaled. "Right," he said. He looked as if he was barely holding himself together. "What...what happened to your leg?" he asked me.

"I was shot," I said, and heard Hal suck in a quick breath.

At Collie's stricken look, I felt a fierce gladness. The sight of my cane hurt him? Good.

"Are you all right?" Collie asked finally.

"I'm alive," I said. "No thanks to you."

He didn't move for a long moment. His knuckles were white in the moonlight. "You're right," he said.

I knew his face so well, but had never seen him look this hesitant, this unsure of himself.

"We brought two autos," he said finally. "We didn't know if one of you might need to go somewhere else. Why don't you and Manfred ride with Hal? You, um…you probably have a lot to catch up on."

The auto's wheels hummed as Hal drove. I'd resisted the urge to ask my little brother if he knew what he was doing, and when I saw how carefully he concentrated – forehead creased slightly, hands on the wheel new-driver steady – I was glad.

None of us had spoken since we'd pulled away from the old house. In the darkness ahead, the other auto was just visible.

"When did you learn to drive?" I asked finally.

"Collie taught me." Hal glanced at me. He and I were in the front seat; Ingo had taken the back. I thought Hal was going to say something about Collie – then he nodded tensely at my cane.

"So…what happened?"

"A guard saw me," I said, and was glad when he didn't ask a guard of what.

"Will you be all right?" Hal's voice squeaked. He coughed and his tone came out deeper. "I mean…you won't always have to use a cane?"

I tried to smile. "I hope not. That would be kind of inconvenient."

"She flew a plane right after it happened," Ingo said quietly. "Your sister's tough. She'll be all right."

Hal stared at me. "You *did*?"

"Yes, but I didn't enjoy it much. Concentrate on your driving."

"I am." He looked forward again. We were still in a wooded area, though I could see lights in the distance through the trees. Hal signalled and slowed for a turn. His profile was older than I remembered, but still my brother.

Keeping strong and well. I thought of the words underlined on a page that had gone soft with too much handling. My throat tightened.

"How's Ma?" I asked softly.

Hal nodded. "She's fine. She really is, Amity. Collie rescued her too. She's in Nova Scotia, where it's safer."

I frowned, rolling my cane between my palms. "What do you mean, 'rescued'? What exactly happened?"

"I mean *rescued* – what do you think? He came to Madame Josephine's and got me the hell out of there." Hal glanced back at Ingo in the rear-view mirror. "I, um...was found Discordant. I was in hiding in a closet for nine months."

"I know," said Ingo.

"You do?" My brother glanced at me.

"He's my friend, Hal. What happened?"

He shrugged. "Collie had a Gun uniform and he came in and took me. At first I thought he really *was* a Gun and I couldn't believe it. He had a Shadowcar. He took Ma too and drove us to their headquarters. Then he snuck us into his own auto and got us out."

When I didn't respond, Hal looked at me. "He could have been killed, Amity. They'd have shot him on sight if they'd caught him escaping with prisoners."

"You'd have been shot too," I said shortly. "Or worse."

Hal's jaw took on an unfamiliar strong line. "Well, that's a chance I was willing to take."

"At least you were safe in hiding."

"Being safe isn't everything. And actually, no, I wasn't. They'd already searched the house twice. They'd have found me before long."

My lips went dry. "Really?"

"Yes, really." Hal shifted gears with a short, jerky motion. "Jo was terrified. So was Ma. I'd hear them whispering through the floorboards sometimes, trying to figure out where else I could go. And I was sitting down there surrounded by all these stupid books and model sets, thinking that if I had any guts I'd leave and put them both out of danger."

I swallowed hard. "I'm very glad you didn't."

"Well, I was about to," Hal said flatly. "I'm almost fifteen – I'm supposed to be the man with Dad gone, not put Ma's life at risk."

Ahead of us, the other auto slowed for a turn. So did we. The dark trees had given way to dark houses. We were in a suburban area, with Topeka still a distant glow on the horizon.

"So you needed out and Collis rescued you," said Ingo from the back seat. "I'm glad of it."

Hal's hands relaxed a little on the wheel. "Yeah, he did," he said, glancing at Ingo in the mirror. "And I'll be grateful to him for as long as I live." Hal hesitated, then added to me, "Listen...I know he's done some really bad things, but he's sorry. He's trying to make up for it."

In my mind I saw again the evidence from Madeline's office going up in flames: the only hope of millions of people. The words "trying to make up for it" couldn't even begin to apply. Yet Collie had saved my family. And he'd had no idea that I'd ever know.

My leg ached. So did my heart, and I hated Collie for it.

Hal glanced at me again. He looked worried, and I stiffened, suddenly knowing what he was going to ask. "Amity, when you were...in that place...were you all right?"

"It wasn't much fun," I said softly. "But we're both okay now."

"How did you escape?"

I didn't want to talk about this. Harmony Five preyed on my thoughts too often as it was. I sighed. As quickly as possible, I described our escape to Hal.

He fell silent for a long moment. "So I guess you're pretty thankful to Rob," he said.

I laughed in surprise. "The boyfriend who taught me how to pick locks," I explained to Ingo, and he smiled too.

"*I'm* grateful to Rob," he said. "I'll buy Rob a drink if I ever meet him."

Hal shook his head, looking dazed. "Seriously," he said to me. "That's just...I'm kind of proud you're my sister, you know that?"

A mental image came: a wooden platform with a crescent moon shining above it – a terrified girl staring at a rifle. And myself not saying a word.

"Thanks, but there wasn't much to be proud of there," I murmured.

Hal's troubled look as he studied me made him look disconcertingly like Dad. I nudged him and tried to smile. "Hey...why didn't you go to Nova Scotia with Ma? I can't imagine she was very happy about you staying here with the Resistance."

"No, she was all right," said Hal. "She knew Collie would look out for me."

"It's dangerous work, Hal."

"Gosh, really?"

"You know what I mean."

"This is my fight too," he said. "I'm Discordant, remember?" He shrugged shoulders that were broader than I remembered. "And anyway, you can't lecture me, Amity. *You* wouldn't have gone at my age."

I wanted to argue with him but couldn't. In the back seat Ingo had stretched out; his eyes were closed.

"I think you know your sister very well," he said drowsily.

We turned onto a freeway. The road smoothed; the tyres whirred over them. Hal looked deep in thought. Finally he glanced at me. "Amity, um...you know—" He stopped short and glanced at Ingo in the rear-view mirror, who'd fallen asleep several miles before.

"It's okay," I said. "He's a sound sleeper."

Hal stared at me, startled. "Are you two…"

I shook my head. "We've just gotten to know each other pretty well, these last two months." It seemed like an understatement. Ironic – I probably knew Ingo far better now than I'd known Collie in all the time Collie and I had been a couple.

Hal glanced back at Ingo again. "What happened to his face?" he whispered.

"His plane was sabotaged."

"Like you said yours was, during your trial?"

I winced. "Did you see my trial?"

"No, but Jo told me things. She didn't want to. I kept asking."

"Yeah," I said after a pause. "His plane was sabotaged in almost exactly the same way. Ingo wasn't as lucky; he was knocked out and then hit by a burning piece of shrapnel."

Hal studied Ingo in the rear-view mirror again. "That's…" He swallowed and didn't complete the thought. "He seems like a good guy," he said finally.

"Hal, what were you going to ask me? It wasn't about Ingo, was it?"

"No, um…" My brother gave me a sideways look. "It's…about Dad."

"What about him?" I said finally, thinking, *Please, no, not this.*

"Did he really throw the civil war Peacefight?"

Outside, the trees slid darkly past for several moments. "Yes," I said softly.

Hal gave me a quick, tight look. "How do you know?"

I felt cold, unable to revisit that night before our father's death. *No one can judge your actions unless they've been there. Got that? Nobody.* "I just do," I said. "I'll tell you about it someday. But yes, he did it." I swallowed. "How...how did you hear?"

"That's what they said about him at your trial," Hal said hoarsely. "Jo didn't tell me. I heard it on the telio, through the floorboards. I was going to ask Ma about it, but..." He trailed off.

"Do...do you think she knows?" he asked. "That he really did it?"

"*I don't know.*" I'd asked myself that a hundred times. All the expensive things we'd had. My father's two airplanes. Peacefighters didn't make much money. Hadn't she ever suspected anything?

Hal was struggling for control. "Why did he do it?" His voice squeaked. In the dashboard's glow his expression was raw. "Amity, why? He was a *Peacefighter.* The whole world trusted him."

"I don't know," I said again. "I wish I did." One of my hands clenched tightly in my lap. *Soon I'll find out,* I vowed silently. *For both of us, Hal. I swear it.*

I cleared my throat and touched his arm. "Listen, maybe...maybe we'll have answers someday. Let's just forget about it until then. Where are you taking us?"

He let out a deep breath. I saw him make a conscious effort to put Dad aside. "To a Resistance meeting point on the other side of Topeka," he said at last. "Vince Griffin will be there – there's a lot going on."

"Like what?"

He slid his hands over the wheel. "I'm not sure. It feels like something big though. Something to do with Appalachia, I think."

My pulse quickened. The Day of Three Suns. If we were lucky, then, we were still in time for our information to help. And we could get Ingo home too.

Hal hesitated. "Listen, I should probably tell you – Vince Griffin is really Mac Jones. I think you've met him."

"*Mac Jones?* But—"

I broke off, remembering my trial. Mac Jones standing there in the by-admittance-only courtroom, shrugging at me with a half smile.

"I thought he worked for Gunnison," I said blankly.

We'd reached a more built-up area. Street lights flickered over Hal's face: light, dark, light, dark. "He does," he said. "So does Collie. I mean, that's their cover."

This on top of thinking about Dad felt like too much. I put a hand to my throbbing head and wondered if my brother even knew what a "cover" was – the tasks that both Mac Jones and Collie would have to do in their work for Gunnison.

"Maybe you'd better tell me everything that Collie's told you," I said finally.

Hal gave me a quick look. "Are you sure, Sis? I mean... maybe you'd better let him tell you himself."

"No," I said. "You do it."

It was still dark when we reached what looked like a factory at the end of a lonely road.

We followed Collie's auto around the back of the large enclosure. There were several other autos parked there: long, rounded shapes in the moonlight. No lights on anywhere that I could see.

Hal parked next to Collie. Silence fell as he killed the engine.

Awake now, Ingo leaned forward. "What is this place?"

"A furniture factory," said Hal. "The owner's a sympathizer. Collie will tell us when it's safe."

Something twisted in my chest. Despite everything, he said it with such simple trust: Collie had always been his big brother.

Collie got out of his auto. He motioned us to stay put, then vanished inside a dark doorway. A moment later he reappeared, beckoning.

I hesitated. "Are you sure this isn't a trap?"

My brother bristled. "*Yes*, I'm sure."

"Hal, you can't blame me for asking."

"I told you: he didn't mean what happened."

"Were you there?" I said shortly.

Hal rolled his eyes. "Well, fine, you can just sit out here in the auto if you want. Think what you like. You always do." He got out and jogged over to Collie.

I sighed and opened my door, unsure how we'd already gone back to our usual sibling relationship. Ingo got out too; he took my cane from the footwell and handed it to me.

"Lena's the same sometimes," he said quietly. "Don't worry about it. How are you?"

My leg was throbbing. I shrugged as we crossed the brief stretch of pavement, leaning on my cane. "Did you hear anything that Hal said on the drive here?" I murmured.

Ingo walked beside me, head down, his hands in his trouser pockets. "A little. And I'd be wary too, for what it's worth."

Everything Hal had said felt like a bruise inside me: our father buying dope from Collie's dad; Collie's father blackmailing ours; Collie being an informer in Harmony Three and then a spy on the Western Seaboard base. He'd thrown Peacefights right from the start. He'd lied to me every single day.

Had I ever known him at all?

Collie stood holding a door open. His eyes rested briefly on my face, then darted away again.

"In here," he said gruffly.

We went down a dimly-lit corridor. Shadowy signs on the doors read things like, *Storage 1-A*, *Sundries*, *Auth*

Personnel Only. At *Storage 2-C*, Collie stopped. "Wait a second, I'll just check…" He knocked and stuck his head inside. Low murmurs.

"*Amity Vancour?*" someone said.

In a sudden flurry of movement Mac Jones appeared in the lit doorway: a few inches shorter than me, a few years older. Just like the only other time we'd met properly, he seemed bristling with energy, his dark hair rumpled.

A bemused look crossed Mac's face as he offered his hand. "Well. This is a surprise. And that's a hell of an understatement. I'm very glad you're not dead after all, Miss Vancour."

I hesitated. We shook. "Amity," I said. "And this feels pretty strange. The last time I saw you—"

"Sure, I get it." Mac gave a crooked smile. "Well, this is the real me. Or as real as I ever get." He turned to Ingo – and I liked him better when I saw him control his reaction to Ingo's face. "Manfred, right?" He put his hand out. "I hear you met Rodriguez in Harmony Five."

"I did," said Ingo as they shook. "I have a message for you…in private. And Amity and I need to show you something."

I had the photos from Gunnison's bomb factory in my coat pocket.

Mac nodded. "All right, give me about twenty minutes. I'm just wrapping something up that can't wait. Collis, take care of them, will you, buddy?" Mac clapped Collie on the shoulder. His brown eyes looked sympathetic;

I wondered what Collie had told him.

Mac went back into the room. Conversation drifted briefly out as the door shut: "So, yes, we can get them out but it's got to be damn quick. Grady's leaving in—"

Collie cleared his throat as we headed down the corridor. "Sorry. Everything's kind of exploded these last few weeks."

My fingers tightened on my cane. *Please* – we couldn't be too late. "The Day of Three Suns," I said.

Collie's head whipped towards me. "You've heard about it?"

"It's what our information's about," Ingo said. "Well, part of it."

Collie fell silent; he looked stunned.

Hal glanced quickly from Collie back to Ingo and me. "What's the Day of..." he started, and then stopped.

We reached a dark break room. Inside, Collie lit a storm lantern. The room filled with a gentle glow at odds with the folding tables and metal chairs.

"The, um...blinds can be seen from the road, so we keep it dim in here," Collie said. He pushed a hand through his hair. "Hal, you want to go read a magazine or something?"

Hal's face was taut but he nodded and went over to a sofa in the corner. Listlessly, he pulled a magazine from the coffee table.

Collie leaned against the counter. "Well, I hope your information's still good, because all hell's broken loose," he whispered. "Appalachia's about to fall. We're busy trying to get everyone out that we can, while the eastern ports are still under free rule."

I glanced at Ingo, thinking of him returning home. "Are you still getting people out?"

"Just."

Ingo's scar was pulling more harshly at his eye than usual, and I knew how tense he was. "Can the Day of Three Suns still be stopped, if our information is valid?"

"Talk to Mac. I sure hope so. If we lose Appalachia, that's it."

We. He sounded like he meant it. I found myself staring at him, anger and pain stirring in me. Why couldn't he have felt this way ten months ago?

Or was this an act too?

Collie noticed my gaze and his cheeks tinged. He hesitated. "Amity, could I...could I talk to you?"

"Go on," I said.

"Not here. Unless—" Collie glanced over at my brother. "Hey, Hal, you want to show Ingo around?" he called. "All right?" he added to Ingo.

"If it's all right with Amity," said Ingo, his voice level.

As I studied Collie I felt made of stone. Finally I glanced at Ingo and nodded. "It's all right."

After Ingo and Hal left, Collie stood tensely. "Um... there's coffee, if..." He indicated a coffee pot. "Or soda, if maybe you'd rather..." He trailed off.

"Just talk, Collie," I said.

He rubbed his hand over his eyes. "All right, look,"

he said hoarsely. "I know that I don't have the right to…to say anything to you. But I'm…" He let out a breath. "I am so glad you're still alive."

He wasn't quite the same Collie after all, I realized: he was a bit broader than before, more muscular. And the vulnerable expression in his eyes made him seem Hal's age – like the smooth-cheeked boy I'd once kissed in our barn.

Shaken, I pushed away the memory. I went to the sofa and sat down. Collie followed and sat in the far corner, several feet of space between us. He sat leaning forward, rubbing his thumb across his palm, as if trying to erase his Harmony tattoo.

"Hal told me everything," I said.

Collie swallowed. He looked down and nodded.

"Thanks for not saying you're sorry," I said after a pause. "Sorry doesn't really cover it."

He choked out something like a laugh. "I know that. Don't you think I know that?" He stared down at his clasped hands. "Look…Hal couldn't have told you about your arrest, because I didn't tell him much. But, Amity, I swear it wasn't like you think."

When I didn't answer, Collie looked at me. His eyes were dark blue in the dim light, full of pain.

"Please believe me," he said.

Chapter Twenty-eight

March, 1941

I headed quickly through the silence of the Zodiac building, the image of Collie burning the evidence still overpowering my senses. I heard his footsteps behind me. He was beside me in an instant.

I didn't look at him as I shoved through a side door and out into the night. He took my arm, glancing furtively up and down the street. "Amity, wait!"

I shook him off and kept going. I heard him swear; he jogged after me.

"Don't touch me," I said.

His jaw was tight. "Fine. But it's dangerous for you here. We've got to—"

"There's no *we* any more!"

"Of course there is!" Then Collie sucked in a quick breath. "*No.*"

My gaze followed his. My veins chilled. A group of Guns were heading towards us across the Zodiac lawn. Over a dozen of them: their coats a shadowy grey that gleamed in the street lights.

Before I could move, a spotlight shone on us. I flinched as someone shouted, "It's Vancour!"

I turned to run. Collie lunged for me, grabbed me. "Don't!" he hissed in my ear. "They'll shoot you!"

I struggled hard against his grip but he had me tight, arms locked around my chest.

"Let go of me!" I cried. Approaching shouts. "*Let me go!*"

"*Shut up!*" He sounded desperate. "Amity, please listen! You can't outrun them – they love having an excuse to kill someone—"

They were on us, spotlights blazing. I was still kicking and bucking against Collie's arms. As the Guns surrounded us I sagged slightly, almost sobbing with anger and fear, hating the fact that Collie was stronger than me.

Then I stiffened as someone I recognized from the telio stepped forward from the group.

Sandford Cain.

I stood stricken as our eyes met. He wore a neat grey suit. His nondescript face looked bland, with a small smile tugging at his lips. From a great distance, I realized that Collie had slowly let go of me.

Sandford Cain gave him a pleasant nod. "Your information is as accurate as always, Reed. She came after it just like you said she would."

I stared at Collie. He stood motionless, avoiding my eyes.

"Yes, I was just restraining her for you," he said.

It was his voice. But I didn't recognize it.

He still didn't look at me. I stood trembling, fingernails gouging my palms. Cain gave Collie a pale-eyed smile. "Good job. Johnny will be very pleased. Enjoy yourself?"

"Not bad, for a Discordant." Collie took a step back. He cleared his throat. "You boys can take her now. I'm done."

"You bastard," I whispered.

One of the Guns struck me hard across the face. A muscle in Collie's jaw leaped, but he didn't move. Cain jerked his head towards me.

"You heard what Sandy said. Do it," he told the Guns.

They surged towards me. The cold steel of handcuffs bit hard against my wrists. "Come on, Wildcat," said one. "You're finally going to get what's coming to you."

As they led me away, Collie didn't speak again.

He didn't protest.

He didn't say a word.

Chapter Twenty-nine

January, 1942

"I didn't set you up," Collie said hoarsely. He sat slumped over on the sofa. "I know it probably looked like that. I didn't expect you to follow me. Then when I saw Cain…I thought of going back to that place and I…"

He gazed bleakly down at his tattoo. "But, Amity, I swear to you, it wasn't only cowardice. Please believe me. I thought…I thought that if I could stay free, keep playing the game, then maybe I could help you."

The small space between us was a chasm. For weeks after my arrest I'd told myself that Collie had only been playing along, that he hadn't really meant to throw me to the wolves.

There had been no help. After they'd taken me away,

I'd never heard from him again.

"What happened?" I asked finally.

"I tried. I kept telling Gunnison how great he'd look if he pardoned you. He wouldn't listen." Collie rubbed his forehead. "I tried to see you; I couldn't arrange it without raising suspicion. I was desperate; I..." He stopped, his muscles tight.

I thought of hiding in the trunk of the auto to enter the country and gave a harsh laugh. "We didn't actually have any problem getting into the Central States, did we? You've got whatever papers you need."

He nodded wordlessly.

"What happened once we got here?"

Collie's hand became a tight fist, hiding his tattoo. Finally he said, "They knew I'd entered the country. I had to stay at the Royal Archer because it's where his people always stay. And I had to meet with them. Pretend I was there alone."

"All those times you were gone from our room." I remembered pacing a trail on the carpet, sick with worry about him.

Tonelessly, Collie said, "I told them that I'd been with you, trying to figure out who you might have told about Madeline's information. But that you got suspicious of me and took off. I said you'd seen the documents on the telio and that we should destroy them. That I was worried you'd try to get hold of them. That's what Cain meant when he..." Collie trailed off, and I knew like me, he was picturing Cain's narrow smile. *She came after it just like you said she would.*

The silence felt absolute.

Collie dropped his head onto his fingertips. "Oh, hell, Amity," he murmured. "It all made so much sense to me at the time: destroy the documents so you'd never see them again. Say someone else had done it and then we could escape. Be safe for ever."

My grip threatened to shatter my cane. "So how does Mac feel about you shoving the evidence in a furnace?"

Collie gave a humourless laugh. "When I first told him I thought for a second he might kill me." He looked down. "I'm not really sure why he trusts me, but...the guy pretty much saved my life. Not that it was worth saving."

"What do you mean, Mac saved your life?"

Collie fiddled with a cuff. His broad shoulders were slumped. "Skip it," he said finally.

I gazed down at my own tattoo, remembering the bite of the needle – the chill air against my naked skin. "Why didn't you ever tell me you were in a correction camp?" I asked.

"Because I was ashamed." Collie's voice was low. "It felt like proof that I was one of those garbage Reeds. And I was ashamed of...of the things I did there."

Melody's body, falling off the platform. The surge of adrenalin as I'd run for it. Could I really tell myself *At least I wasn't an informer* and feel proud?

I didn't know. I didn't know anything.

The minutes stretched past. "What really happened the night Russ died?" I asked.

Collie looked down. "Mac's cover is that he works for Cain," he said finally. "He had to get my report about Hendrix and my thrown fights. But then he kept me talking, hinting around that some trouble was about to go down for Russ. I went to see if I could find Russ and tip him off." Collie cleared his throat. "I, um…I guess that was when I started wondering whether Mac was really with the Resistance."

I couldn't keep sitting here. I struggled to my feet and went to the counter. I found a glass and poured myself some water at the sink, trying to hide my shaking hands.

Collie hesitated, then slowly followed me.

I spun on him. "Did I ever even *know* you?"

"Yes," he whispered. His fist clenched against his thigh. "Amity…those months with you at the base…they were the best thing that ever happened to me."

"But it was all a lie!"

"I loved you. That wasn't. I still…" Collie's throat worked; he looked down. After a long pause, he said, "I know you don't love me any more. I don't expect you to. But…maybe someday I'll deserve you. And then maybe…" He trailed off.

I drank half the water at a gulp. I put the glass down; it made a small sound in the silence. I was amazed that it didn't fly into pieces.

"I can't even think about that," I said.

Collie studied me, his face so familiar that it hurt. “Thank you,” he said quietly. “At least it’s not a ‘no’.”

Storeroom 2-C had shelves with cleaning supplies, and a table that looked as if it was kept folded up against the wall during the day. “No windows, and enough space to spread out a little,” said Mac by way of explanation when he ushered Ingo and me in.

The night-time factory was busier now. A few people had entered the break room while we were waiting for Mac; others were gathered in shadowy groups here and there – men and women, talking in low voices. Both Hal and Collie had left again, presumably to pick up someone else.

Mac shut the door behind us. “Sorry you had to wait. There’s a hell of a lot going on. Did Collis fill you in?”

“A little.” I sat down, clutching my cane. I was glad Collie was gone now – my emotions were too complicated. Ingo sat beside me, his long, angular face tense.

“All right, what have you got for me?” asked Mac.

Ingo and I exchanged a weighted glance. So much depended on this.

“Photos first?” I said, and Ingo nodded. We brought them out.

“There’s a factory that we found a few days south of Harmony Five,” said Ingo, handing them over. “Your Miss Pierce was visiting it. These were on a bulletin board.”

Mac looked at the top photo and his face drained. He sank wordlessly onto the table's edge. As the minutes passed, the slight rustle of paper was the only sound.

At long last Mac put the photos aside. He rubbed his temples. "Holy shit," he whispered. Suddenly he looked no older than me.

No one spoke. Finally Mac let out a breath.

"I knew there was something big being developed," he said. "But I never thought even Gunnison would go this far. To unleash *that* on the world again...he's crazier than I thought, and that's saying something." He seemed to collect himself. "Okay. Where exactly is this place?"

We told him the best we could. Mac took no notes but I had a feeling he wouldn't forget a word. He studied the photos again, all business now, tapping his teeth with a fingernail.

"We've got to release these to the world, and fast," he muttered. "The EA, Africa, everyone. This might be the one thing that'll force other leaders into direct action."

"Not Appalachia?" I asked.

Mac shook his head curtly. "Appalachia's already fallen, pretty much. News of a bomb factory would just make his takeover there even easier." He glanced at his watch. "Wait here."

Mac hurried to the door with the photos and stuck his head out. "Hey, is Grady still here?" he called. He vanished from the doorway. "Good, I caught you. Listen, buddy..."

His urgent voice faded. Ingo and I looked at each other, both too on edge to speak.

Mac returned with only three photos.

"Okay, Grady's one of our best. He's heading out tonight; he'll get those photos to the right people – we're just lucky we got them in time." Mac dropped into a chair and added bitterly, "But even if the world bands together, we won't get military help anytime soon. No one *else* has spent the last twelve years building a goddamn army."

Ingo leaned forward. "You mentioned Gunnison's takeover of Appalachia," he said intently. "You're talking about the Day of Three Suns, yes?"

"It's the Day of Fire now."

My heart clenched. "What?"

"Day of Fire – in just four days," said Mac. "That's why we're busting our asses, because once Gunnison closes off the eastern ports, we're screwed. There are people we've got to get out."

I opened my mouth and closed it again. Collie hadn't mentioned some of this. Clearly it was why he'd told us to talk to Mac.

Ingo was pale, apart from the vivid, crinkled stretch of his scar. "Rodriguez's message was about the Day of Three Suns," he said. "I hope the information's still good."

Mac had been looking at one of the remaining photos; he glanced up sharply. "Oh, buddy-boy, me too," he muttered. He leaned forward. "Let's have it."

"He had pneumonia; he knew he was dying," said Ingo.

"He was hoping I could escape. He told me to tell you that the caterers can smuggle in what you need. I have three names for you." Ingo gave them.

Mac sat without moving. I saw the hope die in his eyes.

"They've all been killed," he said. "It's old info."

Ingo's scar reddened further as his lips whitened. I sat frozen, gripping my cane.

"It can't be," I whispered.

"Believe me, I wish it wasn't," said Mac shortly. "That was from when the Day was originally planned. It was due to take place in Philly then. It's happening somewhere in Washington now. We just got the word a few hours ago – too late to locate the new venue and do anything about it."

"There's no way?" said Ingo.

"No. You wouldn't believe the security measures they've got in place. Those of us in the Zodiac can't even take them out – we're searched every goddamn day."

Despair filled me. Appalachia was still going to fall. Gunnison would continue. All the things my father had set in motion would continue too.

I looked down at my suitcase and felt cold, thinking of what I'd secretly packed.

Mac rubbed his forehead. "Anyway, that's part of what we're doing now," he said finally. "Setting up a network in Appalachia – they're going to need it." He looked up. "What about you two? Are you joining us?"

With an effort, I shoved it all away. Ingo and I glanced at each other. To my surprise, he hesitated. For a moment

I actually thought he was going to say that he'd join the Resistance.

No, I thought, suddenly angry. His brother and sister – his parents – I knew just how much going home to his village near the Med meant to him.

Before Ingo could speak, I said to Mac, "Your man told Ingo that if he delivered the message to you, the Resistance could help him get home. Can you still do it?"

"Is that what you want?" Mac asked Ingo.

Ingo's gaze stayed on me for a moment; after a beat he glanced at Mac. He swallowed. "Yes. It is."

"Shame, pal; we'd have liked to have you. Where's home?"

Ingo's hand was resting on his thigh. It clenched and unclenched, his long fingers flexing. "The European Alliance. Germanic counties, down near the Med."

Mac sat up with a jerk. "The EA? That's where Grady's going. He just had to speak to someone before he – quick, come with me!" Mac scrambled up. When Ingo didn't move, he clapped his arm. "Come *on*, buddy! Those ports could be closed by Gunnison any time – the Day of Fire's just a technicality!"

"Wait," Ingo said hurriedly to me. "I won't go without—"

He didn't finish. He and Mac left the room in a rush.

So soon. All at once I felt shaky. I got to my feet and went to the door. I peered down the shadowy corridor. I could just see Ingo's tall, running form, with Mac's shorter one ahead of him.

"Grady!" shouted Mac, his voice echoing. "*Grady!*"

A third man appeared in the outer doorway; he wore a fedora and overcoat. Mac and Ingo jogged to a stop. Mac spoke to Grady for a few moments. Grady and Ingo shook hands.

My chest tightened. I started quickly towards them, ignoring the pain in my leg. I stopped as Ingo came jogging back to me. He drew me into the dimly-lit break room. No one else was in it now.

Ingo looked dazed. "Grady's waiting for me, just for a few minutes. Mac's getting my bag."

"Ingo, I'm so glad." My voice caught. "You deserve this."

"I..." He pushed a hand over his hair. "This is all so fast...what will you do now? Are you staying with the Resistance?"

"Yes, I think so." With all the confidences we'd shared, all the time we'd spent together, I'd never told Ingo about my Madeline plan. I had no intention of doing so now. I wanted him on that boat when it left, heading home to his family.

"What about Collis?" he said. "Will you be all right?"

I nodded. "I'll be fine. Don't worry."

We were standing so close. We could have touched if either of us had lifted our hands.

Neither of us did.

Silence fell as we gazed at each other. My lips were dry. From the corridor I heard Mac talking.

When Ingo spoke again, his voice was husky. "I don't know how to say goodbye to you."

"Then don't say it. I hate saying it anyway." I managed a smile. "Go on, get out of here, Manfred. Don't come back to this place – promise me."

"I never make promises I may not keep. Who knows what might happen?" Ingo paused, looking uncertain. Then he held out his hand.

I took it. Our fingers gripped each other.

"Take care of yourself," he said softly.

"And you."

"Write to me if you can. Please. Calliposa – just like it sounds."

I nodded, barely trusting myself to speak. "If I can."

"Ingo! Sorry, pal, you've gotta go," called Mac.

I swallowed. I looked down at our two hands, then squeezed his fingers hard and released them.

"Be safe," I whispered. "Now just *go*, can't you?"

Ingo's dark eyes were still fixed on mine. Almost black – you would never mistake them for any other colour.

He hesitated, then touched my face, his thumb stroking over my cheek. He let out a breath and nodded.

He left.

I sank down onto the sofa. I heard Ingo say, "I'm ready," and then rapid footsteps, and the fading murmur of Mac's response: "All right, take care, buddy. Grady, listen, don't forget…"

The building fell silent, despite the other people… a silence as grey and thorough as snow muffling a windowpane.

A few hours later, I sat on a small flight of steps outside a door at the rear of the factory. It looked like the employees came out here for breaks sometimes: there were stubbed-out cigarette tips and a lonely-looking picnic table.

The stars still shone above, though to the east the sky had lightened to a deep, soft blue. There were trees in the distance. I gazed at them, taking in the way they laced against the stars. In the Central States – I could think of where we were in no other way – there was so much beauty. Strange. The land where Gunnison ruled should be a barren desert.

Of course, he ruled the Western Seaboard too now. Soon he'd rule Appalachia. Soon he'd rule the whole world, if no one moved quickly enough to stop him.

Hal's face when we'd talked about Dad. The despair on it, far too much for someone so young.

And everything Collie had told me… I closed my eyes as my leg throbbed. Part of me felt sorry for him and I hated it. I hated *him*, but I still cared about him. How could I not? Collie was my childhood. My first love. I'd thought once he'd be my only love. Why did he have to be here?

Yet he'd rescued my family.

Commander Hendrix had once hinted that Dad had

crashed his plane on purpose. Madeline had been at the World for Peace meeting that he'd gone to earlier that day – the one, according to Hendrix, where they'd told my father that they expected him to throw another fight.

I looked at the trees but instead saw heads on a fence, glistening, grey with frost.

Dad, I thought.

The thing that I'd never wanted to face about my father's thrown fight wasn't a thunderclap when it came. It mixed with the night as if it had always been there, deep and hollow and inevitable. I sat motionless, lost in Harmony Five, my fingers rigid on the cane.

I started as the door opened. Mac Jones came out and sat beside me, dropping onto the top step with a weary sigh.

"Cigarette?" he said, offering me a pack.

After a pause, I shook my head. "I don't smoke."

"No, me neither." Mac tapped one out and lit it with a quick scratch from a lighter. He tucked the pack back into his jacket pocket. "Don't tell my girlfriend, okay?"

We sat in silence for a few moments. The sky to the east was lighter now. Mac's cigarette was a glowing red ember.

"Will Ingo be safe?" I said finally.

Mac blew out a stream of smoke. "Hope so," he said. "Grady's got Class A papers; they shouldn't be stopped getting out of the country. And the Harmony Treaty hasn't been announced yet – the ship in Baltimore should still have spaces. With luck he'll be home in about a week and a half."

Something in me eased a little. *All right,* I thought, still gazing at the trees. *That's it – he's gone for ever but he's safe. Close the door.*

The cool night air prickled at my skin. From somewhere far away, an owl called. From somewhere further, a train rattled past. It slowly faded.

I glanced at Mac. "Do you usually keep my brother working all night?"

"No, not usually," said Mac. "Desperate times, and all that."

"You're aware that he's not even fifteen."

"I'm aware."

"Mac, he doesn't really have any concept of what might happen to him if he gets caught."

Mac propped his elbows on his knees and took a deep drag of the cigarette. Finally he said, "No one can, unless they've been in one of those places. Hell, *I* probably don't – not really. Seeing pictures isn't the same. But if the only people who work for us are the ones who know the consequences first-hand..." He shrugged. "Well, you see the problem."

I did. The stars were high, icy pinpricks, dying one by one. I crossed my arms tightly. "Collie said that you saved his life."

Mac's tone was neutral. "Did he?"

"What did he mean?"

"I'm sure he'll tell you someday, if he wants you to know." After a pause, Mac added, "You know, when Collis asked me if he could join the Resistance…he was taking a hell of a chance. If he'd been wrong about me, he'd have been shot."

My head was throbbing. I studied Mac's profile tensely. "Do you trust him?"

"Yeah. Funnily enough, I do."

"Why 'funnily enough'?"

"Well, I'm sure my boy's told you about his colourful past." Mac glanced at me. "Sephy and I think a lot of him," he said quietly. "The guy's got guts. He told me things that not many men would ever admit to."

"I thought a lot of the Collie I was in love with," I said at last. "I don't know who this new one is."

"I think he's still figuring that out himself."

No. Close the door on this too. Close the door on all of it, for ever, except for the one thing I could never push aside again.

Sing, no, louder, SING! I stared blindly at the trees and saw hair matted with blood on the snow – Melody dropping from the platform – myself scrambling to wrest boots from her still-warm body. This was the abyss that I'd tried so hard to avoid and now I'd fallen into it.

Harmony Five wouldn't have been possible without my father.

I felt strangely calm though my heart was racketing. The shard of glass still lay in my pocket. I rubbed my thumb over its curved edge. I had something better in my bag now, but the hard, glinting shape felt like a friend.

I talked him into…I mean, I talked to *Truce about it…*

I took my hand from my pocket and cleared my throat. "Tell…tell Collie to look after Hal, all right?"

Mac gave me a keen look as he stubbed out his cigarette. "All right," he said. "But I don't think I really need to. He's pretty attached to the kid."

I nodded.

"Can I ask where *you're* going to be? I kinda thought you were joining us, Miss Vancour."

My voice sounded as if I were listening to someone else. "No," I said. "I'm not joining you." I looked at him. "Could you get me into Appalachia? And maybe a little money?"

Chapter Thirty

February, 1942

Kay Pierce stuck her head around Mac's office door and winked. "Any cookies today?"

With less than two days left before Appalachia would be taken over by a pen-stroke, Mac had never felt less like playing the game. He looked up from some paperwork and smiled anyway. "Sorry, kiddo. Mac's Bakery has been too busy working overtime."

"Aw, is Johnny working you too hard?" Kay came in, closing the door behind her. "And here I'm just going to add to it. I feel guilty now."

She held a file in one arm. She came around to where Mac sat and perched herself on the edge of the desk. As always, she was perfectly turned out, today in a stylish blue suit. A golden Scorpio brooch glittered on her lapel. Kay's gaze lingered on Mac's own lapel and for an apprehensive moment Mac thought he'd forgotten his pin. Then Kay reached out and touched it.

"Taurus," she said. "I admire Taureans; I always have. So strong and single-minded." She let her hand fall and smiled sadly. "You know...I really like you, Mac. There are so few people I can trust."

Mac's adrenalin kicked in. What was going on? "The feeling's mutual. Are you all right, kid?"

He drew Kay to the soft chairs in front of his desk and sat her down, thinking, *You knew all about the "atomic Harmony devices" in those photos and you never breathed a word, you viper.*

Weeks before, Kay *had* shown Mac photos though: from Harmony Five, of lifeless bodies with bloody features that were supposedly Vancour and Manfred. Mac, now with the image of the real Vancour and Manfred fresh in his head, wondered how much Kay had paid the camp director to fake them. Why though? It was a hell of a gamble for her to take, if she knew that Vancour was still at large.

Maybe she thought the risk was worth it. Gunnison no longer seemed tormented by the "dark mirror". Just yesterday, Mac had met him in a Zodiac corridor and Gunnison had stopped to chat – smiling, triumphant, though with a too-fixed gaze that had made Mac's skin crawl.

"You see?" he'd said intently. "It's all on the upswing

now, Mac! I *knew* I was right to let the karmic link play out on its own." His voice lowered as if sharing a secret. "Of course, I tried my best to stay on the *up* so that I could push Vancour *down*. But I never interfered with fate, Mac. Not once. Like I said, Lady Harmony would have known."

Gunnison's intimate tone seemed to imply that he and Mac had discussed this often. The whole thing had felt badly off-kilter. Yet the next moment, Gunnison had asked Mac for a report and as they talked had been completely rational.

The memory flitted past. Kay sighed and fiddled with the file she had rested on her lap.

"Oh, I'm fine," she said in answer to Mac's question. "Just awfully busy, with the Day of Fire coming up." She looked up anxiously. "You'll still be there, won't you? You and Sephy?"

"Sure, we'll be there," said Mac, injecting a jolly note into his voice.

Johnny was taking most of the high-level Zodiac staff along. They were all catching a special train out to Washington the next morning – though the event itself was still shrouded in secrecy. Madeline Bark's plans had been shared with no one.

"And Collis?" Kay asked.

"Him too."

"Good," she said. "Well…good about you and Sephy anyway." She frowned. "Mac, I know he's a friend of yours, but are you totally sure we can trust Collis Reed?"

Mac raised an eyebrow, hiding his flash of alarm. He settled back in his chair. "Yeah, I think so. Guy's never failed us yet. Why? What's up?"

Kay wrinkled her nose. "He just rubs me the wrong way, I guess. Forget it – here's why I came in." She opened the file and pulled out some papers.

"These are the names," she said.

"What names?"

"For the Day of Fire." At Mac's questioning look, she said, "Goodness, hasn't Johnny told you? Right after the signing, we're going to begin the Harmonic process and purge any Discordants present. We've been checking Appalachian charts for weeks now."

Mac had always known Gunnison would break his promise to go lightly on Appalachia. They were going to start right there in the stadium though? This on top of the bombs made it difficult to keep his easy smile in place.

"Hey, great idea." He chuckled. "So that's why you've been working my girl so hard."

Kay shook her head impatiently. "No, no, I meant me and Johnny. Look, this is a complete list of the attendees, with the Discordants marked. Am I missing anyone we should be concerned about?"

"I'm no astrology expert, Kay."

"No, but you're a people expert." She gave him a sweet smile. "So tell me if there's anyone else who should be taken, and I'll revisit their chart."

Several thousand names, including his and Sephy's;

hundreds were marked. So Johnny was still making a big show of the signing: no one had been sure whether he would. There couldn't be *that* many venues that would hold so many people, even in Washington.

Once this information would have been vital.

Mac handed the list back, hiding his weary loathing of Kay. "I think you got them all. Very thorough job."

She dimpled. "Well, I've certainly worked hard. We have to make sure that bringing the three countries together again is under the most Harmonic conditions possible."

"Johnny seems much more cheerful these days," said Mac after a pause. "I guess Vancour's death did the trick, all right." It was the first chance he'd had to mention it casually to Kay since he'd learned about her lie.

Her relief seemed unfeigned. "Yes, it was lucky they found her." She giggled. "Tell you a secret," she whispered. "I didn't think they were going to. I went up there to get rid of the camp director and put a new one in place who'd tell Johnny whatever I wanted."

"But then they found her anyway?"

Kay nodded. "I got the call after I had to leave a factory I was visiting." Mac saw anger, as if at some memory, flicker in her eyes and then she smiled again. "Best news of my life," she said. "Seeing the photos just made it even better."

She reached for the lists in Mac's hand. As she opened the file and put them away, he caught a glimpse of another sheet of paper tucked inside.

And of a name written on it.

* * *

"You've got to get the kid out," Mac told Collis in an undertone. "Tonight." They were walking with Sephy through Harmony Park in the twilight, her arm tucked through Mac's.

Collis's face was as pale as his white shirt. "But all you saw was the name 'Halcyon', right? Not 'Vancour'?"

"Just Halcyon."

They fell silent as a woman walking a basset hound passed by, the dog's ears long and drooping. None of them spoke again until they came to a bench beside a duck pond. They sat together; Sephy wrapped her trench coat tightly around her.

Collis looked panicked. He bumped a fist against his lips. "Mac, I swear, I destroyed all the paperwork with his name on it – he shouldn't even *exist* any more."

"And Halcyon's a pretty common name," ventured Sephy. "Maybe..."

"No," said Mac. "Get him out, Collis. I won't have that kid's death on my conscience."

He felt Sephy press close to him; she squeezed his hand wordlessly.

Collis winced and nodded. "Where?"

"Nova Scotia, if it's up to me. Let him join his mother."

"Mac, you can't do that to him! He's desperate to help. Look, what about Appalachia?"

"It's about to *fall*, remember?"

"We could get him new papers again though – he could

work with the Resistance there when we start to build it up. Come Saturday, they're going to need everyone they can get."

"Fine," said Mac finally. "I'll leave that up to you. But he's out of this country before tomorrow."

"He will be." Collis hesitated, looking apprehensive. "What about me? Do you want me to go too?"

Mac let out a breath. "No, you've got to stay. Buddy, I don't know what's going on, but she doesn't seem to like you – so you've got to be careful as hell. But if you leave now, she'll know."

Collis's shoulders relaxed a little. "Don't worry, I don't want to," he said. "I can do a lot more good right where I am. It's just Hal. I'm all he's got, now that..." He trailed off, his jaw tightening. He looked down, fiddling with the brim of his fedora.

The news of Vancour's sudden departure hadn't gone down well. Mac had done what she'd asked. Someone else with Class A papers had been leaving for Appalachia not an hour after her request and he'd gotten her a ride with them – given her a little money.

She hadn't told him what her plans were, and he hadn't asked.

Collis stared at the ducks. He slapped his hat against his opposite hand. "I still can't believe you just let her go," he muttered.

Mac thought he'd kill for a soft bed with Sephy in it and no one else within a thousand miles. With an effort, he kept his voice level: "What exactly was I supposed to do? Come on, tell me, pal. Was I supposed to restrain her? Tell her no, I wouldn't help?"

"Hal will be okay," put in Sephy softly, leaning over to touch Collis's arm. "Look, I've got some friends in Appalachia; you can send him there. Then in a few months, when things calm down, maybe you can go to him."

Collis had his elbows on his knees, his hands buried in his hair. "Yeah," he said finally. "Thanks, Sephy. That sounds like the best thing."

He straightened, visibly trying to collect himself. "So, Mac...you think Kay was lied to about Amity being recaptured?"

Mac nodded. "Looks like it. Whoever's in charge up there now was probably too terrified to admit they couldn't find her. Easy to get photos in those places of bodies with faces too messed up to identify."

Collis looked down at his hands. "And...Amity really didn't say where she was going?"

"I'd tell you, pal. I promise."

The fedora twisted in Collis's grasp. "She still has a hard time even *walking*, Mac. Everything she's been through... oh, hell, I should have known she might go off and do something crazy. I should have—"

"*Hey.*" Mac gripped Collis's shoulder. "Knock it off. This isn't your fault, buddy. She's a grown woman. For all you know, she just wanted some time alone."

"No, I don't think so," Collis said hoarsely. He pinched

the bridge of his nose. "I can't shake the feeling that she's going to go and get herself killed somehow. And that there's not a damn thing I can do to stop it."

None of them spoke. Mac found himself chilled by Collis's words, and was relieved that Vancour didn't know about Gunnison's belief in their supposed karmic connection. What the man might do if he realized the dark mirror was still alive and "taunting" him was anyone's guess.

Finally Collis cleared his throat and stood up.

"All right," he said. "I'd better go get Hal and hook him up with someone who has Class As. It's a long drive."

He held his hand out to Mac; they shook.

"Listen, thanks a million, Mac," Collis said quietly. "I'll make sure Hal stays safe. I'll see you in the morning when we catch the train."

Sephy had been scribbling down her friends' address. She got up and pressed it into Collis's hand and then hugged him. Collis held onto her tightly. Then with a crooked smile, he turned and started away down the path.

Sephy sank back onto the bench. "He just wrings my heart," she murmured.

She pressed against Mac; he drew her close. In the pond, a duck came in for a landing, flapping and ungainly.

Mac gazed at it. When Vancour and Manfred had shown up with their message two days before, for a moment he'd actually had hope. Perhaps Rodriguez had gotten hold of the new, classified venue plans, his brain had babbled; perhaps the assassination of Gunnison and Cain could miraculously go ahead after all.

But why should the Resistance get a break for a change? In less than forty-eight hours the man would take over Appalachia and that would be that: the entire continent would go dark, locked away from the rest of the world.

And judging from those photographs that Vancour and Manfred had brought, soon the rest of the world would fall too.

If Mac hadn't seen the evidence, he wouldn't have believed it even of Johnny Gun. Hell, he wouldn't have believed it of *anyone* of their era. They'd all grown up with the harrowing stories of the Cataclysm. They were all supposed to be better, more enlightened, than this.

Remembering the sight of Vancour and Manfred – the burn scar that dominated the guy's face, the terrible thinness of them both, the haunted looks in their eyes – Mac grimaced inwardly. Yes, so much more enlightened. What a joke that he should even have felt any surprise.

"What do you think Kay Pierce wanted?" Sephy asked finally. "She didn't really need your help with the names, did she?"

Mac shook his head. "To gloat? See whose side I'm on? Or maybe she just likes me and wanted to talk."

Sephy stroked his chest. "Hope so. I hope she's madly in love with you, so she'll help to keep you safe. Take her more cookies."

Mac chuckled despite himself. Sephy sighed and slipped

her arm around his waist. "Day of Fire," she murmured, and shivered. "I wish we didn't have to be there."

"Me too." He gently rubbed her arm, feeling her warmth, the way her body seemed made to fit against his. "Hey," he whispered after a pause. "How about we go home and block out the world for a while?"

CHAPTER THIRTY-ONE

WHEN I WAS A LITTLE GIRL my father sometimes gave flying exhibitions at summer fairs. The big one each year was Monument Valley. It was held in August, in the height of summer, and Hal and I would start getting excited weeks ahead of time.

When it finally came, it was like a birthday and fireworks and the last day of school all rolled into one. The year that I was eleven, I bounced out of bed that morning and raced to my window. A day of blue and gold greeted me, with just a few white clouds drifting high overhead.

I propped my elbows on the sill, drinking it in. Hal ran in wearing his Firedove pyjamas, his dark hair sticking up. He joined me at the window and we grinned at each other.

"Perfect flying weather!" He gave a little whoop.

I nudged him. "You just wait. Dad's going to set that sky on fire!"

The fair didn't start until ten in the morning, and Dad's flying exhibition wasn't until two. We got to the fair right at ten, of course. Ma always looked forward to it too, though I could never understand why she wore such a fiddly dress for a day devoted to fairground rides and prize pigs and toffee apples. I wore shorts and a cotton shirt, and rebelled when she tried to force me into a dress too.

"Amity, you're getting older now," she said as she drove us there in our big black Fraser with its long, curved lines. She shifted gears and winced at the grinding noise she produced: Ma hated driving. "You can't be a tomboy for ever."

Collie smirked at me. "Bet she is."

"Yeah, I bet she is," echoed Hal.

"I bet I am too," I said, irritated. "Who wants to be a girly-girl? Ugh."

"You'll feel differently someday," said Ma.

Some years Collie didn't get to go with us. Some years his awful father chose that day, of all days, to notice that Collie wasn't around much and make him stay at home. But that morning he'd snuck out early and was at our house before Ma even started cooking breakfast. She made pancakes and Collie had had twelve and I'd had thirteen, not to be outdone. I wished now that I hadn't, though I'd die before admitting it.

Dad had been holed up in the barn with his Firedove all morning. He'd declared it off limits and Hal, Collie and I had been fizzing with excitement for hours, trying to think what he was up to. He'd come in for a cup of coffee and had feigned nonchalance when we peppered him with questions.

"Why, I just want some peace and quiet, that's all," he said, leaning oh-so-casually against the kitchen counter. "It's not easy to get some peace and quiet with you three savages rampaging around."

Recalling the glint that had been in his brown eyes, I could hardly think of anything else as Collie, Hal and I wandered the dusty fair, breathing in its heady scents of hot dogs and griddle cakes. Ma had given us some money and gone off to look at the flower arranging, so we did the strong-man test, swinging the mallet to make a bell ring – Collie beat me, even though I did it three times and practically ruptured myself – and then we teamed up together on the shooting range and won Hal a big purple stuffed bear. He didn't really like stuffed toys much, but he was proud of that one because Collie and I had gotten it for him. He named it Lewis and lugged it around all day, its fur getting dustier and dustier.

Finally it was almost two o'clock. We joined the flow of the crowd, all drifting towards the exhibition fields: kids in shorts and sandals eating cotton candy; women in brightly-printed sundresses; farmers wearing overalls and straw hats, and other men hatless, in open-necked shirts.

Everyone seemed loose, happy. There was an excited buzz in the air and my dad was the cause of it.

I gave a skip as I walked. Collie grinned at me, his hands stuck in his back pockets. By this time of summer, his hair was always bleached pale blonde. Today his eyes were as blue as the piece of sky reflected in our swimming hole.

"Tru's gonna be great," he said.

"Better than great," I said.

When we got to the fields, Collie, Hal and I struggled our way down to the roped-off front area, where I could already see Ma standing with some of her friends. She turned and saw us and waved us over. She looked smiling and pretty, her dark hair gleaming in the sun.

"Excuse me, my dad's flying – excuse me, my dad's the pilot," I said seriously as the three of us moved through the crowd. People let us pass. I heard someone whisper, "Her father must be Truce Vancour," and I thought I'd burst with pride.

"He's my father too!" protested Hal.

"Well, of course, stupid." Then I felt bad because Collie had gone quiet and I nudged him. "He's practically your dad too," I told him. "*You* know that. It's not even pretend." And he grinned at me gratefully.

We ducked under the ropes into the special area where Ma stood with a few dozen others. "Where have you been?" she chided, but not as if she really minded. "Here, get in front where you can see," she said – which didn't make much sense because anyone could see what was happening up in the sky, but I wanted to be right up front in case Dad could see us, so I didn't argue. We stood in front of her and she drew Hal up against her and looped her arms around my and Collie's shoulders.

"Now, I recognize Amity and Halcyon. Is that one of the Reed boys?" said the woman next to her with a sickly-sweet smile that made me want to kick her.

"Yes, this is our other son, Collis," said Ma just as sweetly, and I could see the woman's confusion – and that Collie, who'd started out looking embarrassed, was stranding straighter now, trying not to laugh.

I elbowed him. "See?" I whispered. Sometimes my mother was perfect, just perfect.

A ripple went through the crowd as we all heard it: the low, throaty roar of an approaching Firedove.

Ma bent her head down and whispered, "There might be a surprise."

My father's plane came into view. At first I didn't recognize it. Firedoves were blue and grey, with red circles on the wings. This plane was as white as a real dove, with ribbons streaming from its wings and tail. My father brought it low, passing right by the crowd, and I caught my breath, my eyes abruptly widening.

ROSE was painted on the nose of the plane in bright pink. AMITY was across the fuselage in purple, my favourite colour. My father did a one-winged turn, bringing the plane smartly around. On the other side was a red HALCYON and COLLIS in blue.

Dad went into a victory roll, spinning the plane around its propeller. Our names whirled in a rainbow, the ribbons whipping wildly. The crowd cheered. Ma laughed, standing on her tiptoes and waving at Dad. Hal was cavorting in place, shouting, "Amity, Collie, our names! Ma, he painted our names!"

I gazed over at Collie. His mouth was open, his eyes shining. He looked back at me and his grin was threatening to split his face, just as mine was.

The small plane was brilliant against the blue summer sky. A barrel roll, a spin, a loop-the-loop, all as effortless as a fish in water.

Finally Dad brought the Dove in. It trundled to a stop on the field. HALCYON and COLLIS glinted in the sunlight. The Dove's roar died; the ribbons fluttered and went limp. Collie's arm was summer-warm against mine. We all jumped up and down, cheering, even Ma.

My father pushed back the cockpit hood. He peeled off his helmet and waved to the crowd.

Then Dad waved just to us. He smiled and blew a kiss.

"Extraordinary performance," I heard a woman say.

The sun was shining inside of me. It felt as if I'd never stop smiling.

"That's my dad," I told her. "He was a Peacefighter."

Chapter Thirty-two

February, 1942

I was sitting on a bus beside an overweight man with shiny cheeks who told me he was a shoe salesman. He went door to door, he said, showing people samples of his shoes, and if they bought them, then four weeks later – "*...to the day,*" he emphasized, jabbing a finger at me – they'd receive a shiny box in the mail with their shoes all wrapped in tissue paper, like a birthday present.

It seemed a strange way to buy shoes to me. It seemed a strange way to make a living. I pressed my forehead against the window, watching the gentle green hills of Appalachia pass by. The further south we travelled, the more the world seemed to realize it was almost spring. Rain-washed farms looked perfect and new: the barns were red as apples, with white fences. Cows grazed, standing so still they might have been statues.

Occasionally I caught glimpses of ruins. Once we passed what looked like an ancient airport. The control tower lay crumpled along the ground.

When the man told me I looked familiar, I shrugged.

"I guess I just have one of those faces," I said.

Two days after we'd set off from Topeka, we rolled into Washington's Terminus Station. It was unseasonably hot for February and when I rose with the others I felt sticky, my clothes like a second skin. My leg ached. I clutched the railing as I struggled down the bus's metal stairs.

"Hurt your leg, sister?" said a man cheerfully, giving me his hand for the final step.

They don't know, I thought. *They really don't know what's coming.* I stared at the man but didn't realize I was doing it until I saw how uncomfortable he'd become. I gripped my cane.

"Yes, I had a bad fall," I said.

Everyone else clustered around the driver – a crowd of wilted hats and rumpled clothes, waiting for him to swing open the belly of the bus and start hauling out their luggage.

My only luggage was the small, battered case from Arvin's. I'd kept it between my feet on the journey, not willing to let it out of my sight. My fingers tightened around its worn handle.

I turned and walked away.

The station reminded me of Sacrament Station. There was even a similar ornate timepiece over the main entrance, with a motif of Firedoves and real doves, counting the minutes since the Cataclysm. *Lest we forget*, read the florid script.

Outside I found myself on a city street thick with traffic – autos, buses, taxicabs. It also reminded me a little of Sacrament: the same ziggurat buildings, the same billboards advertising toothpaste and cigarettes. An endless flow of people passed by on the sidewalk, some carrying shopping, others briefcases.

No one wore overcoats. The air weighed heavy under a blue sky. My sweater was too warm; dampness dotted under my armpits and along my spine.

I didn't know where I was going yet. Joining the hurried stream of passers-by with my bad leg felt daunting but I did it. I headed east for lack of a better direction, wincing when I was occasionally jostled but trying not to lean too heavily on my cane. I knew I shouldn't depend on it so much. I needed to be more mobile than this.

They had astrologers here too. Once this would have surprised and dismayed me. Now, when I saw the red-and-black Harmony symbol on a side street, I turned off the main road and made my way to it. *Madame Ursula*, read the sign on the door. *Charts cast, futures revealed.*

I opened the door. A bell tinkled cheerfully. I was in a small waiting room with red furniture that had faded to a deep pink. A middle-aged woman poked her head out from behind a set of curtains. "I'll be with you in a moment," she said with a smile.

I nodded and sat down, resting the case at my feet. I liked feeling it against my ankle – the security of what was inside. I rolled my cane between my palms and gazed at the Harmony symbol on the door.

In my mind, I saw a chain-link gate with that symbol in weathered metal, its two halves splitting as the gate slowly swung open against the snowy ground.

I started as the woman emerged again. "Sorry for the wait. Please, step into my consulting room. You're here for a reading?"

I followed her into the inner chamber, keeping my case with me. There were astrology symbols on the walls and a table with a book of planetary graphs on it. A pencil. A ruler. It looked clinical, scientific.

"No, I don't want a reading," I said as I lowered myself into a chair. "Just information. If you were going to do something at an astrologically significant time tomorrow, what time would you choose?"

The woman had been sitting down. She hesitated, a crease touching her forehead, and I realized how flat and intense I'd sounded. I managed a pleasant smile.

"It's for something special," I told her. "A surprise for someone. I want it to be just right."

* * *

The rest of the day passed. I wasn't hungry but knew I should eat so I went to a diner where I picked at my food. It seemed unbelievable that I could ever view a meal with disinterest. Later I went to a movie, my first in almost a year. The story on the screen – a farce involving mistaken identities, instant romance, charming characters leading brittle, clever lives – felt like something from a distant moon.

The audience kept laughing. Nothing about it seemed funny to me.

I wondered what Ingo would think.

That night I slept on a park bench with my arms folded around my case until a policeman moved me on. "You should know better, Miss," he scolded. "Now get yourself to a nice women's hotel. There's one on Hillview."

He gave me directions, holding my arm and pointing up the street – stressing that I should turn right on Baltimore, not left. I nodded and thanked him, and when he was gone I turned and walked the other way.

The streets were quiet now. I felt agitated but knew I should rest my leg. Seven minutes past two in the afternoon, the astrologer had told me. I had to be fit and ready. I found my way back to the station. Almost empty but still open. A cleaner hummed tunelessly as he made his way across the broad expanse of floor with a mop, leaving it gleaming in his wake.

I sat on a bench and looked up at the memorial timepiece. My gaze lingered on a Firedove's sleek lines as I remembered slipping into a cockpit before battle, its metal warmed by the Angeles sun. The faint smell of machine oil in the hangar where our morning meeting was held – how straight and tall we'd stood as we made our vows.

I had really thought it all meant something.

By six o'clock in the morning the station had begun to fill. By eight it was bustling. I stayed on the bench and held my case on my lap. Once or twice I flipped open its scuffed catches and checked inside, though no one could have stolen its contents. I hadn't let that case out of my sight since I left Can-Amer.

What I needed was still there.

Just before twelve o'clock, I rose. I went to the crowded ladies' restroom and struggled my way to a basin. The women on either side were combing their hair, applying fresh lipstick. I splashed water on my face and gazed at myself in the mirror.

My too-thin face looked back: olive skin and light brown eyes. Dark hair that was longer than I'd worn it in years, hanging unfashionably straight to my shoulders. My eyes were so steady, my mouth so unsmiling, that I could see why people had been shrinking away from me these past few days.

I glanced down at the Aries mark: the stylized ram's head etched blackly on my palm. I understood why Collie had always tried to hide his own mark, yet when I let my hand fall it wasn't as a fist. There was no point. The mark would always be there, for however much longer I lived.

I picked up my case again and left the station. It was a brilliant blue day, this last day that Appalachia would taste freedom. I thought of the poem about spring and a wistful sadness touched me.

A taxi rank stood outside the station. A cabbie leaned against a bright yellow cab reading a newspaper. The headline read: *Gunnison and Staff Arrive, President Weir Stresses Nothing Will Change.*

I approached him. "I'm going sightseeing," I said. "Could you just drive me around the city for a while?"

The cabbie glanced up and shrugged. "Sure, sister. No particular destination?"

"I'll know it when I see it," I said.

I gazed out the window with the case in my lap as he drove me through the city streets. At first he tried to make conversation. When I didn't respond he gave up. I saw his eyes flicker to me in the rear-view mirror, curious and a little wary.

I didn't pay much attention to the buildings we passed, not even the rebuilt capitol building with its broad, gleaming dome. It nestled down in a slight dip; the surrounding roads were at a higher level now than in the time of the ancients.

I gave it only a fleeting glance. I was looking at the crowds on the sidewalks, at the traffic itself. It took over an hour of driving, but I was right. I knew it when I saw it.

I leaned forward.

"Here," I said to the cabbie. "Could you stop, please?"

* * *

The cabbie gave a low whistle as we pulled to a stop outside Ranger Stadium. "Hey, I guess this is where the signing's happening."

The vast parking lot was packed. For over ten blocks before we'd reached the stadium, I'd noticed a steady flow of people heading towards it, though there was no game on. That morning I'd read the same paper as the cabbie. It had confirmed that a *specially selected audience* would witness the historic event: the entire continent rejoined under a single flag.

The stadium's main entrance was invisible behind the throng; I could see only the graceful top of an arch. The line going in moved so slowly that it seemed not to move at all. Though it was no surprise, I still stiffened as I glimpsed grey-suited Guns at the door, searching everyone before they went in.

Aries, number seven, hut twelve.

SING!

The cabbie tipped his cap back. "Man, I don't like all the secrecy that's been around this thing. Paper said not even those attending knew where they were going until this morning. Crazy!" He glanced at me. "Ready to move on?"

I shook my head. After a pause, I said, "I think I'll stay for a while and check it out."

His eyebrows rose. "I don't think they'll let you in, sister. You gotta have a special ticket, the paper said."

I came back to myself and managed a smile. "That's all right." I got out my pocketbook and paid him. I gave him the rest of the money I had. It was a big tip and he held the bills uncertainly, gazing back at me.

"Hey, you okay? Want me to wait for you?"

"No need," I said. I opened the door and got out, gripping my cane. I reached back into the cab for my case and shut the door. "Thanks," I told him, lifting the case in a sort of wave.

I could feel his eyes on me as I turned and started towards the crowd. Finally I heard the cab's engine start again and he pulled away.

A ragtag crowd had gathered on the edges of the parking lot, curious about what was happening. They stood in small groups, murmuring, watching the ticket holders go in.

I skirted my way around them. I didn't head for the main entrance. I found a corner of the parking lot that was quiet and propped my case on the back of someone's auto – an old Fraser, just like we used to have when I was growing up.

I opened my case and pulled out the pistol. It was loaded. It gleamed darkly in the sun. I slipped it in the pocket of my skirt and then took something else out too, which I held in the palm of my hand, between my skin and the cane.

I left my suitcase where it was, still open.

I started around the broad, curved shape of Ranger

Stadium. Soon I'd left the buzzing crowds behind. Even the noise of city traffic dimmed. A chain-link fence closed off the stadium's rear section; a cluster of Guns stood guarding it.

It was further away than it looked. My leg turned weak and throbbing long before I got there. I ignored it and kept on, using my cane as lightly as I could. The sun shone too warm on my arms but I didn't really mind. Being warm still seemed like something of a miracle.

Before I reached the fence, the Guns had all noticed me. They stood waiting, watching. I knew I must have seen their warm-weather uniform before – short-sleeved grey shirts with the red-and-black swirl of the Harmony emblem on the breast – but I didn't recall it. To me, Guns would forever be dressed in long wool coats, their faces shrouded by scarves.

Behind them, parked near the back door of the stadium, was a fleet of Shadowcars. I gazed at them, remembering the smell of fear and urine – remembering the places those things took you to.

President Weir stresses nothing will change.

The fence swung open with a *clang*. A trio of Guns strode towards me, their boots black and shining.

"You're not allowed back here," barked one.

I stopped short, letting them approach. My leg hurt and I was glad to stop moving. Just before they reached me, I pulled the pistol out of my skirt pocket and pressed it against my temple.

"My name is Amity Vancour," I said. "I've planted a bomb in this facility. I want to talk to Madeline Bark, or I'll pull the trigger and you'll never find it."

CHAPTER THIRTY-THREE

THEY SENT ONE OF THE GUNS into the stadium. The other two stood nearby and murmured together, watching me with hard eyes. From their body language, one wanted to rush me – the other, maybe his superior, was forbidding it. I stood leaning on my cane. The object in my palm bit against my skin. The pistol in my other hand felt warm. So did the sun on my neck.

It didn't take long. My name meant something, apparently. When Madeline arrived she was walking briskly, almost running, escorted by two other Guns.

She came to a stop in front of me. She wore a grey skirt and a white silk blouse with a string of pearls. Her hazel eyes were wide. As she gazed at me her freckles stood out starkly.

"Amity," she whispered. "But we thought..."

She flinched as I took the pistol away from my head. The Guns leaped forward. I turned the pistol so that the barrel was facing me and handed the weapon to Madeline.

"I'm giving myself up," I said in a low voice. "But I won't tell you where the bomb is until you talk to me. In private."

Madeline stared down at the pistol in her hand as if she had no idea what to do with it. Finally she looked up, her face expressionless.

"Take her to my office," she said to the Guns. "I'll get the information from her and then you can take her away."

Guns grabbed my arms. They hurried me through the gate and across the inner parking lot, past the Shadowcars. I gritted my teeth against the pain – they were walking faster than I could really manage – but said nothing.

Once inside the stadium, the long corridor they took me down was cool and subterranean. Madeline walked behind us, her high-heeled footsteps measured against the concrete. Above, bare light bulbs shone. My pulse beat double-time. Yet I felt tautly focused – oddly calm.

We reached a door. What looked like a temporary sign hung on it: *M Bark, Event Coordinator.*

"Take her in," said Madeline.

The head Gun motioned at my cane. "Not with that."

"It's just a cane," I said. "I can't walk very well without it."

Madeline had the Gun check my cane over. He turned it this way and that, testing to see if the handle came off.

Another Gun searched me, his hands rough and probing as he swept them over my body. I stood motionless, feeling the glass that was still pressed against my palm.

Finally the first Gun handed my cane back. "We'll be right outside," he said to Madeline.

"I'll be quick," she said.

The room was plain and functional – nothing like her World for Peace office. Madeline motioned for me to sit in a metal chair. Keeping the pistol on me, she edged behind the desk and sat down too, staring at me.

"We thought you were dead," she whispered. "We saw photos."

"Then someone was lying to you."

"How did you escape?"

I felt made of stone. She still looked exactly like the woman my father had been in love with – the woman I'd trusted, admired. "We don't have much time, Madeline," I said. "Is this really what you want to spend it talking about?"

Her eyes flicked to a clock on the wall: ten minutes to two. "You can't have planted a bomb," she said. "We – we've kept this venue utterly private. Security has been kept at a—"

"I'm afraid you can't always trust the people you believe in," I said.

She licked her lips and I knew that, like me, she was seeing the note I'd once left on her desk in the World for Peace offices: *I trusted you.*

"What do you want from me?" she asked.

I clenched my cane. I was hyper-aware of the small room and everything in it. Madeline's pearl necklace had a silver clasp showing on one side of her neck. A condensation stain marked the wall behind her.

"Answers," I said in a voice I didn't recognize as my own. "You're going to tell me why my father threw the civil war Peacefight. You're going to promise me you'll get those answers to Hal. And then, if you can't let me go, you're going to take that pistol and shoot me – because I'm not going back to that place."

Her shoulders sagged as if I'd just punched the breath from her. "Amity…I can't…this is so…"

"*Answers!*" I cried. "I know you know! At my trial, you started to say that you'd talked him into it, and then you caught yourself. Don't deny it!"

Her eyes skittered to the clock again. "There's no time!" Her grip on the pistol tightened. "We can *make* you tell us where it is, you know—"

I un-palmed the shard of glass and pressed its sharp point to my neck, in the same spot where my friend had once held a scrap of metal.

"Don't bother trying," I said. "I mean it, Madeline: I'm not going back there. Now *talk*, or your men won't have time to get to the bomb, much less defuse it."

She gave a short, sobbing breath, staring at the piece of glass. "I don't know what you expect to hear. It was all such a long time ago…"

I waited, poised.

"I...Amity, I really don't think there's time. Tell me about the bomb first, and then we can— "

I pressed the glass against my neck hard enough to start a small trickle of blood, warm against my skin. Madeline gasped.

"Start. Talking," I said.

"I don't know what to say!" She stared at the blood as if mesmerized. "We...we were in love. We'd been in love since before he married Rose, but then she got pregnant with you...and then I left Peacefighting and worked for the World for Peace, and got involved in Gunnison's campaign... Amity, this can't be what you want! What if I promise to let you escape if you'll tell me about the bomb?"

"I wouldn't believe you."

"Do you think I *enjoyed* what happened to you?" she cried. "You were like a niece to me!" When I didn't answer, she pressed a hand to her mouth. "I really don't know what to tell you. There's no big story. I asked him if he'd do it and he did."

"You talked him into it!"

"It didn't take much."

"That's not true!"

"It is! He loved me and he wanted the money. He was in debt because of his grandfather's old place and he wanted to fix it up, to have something to give you kids. I don't think...I don't think he really thought about it much apart from that, once he got used to the idea."

I wasn't aware that I was trembling, but I must have been: the glass was shuddering at my neck. "No," I said. "No. He was a Peacefighter. He believed in it with everything he had."

"That came later," said Madeline softly. "Once he realized what he'd done."

Very distantly above, I could hear the thunderous roar of a crowd. More than that, I could feel it: a deep vibration that reached into my bones.

Madeline swallowed and looked at the clock again. Four minutes till two. "Amity..."

I closed my eyes, seeing my father's face as he'd told me over and over about Louise, our ancestor who'd been one of the founders of the World for Peace – the strange fervency in his voice. The sharp-smelling tumblers that I'd found in the kitchen sometimes when I'd woken up in the mornings. A man who could never quite meet our eyes whenever it really mattered.

My fingers pulsed with pain. I'd clenched the glass so hard that I'd cut them. I lowered the shard. I looked at it in my hand – at the blood streaking over the glass and twining over my palm, covering the tattoo.

My throat was tight. I stared down at the glass, the blood, and felt light-headed.

"There's no bomb," I murmured.

Madeline gasped out a breath. "Are you sure?"

I studied her, and wondered how I ever could have thought she looked the same. "Harmony Five changed me,"

I said. "But I'm still not capable of killing hundreds of innocent people."

Our gazes locked. I saw realization dawn in Madeline's eyes: she knew it was true. She grabbed for a talky device on her desk and pressed the button.

"There's no bomb," she said hurriedly. "The situation's under control. Get everyone out to their posts – *now.* They'll be needed soon."

She dropped the talky with a clatter and put her hands over her face. Her shoulders shuddered. Somewhere far above, an audience of thousands cheered – but it wasn't the signing. Not yet. We hadn't yet reached that perfect, astrologically significant moment.

There was a long pause.

"Why are the Guns needed at their posts?" I asked hoarsely.

Madeline slowly lowered her hands from her face. She was still holding the pistol in one, and she gazed blankly down at it. She didn't answer.

"What are the Shadowcars for, Madeline?"

"They..." Her throat worked. "I don't expect you to understand. I know it's – it's all gotten a little out of control. But for a Harmonic society, it's important that..." She trailed off.

"What happened to you?" I cried. "I used to *admire* you."

Her voice was a thin, trembling wire. "Nothing happened. I worked for Gunnison's campaign when he was a senator and saw the good he does – the hope he gives people."

"*Hope*?"

"Yes, *hope.* He made me believe in myself!"

The blood felt slick on my palm. "My father crashed his plane on purpose, didn't he?"

Madeline flinched, her face draining of colour. She opened her mouth and closed it. "I...I don't know."

"Commander Hendrix told me! You asked Dad to throw another fight, and he agreed to it! You knew the guilt had been destroying him for years, but you still..." My words grew tangled with anger, with despair. I stopped. "You killed him," I whispered. "As surely as if you pointed that pistol at him and pulled the trigger."

The weapon in Madeline's hand shook. She watched it with wide eyes, as if the motion had nothing to do with her. Then she straightened her shoulders. She put one hand over the other, steadying it.

She pointed the pistol at me.

"Get out," she said raggedly.

When I didn't move – when I couldn't move, because I was frozen in shock – she shouted, "*Get out!*"

I groped for my cane and stood. I faced her. We were both breathing hard. I could see Madeline's chest rising and falling, though her hands on the pistol were firm.

"I don't know why my father kept having anything to do with you," I said.

Madeline's small, grimacing smile was more like a baring of teeth.

"Because I was the only person he could talk to," she said. "I knew what he'd done."

I left the office. I expected Guns to be waiting outside but there weren't any. To my faint surprise I still held the shard of glass and I stuck it in my sweater pocket. My leg throbbed.

I started down the long corridor, holding tightly to my cane.

The pistol shot was so loud that I cried out; for a heart-thumping moment I expected pieces of wall to explode around me. But then there was silence. Utter silence… except for a faint dripping noise and the rumble of the crowd from above.

I stood staring back at Madeline's office. The door was partly open.

I started to shake. I didn't want to go in there. But what if she was still alive? I forced myself to put one step in front of the other, ignoring the instinct shrieking at me to leave, get away, not look at whatever awaited me.

I got to the doorway of the office and hesitated. Bile rose in the back of my throat: a rich, coppery scent cloyed the air. I took another step.

I looked.

Madeline lay slumped sideways in her chair. The back of her head was gone. The cement-block wall behind her was dripping. Strands of her auburn hair were plastered in the gore.

My cane clattered to the floor. My legs gave way and I

groped blindly for the doorway. I slid against it to the ground and sat shaking, hugging myself, staring at the remains of the woman I'd wanted to be like.

A snapshot of memory: Madeline on our farm. She'd just landed the Gauntlet Jenny, the bright yellow biplane that I first learned to fly in. She paused as she clambered out of it, laughing. Her battered leather jacket was just like my dad's and the freckles across her nose had been multiplying daily in the sunshine.

"Your turn!" she called to me.

The memory faded.

My chest heaved. I gasped and covered my face with my hands for a second, clutching hard at my skin. Yet there were no tears in me. There hadn't been any in so long, and there weren't any now.

When I looked again, Madeline was still there. The back of her head was still gone.

Nothing had changed. Nothing ever would.

I fumbled for my cane and pushed myself to my feet. I felt both electric and numb. I didn't remember walking over to Madeline but my feet must have propelled me there because suddenly I was beside her desk looking down at her, trying not to gag on the heavy scent of blood.

Her hazel eyes were blank. They say the dead look at peace but I'd known for a long time now that this was a lie. The silver clasp of her pearl necklace had a drop of blood on it. She still held the pistol in her blunt, tomboyish hand.

Far above, the crowd roared.

I heard someone's ragged breathing and realized it was my own. It was two minutes past two. In five minutes, Gunnison would take over this country and those Shadowcars would be put into use.

More people taken away.

More heads on fences.

More bodies falling limply from faded wooden platforms against the sunset.

More people killing themselves.

More.

A slow mental drumbeat had started. I reached for the pistol. I prised Madeline's fingers from it and then put her hand gently in her lap.

She'd made her own choices. So had my father. There was no getting away from what they'd done. But there was only one person directly responsible for all that had followed.

No more. It had to stop now.

I slipped the pistol into my sweater pocket. I left the office. It was cool down here but my spine felt clammy with sweat. I leaned heavily on my cane as I walked quickly along the corridor, my uneven footsteps joining the beat in my head. It measured out my footsteps, the seconds, the minutes.

I opened a door and stepped outside. The sun stroked my face with warm fingers and the sky soared overhead: a perfect flying day.

Before me was a long aisle and rows and rows of crowded seats to either side, stretching down to a platform. Gunnison stood on the platform making a speech. The microphone bounced his words against my brain; they were just noise, noise, adding to the drumbeat and my footsteps. Others sat on the platform too but they were blurs. I could see only him, and I could see him so clearly.

No more.

I started down the aisle. My cane thumped rhythmically. Guns stood posted at the ends of each row, arms behind their backs. People were cheering but seemed frightened.

Maybe people began to notice me. I don't know. Maybe the Guns glanced at each other, confused. I don't know.

Gunnison's gaze met mine and he recognized me and he went very still and the words, words stopped, but the drumbeat in my head kept on.

I kept walking.

Melody's body, lying naked on the snow. My brother hiding in a closet for months. Ingo's half-burned face. Collie turning informer to survive.

Guns must have lunged for me then but Gunnison stopped them. His eyes were wide, panicked.

"Don't touch her!" I saw his mouth say. Sound snapped back into focus and I heard him then, his words ringing in the silent stadium: "Let her come. We can't interfere with fate."

I reached the end of the rows of people and stepped

onto grass. I crossed it, my cane sinking into the soft turf a little with every step.

I started up the stairs to the platform and Gunnison's eyes were locked on mine. There were only the two of us in that moment and we knew each other down to our souls.

He took a step back from me. He waved behind him at someone. "Start reading the names," he said hoarsely. "I've got to regain the karmic upper hand."

"Sir, we haven't signed the treaty yet—"

"Read them! Start taking the Discordants away! Do it!"

I took the pistol from my sweater pocket. It felt warm and heavy in my hands. I let my cane fall as I aimed it. People were shouting but all I could see were moving mouths.

No.

More.

No.

I pulled the trigger.

CHAPTER THIRTY-FOUR

FEBRUARY, 1942

THE SHOT RANG IN MAC'S EARS. In the audience near the platform, he sprang to his feet, staring in disbelief at Gunnison's sprawled body – at the dark stain spreading quickly across his chest.

Like everyone else, he'd sat stunned as Amity Vancour had walked slowly to the platform: all of them held suspended in silence, in time. The Guns guarding the stage had rushed towards Amity, then been halted by Gunnison's order. As she'd climbed the platform stairs they'd clustered uncertainly near the seating area, watching with everyone else.

Holy hell, she's really going to do it, Mac had thought, his blood pulsing. Somehow he'd known she had a pistol, as clearly as if he'd seen it hidden in her pocket.

The sound of the shot broke the spell. Amity swayed on her feet, staring down at Gunnison's lifeless form. The stadium throbbed with screams. Onstage a chair fell over as someone jumped up. Shrieking – people scrambling to get away.

"Grab her!"

"She's still got the pistol!"

Dazedly, Amity turned towards the crowd on the stage.

For some reason Mac's startled gaze flicked to Kay Pierce: the only person standing still. Half-hidden, she drew something from her pocket.

A second shot echoed. Sandford Cain staggered and fell. Mac felt dumbfounded, unable to process what he'd just seen.

Only seconds had passed. A Gun charged the stage. He grabbed Amity and hustled her off, half-dragging her, wrenching the pistol from her grip. She cried out in pain, struggling feebly, but was no match for him.

"Cain's still alive! Get him a doctor!" someone shouted. People came running forward; a small, urgent group surrounded Cain.

President Weir of the Appalachian States stepped forward to the microphone. "Calm! Everyone, calm! In light of these…these extraordinary events, the Appalachian States must decline to—"

"No!" The voice somehow carried over the crowd.

Kay Pierce stepped forward, her hands empty now and

her small, pointed face fierce. "I will sign the treaty on behalf of Can-Amer," she said. She motioned to the Guns. "I'm taking control," she told them. "Help President Weir to sign."

President Weir took a step back, his face pale. Guns surrounded him, hands on their pistols. "I…but this is…" he stammered.

The treaty stood waiting on a ceremonial plinth. Kay Pierce signed it with a flourish and turned to President Weir. She handed him the pen. Her face was as Mac had never seen it: hard, uncompromising. Then she covered the mic with one hand and smiled the sweet, pretty smile that he knew.

"Can-Amer still has an army, President Weir," she said, her voice carrying to the first few rows. "Now, would you like to at least get to pretend to stay in charge of your country? Or shall we just add your name to the list?"

President Weir's throat bobbed as he swallowed. He looked at the Guns.

Slowly, he took the pen and signed.

The crowd had gone utterly still. The Guns in the audience stood at attention. Mac thought, *She couldn't have planned this, there's simply no way.* But it had happened just as neatly as if she had.

Kay's eyes met Mac's then: cool, calculating. His scalp winced with sudden realization.

She knew.

He and Sephy were dead.

Kay took out several sheets of paper. "My men are guarding the exits," she said. "Will the following people please give yourselves up to the Guns. This is an unfortunate, but necessary step to ensure that Appalachia continues to be a peaceful, Harmonious place."

She started to read. "Abrams, Harold. Ackerman, Sophia. Borrelli, Clive..."

Protesting, panicked shouts began to fill the air. The Guns seemed to have a list of where everyone was to be found and they moved with mechanical regularity, grabbing people, taking them away.

Mac was wearing his ceremonial Gun uniform. He made his way to the aisle and strode briskly to the twelfth row, where Sephy sat. He reached across someone and grabbed her arm.

"Come on, you Discordant scum," he said clearly.

Sephy sat crying in silent horror, tears running down her smooth, dark cheeks. She had the presence of mind to flinch and shake her head. "No – no, please..."

"*Now!*"

Mac jerked her to her feet and into the aisle; he started hustling her out of the stadium.

"Oh, Mac..." she whispered.

"It's okay, it's okay," he murmured back, and hoped it would be true. Kay's voice still boomed around them, reading name after name.

"...Geroux, Persephone..."

They entered the stadium's foyer area. There was a

hot-dog counter, a popcorn stand – both empty now. The Shadowcars had pulled around and waited in a long grey line outside, silver grilles gleaming. People ahead of them were being shoved into the backs of the vehicles.

"…Jones, Macintyre…"

Sephy shivered as his name was called. Her eyes were locked on the Guns. One stood just outside the main doors, closing up a Shadowcar.

"How do we get past them?" she whispered.

The Gun glanced over. Dread touched Mac. "Shut up," he said loudly, yanking Sephy's arm. She looked down; he could feel her trembling.

They got outside. The Gun headed over to them – thankfully someone Mac didn't know. Before the guard could speak, Mac jerked his head back at the stadium. "Get in there – *hurry!* Vancour had an accomplice; I just passed another gunman!"

He swung open the Shadowcar's rear door and shoved Sephy inside, pushing her hard enough so that she stumbled. He caught a glimpse of a dozen pale, frightened faces as he banged the door shut again.

"Go! I'll take the prisoners!"

The Gun hesitated. "But—"

Another Gun had overheard. He spoke urgently into a talky. "Vancour had an accomplice! Near the main entrance. Start searching; we're heading back in." He glanced up. "Sectors three through eight, back to your posts! *Now!*"

Several Guns took off. Mac heard them shouting once

they got inside. The man in front of Mac hadn't moved. Mac grabbed the keys from his hand. "Get back in there or join the prisoners," he hissed.

The Gun almost stumbled over the kerb in his hurry to run after the others. Mac rushed to the front of the Shadowcar, wrenched open the door. He twisted the keys in the ignition and pulled away with a lurch, spinning the steering wheel.

In the rear-view mirror, he could see a trio of Guns watching, frowning uncertainly. But they didn't move and a moment later Mac was gone, speeding down the city streets. He let out a long, shaking breath, watching the stadium grow smaller behind them.

A grilled opening connected the cab to the back of the truck. Mac heard Sephy talking urgently: "…so please try not to worry; with luck we'll get away and it'll all be fine…"

"Sephy!" he called. He didn't take his eyes from the road but reached up and stuck his fingers through the grille. A moment later he felt her grip his hand tightly.

"I'm here," she said.

He looked at her in the rear-view mirror, taking in her eyes, the elegant line of her neck.

"Number twenty," he said. "Will you marry me?"

She pressed her cheek against his fingers.

"Maybe," she said.

Epilogue

April, 1942

"Mac wants to know if you're ready," said Hal.

I turned from the bedroom window. I'd been gazing out at the view one last time. Sephy's friends' house was deep in the Smoky Mountains. These last two months I'd spent a lot of time sitting alone on this window seat, watching the leaves change from vulnerable green curls to full, lush foliage.

It made a welcome change from what was happening on the telio.

My brother stood in the doorway, waiting for my answer. He looked so mature and so young at the same time. I hesitated, then put my hand on his shoulder.

"Almost," I said.

Hal tried to smile but his expression was conflicted. "I'll go help Mac," he mumbled. Suddenly I was standing alone and Hal was jogging down the stairs.

Sephy was just coming out of the bedroom that she'd been sharing with Mac. She touched my arm.

"Hey, he'll forgive you," she said. "He loves you a lot, you know. Just give him time."

I nodded. I hoped she was right. The first night I'd come here, I'd been unprepared for my brother's anger. "Do you have any idea what it was like to come back and find that you'd just *left*?" he'd demanded.

"I'm sorry," I'd told him. "I was trying to get answers for us…about Dad."

Hal had stared at me in disbelief. We'd been sitting alone at the kitchen table, with rain beating against the windows. "What the hell good would answers have done me if you'd been killed? I'd only just gotten you back, Amity! It was like you didn't even care!"

"I'm sorry," I'd repeated. There was a vase with flowers on the table; I'd pushed my hair back with both hands, gazing at it. "I guess…I guess I wasn't thinking very clearly," I said softly. "Getting answers seemed like the most important thing in the world at the time."

It was the only explanation I could give him. It was true, but it didn't seem to help.

Hal had looked away from me. "So did you find out why Dad did it?" he asked finally, his voice stilted.

I slowly shook my head. "I don't think there *was* any

reason, really. Or at least no good one. He just…made a mistake."

That didn't seem to help either. But I knew that what didn't help most of all was me.

The moment of the shooting felt like a dream now. Yet since then, I'd been remote. Distant. It was nothing I could control. I felt locked apart from myself, observing everything from far away, and no matter how much I told myself that my brother needed me, I couldn't seem to find my way back to him. I couldn't seem to find my way back to anyone.

After I'd pulled the trigger, everything had shifted to slow motion.

The report had kicked through me, stinging my palms. The gunshot hurt my ears. John Gunnison crumpled and fell to the platform floor: the man I'd seen in a hundred newsreels, a thousand newspaper stories. He'd always been in grainy black-and-white and now here he was in colour. His thick blonde hair was greying at the temples and the life was draining from him as I watched.

I'd stood frozen and cold, gazing at a tiny bubble of blood at the corner of his mouth. His blue eyes slowly went blank.

I've killed a man, I thought.

The world dimmed at the edges then. A Gun tackled me and dragged me away. I may have struggled – I don't remember. The next thing I really recall, I was in a Shadowcar, being driven somewhere. I sat huddled on the bench as the engine vibrated, and thought of the shard of glass.

It was in my pocket. I took it out and gazed down at it in the gloom. What I had to do seemed so clear to me, but all I could see was Gunnison crumpling, falling. The glass glinted.

The Shadowcar stopped. I clutched the glass and looked up sharply, fear pulsing through me.

Footsteps. The back of the Shadowcar swung open.

Collie.

I gasped out a breath. "Was…was it you?"

The Gun who'd grabbed me had shouted so loudly – *You'll pay for this, Discordant scum! No, I've got her! Help Cain!* – that I could hardly make out his voice. He shoved me in the back of the van. I'd been in such a daze that I hadn't even looked at him, not really.

Collie's eyes were bright. He cleared his throat. "Yeah, it was me."

He helped me from the van. I emerged into the sunshine. Somehow his arms were around me and he was holding me tightly.

"Are you all right?" he said, his voice hoarse.

He still smelled like Collie. I heard myself moan. I closed my eyes and pressed my face against his warm neck, willing none of this to have happened – for it to be eleven months ago, and for us to be dancing at The Ivy Room with Van Wheeler singing and the Western Seaboard still its own country.

"Amity?"

I pulled away and stared at him, taking in his crisp grey clothes. Collie had been the Gun. He wore a Gun's uniform.

My eyes were still dry. So was my throat, my chest, my very soul.

I turned away and rubbed my arms. "I killed him," I said finally.

Collie started to touch my face. He hesitated and let his hand fall. "I know," he whispered.

I noticed where we were then: what looked like a little-used service road not far from Ranger Stadium. The dirt road was dusty, with weeds growing beside it. The curved shape of the stadium rose in the distance.

I gazed fearfully at it. "Why are we still here?"

Collie glanced at the stadium too; his jaw tensed. "I've got to hear this," he said. "I could hear what was happening through the loudspeakers as I was driving away."

A woman's voice was booming faintly, calling out names.

I clutched my elbows, staring over at the stadium. "They're arresting people," I whispered. "*How?* Gunnison's gone!"

"Kay Pierce has taken over," Collie said.

He'd winced at *Geroux, Persephone;* now *Jones, Macintyre* was called and Collie dropped heavily into the still-open van. His shoulders slumped. He gripped his face with both hands, his knuckles white.

In a daze, I sat beside him. *Kay Pierce.*

The list went on in that slow, steady voice. Dozens of names. Dozens of them, all pounding at my brain. My leg throbbed and I thought how crowded the trains heading up to the camps would be and how tragically easy it was to kill a man but how hard it was to make any difference.

How hard it was to make any difference at all.

Suddenly Collie stiffened. He briefly closed his eyes and then stood up.

There was a notepad in his front breast pocket; he took it out and scribbled something in it. "This is where Hal is," he said hurriedly, handing the page to me. "He's here in Appalachia, with friends of Sephy's. Go there until you can figure out what to do."

I glanced down at the scrap of paper. "What? But—"

"Listen!" He took out his wallet and drew all the bills from it. He thrust them at me. "Take the Shadowcar! Ditch it once you're out of the city. Buy a used car, *soon.* I'll stall them as long as I can, but they'll be showing your image on every telio set in the country in a few hours."

A chill touched me. "You're going back there. To work for Kay Pierce."

Collie gripped my arms. "I've got to! I wasn't called. I'm the only person the Resistance has got who's still on the inside. They're going to need all the help they can get now."

I felt empty. I slowly folded the scrap of paper and part of me wondered if that was why he was really going back.

Guilt touched me at the thought, and then anger that I felt guilty, after all that had happened.

Collie had my pistol tucked in his belt. He handed it to me with tense fingers.

"Shoot me," he said.

"*What?*"

"Shoot me! Just in the arm, or leg! If they suspect I let you go, I'm dead."

I shuddered at the feel of the weapon, remembering how it had kicked against my palms. Bile rose. "I can't do that."

"Amity! You have to!"

"No. I can't." I was shaking. I gave the pistol back to him.

"All right, fine; I'll do it myself." Collie glanced down the road, breathing hard. He took a handkerchief from his pocket. "I'll wrap this around it," he muttered. "Then cut across to the main road…then I'll lie down like I've collapsed from loss of blood…"

"Collie…" There were still no tears, but heaviness weighed like lead around my heart.

"Be careful," I said finally. "Don't…don't really collapse from loss of blood."

He went still and looked at me. His eyes were very blue in the sunlight. "Would you care?"

My throat clenched. "I never stopped caring. That was never the point."

Collie let out a long breath and stepped close. "I love

you," he said. "I'll see you again. You and Hal both." Before I could stop him – before I could decide if I wanted to stop him – he took my head in his hands and kissed me.

His lips were warm, slightly rough. So familiar.

He pulled away and gazed at me. His thumb stroked the corner of my mouth and from nowhere, I thought of the day that Dad had painted his plane with our names. I swallowed hard.

"A man can change," Collie whispered.

He stepped away from me. I felt frozen. Distantly, the names were still being read. Collie steeled himself and took the pistol. He pointed it at his right bicep and he pulled the trigger.

"Hey, Amity, I almost forgot," said Mac.

We'd just pulled away from the house in the beat-up Bennett that Mac drove now. Leslie and Beatrice stood with their arms around each other, waving at us from their front yard: a kind couple who I'd spent too little time talking to these past two months.

I was in the back seat with Hal. "What?" I said.

In the front, Sephy twisted to wave at her friends. Mac waved too, then glanced back at me. "That pal of yours is going to be there."

We were on our way to Bayon – just across the Hudson from New Manhattan, where someone could sneak us into the city.

Since taking power Kay Pierce had been touring Appalachia, "consolidating the new alliance". In fact, she'd been putting new officials in place. As expected, Appalachia was now its own country in name only. The entire continent was under Pierce's rule.

My taking a man's life hadn't helped. The Shadowcars still prowled. So-called Discordants were still taken away in broad daylight. No matter how often Mac reassured me that killing Gunnison had done some good – "Kay won't be able to hold on to it, Amity. You've dealt that regime a death blow" – it was clear that Kay Pierce loved power and was learning the ropes fast.

Sandford Cain was still alive, despite the fact that Pierce had taken advantage of my shooting to try to do away with him as well. The fiction was that I'd shot both men. Whether Cain realized the truth or not, I didn't know, but his pale-eyed gaze still chilled me whenever I saw it.

That morning Kay Pierce had announced on the telio – in that thin little voice of hers that I'd learned to hate – that the headquarters for her regime would now be based in New Manhattan, the largest city on the continent.

It was the announcement we'd been waiting for. We'd be wherever she was, trying to bring her down. Like my brother, I'd agreed to work with the Resistance, though the thought of the fight ahead made me feel weary before I'd even started.

Mac had managed to speak to Collie. He was all right, Mac said – he'd gotten back safely and hadn't been suspected. With his help from inside Pierce's regime, along with whatever aid the rest of the world could offer, Mac hoped we'd be able to defeat her.

Now, in the auto, I stared at Mac, wondering if the "pal" of mine he meant could possibly be Collie. The rush of conflicting emotions felt more complicated than I knew how to deal with.

"Who?" I said apprehensively.

"Manfred."

I was silent for a long moment, clutching my new cane. "No," I said. "Ingo went home."

Mac shook his head. "Nah, he didn't make the ship. Just found out this morning when I finally managed to connect with Earl. He's going to be in New Manhattan with us."

When I didn't respond, Mac raised his eyebrows at me in the rear-view mirror. "Hey, that's not a problem, is it? I thought he was a buddy of yours."

My chest felt like a clock that had been wound too far. I stared out the window at the passing trees, aware of Hal gazing at me.

"He is," I said. "It's not a problem."

They said I'd find him up on the roof, and I did.

I paused at the door that led out to it. Faintly I could hear a guitar playing. My muscles were clenched. I turned the doorknob and stepped out onto the flat, soaring world of the roof.

A weathered picnic table sat up here. In the distance was a view of New Manhattan, its buildings spiking up at the sky. Ingo sat on top of the table, his dark head down as he played. His hair was longer now, starting to curl. He looked much healthier, his shoulders less narrow – thin instead of skinny.

He was the last person I'd ever wanted to see again.

I went slowly over, tense with anger. I was carrying my cane, though I didn't really need it now, unless I'd been walking for a while.

As I approached Ingo stopped playing and looked up. The scarred half of his face was just as horrible as before. His almost-black eyes were just as direct. He smiled and raised his good eyebrow.

"You barge in on my table and you don't even bring me champagne?" he said.

My voice shook. "Don't you dare joke. Why are you here?"

Ingo laid the guitar aside. "Is that really the greeting I get, after two months?"

I sank down onto the bench. I felt so empty suddenly. "You're supposed to be home!" I cried. "You're supposed to be with your family! You're supposed to be…"

I choked to a stop. I covered my face with my hands. "…to be happy…"

The tears came from nowhere, wrenched from someplace deep inside of me. My shoulders heaved as I sobbed raggedly, crying like I hadn't cried since I was a little girl.

No. Not even then. I'd always prided myself on being so tough.

I felt Ingo sit on the bench beside me. He wrapped his arms around me and held me tightly. He didn't speak. I slumped against his chest and cried and cried until there was nothing left.

Dad.

I sat where I was for a few moments, feeling Ingo's steady heartbeat under my cheek. I felt limp, drained. Finally I drew away. I stared over at New Manhattan, sparkling in the twilight.

"I thought it would help," I whispered. "But nothing helps."

"Shooting Gunnison?" Ingo produced a handkerchief and dabbed gently at my face. He gave a small smile. "You're determined to remain infamous, aren't you, my friend?"

I swallowed, remembering. "I...didn't really plan it."

"I never thought you did. Are you all right?"

I let out a breath and nodded. "Why *are* you here?" I said after a pause. "I thought..."

Ingo drew away and leaned his forearms on his knees. "There was a rumour in Baltimore about the treaty. The docks were mobbed; people were bribing the ship's steward to get on board. There was only one berth left, so Grady had to take it." He shrugged. "It was more important that the photos get to the EA than I did."

"*You* could have taken them!"

Ingo studied his hands. "Yes, maybe. But if you want the truth…I'd changed my mind before then anyway."

I felt taut. "Why?"

He shrugged. "I couldn't just go home to Calliposa and my safe little vineyard with all of this going on. I couldn't just leave you to fight and do nothing myself."

"How did you know I was going to fight? I didn't even know that myself."

Ingo gave me a dry look. "Because I know you. You're as stupid about these things as I am. And look: here you are."

I smiled slightly. I couldn't remember the last time I'd smiled. "All right, I can't really argue with that."

"Well, that makes a nice change." Ingo nodded at my leg. "You're walking much better," he said.

"Yes, I've been practising. I don't need the cane too often now."

"Just carry it around to batter people into submission?"

I snorted; it turned into a chuckle. "Don't make me laugh. I don't feel like it." I sat gazing at him, with New Manhattan in the distance. After a moment I cleared my throat. "Were you able to get news to your family?"

Ingo nodded. "Grady took a letter from me that he was going to post when he got there. I haven't heard back, but it's difficult. I've been moving around a lot…" He shrugged and looked down.

"They're fine," I told him. "You'll hear from them."

The corner of his mouth lifted, tugging at his scar.

"I thought we didn't do platitudes."

"We don't. That was a statement of fact."

"Anyway, speaking of letters...I have something for you." Ingo dug into his back pocket and handed me something: a folded piece of paper. He cleared his throat. "I couldn't make myself trade this. I thought it was probably important to you."

I stared down at it. I knew what it was without opening it, but opened it anyway, carefully. The faint, pungent scent of disinfectant wafted out.

Dear Amity,

Darling, I've tried so hard to get to see you...

My throat closed.

"I should have given it back to you a long time ago," Ingo said into the twilight silence. "I suppose I didn't want you to know I'd read it. I'm sorry. It was private; I had no right."

"But how did you get the wire for me to pick the lock?" I said in a daze.

Ingo made a face. "It doesn't matter."

"It does. Tell me."

"All right," he said finally. "I traded my breakfast that morning."

I stared at him, remembering Harmony Five – the magnitude of such a gesture there.

Slowly, I refolded the letter. It collapsed back into time-softened creases. As I slipped it into my skirt pocket, I touched the shard of glass. It had always been there, from the time we'd escaped. Each morning I'd felt naked, vulnerable, unless I had it nearby.

I took it out and looked at it. I brushed my thumb over the sharpness of its tip.

Very lightly, I tossed the shard into a trashcan that sat nearby. The can must have been empty; I heard the glass shatter. Something eased in my chest.

"Thank you," I said. "More than I can tell you."

Ingo's expression as he studied me was one I'd never seen him wear before. "You're welcome," he said quietly.

Neither of us seemed to know what to say then. I gazed out at the jagged, sparkling skyline of New Manhattan: home of Kay Pierce's new regime. Soon to be our home too.

Collie was out there somewhere, in one of those glittering buildings. I thought of the moment he'd kissed me and tensed. I'd encounter him again, and probably soon. Mac trusted him. The Resistance trusted him.

A man can change.

Did I believe that?

I pushed it away and rocked sideways, nudging Ingo. "Hey. Do the dramatic chord."

He gave me a look. "Am I supposed to know what that means?"

"Yes, actually. The Peacefighting-story chord."

"Ah, of course." Ingo picked up the guitar and strummed it with a quick motion; the vibrant notes hung in the air. He intoned, "Amity Vancour became a Peacefighter because..."

I took a breath. “Because she wanted to make her father proud,” I said. “Only he was already dead…and so he never knew.”

Ingo hesitated, then laid the guitar aside and rested his hand on my shoulder. He gripped it gently, his thumb rubbing back and forth.

“Thank you for not choosing this particular moment to start spouting platitudes,” I said.

His hand tightened. “You know me better than that,” he said. “But I do think the man would have to have been insane if he wasn’t already proud of you.”

I gazed at Ingo. I felt my mouth relax into a smile.

“I’m glad you’re here,” I told him.

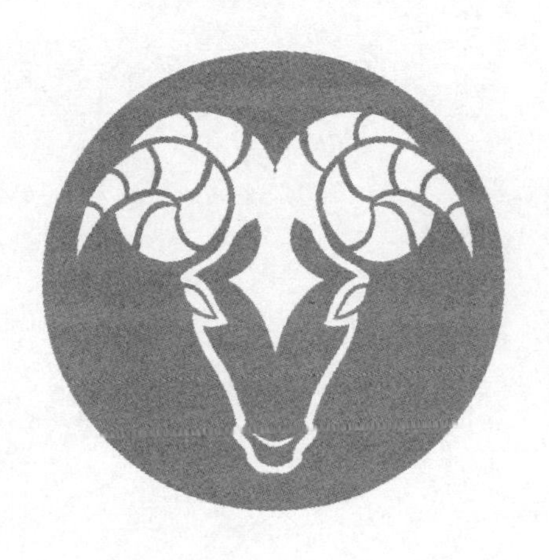

Coming in Spring 2017

Book Three of the Broken Trilogy

BLACK MOON

ISBN: 9781409572046

Welcome to a "PERFECT" world.

Where war is ILLEGAL, where HARMONY rules.

And where your date of birth marks your DESTINY.

BUT NOTHING IS PERFECT.

And in a world this BROKEN,
who can Amity TRUST?

An exhilarating epic of DECEPTION,
HEARTBREAK and REBELLION.

ISBN: 9781409572022

Praise for

Broken Sky

"Full of tension and foreboding...so cinematic and vivid. Broken Sky is a book that will blow you away. 5/5"

Reality's a Bore

"Broken Sky just left me "broken" and elated and in awe. Amity – she's my girl. 5 stars"

Beatrice Learns to Read

"Feels utterly fresh and unique...
So, so, soooo good."
THE ZOE-TROPE

"Action, romance, heartbreak, betrayal, agonising guilt and heart-stopping tension: BROKEN SKY has it all. And TWISTS; dear Lord, the twists."
AWFULLY BIG REVIEWS

"Brilliant...a gripping story with heroic characters."
ARMADILLO

"Written with Weatherly's trademark style, suspense, creativity and energy, this is a gripping, fascinating thriller."
LANCASHIRE EVENING POST

Acknowledgements

Though it may sound strange given how gritty *Darkness Follows* is in places, this book was a joy to write – one of those magical writing experiences where the characters did all sorts of things the author didn't expect. I followed where they led me and loved the journey.

Other, non-fictional, people came along for the journey too, and I'm extremely glad they did.

First, my dream team at Usborne. I truly couldn't ask for a better editor: Stephanie King, to whom this book is dedicated, unfailingly provides keen insight, inspiration and calm wisdom. "Thank you" is an understatement! My heartfelt thanks also to Rebecca Hill, Anne Finnis and Sarah Stewart. As always, your spot-on feedback made

Darkness Follows a much better book. My thanks also to Katharine Millichope for the gorgeous front cover, and to Amy Dobson and Stevie Hopwood for their stellar efforts in promoting the series. Though *Darkness Follows* is a challenging book in some ways, Usborne were behind it right from the start. So to everyone there, thank you for your faith in the story and in me.

I must also give a nod of thanks to the memoirists and historians – some of whom are no longer with us – whose work was so valuable in helping me shape *Darkness Follows*. The fictional "correction camps" of Gunnison's regime aren't meant to represent any specific real-life concentration camps, but they do borrow elements from examples across several cultures. Especially useful in my research were Primo Levi's *If This Is a Man*; Agnès Humbert's *Résistance*; Paul R. Gregory's *Women of the Gulag*; Anne Applebaum's *Gulag*; and Kang Chol-Hwan's *The Aquariums of Pyongyang*.

My usual posse of writing pals, plus some new ones, have provided feedback, laughter, cappuccinos and gin – you all keep me sane, as you know! My love and thanks especially to Christi Daugherty, Keren David, Fiona Dunbar, Hilary Freeman, Candy Gourlay, Helen Grant, Helen Graves, Nick Green, Emma Haughton, Melissa Hyder, Inbali Iserles, Katherine Langrish, Zoë Marriott, Gillian Philip, C.J. Skuse, Keris Stainton, and Sheena Wilkinson.

To all the readers, bloggers and reviewers who've

enjoyed the series so far, thank you so much! I love hearing from you, and I hope that *Darkness Follows* meets expectations. Thanks also to my agent, Jenny Savill – I feel that we're poised on the verge of a great adventure.

Finally, hugs to my family for being there, especially my sister Susan Benson Lawrence. And an extra-special, you-are-amazing thank-you to my husband. "Peter" means "rock"…and you both rock and are my rock. I love you.

About the Author

L. A. WEATHERLY was born in Little Rock, Arkansas, USA. She now lives with her husband and their cat, Bernard, in Hampshire, England, where she spends her days – and nights! – writing.

L. A. Weatherly is the author of over fifty books, including the bestselling *Angel* trilogy. Her work has been published in over ten different languages.

Catch up with L. A. Weatherly on facebook

@LA_Weatherly

laweatherly.tumblr.com

Can't wait for Black Moon? catch up with L. A. Weatherly's

"Heart-stopping romance." *Mizz*

"Wonderful, original." *The Sun*

"Packed with suspense and drama." *The Daily Mail*

"Sparkling." *Books for Keeps*

"Awesome." *Once Upon a Bookcase*

"Will leave you breathless." *Daisy Chain Book Reviews*

"Stunning." *Book Angel Booktopia* for *Chicklish*

"Made me laugh, smile and cry." *Open Book Society*

"Fresh, imaginative...highly addictive." *Empire of Books*

"Will suck you in and take you on a thrill ride."
Feeling Fictional

"Pure perfection." *Dark-Readers*

"Unmissable." *Jess Hearts Books*

"Mind-blowing, spine-tingling, absolutely brilliant."
Book Passion for Life

ISBN 9781409521969

Willow knows she's different from other girls. She can look into people's futures just by touching them. She has no idea where she gets this power from...

But Alex does. Gorgeous, mysterious Alex knows Willow's secret and is on a mission to stop her. But in spite of himself, Alex finds he is falling in love with his sworn enemy.

Only Willow has the power to defeat the malevolent Church of Angels, and they will stop at nothing to destroy her. But when Willow and Alex join forces with a group of Angel Killers, Willow is still treated with mistrust and suspicion. She's never felt more alone...until she meets Seb.

He's been searching for Willow his whole life – because Seb is a half-angel too.

ISBN 9781409522393

Training a new team of AKs, Alex and Willow's love grows stronger than ever. But with the world in ruins, the angels are enslaving humanity, moving survivors into camps where they devour their energy, causing slow but certain death. When Alex is forced to embark on a deadly solo mission, Willow is left to defeat the angels with Seb – and she has no idea if Alex is ever coming back...

www.angelfever.com

For my editor, Stephanie King

First published in the UK in 2016 by Usborne Publishing Ltd., Usborne House, 83-85 Saffron Hill, London EC1N 8RT, England. www.usborne.com

Cover photo of pieces of demolished or shattered glass isolated on black © Arsgera/Shutterstock
Aries and Taurus artwork by Ian McNee.

A CIP catalogue record for this book is available from the British Library.

ISBN 9781409572039 03207/1

JFMAMJJ SOND/16 Printed in the UK.